TASK FORCE THUNDERBOLT

Global Response Force Book 3

GALEN D. PETERSON

Knight Books

Published by Knight Books, Erie

ISBN 979-8-9901304-7-0

Publisher's note: This is a work of fiction. Names, characters, places, and incidents either are the product of the author's imagination or are used fictitiously. Any resemblance to actual events, locales, or persons, living or dead, is entirely coincidental.

Additionally, the organization of Lightning Troop is further fictionalized in order to explore how various war fighting functions could interact, instead of how others dictated.

A glossary can be found in the back.

Edited by Kristen Corrects, Inc.
Cover art design by Ivan Zanchetta

For Dave

AUTHOR'S NOTE

The US Army maintains an armored company-size force capable of deploying anywhere in the world within ninety-six hours. The tank- and armored-vehicle-equipped team provides the firepower, protection, and shock power for rapidly developing contingencies against formidable foes. This team is known as the Global Response Force (GRF).

This story is fictional and any parallels to real events or real people are unintentional.

BELARUS
POLAND
UKRAINE
RUSSIA
MOLDOVA
ROMANIA
CRIMEA
Kursk
Voronezh
Chernihiv
20th Combined Arms Army
Western Military District
Lutsk
Belgorod
Kyiv
Myrhorod
Vorskla
1st Guards Tank Army
Kharkiy
Airborne Corps
Lviv
Poltava
Donets Pocket
Dnipro
Vinnytsia
Oril
Kobelyaky
Pereshchepyne
6th Combined Arms Army
Pavlohrad
Bug
Dnipro
Luhansk
Donetsk
Kryvyi Rih
Zaporizhzhia
Southern Military District
Don
Mariupol
Rostov-on-Don
Mykolaiv
Melitopol
Kherson
Berdyansk
Odessa
50 100 200 km
50 100 150 mi
Krasnodar
Sevastopol

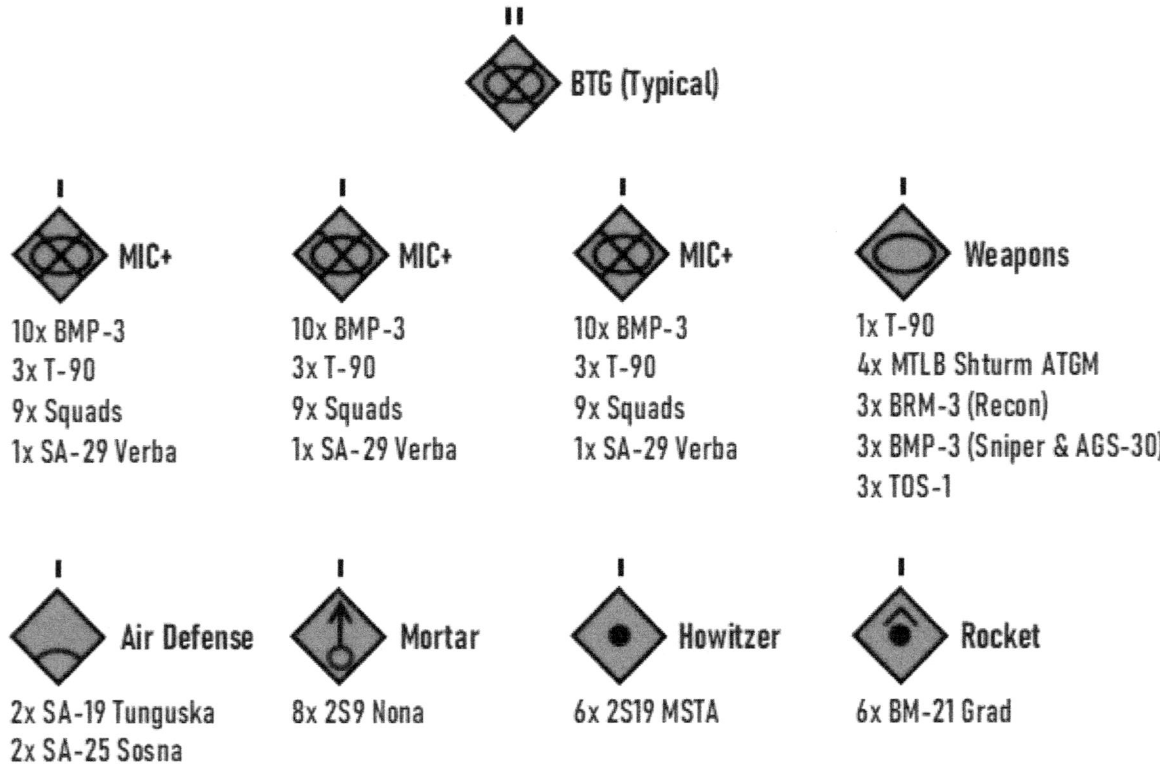
II
BTG (Typical)
I
MIC+
10x BMP-3
3x T-90
9x Squads
1x SA-29 Verba
I
MIC+
10x BMP-3
3x T-90
9x Squads
1x SA-29 Verba
I
MIC+
10x BMP-3
3x T-90
9x Squads
1x SA-29 Verba
I
Weapons
1x T-90
4x MTLB Shturm ATGM
3x BRM-3 (Recon)
3x BMP-3 (Sniper & AGS-30)
3x TOS-1
I
Air Defense
2x SA-19 Tunguska
2x SA-25 Sosna
I
Mortar
8x 2S9 Nona
I
Howitzer
6x 2S19 MSTA
I
Rocket
6x BM-21 Grad

Chapter 1

Sudivka, Ukraine – January 4, 0900 hrs

Logan's teeth chattered to the point of pain as he huddled in the troop compartment of the command post. He couldn't remember how many hours it had been since he last felt his toes. The M1283 Armored General Purpose Vehicle that served as the command post for Logan's Troop L, 3rd Squadron, 3rd Armored Cavalry Regiment, had a fully functioning heater, but it was off for safety. The glowing thermal signature of a warm armored vehicle was asking for detection and destruction.

"I gotta get some blood flowing. Who wants to come check the line?" Logan looked at the other soldiers huddled around him.

"I'll go." Specialist Pezo held up a hand.

"Top," Logan said, looking to the troop's first sergeant, Bob Harris, "I'll work north to south, taking my truck. If we run into contact, have First Platoon come to us. If you take contact here, manage the fight and I'll get to the nearest platoon and fight back with them. If I miss a comms check by more than thirty minutes, have the platoons use a drone to find me."

Top Harris nodded. "Right." His dark eyes closed as he rubbed his temples. Rings around his eyes were pronounced, even on his charcoal skin. He reopened his eyes. "Be careful, sir."

Logan cracked open the troop door and climbed out. Squinting in the bright sunlight, Logan pulled sunglasses from a pouch on his kit and donned them. The relief was immediate. The command post vehicle was tucked into a dug-in position and covered with camouflage netting. Enemy drones were the biggest threat.

"Cold as my ex." Pezo's crack elicited Logan's grin in the frosty air.

"Weatherman says it will warm up next week. We might even stay above zero a few days." Logan trudged up the ramp until he could see above ground level. There, he scrutinized the sky and then the horizon.

"Don't see nuttin', sir."

"Yeah. Let's go." Captain Logan Trondfjell briskly strode along the tree line to another ramp down. Snow crunched under footsteps. Logan's M1280 Joint Light Tactical Vehicle (JLTV) was hidden under its own camouflaged netting.

"Hey sir," Sergeant Ekman called from the gunner's hatch of the truck as they approached. Ekman resumed looking out at the empty field in front of the woods.

"Time to crank up the windchill."

"Ah..." Ekman grimaced.

Pezo jumped in the truck and started the motor.

"Sir, you think it's gonna be a red air day?" Ekman asked as Logan climbed in the front seat.

Logan checked to make sure the communication systems were on and ready before responding. "When was the last time it wasn't?"

"Touché." Ekman also had been with Troop L since the beginning. Not a day had gone by without a Russian fighter-bomber, helicopter, or drone in the area.

Logan caught his reflection in the side mirror. After 176 days into the war, Logan's old scar on his left cheek no longer seemed out of place. Many troopers under Logan's command had their own new scars. Pezo was one of the lucky ones without.

Logan keyed up the radio. "Lightning X-ray, Lightning Six, SP."

The speaker crackled back after a beep. "Roger."

Pezo pulled the truck up the ramp and followed the path through the leafless trees. At the north edge of the woods, Pezo paused and all three scanned the surroundings. Satisfied, Pezo pulled out into the field. The path followed the trees on the edge and dipped into a ravine. Two kilometers down, Pezo pulled into an unoccupied hide spot ramp.

Ekman broke the silence. "Remember the day you said we needed visitor parking?"

"I'd rather not," Logan whispered. In October, Lightning Troop began a screening mission along the Vorskla River. The troop now had observation posts strung out along nine kilometers of frontline. Russian artillery thrashed the troop daily. A barrage had caught Logan while checking on the troops. Shrapnel killed two soldiers as they piled branches on the truck to hide it. That was even before the Russian drones proliferated.

Logan barely had time to quietly ease his door shut before 4th Platoon's leader met him.

"Sir, morning." First Lieutenant Landon "Squeaky" Ewell's voice betrayed the origins of his nickname.

"Hi Squeaky." Logan followed Squeaky to his M2A3 Bradley fighting vehicle. "What's new?"

"Ivan changed out his combat security outpost at oh eight hundred again. That makes three days in a row. Same manner each time."

"Whole platoon?" Logan's eyebrows rose in interest.

"Yup. You thinking of hitting them?"

Logan nodded. "Catching two platoons might be worth the howitzer battery displacing."

Squeaky rubbed his hands together and ducked through the Bradley's troop door. Logan followed. A cup of hot coffee waited for Logan to take a seat.

"You always brew coffee when you hear me SP?" Logan asked the young platoon leader. Squeaky grinned and took a sip from his own cup. Logan took a sip and savored the burning liquid sluicing down his throat. *There is something magical about a cup of coffee.* "How is your platoon?"

"Good. Cold. Last week's firefight served as a good reminder for field craft."

"It was a cheap lesson. A good lesson. You need anything, Landon?"

"Going through batteries on the Ravens faster than we can charge them with this cold. At least we haven't lost one to icing."

"Yet," Logan countered. The high humidity and low temps had claimed many drones, friendly and enemy.

"Sir," Landon said after another sip, "bumped into a patrol from Ironhawk Troop this morning. Heard a rumor."

"Oh?" Logan never ceased being amazed at the lieutenant intelligence network.

"Major operation coming up. Like maybe we're going to break through to the Ukrainians in the Donets Pocket." Landon's face hardened.

"Hmm." Logan held his coffee cup under his nose and thought. When the Russian invasion conquered nearly a third of Ukraine, it trapped six Ukrainian brigades. Those brigades continued to deny Russian squeezes east of Kharkiv. The Donets Pocket consumed Russian equipment and lives at a disproportionate rate. It was the reason the Russians were unable to expand their grip on Odessa and Mykolaiv. Only diminishing supplies would keep the pocket from holding out forever.

"Supposedly, squadron is gonna give the order soon."

A beep in Logan's radio earpiece interrupted. "Guidons, Thunder X-ray, orders group at ten hundred."

Logan marveled at Landon. "Speak of the devil. Gotta go." Logan gulped the rest of his coffee and climbed out of the Bradley.

Pezo had the truck running and Logan scrambled in.

"To squadron?" Pezo asked.

Logan nodded and gestured for him to drive. Thunder Squadron's Tactical Operations Center (TOC) was several kilometers west. Pezo drove back down the ravine.

"Red air! Red air!" a voice on the radio called. "X-ray, Four-Four, contact drones east. Out."

"Pezo, park it in these trees!" Logan pointed at a clump of trees right in front of them.

Pezo quickly drove under the trees and stopped. Movement always catches the eye.

"What are they?" Sergeant Ekman called, scanning the sky.

"Patience." Logan held his breath, then slowly pushed it all out, forcing himself to remain calm.

"X-ray, Four-Four, one Orlan and ten delta wing kamikazes."

Pezo whistled.

"Yeah. Playing for keeps," Ekman answered.

Logan keyed up the radio. "Guidons, Six, knock down as many kamikazes as possible before we take the Orlan with a Stinger."

"Won't they just target us then?!" Pezo glared at Logan.

"Our mission is to protect those behind us from Russian eyes and weapons."

Logan looked out the window toward the east. Detecting tiny drones strained the eye, but at least it was a blue sky and the sun already swinging southward. *There!* Movement caught his attention. The drones were high, kamikazes following behind the higher and larger observation drone. *There should be a second Orlan. They operate in pairs or more...*

"Drone above us!" Ekman's cry startled Logan. "Directly above us!"

"Okay. Okay. Maybe it doesn't see us." *Fat chance.* "Pezo, stay sharp—if I say go, drive like your life depends on it. But don't crash!"

Logan looked back at the flock of kamikazes clawing into the western breeze. *Jeez, they are getting close.* One dropped out of formation and fluttered down like a leaf. Another floundered out of the air. The Drone Defenders in 4th Platoon worked quickly as the drones entered their range. A third kamikaze fell. A fourth. The drones were very nearly to Logan. *Too high to shoot with a rifle.* A fifth drone spiraled out of control. Five left.

"Pezo, put it in gear. Stand by..." Logan yelled over his pounding heart. Another fell out of the sky.

"Incoming!" Ekman pointed at a kamikaze breaking formation and diving for them.

"Duck into the armor!" Logan yelled back. He crossed himself and cringed.

BOOM! Blinding light and choking dust enveloped the truck.

"Everyone okay?" Logan coughed.

Pezo spoke first. "Shit!"

"Ekman? You okay? Ekman?"

"I think so," Ekman finally answered. "It hit the tree first."

The dust and snow cleared from the air and Logan leaned against the windshield to look up. The Orlan circled like a hungry shark, three kamikazes following like remoras.

"Hold still, maybe they think they killed us."

A kamikaze fell as the drone parade made another turn west.

"Come on, guys!" Ekman cheered on 4th Platoon as he peeked back through the gunner's hatch.

A white smoke trail from the south rushed into the sky behind a Stinger missile. A flash and puff of smoke punctuated the union of the Stinger and Orlan. One kamikaze followed the smoke trail down. The last turned and dove at Logan's truck.

"Go! Head west!"

Pezo floored the gas pedal and the truck accelerated. Each bump jolted loose items around.

"Faster!" Ekman cried out.

The drone angled lower as it closed in with the speeding JLTV truck. Pezo took a corner in the ravine hard and the truck threatened to tip. Ekman ducked down as Pezo aimed for an exit into a field.

BOOM! The truck careened out of the dust cloud and Pezo aimed for a line of trees.

"That was the last of them!" Ekman called.

The radio crackled to life. "X-ray, Five-Four, engaged and destroyed one Orlan. The second moved north out of range. Negative casualties or damage."

"Ekman, how do we look?" Logan thrust his thumb toward the back end.

Sergeant Ekman climbed higher in the hatch before responding.

"Spare tire gone. Cargo is a mess."

"That was close," Logan muttered before keying up the radio. "X-ray, Six, took two hits, still rolling but we have damage. Negative casualties. Heading to Thunder."

Pezo slowed down and turned onto an asphalt road. "Yeah..."

Poltava, Ukraine – January 4, 0945 hrs

The small space heater in the corner barely kept the room from freezing. *Warmer than outside...or in one of the company's fighting positions*, Captain Michael King grumped as he pulled his sleeping bag tighter. Wearing the bag like a robe looked ridiculous, but it was warm.

Nobody would say anything to him. *The perks of command.* Michael was vaguely aware that nobody would approach him if they had a choice. He was not privy to the nickname his troops gave him: King Permafrost.

Michael stared at his laptop. The latest operations order handed down from higher stared back. V Corps planned an attack to penetrate the Russian lines to relieve the Donets Pocket. So, the 11th Airborne Division would attack east from Poltava to clear the city and woods of Russian forces. Thus, the 173rd Airborne Brigade would attack to clear a portion of Poltava on the east side of the Vorskla River. 1st Battalion of the 503rd Airborne Infantry, Michael's company included, would have to seize the central railyard. *It has to be an attack. Not even a combat jump. Why me?*

"Sir, check this out," a soldier looking at a small tablet called to Michael.

Michael waved the soldier over. Moving without taking his eyes off the screen resulted in him knocking over a folding chair. The crash of metal on concrete grated Michael's nerves.

"I found this with the Raven," the soldier proudly announced. He had become adept at flying the small drone low between buildings to penetrate the east side of the city and get beyond the Russian anti-drone defenses.

Michael looked at the screen. A group of Russians gathered around a map held against a wall. Two soldiers with cameras filmed the group. A BTR-82 with an impressive collection of antennas protected them from the street. "Where is this?"

"That yellow wall belongs to the train station. Just across the bridge." The grid location of the Raven was displayed in the corner of the tablet screen.

"That's a general. No question." The soft voice of First Sergeant Kim irritated Michael. Michael had not heard Kim enter the room. *Fricking ninja.*

"If I zoom out, you will see three more of those command BTRs." The soldier paused. "I think those dudes in the middle are all generals. Sir."

"Our mortar section can reach them. Take out some generals. Hell yeah." First Sergeant Kim popped his fists together.

"How did they get there without us seeing them?"

"They can move on the far side of the buildings easily enough. Hell, we do the same thing. Sir." Kim was wary. "Let's hit them. The balls to visit this close!"

"If we fire our mortars, Russian counter-battery fire will follow. And this building is too close to the mortar position. Not worth it." Michael glared at Kim.

"Generals with film crews are high up. Sir, this is a rare opportunity."

"Thus, the Russians have counter-battery on standby. We need to move the mortar squad before we fire and then they would have to displace immediately." Michael crossed his arms. The discussion was older than he cared.

"It'd be worth it, sir."

Michael stared back. "Give me a moment to think." He pushed out of the chair and paced the room. *Perhaps we can make a run for a different building as the mortars fire? No, that won't work. The Russians will pulverize this whole area.* Michael saw Kim's eyebrows twitch. "I'm still thinking. Have the Raven make another pass and confirm the grid."

"Roger, sir." Kim's shoulders slumped and he watched the Raven pilot zoom in on the Russian generals. On cue, the generals faced the Raven. A push of a button and the Raven captured a still photo of three identifiable faces. The soldier would look up the faces later. His buddy in the battalion intel shop would help.

"They saw me." The drone operator's voice fell flat. "And there they go."

Michael turned to the screen and watched as the Russians ran for their vehicles. *Well, no sense trying to hit them now.* In just ten more seconds, the BTRs fled down the street.

Kim sighed and sat down in a chair. The drone operator shook his head and shifted noisily in his seat.

Michael ignored them and continued reading the operations order. The son of a governor, Michael was going places. He just needed to survive this important ticket punch of company command. Michael hadn't planned on the war and was horrified to take command just four days in. He never forgot the commander before him died. *At least we got to stay in bunkers all this time. But now... At least I'm not a platoon leader.* Michael's chest tightened.

Bairak, Ukraine – January 4, 1000 hrs

3rd "Thunder" Squadron TOC was set up in a large shed. The armored command post vehicles parked with their ramps facing in. The sides of the enclosure between vehicles sported thick sandbag walls, and mechanics had welded a frame to add sandbags on a ceiling. From inside, the comforting protection of the bunker was obvious. Only a nondescript shed showed from above.

The communications specialists ran wires from the TOC to antennas as far away as possible. All other vehicles parked under another shed. Nothing was too much in the quest for survivability.

As Pezo pulled into the shed, Logan saw Top Harris's truck. They could travel together for the trip back. *Safety in numbers.* Logan left his rifle in the truck, taking his map and notebook.

"Wow, you got lucky, Logan." Captain Eli Hood, the howitzer battery commander, put his hand on Logan's shoulder. Logan surveyed the damage to the truck.

"Yup. How are you, Eli?"

"No complaints anyone would listen to."

"Same." Logan pulled up his map. "Hey, we have an opportunity to bag two platoons of Ivans. They've been sloppy in their outpost relief. Catch them in the open." Logan explained further, detailing the observations.

"Worth it. How confident are you on the grid coordinate?"

"Very. Landon's platoon reverified using different methods. Same coordinates every time."

"Right on. Tomorrow, then."

A truck pulling into the shed interrupted them. Logan and Eli waited for it to turn off. A stranger got out and walked over. The rank and nametape identified him as Captain Larrabee.

"Hi guys. I'm Dakota, Regiment Three Shop." The captain held out his hand to Logan first.

"Logan. What brings you here?"

"You're Logan? You don't look like a Trondfjell. Anyway, bringing some new maps down and getting a feel."

Logan snorted. It wasn't the first time someone commented on the strong Hispanic features passed down by his mom's bloodline.

"Feel for what?" Eli shook Dakota's hand.

"Supposed to take command of a troop."

Eli and Logan shared a glance. "Whose?"

"Yours. Logan, you've been in command for over twenty months."

Logan stared blankly at Dakota. *Really? Now? Helluva way to find out.*

Dakota nodded and continued, "Two months beyond the required tour. You've already made a name for yourself. Time to let someone else get a chance."

Logan snorted. "No, the troop earned its reputation. Not me."

"Relax. I wouldn't want to give up command either." Dakota put his hands on hips. "You know the directive came down to get personnel movements going again. Can't have half the Army's timelines jacked up."

"Sure." Logan turned and walked to the TOC. *Awesome day so far.*

Inside the TOC, the din of conversations carried a tone of excitement. Logan slumped into a chair and looked at the map posted on the wall. Top Harris sat down next to Logan. His silence meant he too just learned the news.

"Seats. Let's go. Seats," Major Noyes, the squadron executive officer, called out. Voices died out and the gathered leaders sat down.

Lieutenant Colonel Pacheco finished his private conversation with the operations officer before addressing the room. "Folks, the operation we've been anticipating for three months is finally here. Captain Baldwin, you may begin your intelligence update."

The baby-faced captain stood and walked to the map. It took nearly fifteen minutes for him to distill the enemy situation. The Russian lines followed the Vorskla River from Russia to the Dnipro River. From there, the frontline continued southwest across the river to just north of Mykolaiv. A twenty-kilometer-wide strip of Russian-occupied coast connected to Moldova. Twenty Russian divisions held the line. The Donets Pocket, centered on Izyum, faced another seven Russian divisions. Directly across from Logan's troops was the Russian 4th Tank Division.

To its south was the Russian 2nd Guards Motor Rifle Division. Behind was the 47th Guards Tank Division, and the rest of the 1st Guards Tank Army was farther south. The Russians recognized the importance of the Poltava sector, assigning their best units to it. The Russians had nearly made up for all equipment and personnel losses during the initial invasion.

None of this information was news to Logan. His troopers' patrols and observations provided most of the intelligence on the Russians across the valley. He even knew the locations and specifications of the Russian minefields.

Major Douglas, the operations officer, followed. "Fifth Corps attacks no later than twenty January, zero four hundred hours, to rupture the Poltava front in order to allow linkup with the Ukrainian forces in the Donets Pocket."

The collective breath paused Major Douglas. The corps and regimental concept of operation took another five minutes to detail. As he finished, Lieutenant Colonel Pacheco stood to deliver the squadron mission.

"Thunder Squadron guards the corps' right flank in order to protect it from Russian counterattack. My intent is to find and destroy any and all Russian forces that come within range of our weapons as we extend along the flank. The Kharkiv to Dnipro lines of communication are vital to the Russian forces. Cutting those will get an immediate and powerful response. The Russians don't have much north of our axis of advance. Their power is south, in front of us." Pacheco paused to look each troop commander in the eye before continuing.

"Now, the key elements are going to be one: the forward passage of lines with First Armored Division to breach the obstacle belt. Second, the linkup with the Eleventh Airborne Division's left flank on the shoulder of our penetration. Third, maintaining enough maneuver space to destroy Russian counterattacks before they threaten our own lines of communication. Lightning Troop has the most experience. You know the airborne from last summer. You will be our pivot."

Butterflies took flight in Logan's stomach. Major Douglas took over the briefing again and detailed the operation. Logan's hand cramped from furious note-taking. Despite the detail of the plan, one nagging question remained. When the briefing was over, he pulled Lieutenant Colonel Pacheco aside.

"Sir, can I talk?" Logan waited as Pacheco led him into one of the armored command post tracks and took a seat.

"Logan, what's on your mind?"

"Am I getting replaced? A captain said he was taking my troop."

"I'm sure you heard of the directive."

"Yes sir. But now? Pretty bad timing, don't you think?" Logan crossed his arms.

Pacheco nodded. "It's not ideal. Even Colonel Ollerich's hands are tied on this. Logan, I already fought and lost. So did the old man. He probably lost his chance at a star over it. Anyway, we'll do the change of command in two days. That gives you time to get the initial plan going and Dakota time to get his feet under him."

"How long have you known, sir?"

"We got the directive a month ago, but I've been fighting it. I thought with this attack coming, we could leave you in command. I really did, Logan." Pacheco's shoulders and voice dropped. "I'm sorry."

"Nothing I can do?"

"Can't stop it. You'll move to our S3 shop. If it softens the blow, I found out this morning the 173rd put Lightning Troop in for a Presidential Unit Citation and you in for the..." Pacheco trailed off, as if he wasn't supposed to share something. Logan stopped listening, his mind racing.

Pacheco's hand on Logan's shoulder pulled Logan back. "Logan, Lightning Troop will be okay. I know it's hard. You have been a phenomenal commander. It's time to move forward with your career. Keeping you in the squadron means you will be able to mentor Dakota. Big shoes for him to fill."

Logan nodded, his chin touching his chest.

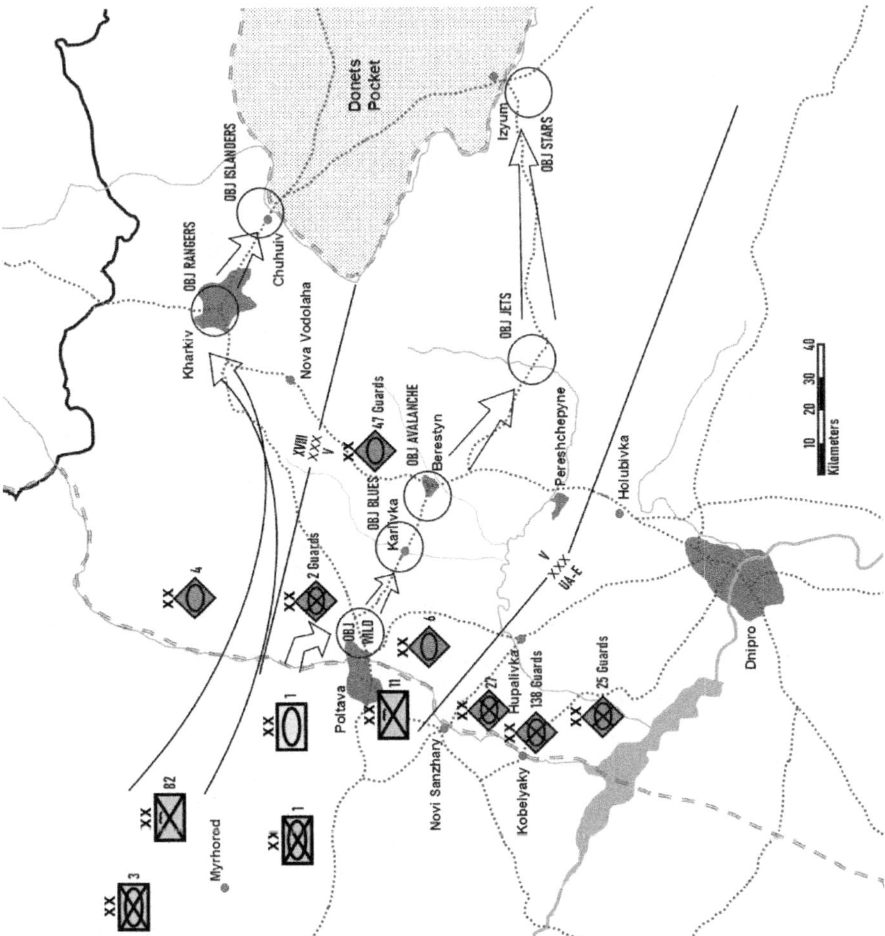
Donets Pocket
OBJ ISLANDERS
OBJ RANGERS
Chuhuiv
Kharkiv
Nova Vodolaha
Izyum
OBJ STARS
OBJ JETS
47 Guards
OBJ AVALANCHE
Berestyn
OBJ BLUES
Karlivka
Pereshchepyne
Holubivka
2 Guards
OBJ WILD
Poltava
Hupalivka
138 Guards
25 Guards
Novi Sanzhary
Kobelyaky
Myrhorod
Dnipro
XVIII
XXX
V
UA-E
Kilometers
10
20
30
40

Chapter 2

Kharkiv, Ukraine – January 4, 1400 hrs

"Relax, sit." Minister of Defense Andrey Vladimirovich Popov waved his hand to the room as he stepped through the door. As one, the room sighed and recovered from the stiff position of attention his entry elicited. Popov's bald head and overweight body did not command the respect of generals, but his harsh ways demanded it. The generals obliged. This was Russia, after all.

"Minister Popov, welcome." Army General Golovko spoke first and gestured to sit at the head of the table.

"Sir, we have tea," Lieutenant General Mikhail Borisovich Kiselyov offered as the host of the meeting. The field headquarters of the 1st Guards Tank Army lacked the polish of the higher echelons, but aligned with Popov's desired image.

"General Golovko and Colonel General Dronov, thank you for coming forward to meet with me," Popov acknowledged the head of the Russian Ground Forces and commander of the Western Military District. "Where is Colonel General Lipilin?"

"His aircraft diverted due to enemy air activity," Golovko answered, shaking his head.

"Our chopper had no issues getting us here from Poltava," Popov wryly countered.

"Ah, the Southern Military District does not have as good of luck with their air defenses as young Mikhail Borisovich has." Dronov smiled and looked at Kiselyov.

Golovko took a sip of his tea. "How was your excursion to the frontlines?"

"Uneventful, really. We saw an American small drone, but it was unarmed and nothing came of it. In fact, the Americans seemed oblivious or apathetic about us being right up near the river," Popov answered. "I understand the Ukrainian drones are more lethal."

Kiselyov nodded. "Correct. They equip many of their small drones with grenades and small bombs. Had we been in a sector with Ukrainians, I would have had us scatter at first report of the drone."

"Well, the footage of our visit will air tonight and boost morale." Popov stopped and sipped his cup.

Dronov looked around the room before asking, "So the rumors are true?"

Popov nodded. "Unfortunately. The younger generation seems more skeptical of our efforts here in Ukraine than necessary."

"They will come around." Dronov snorted.

"It is still a problem. We need a unified nation to face a challenging war." Popov wagged his finger at Dronov. "General, you forget it was a revolution that forced our nation to quit the first world war."

"I'd rather we don't see a revolution in my time," Kiselyov whispered.

"Yes. Now, our young star, let us talk of realities. Colonel General Dronov, what is your prognosis of the Donets Pocket?"

"We will smash it."

"By when?" Popov asked.

Dronov looked to Golovko for support, seeing none, before warily answering, "Soon enough."

"No, dammit. Give me a date. I want a date that you believe in. I want a date you will bet your own life on. Not some half answer." Popov pounded the table.

Kiselyov flinched, thankful he wasn't the one answering.

"We are winning the war of attrition. The Ukrainians in the Donets Pocket are using their weapons faster than they can obtain them. My staff calculates the resupply flights that leak through to the pocket deliver just three tons per day. They are consuming five tons of ammunition per day."

"Cut to the point, General," Popov interrupted.

"We need the pocket low enough on ammunition to successfully attack. My staff estimates that point will come in March." Dronov looked down at his hands as he answered.

"March?" Popov's bushy white eyebrows flexed upward. "So, you are waiting until General Mud forces a delay until May?"

Dronov nodded slowly. "Pushing the attack sooner will only see the same results as previous attacks. Until then, we keep up the pressure locally. As pulverized as the pocket frontlines are, the mud problem will be considerable."

"I see. Thank you for being honest." Popov's icy stare melted slightly before turning to Golovko. "General, what do you see NATO doing?"

"NATO will attack. We underestimated its resolve to defend Ukraine last summer. I suggest we don't make that mistake again. The right bank of the Vorskla River now has some one hundred fifty thousand NATO soldiers. There is even an Australian brigade integrated into the US First Infantry Division, alongside the British brigade and Canadian battalion. At least our strength in air defense missiles denies the NATO aircraft control of the skies."

"Yes, I know," Popov interrupted.

"As I was saying, I see NATO attacking in February. Their First Cavalry Division—really another armored division—will arrive by the end of this month. If I was them, I would wait for it and then strike through Kharkiv to the Donets Pocket. That will cut our lines of communication to the entire northern half of the front. The Yankees especially love to use sweeping flanking movements. They would continue their attack through the Donets to Mariupol. If they reach the Sea of Azov, it's over for us. That would be NATO's most dangerous move."

"And to stop that attack?" Popov turned back to Dronov.

"We have good defenses and deep obstacle belts. We can attack their flank from the south. Lieutenant General Molchalin's Sixth Combined Arms Army has contingency plans ready. My counterattack would be especially powerful if you make Colonel General Lipilin give me his Fifty-Eighth Combined Arms Army. Give me his Second Guards Tank Army and I can counterattack NATO all the way back to Kyiv." Dronov leaned forward, sweeping his arms across the table. Two chairs over, Molchalin maintained a stony mask.

"Victor Aleksandrovich, what is your contingency for a NATO attack north of Poltava?" Golovko asked Molchalin.

Molchalin carefully chose his words. "General, I will have my reconnaissance battalion screen the Vorskla line, with two BTGs in support. I would then attack north with my divisions."

"We've explored options to give Victor Aleksandrovich operational control of the Forty-Seventh Guards Tank Division if NATO penetrates far enough to hinder Mikhail Borisovich's control of the powerful division. But..." Dronov smiled. "I have full confidence local counterattacks by the First Guards Tank Army will be sufficient to defeat a NATO offensive."

"General, you know President Voroshilov withholds that sort of realignment authority."

"You can persuade him. I can make it to Kyiv. Lipilin has three more combined arms armies than I do."

"And three times the frontage. Let's not forget your Twentieth Combined Arms Army defends the Russian border and NATO is highly unlikely to risk nuclear war."

"I agree, Minister Popov. But we cannot risk NATO surprising us with such an attack should I pull those troops for a counterattack."

Popov stared at Dronov.

"Can we end the war before NATO attacks in February?" Kiselyov ventured quietly.

Popov shook his head. "No, Ukraine and NATO are confident they will retake all of their territory. The Chinese have forwarded an offer from us to allow Ukraine NATO membership as long as we retain all of the territory we seized."

Kiselyov stifled a smirk.

"Yes, you know why Ukraine won't agree to that."

"Did they offer anything back?"

"They gain NATO membership and get all their land, including the Donbas, back."

Golovko laughed. "No."

"In the end, I believe if we can defeat the coming NATO attack before they reach the Donets Pocket, Ukraine will accept any peace offer. Another year of war will destroy them beyond recovery."

Kiselyov nodded at Popov's assessment. He had seen the casualty figures for both Russia and what the GRU estimated of Ukraine. While Russia had lost some four hundred fifty thousand men, Ukraine's three hundred thousand was a much larger percentage of their population. *Still, that is more than Afghanistan, Chechnya, and Georgia combined and multiplied by three. And how many casualties will NATO sustain before this war is too expensive for them?* "Then our fate hangs on defeating the NATO offensive."

"Yours especially." Popov wagged his finger at Kiselyov and Molchalin, then pointed it at Dronov.

Winter Offensive Looming

(Reuters) Kyiv, January 4 - The Ukrainian minister of defense update included over twenty Russian vehicles and nearly a thousand Russian soldiers destroyed over the last twenty-four hours. The Ukrainian drone units continue to pinprick the Russian frontlines and raid deep into enemy territory. "Death by a thousand cuts until our counteroffensive removes the enemy from our soil once and for all," Ukrainian President Lytvyn commented during a visit to a forward command post.

Military Analyst Tony Davids of the Global Warfare Institute expects a NATO and Ukrainian combined counteroffensive is likely within the next four or five weeks. "The ground is frozen solid. The marshes are frozen solid. While the cold is hard on soldiers and equipment, deep winter offers the mobility needed for a major offensive." Davids pointed out that by February, the NATO forces will be overwhelmingly strong.

Signs of the coming offensive were apparent across Ukraine as supplies and new equipment streamed east to the front. Citizens in cities throughout the country were seen boarding up and sandbagging buildings in anticipation of the Russian reaction.

Speculation on where the hammer will fall is a constant conversation topic. Many Ukrainians expect the offensive will regain the pre-2014 borders. Others worry Russian nuclear weapons will prevent crossing into the areas lost prior to last summer. All agree the end must come soon.

In Davos, peace negotiations have remained as stagnant as the front lines. Officials, speaking off the record, expect negotiations will renew in earnest once the military situation changes.

Sudivka, Ukraine – January 4, 1500 hrs

Word traveled fast. By the time Logan was ready to issue his warning order, the whole troop knew he would leave. They also knew the attack was coming. Captain Dakota Larrabee arrived with his bags just in time for the warning order.

"Logan, I'll just sit in the back and let you issue it. I want to see how you run the troop."

"Fair enough." Logan led Dakota from the command post to a farm house fifty meters through a grove. Inside, the house was reinforced with sandbags and heavy timbers. It was the only way the troop's leadership could gather for briefings in a concealed and covered location. Everyone sat around a table fashioned from a door when Logan and Dakota entered.

"Gentlemen." Top nodded to Logan before finishing his discussion with the troop leadership. "As I was saying, keep checking the troopers' feet. Make sure we are changing socks with this cold. The squadron sergeant major is digging into where our last laundry push disappeared to." Top closed his notebook and looked around the room. With eyes as dark as his charcoal skin, it was always hard to read his mood. "Sir, I'm all done and we are ready for the WARNO."

"Let's start with the obvious. This is Captain Larrabee. He takes command in two days. We have a major operation coming up, so gonna be busy."

Logan patted the troop executive officer on the back. "This is your XO, First Lieutenant Savvy Kraemer. She has the property book in great shape. Savvy is a procurer of the impossible and a tenacious fighter."

Savvy looked at her feet.

"Standing in the corner is Sergeant Doc Koss. We prefer if he and his medics are bored." Logan stepped around the table to left. "First Lieutenant Landon Ewell. Some affectionately call him Squeaky. He started the war with First Platoon's tanks and now has Fourth Platoon's scouts. Solid. But don't let him trick you into a footrace.

"Sergeant First Class Torres is Fourth Platoon's platoon sergeant. I go to him with scouting questions. Fifth, the fires platoon, is led by Second Lieutenant Lucas Donizetti. He is our newest member, coming just three weeks ago. If you want to put artillery in Ivan's coffee cup, fires platoon can do it.

"Brings us to his right-hand man, Sergeant First Class Orrego. Orrego grew up air defense so his experience and knowledge are invaluable." Logan paused and looked around the room. "Forgive me, I should have had everyone sit in order, but it's okay."

He continued. "First Platoon leader, Second Lieutenant Seth Chomsky. He has the distinction of being our very first replacement, joining us in July. Motivated and a quick learner. Next, we have his platoon sergeant, Sergeant First Class Floyd. He joined us in October. He has done well mentoring Seth. Staff Sergeant Hamasaki held down the fort until Sergeant Floyd arrived."

Logan paused, seeing Dakota furiously taking notes. When Dakota looked up, Logan continued. "Sergeant First Class Running Bear, Second Platoon. This is my second war alongside him. The definition of a warrior."

Dakota looked at the large and muscular Lakota and squirmed. Logan ignored him. *He'll figure out what I mean.*

"Running Bear is paired up with Second Lieutenant Gene Sinclair. Gene is steady and resourceful."

Logan stood behind the last lieutenant at the table. "And that leaves Third Platoon, led by First Lieutenant Joey Blazkowitz and his platoon sergeant, Sergeant First Class Ratty Ratatuev. Joey is our most experienced PL. Sergeant Ratty is a skilled scout, and fluent in Russian."

Logan stood next to the only other team member standing. "Last, and definitely not least, is our maintenance team chief, Sergeant First Class Heydte. He is the reason the whole troop isn't sitting in a gulag. He kept our vehicles running so we could fight back to friendly lines."

"Got that right," Top echoed.

"And you've met First Sergeant Harris. Top takes care of the troops and as good an advisor as they come." Logan locked eyes with Top, wondering if Top's advice would be enough.

Half smiles and long looks at Dakota accompanied introductions. *At least Dakota seems humble enough. I just hope he has what it takes.* Logan knew they would find out soon.

Sudivka, Ukraine – January 5, 1830 hrs

Two hours after the sun slid under the western horizon, the temperature dropped like a rock. Logan stamped his feet to keep blood flowing as he waited for the next vehicle's arrival. The metal deck of the troop's cargo five-ton truck sucked the heat from a body. The daily logistics package (LOGPAC) was Logan's best opportunity to see most of the troopers. Pulling the M1A2 Abrams and M2A3 Bradleys out of their hide sites for fuel and supplies was risky, but vital. Without the LOGPAC, the armored vehicles were little more than bunkers. Changing the timing and location of the LOGPAC mitigated the risk.

A rattle of tracks and whine of turbine engines carried in the frigid air. In the green veil of night vision goggles, Logan watched as 1st Platoon's tanks pulled into the LOGPAC. The service station started with fuel, and Top Harris and Doc Koss liked to post there and talk with crews as they filled up. Savvy and Logan served chow out of insulated boxes. By the time it was their turn to eat, the stew would be near solid. Dakota watched alone from Logan's truck. Logan thought the new captain was letting Logan say goodbyes.

The first tank finished taking fuel, skipped the ammo station, and pulled up to the food station.

"Evening, Sergeant!" Logan stepped across the gap to the tank.

"Sir, I'll miss you. You have been awesome to work with." Staff Sergeant Dani Hamasaki hopped out of her hatch to shake Logan's hand.

"I'll miss you too. Learned a lot from you. Gonna miss Lightning Troop." Logan's smile lacked joy. Inside, his heart ached.

"Fiery Cross. Dnipro. Here," Dani said, sweeping her arm out at the snow-covered wheat stubble, "you've seen me through hell and back. I'll fight alongside you anytime, anywhere."

"I appreciate that." Logan sighed. "Humbled and honored." Dani was a legend in the Army because of her actions on Fiery Cross. Now, Dani's crew was only one of two tanks in the troop with the original crew from day one of the war. Furthermore, their cannon sported twenty-seven half-inch white rings, the most in the troop. Once the frontlines stabilized in August, Logan authorized a kill ring for every Russian armored vehicle destroyed. The Abrams wore their rings on their cannon's gun tube. The Bradleys sported their kills as hashmarks on the TOW missile launcher, and hashmarks on the rear sponson box for kills by the scout team. Each kill was adjudicated by Top Harris, awarded only if confirmed and corroborated.

"I mean it, sir." Dani grabbed Logan's shoulder and squeezed it.

Savvy handed over the stack of food trays for the crew. "Beef-flavored slushies." She grinned. "You need anything?"

Dani shook her head and relayed the trays to her loader.

"Take care of yourself, sir."

"You too." Logan smiled and stepped back to the truck. He watched as Dani dropped back into her hatch and the tank pulled away.

"Sir..." Savvy's voice was soft. "I wish we weren't losing you on the eve of this attack. Captain Larrabee doesn't have your experience."

"I wish I wasn't leaving either. Give Larrabee a chance. We all start with no experience."

"You came with combat experience from Fiery Cross, though." Savvy's counter ruined Logan's argument. "It was your experience and wasta that let us survive and succeed the first week of the war. You made us—the whole squadron, too—fortify early. We'd have taken more casualties without you. Don't pretend you don't see it."

"Well, Fiery Cross came with a lot of hard lessons. But now, the troop is battle hardened. I have confidence in you all."

Savvy nodded. "We do have a good troop."

"You deserve as good a team when you become a commander. And I know you will, and you will be a great commander. I hope you'll keep in touch."

Savvy blushed and looked down. "Thank you. Means a lot coming from you."

The next tank clattered up to the truck. The loader quickly reached over to grab the food trays before it drove off. Logan watched it go. *Seth's tank. He still hasn't completely settled into his platoon yet.*

Savvy changed the topic to updates on her family. Her husband was in 1st Squadron's howitzer battery. Second Platoon arrived, with Running Bear's tank at the end.

"Sir, can we take a short walk? Third Platoon is still a ways out," Running Bear called as his tank pulled up to the truck. He pulled off his helmet and slid to the ground.

"My legs would appreciate some blood flow." Logan hopped over to the tank and slid down.

"I thought so." Running Bear waved for his tank to follow.

"What's on your mind, Running Bear?"

"I hate to see you leave us. But also, I wanted to tell you it's been an honor. You don't seem to see it, but you are a warrior."

"I hate leaving. Especially now."

"You're paying the price of officers."

"Moving upward and onward? I wish it wasn't so. Your time in a tank is just about up too. I'd be shocked if you aren't on the promotion list this summer."

"Sir, you're making some big assumptions. This attack carries increased risk. I came through Fiery Cross without a scratch. Somehow through this war so far. How much longer can my luck hold out?"

"Luck mixed with skill is potent. You think you're gonna get hit?"

"I had a dream. The three of us—you, Dani, and me—were cresting a hill. Only one tank made it to the top. I woke before I could see which one of us it was."

"Jeez." Logan listened to the snow crunching under their steps.

"Just a dream, but I want you to be careful. I know you're going to staff, but I won't be there to keep an eye on your back. Sir, you are an exceptional tanker and leader."

Logan stopped and met Running Bear's fierce eyes. "I'd say the same about you. I'll be careful. But you gotta promise me the same."

"Deal. Akicita, my brother." Running Bear offered his upward hand. Logan grasped it in a warrior's handshake.

"Ah-kee-chee-tah, Running Bear." Logan grinned. "I say it right this time?"

Running Bear grinned and nodded before turning and nimbly swinging up onto his tank.

Logan waved and crunched his way back to the truck.

Top walked over to the truck as the last platoon finished LOGPAC.

"Well, surprisingly no new frostbite cases, sir."

"We're getting used to the cold," Logan replied as he climbed down.

"True. Once we start the attack, faces will be my big concern."

"I wish I could lead you then."

"We'd take you back in a heartbeat, sir." Top paused. "Captain Larrabee will be okay. Don't worry about us."

"Yeah, he's eager to learn. It's just that he has so much to learn. That's harder on the troops."

Top stared back at Logan, nodding. He sighed. "We will be okay. You've been a great commander. I'm sad to see you go. Good ones never stay as long as I like." Top smiled. "But the crappy ones linger past my patience."

"I couldn't have asked for a better first sergeant. Thank you for everything you've done for the troops."

"Same. At least you're only going as far as squadron. Be easy to visit you."

"Definitely."

"And after I retire next year, you better come visit."

Logan grinned. "Of course. As long as it isn't Barstow."

Top laughed. "Yeah, no way! Nope, I'm staying put. Another twelve years and my house is paid off. Besides, Candi loves Colorado Springs."

"Well, no clue where I'll end up next, but you're always welcome in my home."

Bairak, Ukraine – January 6, 1900 hrs

"Logan, welcome to the Three Shop." Douglas clapped Logan on the back as Logan set his bags down next to the ramp to the TOC.

"Thank you, sir." Logan half smiled. "Where do you want me to start?"

"We'll get to that. How is Erin?"

Logan gave a toothy smile, his first of the day. "She's good. Finally healed up all the way and will resume flying soon." Logan met Captain Erin Haag at the beginning of the war and their chemistry was unstoppable. Shot down the first night of the war, Erin survived the Black Hawk's crash. Alone, she was able to find her way to Logan's troop and together they fought over a hundred kilometers back to friendly lines. A Russian kamikaze drone wrecked Erin's leg with just a few kilometers to go.

"That's good to hear. She gonna stay on their rear detachment?" Douglas knew Erin was with the remnants of the 12th Combat Aviation Brigade in Germany. Nearly all the brigade was captured with the fall of Dnipro.

"Yes, sir. Erin's helping track down the missing from that first week. Still thinks the Russian prisoner reports are questionable."

"I've heard rumors." Douglas slipped into the plans vehicle and gestured for Logan to sit next to him. Logan sat and looked at the computer set up in front of him. His cheek twitched.

"Logan..." Douglas lowered his voice. "I feel for you. Giving up command on the eve of the offensive is a tough pill."

"It's not fair to the troops. Larrabee is a good guy, but has no experience with tanks. His lieutenant time was in a Stryker cavalry unit. I'm worried. Why force the change now?"

"If I explain, promise you aren't going to continue to mope about it and bother the colonel?"

Logan's eyes hardened but he nodded.

"I was present when Colonel Pacheco asked Colonel Ollerich. Remember everyone at that rank and higher cut their teeth in the War on Terror. Okay? Well, in Iraq and Afghanistan, we would take heavy casualties for a short time, and then it would taper off. Rotating commanders in theater got more officers combat experience. No correlation between the changes of command and increased casualties. Well, now we took heavy losses in the first month. You know. You were part of that more than anyone in the regiment. By the way, it was your experience and sharing of your lessons that helped us all. Since things stabilized, losses have tapered off. Time to return to the old playbook." Douglas paused and looked at Logan. "Don't shoot the messenger. Like it or not, that's the deal and we'll drive on."

"Roger." Logan sighed. "Okay, where do I start?"

"I want you to get with Andy. Refine the Russian most likely and most dangerous courses of action we will face during the flank guard. Then develop two contingency plans for each. I gave these instructions to Andy before you got here. Captain Baldwin! Join us!" Douglas's change in volume caught Logan off guard.

"Coming sir!" Andy called from the intel vehicle.

"Sir. Hey, Logan." Andy shook Logan's hand.

"Right. Get to work. XO has you two on the night shift so there will be fewer Russian interruptions." Douglas got up and let Andy take his seat.

"Roger, sir. Okay, Andy, show me what you got so far." Logan pulled up the map on the computer and Andy explained.

Logan tapped his finger on the town of Stepne. "I agree the Second Guards Motor Rifles will hold the Russian shoulder, but I think at least one Battalion Tactical Group from the Sixth Tank Division will counterattack us at Objective Wild." Logan traced an axis of advance from the south. If he was leading that Russian BTG, it was the axis he would use.

"Makes sense. Call it the Russian most likely. Figure they can do that in about twenty-four hours? Maybe eighteen?"

Logan hesitated before answering. "Yeah."

"Then for the Russian most dangerous, what do you think of what I outlined?"

"Um, I agree they will would use at least two motorized rifle divisions in the Sixth Combined Arms Army to counterattack, but I think they axis would go from Objective Blues before pivoting toward Objective Avalanche with one MRD." Logan traced his finger from the south to Karlivka, then east to Berestyn. "The other MRD would continue northeast to cut our lines of communication."

"But Berestyn is the key terrain, Logan. That's the rail line and Highway 105."

"True, but the ground is frozen so they can follow easier ground to Karlivka. They will want to rupture our lines without risking destroying the rail bridges in and near Berestyn. Also, the terrain is easier to fight eastward than west on."

"Right. Let me flesh this out." Andy got up and returned to the intel vehicle.

Logan sighed and opened the computer's email and set it up. *Switching computers is such a pain.* Once everything was set up correctly, Logan downloaded his inbox. A new email from Erin caught his eye.

Dearest Logan,

I love you so much! I wish you weren't so far away. Especially right now. I can only imagine the emptiness you must feel after giving up Lightning Troop. You have led the troop through hell and back. Perhaps without you, they—me too—might all be stuck in a POW camp in Russia or the occupied areas.

Speaking of camps, I found some intel there is possibly an off-the-record POW camp not too far from you. We found some social media indicators that put a camp in Pereshchepyne. Digging deeper, we found the Russian logistics are supplying more food to the unit there than their mouths alone can eat.

Anyway, the team here thinks it could be somewhere between 150 and 250 POWs. That's nearly all of our missing. We did a head count of the photo of the Dnipro POWs from 13 July and compared with the list of official POWs held by Russia. We are missing 273 from that photo alone. Anyway, I passed the info up to higher.

I'm ready for this war to be over. For you to be safe. To be home. To be able to go on a date with you again. I now have the photo of us in Vienna on my desk, my phone, my bedside table… I miss you.

In the meantime, be safe. I know you are still doing great things for the troops. Your competence has always impressed me and you are too talented not to move upward and onward.

When you see anyone from Lightning Troop, please continue to give them my best. And tell Dani and Savvy I send a big hug. Perhaps one day I will tell you what Dani told me about you. I hope one day we will be able to reunite at home. I owe my saviors a beer.

Love,
Your Erin

Closing his eyes, Logan imagined Erin's arms wrapped around him tight. Smiling, he returned to the present. He closed his email and focused on the map. *First, we choose where to stop the Russians.*

Chapter 3

Poltava, Ukraine – January 6, 0800 hrs

Below-zero air kept the cloudless sky pink well after the sun climbed out of the horizon. The morning stand-to had been as uneventful as the previous ten. Michael smiled in thanks at the thought. He looked out the fourth-floor window to the Vorskla River. The bridge was covered in a briar patch of wire. More wire lined the riverbanks. Huge piles of rubble remained where tall buildings once looked down on the sixty-meter-wide river. Michael hmphed at the memory of Russian artillery collapsing the one across the street. *Pure luck. Could have been me.*

A rifle shot cracked the icy calm. Michael looked north to the source. More shots followed. A machine gun joined.

"Now what?" Michael turned away from the window and ran down the hallway to his command post. "What is going on?"

"Sir, troops in contact. OP3 engaged a Russian patrol at the north end of the beach," Michael's radioman answered, pointing to the spot on a map. Michael grabbed the radio hand mic out of the soldier's hand.

"Three-Six, Six, can you handle your mess?" Michael didn't see the soldier flinch at his tone of voice.

The radio crackled back, "Yeah, I think so. Killed three of the ten or so. They're on our shore. Gonna use two squads to clear them."

Michael shuddered. *Russians are in our wire.* "Do it." Michael tossed the radio hand mic back to the radioman and then snapped his fingers at Kim. "Get the reserve squad here now!"

Kim flashed a thumbs-up and took over the radio.

Small explosions added to the battle. An auto-cannon in the east opened fire.

"Sir, Third needs some help! A BTR has OP3 pinned down but they can't get into position with a Javelin." Kim pointed on the map.

"Where is our FO? He needs to get a fire mission going. I want HE on it!"

"We can reach them with our mortars," Kim offered. Running footsteps in the hallway were probably from the company's forward observer, Second Lieutenant Padilla.

"That will result in counter-battery." Michael glared at Kim.

Kim listened to the radio a moment before responding. "Sir, they need help right now."

Michael stared at Kim. Padilla entered the room, breaking the spell.

"I think the BTR is next to a pre-plot target. I can get rounds quick," Padilla announced after looking at the map.

"Who's guns?" Michael asked.

"It's a one-oh-five battery. Sir."

"Do it. And where were you?"

"Had to take a dump, sir. Sorry. Sir."

Michael grabbed a walkie-talkie and strode down the hallway to the far end of the building. *Padilla hasn't earned my trust yet about not using our mortars. And our mortars are too close to the command post. I need to move the mortars today. Or the command post.*

At the far north end of the building, Michael found a window he could look out and see only the west side of the river. No sense in risking a Russian sniper or BTR seeing him. Tracers from the BTR ricocheted up and away. Dust and smoke marked the street the fight was on, but Michael didn't see anyone.

The radio squawked. "Six, Seven, I have the reserve squad with me. You want to take them to OP3?"

"Negative. Wait. Have them secure our building for now." *The whole point of that squad was to protect me from any other Russian infiltrators!*

Ripping linen preceded a large explosion across the river. Padilla's fire mission arrived. The BTR stopped firing and the tempo of rifle fire slackened. Distant yelling echoed in the distance.

Michael grew impatient and keyed up his radio. "Three-Six, Six, sitrep!"

There was a pause before the reply crackled back. "Six, Three-Seven, secured our bank. We are conducting actions on the objective." Staff Sergeant Ganahl's tense voice hinted there was more to the story.

Michael stared out the window. *It's not that I prefer the damn platoon leader answer when I ask for them—I do. It's that Staff Sergeant Ganahl just pisses me off. Of course, First Sergeant Kim will say something to me if I put him in his place again.* Michael drummed is fingers on his chest, opting to wait another minute.

"Seven, Three-Seven, sending two WIA to the collection point," the radio crackled.

Kim immediately radioed back, "Roger, I'm waiting here for you."

Michael turned from the window and headed back to the command post. It was too cold. The brisk pace through the hallway reinvigorated him.

"Why hasn't Second Lieutenant Zaman come up on the radio yet?" Michael snapped as he entered the warmer room.

"Not sure, sir," Michael's XO, Lieutenant Burton, answered.

Michael glared back before keying up his radio. "Three-Six, Six." When no reply came immediately, Michael repeated himself.

"Six, Three-Seven, he is down. I'll have an update for you in about two minutes," Ganahl answered.

Michael blew out a big breath. *Of course*. He sat down in a chair and looked at the map as Burton plotted the last known location of the Russian BTR. Two minutes passed too slowly.

"Six, Three-Seven, okay, we are secure here. Two wounded. One litter urgent, the other ambulatory. Recovered one Russian body. Seven more bodies are out in the open. A Russian sniper shoots at us every time we try to check on them. We've already replenished ammo."

"Are you confident we have no other Russians on our bank?"

"Roger."

"Double check. I want all platoons to thoroughly patrol our sector. Out." Michael set down his radio and looked at the map. *Where was that Russian patrol heading to?* Michael traced the line of buildings that ran from the river to the command post. *They were coming here. I know it.*

"XO." Michael snapped his fingers then circled a building on the map. "I want to move our command post. We've been in this building too long and it's too obvious. I want to move to here."

"Yes, sir."

"I'm going to the aid station to check on our wounded. I want you up and running in the new location by the time I return."

Burton looked at his watch, then nodded. "Roger, sir. Okay gang, let's move it."

Michael strode out of the room and yelled, "Reserve squad! Give me a fire team!" There was no way Michael would risk movement to the aid station without some soldiers to provide security.

The trip to the aid station was quiet. The paratroopers moved from building to building for several blocks. Once on the bluffs, they could move openly. Still, everyone carried their rifles at the ready.

The battalion surgeon was working on Zaman when Michael arrived. Michael watched from the doorway, tuning out the surgeon's urgent directions. A touch on Michael's elbow pulled him out of the trance.

"Sir, you okay?" Kim pulled Michael away from the doorway.

"Yeah. I'm fine, First Sergeant." Michael leaned against the wall in the hallway. "What happened?"

"Wade was shot in the upper arm early on. He'll be okay. Lieutenant Zaman got hit by the BTR when they were moving to flank the Russian patrol. He'll be very lucky if he doesn't lose his leg. It's pretty messed up. He'll live, though. Thank God for tourniquets."

"I see. Terrible timing. I need him for the coming attack." Michael spat on the floor before taking a sip from his canteen.

Kim just stared at him and shifted his weight. He spoke after a long pause. "Sir, it is never good timing to suffer a life-changing wound."

"You know what I mean, First Sergeant." Michael turned and walked out of the aid station. *I need to let battalion know I moved my command post. Oh, and about Zaman.* Michael snapped his fingers at his paratroopers and pointed them toward the battalion TOC.

Pereshchepyne, Ukraine – January 6, 1800 hrs

The café was dark and quiet as Kiselyov stepped in out of the cold. Out of habit, his eyes swept across the room, studying every face and pair of hands. Only uniformed Russian soldiers occupied the space. *Ah*. Kiselyov recognized the back of a head sitting at the corner table.

"Victor, good to see you." Kiselyov greeted his old friend as he approached, allowing Molchalin to turn and see him.

"Mikhail, you too." Molchalin stood and hugged Kiselyov. "I saved you the seat facing the room."

"You are kind. Have you ordered?" Kiselyov took off his coat and hung it on the back of his chair before sitting.

"Just tea. I'm told they make good stroganoff here though." Molchalin returned to his seat and took a sip of tea.

"And the cooks? They are...?"

"The family of an officer from the supply depot here. They liberated this café from its nazi owners. Now it offers safe food."

"Ah, good. I don't trust the locals."

"Chechnya's legacy."

"One of many, Victor."

Molchalin nodded and closed his eyes. When he opened them, a waitress approached.

"Generals, what can I get for you?"

"Vodka, and my friend says your stroganoff is good."

"Yes, General. And for you?" She looked at Molchalin.

"Stroganoff as well."

"Of course."

Kiselyov watched the waitress go to the kitchen before talking again. He nodded toward a table of officers standing up to depart. "What is the GRU doing here?"

"Ah, them. They have a camp northwest of town. I'm not supposed to know what it is." Molchalin's face slid into a sly smile.

Kiselyov waited for the GRU officers to leave before continuing. "Those weasels clearly are not Spetsnaz."

"No. Their camp has machine gun positions facing inward."

"Ahhhh... I was not aware we had any prisoner camps here. We sent all of our prisoners back to the camp at Saratov."

"We don't, and Mikhail, remember we don't have a camp here." Molchalin winked.

Kiselyov nodded and Molchalin shifted in his chair. The waitress returned with a glass of vodka.

"Your back any better?"

"No. It is a good reminder I'm still alive."

"We survived. You want a sip? It would soothe the pain." Kiselyov pushed the glass to the middle of the table.

"I won't. I can't. Remember I almost lost my division."

"Your reputation from Grozny saved you. I admire your strength and dedication to pull out of the complete grip of the vodka. I would not have done the same."

"Ah, but you handle it better."

"Good vodka, yes. The memories, perhaps, no better than you."

"There are times when I feel I actually died with my regiment on that street and only my ghost is here today."

"But you saved me from certain death that day."

"You would have done the same for me."

Kiselyov winked. "Tanya would vouch you are no ghost."

Molchalin laughed. "Hard to make a child as a ghost."

"Please give her Mila and my regards."

"Yes. How is Mila?"

"She is visiting her family in Kazan. She is worried."

Molchalin lowered his voice and looked around. "Worried?"

Kiselyov nodded and leaned in. "She told me some of what she has seen on her travels. What she has heard whispered."

"What are they saying in the cities?"

"Victor, it's not good. People wonder how the West can have such consistent and vast propaganda. Perhaps it isn't just propaganda. There is doubt. The mood seems to be this war is perhaps unwinnable."

"Tanya has told me the same."

"But we cannot lose this war."

"And we won't. NATO will never invade Mother Russia. That would result in immediate nuclear holocaust."

"Yes. But if NATO's attack should succeed, the fear at home is we won't be able to stop NATO from capturing nearly our entire army. We have no reserves. And you know we won't be able to withdraw via the Crimea. That bridge doesn't last five days between hits," Kiselyov finished with a frown.

"Partisan strikes on the railway through the Donbas have been worse than those in our sector. We are lucky to have a shorter supply line."

"Indeed, Victor. We can hold. I have faith. But the people at home seem to have less and less."

"I know. Tanya has shared some of the same observations with me, my friend. She worries that if NATO can defeat us in the Ukraine, it will cause the fall of Nikolai Voroshilov. That would unleash unrest and purges of the high command. Tanya worries where we would stand in that mess, even though you and I have managed to remain carefully politically neutral."

"If NATO breaks our lines completely, you and I won't be around to see the political fallout. This is why we must crush them west of Kharkiv."

"You agree with General Golovko's assessment of NATO's plans?"

"I think they will strike on my boundary with the Twentieth Combined Arms Army. I've had the Fourth Tank Division concentrate its obstacle efforts there. The Sixth Tank and Forty-Seventh Guards are ready to counterattack north into their flank and drive them toward the border. NATO can't afford getting close to the national border. No depth will be their death."

"And if NATO should penetrate to Kharkiv?"

"Then, Victor, I would have you take control of my troops south of the salient and smash them as I know you can do. A five-division counterattack under your command would destroy NATO's forces before I got my headquarters established at Belgorod. The field bunkers we made last summer are still available."

"May it not come to that."

The waitress arrived back at the table with their meals and the two generals turned to reminiscing of younger years.

Bairak, Ukraine – January 7, 0200 hrs

The laptop screen glared back at Logan as he contemplated the map. After spending all night developing their vision of the Russian counterattack, Logan now focused on how to defeat it. Without looking, Logan raised his coffee cup to his lips. No liquid life flowed and Logan looked into the mug. *What was that? My third cup? Fourth?* Logan turned in his chair and poured another cup from the pot in the corner.

"How is it coming, Logan?" Andy sat down next to Logan and waited for him to take a sip.

"You know, last summer, I never had time or the desire to come up with multiple courses of action." Logan waved his hand at the laptop. "I've come up with my best idea, creating a second one now... Well, this second idea sucks."

"Major Douglas usually has us focus on the better plan and the second is just a throwaway."

"Kinda defeats the military decision-making process."

"Welcome to staff. As long as we defeat the enemy." Andy winked.

"Geesh."

A soldier poked her head in the doorway. "Sir, Captain Baldwin, we have something to show you."

"Oh?" Andy looked at Logan and nodded for him to follow. "Take a break and let's see what new intel my troops found."

Andy and Logan followed the soldier to the intel vehicle. The soldier sat down in front of her laptop, waiting for Andy and Logan to gather behind her.

"So, sir, I got this email from my basic training battle buddy." She opened the attached picture. "A Raven in the 173rd took this a few days ago."

Logan looked hard at the picture of three Russian generals. *That dude looks familiar. Where have I seen that face?*

"Where was this taken?" Andy asked.

"Poltava, near the river."

Andy pointed at the picture. "Those faces look familiar. Please tell me we identified them."

"Now, let me show you this." The soldier opened another picture and moved it next to the other. "That, sir, is the Russian Minister of Defense Popov. Less than a klick from the front lines, owning it like a boss."

"If only I could have been watching that Raven real time. I'd have dropped a mortar round on his head." Logan noticed the grid location displayed on the picture. *Someone totally could have.*

"Who are the other two?" Andy interrupted.

"Sir, pretty sure the guy on the left is Lieutenant General Kiselyov, commander of the First Guards Tank Army. On the right is definitely Lieutenant General Molchalin of the Sixth Combined Arms Army."

"If only." Andy shook his head. "Killing them would make this offensive a lot easier."

"Interesting." Logan scratched the whiskers on his cheek.

"What's that?" Andy looked at Logan.

"Ivan seems pretty confident in his front line. That we won't attack. That we won't try anything. For them to be that close? And the cameras accompanying him? Gotta be a propaganda op."

"That jives with the complacency observed among the Russian outposts."

"It does, Andy. Explains why the Russians would have a secret POW camp a hundred klicks from the frontline."

"Huh?" Andy cocked an eyebrow.

"Erin emailed me about finding indications of a secret POW camp near Pereshchepyne. The Russians didn't disclose this camp and we think they aren't disclosing over two hundred POWs."

"What would they gain from keeping them off record? And why so close?"

Logan shrugged. "Maybe the farther they moved them, the more likely to get noticed?"

"Hmmm..." Andy's eyes narrowed. "Who are these POWs that the Russians would keep them off the books?"

"I'm not sure."

"Doesn't seem like the Russians are planning on giving them back, does it? Our plans are going to get within ten klicks of Pereshchepyne. Wonder how the Russians will react to that."

Logan scrunched his face. *Not good. Probably a mass grave.* He kept his thoughts to himself, but looking at Andy and the soldier, Logan knew it was a shared thought.

"Sir," the soldier quietly asked, "you want me to take a good look at Russian defenses around Pereshchepyne?"

"Do it." Andy tugged Logan's sleeve and nodded to the doorway. Both went out into the briefing area of the shed.

"Logan, if you were gonna try to rescue them, how would you do it?"

"Depends, I guess. With the Forty-Seventh Guards Tank Division north of the camp, I'd want to swing around from the west. But the timing of the Russian counterattack matters. That's the same ground they're gonna use."

"Right. Maybe keep that thought handy."

Sudivka, Ukraine – January 17, 0900 hrs

A gust of icy air rushed across the room as Savvy entered the house. Top and Larrabee leaned on the table, studying the map together and in earnest discussion. She took off her helmet and quietly set it down before joining on the opposite side of the table.

"Sir," Savvy murmured when there seemed a break in the dialog, "I heard them SP." *Them.*

"Right. Still not comfortable about this at all." Larrabee looked up at Savvy.

"I'm not sure anyone ever is initially. But it might not be all bad. At least it's just one reporter and not a whole camera crew," Top offered.

"Well, still, I have too much to do. I don't have time for a reporter. I want you to keep her away from me. Were either of you able to find out what her angle is going to be?" Larrabee pointed at Top.

Top and Savvy shook their heads.

"Well, where are you sticking this reporter?" Larrabee looked at Top.

"I'm thinking I'll have her go with Sergeant Heydte. Keeps her in less danger, and at the same time, mostly away from you."

"With Heydte? Sure that's a good idea?"

"Why not?"

"He's kinda a redneck. Can we trust him to not say something that will get us in trouble?" Larrabee recognized the respect the troop had for the chief mechanic, but noticed his rough edges.

Top laughed and Savvy smirked.

"When we get home, you'll see his smooth side come out. Heydte can polish up around civilians and family. Don't worry." Top patted Larrabee's back.

"Okay. I'll trust you, Top." Larrabee's face was blank, though. "Anyway, back to the guard mission. Who is going to physically tie in with the paratroopers on the flank?"

"Sir, knowing Lieutenant Ewell, he'll do that himself."

"Hmmm...not XO?" Larrabee looked at Savvy.

"I can if you want, sir. Captain Trondfjell liked keeping my track centered since we often end up with a wide front."

"Oh yeah, that's a good point. Well, let's do that. Maybe I'll swing over to the flank at linkup and get a feel for the paratroopers myself."

Top frowned. "Lone tank? Maybe we better pull a section from First or Second Platoon to roll with you."

"No, keep the tank platoons massed in the center. My tank's an Abrams. And I'll be with Fourth Platoon's Bradleys—not really alone. Anyway, moving on." Larrabee flipped his hand to dismiss Top's worry.

The rumbling of diesel engines outside stopped the discussion. The three exchanged looks.

Larrabee sighed. "I guess I better go play host." He pushed off the table and crossed the room to grab his helmet and rifle.

The door flung open and Pacheco stomped the snow off his feet as he entered. Behind, a well-bundled-up female with a civilian hiking pack on her back and a Pelican laptop case followed. Savvy expected the civilian to have the traditional blue helmet cover and body armor press members normally wore. This one had the same camouflage as a soldier and just a patch with PRESS. *She looks professional enough.* Savvy read the writing on the press pass hanging from a neck lanyard. *Who or what is the IFJ?*

"Room, attention!" Larrabee called out, and everyone snapped to attention.

"Carry on." Pacheco smiled and took his helmet off. "Dakota, how are you?"

"Good, sir."

"First Sergeant, good to see you. How is Candi?"

"Ready for me to come home. Good to see you too, Colonel."

Pacheco pulled a package from behind his back and handed it to Savvy. "Colonel Ollerich dropped off this for you."

Savvy took the package and saw Tye's handwriting on it. She blushed. *I can't believe the regimental commander is playing mailman for my husband.* "Thank you, sir." Savvy would wait for a private time to open the package from her husband. Savvy glanced over at the reporter setting her pack down in the corner.

Pacheco waved his hand over at the reporter. "Team, this is Kristyn Rhodes, a print journalist. Ms. Rhodes, this is Captain Dakota Larrabee, commander of Lightning Troop, First Sergeant Bob Harris, and Lieutenant Savvy Kraemer, the XO."

"Good to meet you. Call me Kristyn." Kristyn shook their hands. Savvy noticed a firm grip and flint in the eye. *Maybe not a powder puff civilian?*

"Kristyn, you are in good hands. Dakota, walk with me please." Pacheco nodded to Kristyn and waited for Dakota to finish putting his helmet on, then the two went outside. Savvy waited for the door to close before turning back to Kristyn.

"Okay, Kristyn, welcome. Interesting accent. Where are you from?"

"I was born in Colorado." Kristyn flashed both eyebrows up and down and smiled.

"I was gonna guess somewhere overseas. Not the UK or Australia. Maybe New Zealand?"

"I've lived in South Africa for the last twelve years. I think that's what you're hearing."

"Sometime I'll have to hear that story. What are you hoping to report on?"

Kristyn pulled a packet of paperwork from her laptop case and handed it over. "I'm read in on the coming offensive and will cover it from your perspective. I will tag my reports with a nearby city that hasn't recently changed hands. Over the years, I've learned to discern between sensitive information and what won't risk you. When in doubt, I'll ask you to review my work before I send it out. I know the consequences of leaking info."

"Not your first rodeo, is it?" Top smiled at Kristyn.

"No. That's why I don't wear the traditional blue on the battlefield. Not that the Russians even care to discriminate between soldier and non-combatant. I know my own survival is closely linked with yours."

"We appreciate that," Savvy replied, and pointed to Kristyn's credentials. "Who is the IFJ? That a magazine?"

"International Federation of Journalists. I'm a freelance journalist. The IFJ provides vetted credentials. Without credentials, a journalist doesn't get in the door."

"What is your background?"

"I started out with the *Denver Post*, then joined the AP. Five years ago I turned to freelancing. Nearly my whole career has focused on conflicts. Afghanistan. I was in Kabul during its fall. Syria. Sudan. Mali. Some of my time has been imbedded, most not. I've been a war correspondent for fifteen years now. Others focus on the policy and strategy; I bring home the human side stories. You soldiers are still family, neighbors, and such to people. And the rest of the nation wonders what it's like to be on the front lines."

"Interesting. Who prints your stories?" Savvy was surprised. Kristyn looked much younger than that.

"Mainly periodicals. A few online-only outlets. Lately, Colorado and Texas outlets have been my most reliable customers."

"So, you are writing about the troopers and not the events?"

"Both. I'm covering how the soldiers handle the events. Colonel Ollerich told me he wanted me with Lightning Troop because you have the most interesting story so far."

"Oh? What did he tell you?" Top responded first.

"You've been here since the beginning, coming over as the GRF. Ollerich said you played a big role in the initial defense. That you were cut off by the Russians and fought your way back. He also mentioned some of the best tank commanders in the whole Army are in your formation. Ollerich didn't say who, but that I would probably recognize names from the South China Sea war."

Savvy looked over at Top. *Fiery Cross? I'm not volunteering info. Dani and Running Bear wouldn't like that.* Top seemed to read her mind and nodded back. Savvy turned back to Kristyn, who had a raised eyebrow.

"Did I intrude into something?" Kristyn asked after a pause.

"Well..." Top cleared his throat. "Kinda. I think I know who ol' Remington Six was referring to, but I'll tell you those warriors might not be super talkative about it."

"You mean Colonel Ollerich, right? Remington Six?"

Top nodded.

"Well, he told me the same thing too."

Savvy turned her attention to the papers. She quickly read through them. "Kristyn, says you're staying with us until at least the end of the month? Is this all your gear?"

"Yes, that is correct." Kristyn gestured at her pack. "I have everything I need in that pack and the Pelican case. All I ask is a seat to ride in, a place to write on my laptop, and means to charge my batteries. I can sleep anywhere."

"Fair enough, ma'am. You'll ride with our troop's maintenance team chief, Sergeant First Class Dave Heydte. He has an open seat and it is probably one of the safer places to be."

"I'm not looking for the safest place to be. I'm here to learn about you all. Am I allowed to move around in your formation?"

"Let me ask Captain Larrabee on that. Let's get you linked up with Sergeant Heydte." Top waved for Kristyn to follow him.

"Good to meet you, Kristyn." Savvy smiled at the reporter.

"You too." Kristyn collected up her stuff and followed Top.

Savvy waited for the door to close before ripping into the package from Tye. Inside was a wooden nesting doll wrapped in a shawl, and a note. Savvy put the shawl on. She held the doll in one hand and cherished the note, reading it several times before opening the doll. Savvy sat down and allowed herself to daydream. There was still time.

Myrhorod, Ukraine – January 19, 1200 hrs

The wail of the air raid siren stopped everything. Faces turned toward a blinking red light above the doorway of the large warehouse.

"Go! Get to the bunkers!"

As one, over a hundred bodies snapped into motion, streaming for the doorway, most picking up their helmet and body armor.

At the back of the crowd, one soldier lingered behind, her ponytail swishing as she checked sleeping bags for anyone left behind. Satisfied, she joined the mass of soldiers flowing out the doorway.

Exposure to the blinding sunlight and searing cold was momentary as they all rushed into the doorway of the bunker. It was a concrete-encased ramp leading down to a larger room.

"Last one!" Captain Sam Gentry called as she entered the bunker door. Two soldiers closed the heavy metal doors and then retreated into the bunker. The soldiers milled, organizing themselves into their squads and platoons.

"Ma'am, we are accounted for. Commander and First Sergeant still haven't returned from their meeting."

"Thank you, Sergeant Yates." Sam forced a smile. Even in the dim light of the bunker, she could see tension. Eyes looking at the ceiling. Shoulders hunched slightly.

"What do you think they're targeting?" Sergeant Yates asked.

"The airfield. We are safer here. This is a good bunker and we're far enough from the aircraft, the fuel, the runway and such. I've survived with less." Sam forced another smile. *God, that sucked.* Sam remembered how terrified she was at Fiery Cross. Unstoppable enemy air raids and artillery made her little better than a rat. *This is different. We have air defenses now. Breathe.*

A muffled explosion in the distance silenced the room. Another explosion. A third was quickly followed by a ripple of explosions.

Sam looked around the room. Eyes stared at the ceiling, others at the floor.

"Those sound over a klick away," Sam announced. A few nods and shoulders easing down rewarded her effort.

"The XO would know," a voice called from the back corner. Murmurs of agreement followed.

"Ma'am, what do you think of this mission?" Yates whispered.

"This is the sort of mission we live for. Rescuing prisoners is as good as it gets. And you know a secret camp means they won't come home if the Russians were left to their own devices. Ever."

"Hooah." Yates nodded. "I meant the op itself."

"Intel seems legit. As long as we get there before Ivan reacts to Fifth Corps. Which is why we gotta make this happen. Timing will be everything. The window of opportunity opens when we rupture the Russian defensive belt, but closes when the Russians react."

"Right? Pretty long infil from the LZ to the objective, though."

"I'd rather march up the Oril River valley than get shot down by that heavy cluster of air defenses. On the ground, nobody can match a company of Rangers." Sam grinned. A whole air defense regiment defended Pereshchepyne. SA-27 missiles, which the Russians called Buk, backed by SA-22 missile and cannon systems, would be lethal to anything that tried to fly close to the city. The western approaches were blocked by minefields and a company of Russian motorized infantry. *The supply depot on the east side of Pereshchepyne means that much to Ivan.*

"Damn straight, ma'am. Why not just do the one flight in, land on the objective, then exfil directly with that SEAD mission?"

"The worry is a major effort to destroy the Russian SAMs will tip off the mission. A loss of surprise might give the Russians time to kill the POWs. Also, I'd bet a month's pay the camp has some SA-29s on the roof. A SEAD mission can't eliminate those. But we can't expect the POWs to march out, so the SEAD mission leading the Night Stalkers is necessary for exfil. And if exfil fails, Plan B is we hide nearby until 3ACR pushes south to us. Either way, we will get our people home."

"How long will it take for 3ACR to move that Russian tank division out of the way?"

"Doesn't matter. This mission is worth it."

"Hooah, ma'am." Yates bumped fists with his company XO.

Sam pulled her intel packet out of her cargo pocket. Yates and a couple other Rangers gathered around it. She flipped to the satellite photo of the objective. The secret POW camp was in an abandoned mill secluded near the western suburbs of Pereshchepyne and the canal north of town. A new wire fence shining in the sunlight betrayed the purpose.

"I bet it sucks climbing to the position on top of that water tower," Yates quipped as he pointed to the tall water tower in the compound's southwestern corner. A pair of Russian soldiers were clearly visible with a machine gun and a MANPAD—a man-portable air defense missile system. "That a PKM?" The PKM was a reliable and effective 7.62mm machine gun.

"I think so. The ones on the mill roof appear to be a mix of PKM, NSV, and AGS-30s though." Sam put her finger on the roof of the four-story mill.

"Probably a PKM in this little guard tower they built on the northeast corner."

"Yes. Figure one soldier in there. Too small for a pair of soldiers, and it doesn't have the vantage point the water tower or roof have. Three Tigrs and two cargo trucks. Figure forty enemy soldiers." Sam looked at Yates, watching his brain turning.

"Yeah, I'd have the snipers take the two tower positions out and the mortars hit the roof." Yates nodded to himself. "Yeah, that's how I would do that. Gotta put the support by fire to the northwest, where it can engage all three positions. Figure security on the road from each direction. Then breach the fence in the corner and assault like so." He traced his finger across the compound.

Sam smiled. Yates was pretty close to the commander's plan.

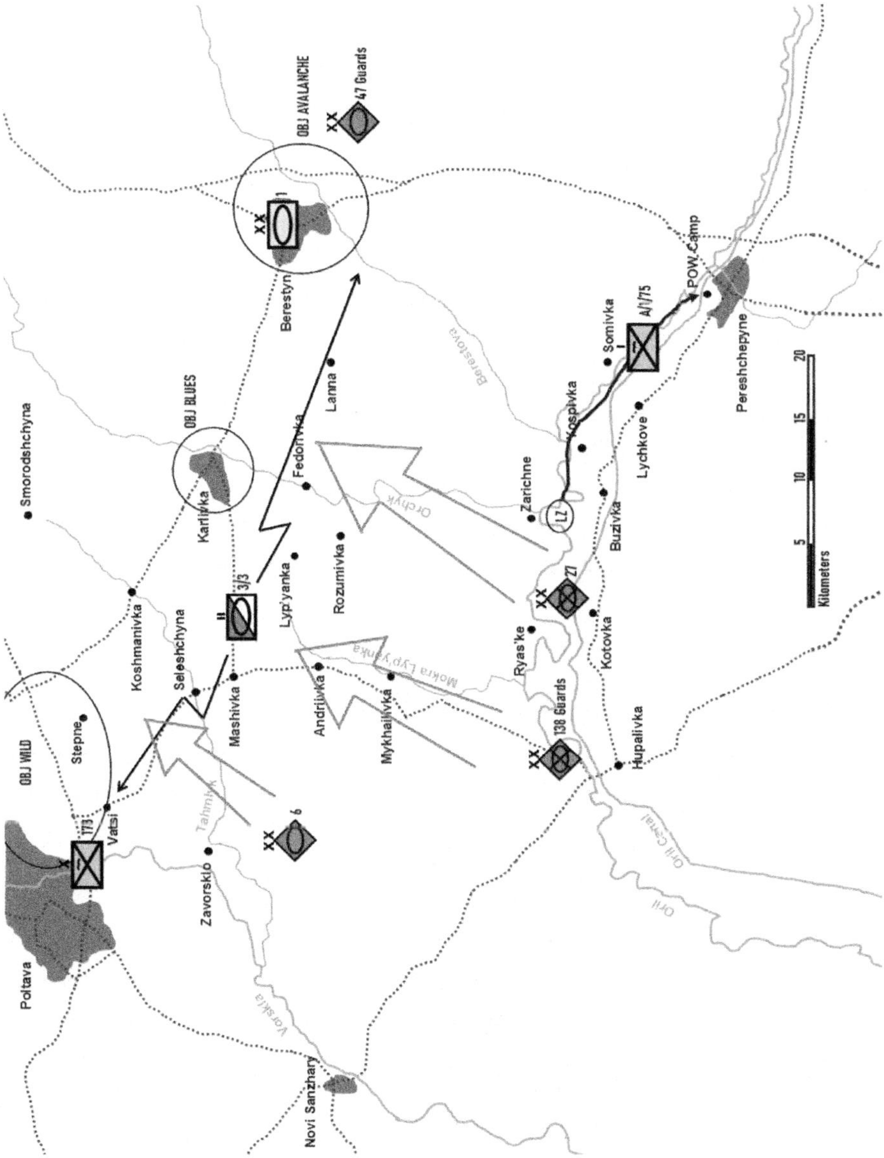
OBJ WILD
Poltava
173
Vatsi
Stepne
Zavorsklo
Koshmanivka
Seleshchyna
Mashivka
6
3/3
Karlivka
OBJ BLUES
Smorodshchyna
Lyp'yanka
Rozumivka
Andriivka
Mykhailivka
Mokra Lyp'yanka
Fedorivka
Lanna
Orchyk
Berestyn
OBJ AVALANCHE
47 Guards
Berestova
Zarichne
LZ
Kospivka
Somivka
A/1/75
POW Camp
Pereshchepyne
Lychkove
Buzivka
Kotovka
Ryas'ke
27
138 Guards
Hupalivka
Oril Canal
Oril
Vorskla
Novi Sanzhary
5
10
15
20
Kilometers

Washington, DC – January 19, 1300 hrs

The Situation Room at the White House was standing room only. Every statutory member was present and flanked by multiple aides. Nobody wanted to be unprepared for this afternoon's meeting.

"Let's get started," President Kayla Tribolet announced before she even crossed the threshold of the room, waving her hands for everyone to keep their seats. Normally, she enjoyed the pomp, but today, her mood was too dark to relish in civilities.

"Yes, Madam President, we are ready. The attack begins at eight p.m. our time. The troops are ready. We will prevail," Secretary of Defense James Arnold responded as Tribolet took her seat.

"Would you say otherwise?"

Arnold blinked and flinched back in his chair. "Of course, Madam President. This offensive is well planned. I have seen every last detail."

"James, if you are so confident, why are you still sending the First Cavalry Division to Poltava, scheduled to arrive two weeks from now? Why ask to send another division over?" Secretary of Energy Tomas Gonzales asked, continuing his habit of being a thorn in the former general's neck.

"Tomas, as I told you before, the Russians know we are going to attack. The point of attack is dictated much by terrain and the situation. The only way we can surprise Voroshilov is through timing. Having fresh divisions arriving after the attack provides us with reserves to follow up success. Remember the Russians have no reserves." Arnold had the same face he used when explaining life to his grandchildren.

"After this attack, Russia won't have much left at all. The remains of their navy are trapped in port. This attack will draw their air force into the open and their army will be trapped. Voroshilov will have no option left. He will accept our peace terms." Jasmine Simons, the National Security Advisor, flashed her disarming smile. "Ending the war soon enough to have the troops home before the general election."

"And if Voroshilov has no navy, no air force, no army, that leaves him with only his nuclear forces." Gonzales leaned forward. "We are taking a risk he won't resort to his last weapons?"

"Tomas," Director of National Intelligence Ed Surles immediately answered, "our sources indicate that will not happen. There is nothing to suggest the gentlemen's agreement is broken. Unless we cross the Russian border, the Russians will not use their weapons of mass destruction. Even if Voroshilov loses his cool, it is hard to imagine the rest of their security council would also. We know the Russian officers controlling those nuclear weapons have the same gravity and professionalism our own do. We see Voroshilov's control over his military—all of it—waning with our offensive's success."

"And we will not cross into Russia. Correct?" Tribolet raised an eyebrow at Arnold.

"No, Madam President. Our operation will maintain a five-kilometer buffer. Our aim is to destroy the Russian army, not grab every square inch of Ukraine back."

"I know. You have no idea how exhausting Lytvyn has been about it." Tribolet had spent more time convincing the Ukrainian president to trust NATO's method of warfare.

"Speaking of Lytvyn, do we want to discuss the latest offer the Chinese suggested?" Secretary of State Elliot DeBever interrupted.

"Sure. Why not?" Tribolet sat back, sure the latest proposal was as impossible as the previous.

"This one would have Russia accept Ukrainian membership into NATO and the EU, while establishing the national border along the current lines of military-controlled territory."

Several snorts from the back row of chairs joined the smirks. Six months into the war and the Russians and Ukrainians refused to sit down in the same room for peace talks. Each proposal was as completely unacceptable to the other as possible.

"Elliot, are the Ukrainians still planning on insisting on regaining everything, including the Donbas and Crimea, once we have destroyed the Russian army for them?" Arnold asked.

"Well, we are going to have it soon enough under our own military control." DeBever shrugged. "It would make sense."

"Did we forget Voroshilov formally annexed Crimea and the separatist areas of the Donbas before he invaded? Won't our attack into those areas trigger the criteria for nuclear war? And if we don't take those areas, won't the Russian army have an escape route?" Gonzalez countered.

Silence gripped the room.

"Tomas has a valid concern." Tribolet broke the silence.

"I don't think we need to stress the importance of keeping the Russians from resorting to nuclear weapons." Simons cleared her throat. "They use one, we use one. A detonation on Russian soil triggers Dead Hand and the whole world turns to ash and glass."

"We need a good peace offer that Voroshilov would accept before we reach that point." DeBever nodded as he spoke, leading others to nod also.

"And what would be acceptable to Russia and us?" Tribolet asked, still shuddering.

"The Russian objectives for this war were to destroy Ukraine's military and industrial capabilities, to seize the industrial southeast and the ethnic Russian areas, and create a buffer space. Let's consider those in our offers," Surles offered.

Arnold scoffed. "Yeah, well we will have defeated Russia, so they lose their demands."

"Yes, but if we can build our offer with a token of what they aimed to gain, they can accept defeat and save face. Voroshilov has to have something to claim for the half-million Russian widows and orphans." Surles glared at Arnold.

"What if," Gonzales offered, "what if we propose the following terms: Ukraine gains back all the territory they lost since July 12. Russia gains international recognition of Crimea and the breakaway portions of the Donbas. Ukraine gets NATO membership. Russia gets a twenty-mile DMZ along the border with NATO."

"Well, I can tell you Lithuania for sure won't agree to that. Vilnius is maybe twenty miles from the border," Arnold countered. "And I'm sure Lytvyn won't accept loss of any territory."

"I like Tomas's idea," Tribolet chimed in. "What would be a proper DMZ width, James?"

"Perhaps three kilometers on each side of the border. It would probably end up like the Korean DMZ."

"I think this is a fair deal to both. Especially since it could prevent the death of all humanity," DeBever agreed.

"We have to get Ukraine to agree also."

"I'll call Lytvyn and tell him to agree or we don't attack." Tribolet crossed her arms. "I want Elliot and Jasmine to press hard on our allies. I want to give Voroshilov this offer as soon as it is obvious our attack will succeed."

"Cutthroat." Surles smiled.

"Okay, shall we get back to the agenda?" Simons asked.

Tribolet nodded and the meeting turned back to the attack plan.

Chapter 4

Poltava, Ukraine – January 20, 0300 hrs

Michael looked at his watch for the third time in less than a minute. *Any second now.* His stomach soured and the urge to urinate again gripped him. *I just pissed fifteen minutes ago. Can't show any weakness.* Michael looked around the room. His radio operator and Kim looked back at him in the dark. The eerie green world in the night vision goggles served to further unnerve Michael.

A beep in the radio earpiece preceded a single word. "Rock."

Michael took a breath and nodded at his company before keying up his radio and releasing the button three times. The release of the attack lifted the tension from his body. Seconds ticked by in silence. Minutes. Michael remained still, leaning against the wall.

"Six, Two-Seven, secure." Out in the frozen darkness, the paratroopers of Second Platoon moved through buildings on the Russian side of the Vorskla River. So far, not a shot ruptured the night. Michael smiled. He reached out and tugged the sleeve of his radio operator and moved toward the door.

As he stepped into the street, Michael's breath fogged his night vision goggles and he paused to let it clear before moving toward the river. Ahead, he could see the paratroopers of Third Platoon dashing across the ice in teams. The glow of chemlites marked the passage through the Russian minefield. Careful observation over the last month tracked Russian patrols using the path.

Snow crunched under Michael's feet as he sprinted across the ice. He slowed to a jog as soon as he was in the trees on the far side. The empty houses of the riverside neighborhood offered plenty of places to hide—to hide Russians or Americans.

"This is our casualty collection point." Kim opened a new chemlite and shook it before cracking it and tossing it next to the gate. Michael had been so focused on crossing the river he forgot the first sergeant and a pair of medics had followed right behind him. The lapse in awareness sent a shiver up Michael's spine.

"Right," Michael whispered back. A nod to his radio operator and Michael continued east. As he came to a bend in the street, he saw the outline of a pair of paratroopers and joined them. One turned and Michael saw it was Padilla.

"Sir, Ganahl just led two squads into the first school house." Padilla pointed at a three-story building ahead. The school was suspected to be where a Russian outpost platoon was living. It was also the stepping stone to the eight-story building across the street. That tower dominated the Myru Street bridge and the train station area.

"Right." Michael looked at his watch. *Still on schedule.*

"You still think there's a Russian OP in the tower?" Padilla asked after a pause.

"I don't think they would give it up, even after all the missile strikes."

Padilla nodded and continued watching down the street.

The ripping crash of gunfire from the school shattered the quiet. Michael's ears sorted out the sounds of both American and Russian rifles and automatic weapons.

Padilla tensed up. "Here we go."

Running feet from the west pounded the brittle asphalt. First Platoon quickly moved past Michael and filtered through the houses nearby.

"Six, Three-Seven, we are secure and set," Ganahl gasped on the radio through heavy breathing. His platoon was ready to support First Platoon's assault across the street to the tower.

"Roger, team, execute," Michael responded.

"Shot," the company mortar squad answered on the radio and the hollow *thunk* of the 60mm mortar firing carried through the darkness.

Michael cringed for the coming explosion in the street ahead. The blast was blinding as smoke rounds burst and the smoke billowed in the street.

Padilla suddenly got up and ran to the school with his observer, leaving Michael. *We are gonna take incoming now,* Michael realized. He tugged his radio operator and jogged to the school doorway marked with another chemlite.

A single shot rang out from the tower. Machine gun fire from Third Platoon answered and the sound of the battle escalated as Third Platoon fired grenades. *Must have pinpointed the Russian position in the tower.* Michael leaned against the interior corner of a room on the backside of the school. He had no desire to see what was happening.

"One-Seven, we are assaulting," the radio cracked. The volume of fire from Third Platoon increased as Ganahl's paratroopers sought to completely suppress the Russians in the tower. Only by keeping Russian heads down would First Platoon make it across the street in one piece.

This time, the incoming artillery offered no warning sound. Deep explosions shook the building. Michael crouched down lower as the drumbeat continued. The company's mortars seemed so puny in comparison. *A bunker would be really nice right now.* The bombardment ended, but Michael remained still.

"Six, One-Six, there are three BTRs in a warehouse northeast of us!"

"Well destroy them!" Michael snapped back. *Seriously?*

Michael moved farther into the school. No sense being near an exterior wall. The BTR wouldn't be able to penetrate more than one wall. *Probably.*

"One-Six, Three-Seven, I'm sending my Carl Gustav team for those BTRs." Ganahl's unsolicited radio traffic reminded Michael that First Platoon was organized and equipped to clear the tower, not to take on armor. Their Javelin missiles and Carl Gustav recoilless rifles were back at the attack position. Michael frowned. The sound of battle tapered off, signaling Third Platoon lifting their fires on the tower as First Platoon worked up the floors. A ripple explosion interrupted.

"Six, Three-Seven, those BTRs are destroyed. Returning to position with my team." Ganahl's report caused Michael to blow out a breath of relief.

A smattering of rifle fire from the tower refocused Michael. First Platoon had to be nearly done. Michael keyed up his radio, "One-One, sitrep!"

The platoon leader responded immediately, "Clearing the last floor now. We've killed three Russians and have five casualties."

Michael nodded to nobody. *This is why I don't follow with them!* Still, there was much to do. With the tower secure, the rest of the battalion could exploit the momentum. Burton was already at the passage point, ready to pass Company B forward and left. Company C would pass forward and southward. With the railyard district secure, the rest of the brigade would be able to attack the Russian main battle position straddling the freeway bridges from behind. The great offensive was in motion.

Nova Vodolaha, Ukraine – January 20, 0700 hrs

Cigarette smoke choked the room, adding a layer of chaos to an already tense staff. Kiselyov waved his hand in front of his face to clear the smoke. He moved closer to the map posted on the wall. A staff officer marked updates to the situation with a grease pencil.

"Someone find out why the ventilation isn't working properly. I can barely see the map." Kiselyov snapped his fingers at his chief of staff, Major General Sergey Vladimirovich Pyataev. Kiselyov waited for the general to relay the order to another officer.

"Sergey Vladimirovich, this attack at Poltava is no raid. NATO is coming. They are farther south than I anticipated, but perhaps they don't trust the frozen Vorskla floodplain and want the highway bridges."

"I agree, General. Intelligence shows the American 173rd Airborne Brigade is the unit across the Vorskla in Poltava and the 3rd Brigade of the American 1st Armored Division is in our obstacle belt north of the city."

"I love having near-real-time feed from their own tactical displays. I hope we don't lose this vital source of intel again soon."

"This is day two of having it back up. By my math, we will lose it again in two more days. NATO has been consistent in changing their encryption weekly. It took us three days to break it this time. Keep in mind, sir, we only have a partial feed. We know of seven American battalions that somehow don't show up. We cross-referenced callsigns captured in radio recordings. It would be nice if we could decipher their voice communications faster and more completely." Pyataev raised his eyebrows hopefully. He had deep faith in kids intercepting and interpreting the enemy signals.

Kiselyov nodded and turned back to his desk. He picked up the phone and called Molchalin.

"Mikhail, I understand the Yankees crossed the river early," Molchalin answered without a hello.

"They did. Infantry in Poltava and tanks north of the city. They are trying to breach the obstacle belt. What are you seeing in your sector, Victor?"

"Artillery and drone activity is up a little. There is a definite attempt at local air superiority above us. My SAM batteries are taking damage, but are also inflicting heavy losses. Do you think you are facing a diversion or probe, or is this their main attack?"

"We think this is their main attack. I don't know why they didn't wait for their cavalry division. I would have."

"You know, when that division gets here, the American Fifth Corps is going to be really annoying to track with three divisions that are all 'First.' Perhaps we can call them the infantry, the armor, and the cavalry."

"Ha! If we can get NATO to stick its neck out far enough to chop it off, it won't matter because then it will be only the First Cavalry. They won't be strong enough to matter at that point."

"You need anything, Mikhail?"

"Perhaps if your long-range rocket battalions are not busy, they could target enemy command posts if mine have to displace around the enemy salient."

"Happy to kill for you."

"Thank you. Be safe." Kiselyov hung up. He returned to the map and studied it a minute.

"Sergey Vladimirovich, I want the Forty-Seventh Guards Tank Division to move to attack from the south in conjunction with the Sixth Tank Division. Assemble them near Hupalivka and their axis of attack will be north: Mashivka, Stepne, Runivshchyna. I want them ready to attack not later than tomorrow morning at first light." Kiselyov traced his finger up the map.

"What are your orders for Second Guards Motor Rifle and Fourth Tank Divisions?"

"I want them to hold the shoulders of the salient. Force NATO to string out."

"Second Guards is nearly spent, Lieutenant General. I'm not sure they can hold much anymore."

"Give them a BTG from Sixth Tank Division."

"Yes. I will make that happen." Pyataev paused and lowered his voice. "I don't understand why NATO didn't wait for their cavalry division. They just needed to wait two more weeks."

"Indeed. Two more weeks would have allowed us to complete our obstacle belts."

"Our positions are strong already though."

"Yes. We have good defenses and our air defense systems have been effective. Sergey Vladimirovich, has the 112th Artillery Brigade reported any activity?"

"No, General. They have not engaged yet."

"Have them load scatterable mines in their BM-27 Uragans and hit the highway interchanges at Poltava. When they reload, I want half to be mines and half to be cluster munitions. If the NATO armored forces attempting a breach north of Poltava succeed, we will plug the hole."

"I will make it happen."

The ground trembled and a rumbling explosion made the staff pause. Dust filtered down out of the vents. Another followed. And another. A fourth was close enough Kiselyov had to grab the wall for balance. Smoke choked the room. Kiselyov coughed.

"I suspect our decoy bunker is dead," Pyataev remarked between coughs.

Kiselyov nodded and went to his desk. He pulled a canteen out of a drawer and took a sip. "We better switch to the alternate antennas and have a repair crew check on the others."

Pyataev turned to the staff and snapped his finger. A scurry of officers instantly returned to work.

The phone rang. The number belonged to the Western Military District Field Headquarters. Kiselyov picked it up and answered, "Lieutenant General Kiselyov."

"It's me," Dronov responded. "What is happening in your sector?"

"General, NATO is forcing the river at Poltava. They have two brigades across the river and in our obstacle belt. I'm targeting their rear with scatterable mines now and having the Sixth and Forty-Seventh Tank Divisions assemble for a counterattack."

"What? No. It is too early. The rail lines from Kharkiv to Dnipro are too important to prematurely pull the Forty-Seventh from its defensive positions."

"We need to have them in place to hit before NATO can consolidate any foothold they get. I need to move now, General."

"I disagree. Patience. Hammer NATO's assembly areas now. Keep in mind NATO still has two airborne divisions here. It would not be impossible for them to try an airborne or helicopter landing to cut the rail lines."

"Yes, Colonel General Dronov. If I am to counterattack an exposed enemy flank, I need to move a division now. If we wait, I won't have any BTGs in the right place. The opportunity could slip away."

"Okay, Mikhail Borisovich. I will compromise. You can have the Sixth Tank Division prepare a counterattack. I will also have Lieutenant General Molchalin pull his Twenty-Seventh Motor Rifle Division and prepare it to attack also. It will remain under his control for now. But having it move north will put troops in position for a strong counterattack if we need it."

"Thank you."

"Stop the enemy before they cut the rail line." Dronov hung up.

Kiselyov looked the phone a moment before setting it down on the desk.

Pyataev looked expectantly at Kiselyov.

"Well, how far did you get putting the Forty-Seventh in motion?"

"Not far."

"Tell them to disregard for now. Then I will fill you in." Kiselyov waved his hand to dismiss Pyataev and returned to his map, scratching his cheek.

Sudivka, Ukraine - January 20, 1400 hrs

The drumbeat of artillery in the southeast carried far in the near-zero temperatures. Kristyn shivered as she walked around the maintenance laager, trying to force blood into her limbs. *Impossible to write when I can't feel my hands, much less my fingers. If I had something better to write about...* Kristyn had gotten to know the mechanics quite well. So far, Larrabee had been reluctant to allow her to spend time anywhere else. *Maybe once we are moving. Sounds like the penetration of the Russian defensive line went well. Maybe Larrabee will relax some once we get going on the flank mission and the worry passes. Then he will let me talk with the rest of the troops.*

Surprisingly, Kristyn's best source of information on what Lightning Troop had done during the initial week of the war came from a soldier who wasn't even there for it. Private Paige Webster joined the troop in October. A supply specialist, Paige was the only other female in the troop's maintenance laager and seemed to need female conversation. Through Paige, Kristyn learned secondhand stories of the battles along the Dnipro and the wild long fight north that culminated south of the Vorskla River. Kristyn was fascinated by the humility of the troopers. Only with Paige's information could Kristyn ask direct and probing questions to tease the full story out of the mechanics. So far, her interactions with scouts and tankers of the troop had been very limited.

The tension was palpable. All morning, the soldiers had been quite unwilling to talk. Most were busy making one last check of their equipment. Kristyn watched quietly. The rattle of tracks in the north made Kristyn turn and watch. The mechanics seemed to burst into activity.

"Ma'am, you mind coming over here out the way? We gotta pull the engine from a tank. He will stop right where you are," Heydte called from near his truck.

Kristyn jogged over to him. "It's Kristyn. What is going on?"

"Yes, ma'am. Running Bear's tank keeps going into protected mode. Sergeant Baker narrowed the fault to the engine pack. The part we need to check is on the bottom."

Kristyn shook her head and smiled. *Pretty sure he will never call me anything other than ma'am.* "Running Bear? I'd like to meet him."

"I would imagine so, ma'am." Heydte turned and strode off, yelling at his soldiers, "Better put those sockets in your pockets so they don't break! Damn cold makes metal more fragile than a Karen!"

Kristyn snorted. She watched as a tank pulled into view through the woods, the whine of the engine alternating between a high pitch and a lower one. *That engine sounds sick.* The ground rumbled as the large M88A2 Hercules turned on. A moment later, Kristyn watched as the A-frame raised over the vehicle and the massive armored beast moved to the tank. Four soldiers quickly pulled open hatches on the back deck of the Abrams. The flurry of activity was impressive to Kristyn. She found herself walking closer without realizing it.

"Why this tank waited for the eleventh hour to break down is beyond me," the massive tank commander yelled as he climbed out of his hatch.

"Did you stop whispering sweet nothings to it?" Heydte called back over the roar of the engines.

"Ha! You know me better than that! She's the only girl I got now." The man climbed down and stood next to Heydte. "How far back is the nearest engine if this fix doesn't work?"

"They have one in the combat trains. We'll have you back up before LD."

"Fair 'nuff."

"What is LD?" Kristyn asked, now standing next to Running Bear.

"Oh, hi ma'am. LD is line of departure. Not just the starting line, but also the time of an attack." Running Bear turned to answer. "You must be the reporter?"

"Guilty. I'm Kristyn Rhodes."

"I'm Sergeant Running Bear. Pleased to meet you, ma'am." Running Bear held out his hand. Kristyn noted his gentle but firm grip, despite appearing like he could crush the hand of a marble statue. She smiled up at him.

"I've heard much about you." Kristyn's reply erased the easy smile from Running Bear's face.

"Probably none of it is true. People tend to exaggerate things, ma'am." His tone was polite, but Kristyn sensed his guard going into high alert.

"Perhaps. I've only heard good things. Please call me Kristyn. Not *ma'am*. I work for a living." Kristyn winked and smiled, using the same line she heard sergeants tell her. After hearing some of the initial stories from Paige, Kristyn had asked the *Post* to research the Fiery Cross background and send the information forward to her. *Might be onto a really good story.*

"Like I said, ma'am, people exaggerate." Running Bear seemed more focused on the mechanics working. Kristyn let him be a few minutes. She needed to put Running Bear at ease if she was to gain a conversation.

"Running Bear, that's your last name. What is your first name?" Kristyn already knew it was Jonny from the files. *Let's start with the basics.*

"Ma'am, just call me Running Bear. Nobody uses my first name."

"Oh, I see. Running Bear is a pretty awesome name. But it will cost you. You can't keep calling me ma'am." Kristyn flashed a disarming smile.

Running Bear tilted his head and half smiled back. "Okay. Deal."

Kristyn held out her hand to shake on it. He met her.

"Okay Kristyn, what story are you here to get?" Running Bear seemed to tackle the conversation head on.

"Well, I'm writing on the experiences of the soldiers on the front. I wanted a unit with the most experience."

"Well, we are that." Running Bear pointed at a soldier and waved him over. "Hofi, go get a new scraper from supply. Go. Quick."

Kristyn tried again: "I understand you are based in Colorado. How long have you been at Fort Carson?"

"I've been at Fort Carson most of my career."

"You are lucky. I understand Carson is considered a choice assignment."

"It is. I didn't ask for it. Not once. I go where I'm sent, but I just got lucky."

"What is the best part of Carson?" Kristyn was happy words were flowing.

"That's easy. Close to home as I can get. Well, maybe Riley in Kansas might be similar."

"Where is home?"

"I grew up in Pine Ridge, South Dakota."

"That in the Black Hills, or out on the plains?"

"Neither. The Pine Ridge is kinda hilly, with pine trees. A bit like Fort Carson's training area."

"Must be beautiful."

"It is, Kristyn. I'm surprised you know about the Black Hills." Running Bear seemed to stare into the distance a moment.

"Oh, because I don't sound like I'm from around there?"

Running Bear turned red and gave a single nod.

Kristyn laughed. "I wouldn't be embarrassed about noticing things. You have family?"

Heydte whistled. "Oh man, don't go there."

Kristyn startled. Running Bear's face tightened. She wasn't sure what just happened.

Running Bear sighed before answering, "Yeah."

Kristyn didn't respond, seeing Heydte put his arm around Running Bear. *What the heck?*

"It's okay." Running Bear sighed again.

"Sorry I touched on something painful." Kristyn's mind raced to fix the conversation. "Your tanks break down often?"

"Not too often. My first tank had some issues, especially after abuse of the retreat to the Vorskla. But this tank I drew from the prepositioned stocks has been great."

"The abuse?" Kristyn hid her relief at getting back on track.

"We put a lot of hard miles on them and had to use diesel instead of JP8 fuel."

"Must have been hard on soldiers too."

"Yes. In many ways. Yeah."

"How are you feeling about this attack?"

"Glad to get things going. You don't win wars sitting around."

"I suppose not. How does the anticipation compare to right before the Russian invasion?"

Running Bear scrunched his face a moment before answering, "Well, I think there is more confidence. Even though half the platoon are replacements, even the newest has seem some action this last month."

"Half? I didn't realize you lost so many during that first week."

"Yeah, nine of sixteen in the platoon. Combat is high risk."

"You sound like you accept that risk."

"Personally, I do. I hate losing soldiers, but I'm okay with the chances of my own death."

"I see. What makes you okay"—Kristyn caught herself trying to circle back to family—"okay with your leadership?" Her shoulders slumped with the hasty recovery.

Running Bear looked at her funny, then his facial muscles relaxed. "Good leadership is competent and cares for the soldiers. Is honest. And has some character."

"Mind if we step over to the side so we can explore this more?" Kristyn had learned sergeants and higher would not be forthcoming on certain topics in front of troops.

"Uh...okay?" Running Bear walked over to where he could see the work on his tank but they could talk quietly. Kristyn followed.

"So, Running Bear, I get the impression this troop has been very lucky with leadership."

"We have."

Kristyn rolled her wrist, asking him to elaborate.

"Just like Fiery Cross, we had a great commander. Actually, Captain Trondfjell was with us at Fiery Cross also. He really took the lessons from there and used those to protect the troops. Top Harris is great and our XO is also good. My platoon leader has been solid since day one. You've seen many units. What have your impressions been of our leadership?"

"You all seem to continue the American tradition of strong leaders, especially the sergeants. Perhaps because I haven't spent a lot of time with a bad American unit. As I was asking, Captain Trondfjell—how long ago did he change out with Captain Larrabee?"

"A couple weeks ago. Kinda unfortunate timing. I think everyone would prefer having a tried-and-true commander and Captain Trondfjell was awesome. Maybe one of the best ever. We will see how Captain Larrabee does. You haven't spent a lot of time with a bad American unit?"

"I've not spent a lot of time with any bad unit. When I find myself among questionable ones, I leave. No sense needlessly risking my life to see a terrible perspective." Kristyn raised her eyebrow. *Who is interviewing who?* "I wish I could have met Captain Trondfjell."

"Maybe when this all is over. He's up at squadron now. You ever spend time with the Russians?"

"Never. I don't speak their language. They also aren't known for their love for the press. Why chance it? I've been on the ground in Syria in their areas. I've seen their methods. What do you think of Captain Larrabee?" Kristyn didn't think she would get a straight answer, but would go off body language.

"Still too new to know," Running Bear answered without any noticeable change.

"I see. Time will reveal?" Kristyn followed. *It seems like nobody has much of a read on Larrabee yet.*

"We LD in nine hours. Where are you based out of? Or who do you write for?"

"My pack is my home. I've been a nomad. My few possessions not with me are in storage units in Denver and Jo-burg. But I don't write for a specific outlet. How do you feel about the plan Captain Larrabee came up with?"

"Well, I suspect nearly all the plan came from our old CO. The plan is solid. Well considered and I see some of his trademarks on it. Definitely not a rookie plan. You talk with the CO about it?"

"Well, Captain Larrabee seems to be avoiding me. He isn't the first." Kristyn smiled. Running Bear smiled and gave a curt nod of agreement. "You've seen other commanders do the same?"

"Well ma'am, I had one commander who did his best, right up until the chain of command told him he was no longer allowed to hide."

"We have a deal. It's Kristyn."

"Sorry. Kristyn."

"Must have been a commander with a really good story."

"You might say that. I'd say he was just a great commander. But that is a story for another place and time."

The sound of the tank engine starting stopped the discussion and they both watched. Heydte turned around and waved a thumbs-up.

"Looks like they fixed it. These guys are really talented." Running Bear walked back to his tank. Kristyn stayed by his side.

"Well, thank you for talking with me. I hope we get a chance to talk some more soon. Running Bear, it was an honor to meet you." She placed her gloved hand on his arm briefly.

"For a reporter, you seem all right." Running Bear's face showed no indication what he meant by that. Kristyn studied it. *This guy's interesting. I hope he stays safe.*

The mechanics finished their work and Running Bear climbed back on his tank. A few minutes later, the tank was gone and the mechanics quickly packed up their tools. Kristyn returned to her seat in Heydte's truck and sat down. She pulled out her pencil and notebook to jot down notes.

"Well, you met Running Bear," Heydte remarked as he sat in the driver's seat.

"He seems very polite and kind. Seems like there is a lot going on in his mind."

"Ma'am, Running Bear is quite the gentleman. But he is also quite the warrior. It is amazing how he can flip the switch and stay in the right mindset at the right time. I've seen him in battle, I've seen him at home. My family used to live next door to his and my kids love him too."

"Used to?"

"Yeah. The divorce ended that. I don't want to talk about it. Not my right to."

"I see. Well, then we won't talk about it." Kristyn stared out the window at the woods, letting her mind sort through everything she had learned.

Chapter 5

Moscow, Russia – January 20, 2345 hrs

"Okay, tell me what the latest is," Voroshilov snapped as he sat down, "and someone bring me a vodka." He rubbed his temples and closed his eyes.

"President, are you okay?" Prime Minister Dmitry Zubkov asked quietly as he leaned close.

"This headache is brutal, Dmitry Pavelovich," Voroshilov whispered.

Around the table, the rest of the security council waited as an orderly placed a glass of vodka in front of Voroshilov. They watched silently as Voroshilov took a sip. Voroshilov set the glass down and glared around the room. "Well?"

"President Voroshilov, NATO troops breached the obstacle belt in the Poltava sector. They have also effectively seized local air superiority, though our air defenses have succeeded in limiting the area. Partisan attacks in the Donbas increased today, severing the rails through the region." Popov clicked the pointer to bring the map up on the screen.

Voroshilov held his hand up to stop Popov as he studied the map in quiet.

"What happened to the Second Guards Motor Rifle Division's local counterattack this afternoon?"

"The attack? The Second Guards were forced out of Poltava with heavy losses and were in no position to counterattack. None was ordered," Popov answered, looking at the ashen faced Dronov and Golovko.

"Were they poorly led?" Voroshilov looked at Dronov.

"They were properly led. Until their commander died a hero's death. The attack ran into a concentrated kill sack. It happens sometimes with urgent and hastily planned counterattacks. Lieutenant General Kiselyov's main counterattack is tomorrow at first light," Dronov explained.

"It better be. It better throw NATO back across the river." Voroshilov pointed west.

"Yes. We are doing everything possible." Dronov nodded.

Voroshilov squinted at him then turned to the video feed. "Colonel General Lipilin, what is the enemy doing on your front?"

Popov clicked to the next map as the Southern Military District commander spoke on the video screen.

"We had no major enemy ground attacks, but Ukrainian drone attacks quadrupled over the last twenty-four hours. Additionally, cruise missiles, probably submarine launched, struck the Crimean Bridge. My engineers are working to replace two spans. The missiles also targeted the barges in Kerch and Taman. Additional strikes hit the rail bridge at Kherson. It will be repaired by morning. Partisans heavily damaged the bridges at Nova Kakhovka and Zaporizhzhia. Additional terrorist acts throughout my entire sector have hampered efforts to move supplies forward."

"Hmph." Voroshilov closed his eyes a moment before turning to Dronov. "Why are you here in Moscow when Colonel General Lipilin is in his own headquarters? Wouldn't your counterattack benefit from personal leadership?"

"I was meeting with General Golovko when the attack commenced. My time is better spent commanding at a command post instead of traveling back to Saint Petersburg or the forward command bunker at Bryansk."

"A helicopter could have you to Bryansk in under an hour. And. Yet. Here. You. Are." Voroshilov punctuated each word with a finger stab. He stopped and took another sip of vodka. "Let me make myself clear. If so much as one Western boot steps onto Russian soil, you will die. I will personally make sure you are strapped to the first nuclear missile I launch. If you do not defeat this NATO attack, I will have you arrested. You will be charged with treason. Is that clear?"

"Yes, President Voroshilov." Dronov sat still.

"What are you waiting for?" Voroshilov slapped the table. "Get to the front now!"

Dronov stood rapidly, nearly knocking over the chair. He snapped a salute and scurried out of the room.

Voroshilov closed his eyes, waiting until the clicking footsteps faded away. He slowly opened his eyes and wagged his finger at the security council. "We will defeat the West's attack at Poltava. I will not stand to see Western imperialism trample our nation's soil. I will destroy them. All of them. If they damage Russia, I will repay them with fire until their cities and countries resemble hell. And you, you, you will see that we win this war. We will reconvene tomorrow. I need some Analgin."

The security council remained silent, blinking. Voroshilov tossed down the last of his vodka and quickly left the room.

NATO Forces Attack

(CNN) Kyiv, January 20 - BREAKING NEWS. NATO forces in Ukraine attacked near Poltava. Intense fighting along the Vorskla River and heavy air attacks shattered the stalemate. Anonymous sources state the attack is progressing well, but could not offer details.

In Beijing, the Chinese premier expressed hope that both sides could quickly come to a resolution before the fighting escalated further. "Escalating fighting between nuclear armed powers is fraught with danger to the whole world. We continue to find middle ground between the sides to make peace possible before the unthinkable occurs."

```
Updates from the front will come
as soon as our imbedded reporters
are able to provide information.
```

Semianivka, Ukraine - January 21, 0200 hrs

Logan waved at a British Warrior infantry fighting vehicle as it spun on the cold asphalt to head east on a side road. In the darkness, the gold and red flash of the 5th Royal Fusiliers painted on the sides of the Warrior was just different shades of green. Exhaust hung like fog in the ten-below-zero snowstorm. Tiny and dazzling flakes fell, covering the tracks of the many vehicles that had passed already.

Logan's mind wandered. Thirty-six hours ago, Pacheco threw a curveball at him and had Logan take the liaison section to the forward passage of lines linkup. *I suppose I wouldn't want to trust this critical task with a brand-new second lieutenant either.* The lieutenant was new enough to not even know he had been slighted. Once the last of the 20th UK Armored Brigade passed forward, Logan would return to the squadron TOC, leaving the military police squad providing traffic control in charge of the entrance to the lane.

"That's the last of us. Best of luck, mate." The British major shook Logan's hand. "It has been good chatting with you."

"Thank you, sir. Take care." Logan nodded and the two climbed back into their respective vehicles.

"Sir." The driver immediately got Logan's attention once he closed his door, "Lightning, Killer, and Ironhawk all called up REDCON-1."

"Thank you, Li." Logan studied the tactical display. The stream of blue icons flooded east across the Vorskla. Once the 11th Airborne Division cleared Poltava's eastern half and the 1st Armored Division breached the Russian lines north of Poltava, momentum grew. The lead brigade already seized Objective Wild. The 1st Infantry Division, reinforced by the 20th UK Armored Brigade, the 3rd Australian Brigade, and the 1st Royal Canadian Regiment, widened the gap. In just another hour or so, they would smash the exposed left flank of the Russian 4th Tank Division.

Then the XVIII Airborne Corps would thrust to Kharkiv and V Corps would rupture the rear of the Russian lines facing the Donets Pocket. Logan sensed energy.

"Back to the TOC?"

"Yup. You already let them know we're complete on the passage of lines?"

"Yes, sir." Li put the M1280 JLTV into gear and the large truck crunched through the snowy field. The roadways were designated for eastward units, so backroads and fields it was. At least the snow wasn't that deep.

Logan reached over and turned the radio volume up, just in time to hear a familiar voice on the radio: "Thunder X-ray, Lightning Five, SP." Logan looked out the side window. *Miss them. I hope Larrabee does all right for them.* It felt weird listening to his troops moving forward. Logan frowned. They traveled back to the TOC in silence, only the radio crackling more units in motion interrupting.

The TOC buzzed with energy as Logan entered. He took his familiar seat and opened his laptop. Two minutes of studying the situation and comparing to the operations order left Logan feeling slightly unnecessary at the moment. He opened his secure email and composed a new message.

Sweet Erin,

I love you! I miss you. We are finally in motion. Of course, you probably see that already. Moving toward the enemy is such a great change of pace. It just feels right to finally be on the attack. It means we have hope of seeing the war end a little bit sooner. Wouldn't it be amazing to end this war early? Without us having to reach the beach on the Sea of Azov? Without us having shed so much blood as we battle across the old fieldworks of the Donbas?

I'm so thankful I was able to get to see you in Vienna. My mind constantly returns to the memories we made there. I hope to see you again soon, with the war over so we can relax without the specter of pending combat hanging over the entire experience. We will win this war. We will return home. And I will excitedly await our opportunity to be together again.

Know that I'm being as safe as I can, that we are not taking unnecessary risks. I love you.

Love,
Your Logan

Logan clicked send and sat back with a massive grin on his face. He opened his jacket pocket and pulled a Ziplock baggie out. Inside the baggie was the silly photo Logan and Erin took in a Vienna photo booth. Logan kissed the baggie, then carefully returned it to his pocket.

Vatsi, Ukraine – January 21, 0600 hrs

Michael rotated his night vision goggles up and rubbed his eyes. Sunrise was still an hour and a half away, but he wasn't sure his eyes would handle much more of the goggles' green glow. *Or another kilometer.* Normally, fifteen kilometers was an easy movement, but this one had been one marathon of firefights, with many zigs and zags for position. After clearing the railyards, Michael's company attacked east and south. No less than seven times, a platoon encountered Russians and a fight brewed.

Frost clinging to Michael's neck gator stung his chin. He had long given up on his clear ballistic glasses, as they iced over.

"Another band of snow moving in," Kim whispered and pointed to the west. Michael turned and squinted. *Even my eyeballs are freezing. This sucks. Let's hurry up and get somewhere to warm up. Why did I feel the need to follow grandfather's footsteps into the infantry? Why didn't he tell me how much this sucks? Is the prestige worth this?*

"First Platoon ever gonna get their OP set? I want to beat the Legs to the linkup."

"Any minute, I think." Kim looked at his watch.

"Too slow. I'm gonna put a boot up their ass." Michael repositioned his night vision goggles and got up. The gardens inside the block were eerie. Only the sound of snow crunching under his feet broke the spell. A few minutes later, Michael reached the house 1st Platoon's leader was at. Michael shrugged his shoulders and tried to wiggle his rucksack. He yawned and pushed open the door. Warm air greeted Michael and he stepped in, not noticing the water pooled on the floor.

"Oooof." Michael slammed down on his rucksack, tweaking his back. "Damn it. Mop the floor someone?"

"You okay?" A soldier asked and pulled Michael to his feet before recognizing him, "Sir. You okay?"

Michael glared back. It was one of the newer soldiers, one he couldn't remember the name of. "Just mop the floor. You trying to kill me?"

"No sir." The soldier backed away into the house.

Michael pushed past the soldier and found the platoon leader looking out a back window.

"What's the holdup?"

"Sir, Sergeant Asti thinks they found a Russian outpost. He is maneuvering to confirm."

"I don't hear any shooting," Michael responded. "So, what's the problem?"

"Just trying to verify the possible enemy sighting. Sir."

"Okay…where is this possible Russian position?"

The platoon leader pulled out his map and pointed to an intersection of tree lined fields. "Here, sir."

"Well, that's on the other side of our boundary, is it not?"

"Yes sir. It is."

The radio crackled and the platoon leader took notes in his notebook. Michael zoned out, not listening to the platoon radio traffic. He leaned his rucksack against the wall and rotated his head and neck.

"Sir, confirmed the Russian outpost. Seven Ivans with one anti-tank missile launcher, an AGS-30, and a PKM. We can't find their vehicle."

"Okay." Michael stared at the lieutenant looking back at him.

"Sir, you want us to do a call for fire?"

"No, it's on the other side of the boundary. Remember? I'll have the cavalry take care of it."

"You want me to radio this to the command post, sir?"

"No, I'll take care of it." Michael yawned. "Okay, how long until your OP is set? That's what is holding me up."

"Sir, Sergeant Asti says he will just use his current position as the OP. Good vantage point."

"Okay. Finally." Michael shook his head and stomped off. A soldier was wiping the floor with a blanket and Michael put his hand down on the soldier's head for balance as he stepped over the wet spot and opened the door.

The cold air slapped Michael and gave him a momentary burst of energy. He quickly followed his tracks in the snow to find Kim.

"Okay, they're finally set. I need some sleep. Where did First Lieutenant Burton set up the command post?" Michael couldn't remember. *Must get sleep.*

"This way, sir." Kim moved down the street and entered a small house a block farther back.

Once again, the warm air pulled Michael in. Two soldiers were already asleep in the corner.

"Sir, all platoons are set. Battalion has new graphics for us. We'll push south again at fourteen hundred hours."

Michael set his rucksack on the kitchen counter and slipped out of the straps. *Oh man. That feels so nice.* Burton was staring at him, but Kim moved into another room and Michael could hear him talking to another soldier. *I need to sleep right now.* Michael turned around and pulled his sleeping back from his rucksack.

"Wake me at ten." Michael brushed past Burton without waiting for a response and found a bed. He flopped down and pulled the sleeping bag over himself. A minute later, he was snoring, having completely forgotten telling 1st Platoon he would take care of reporting the Russian outpost.

Outside, the snow continued to fall, covering tracks. Three thousand meters away, seven Russian soldiers readied their weapons. They believed when the sun came up, the right flank of the BTG hinged on their successful disruption of the inevitable American attack across the fields around Stepne.

Stepne, Ukraine – January 21, 0700 hrs

Larrabee sat back down in the commander's seat of his tank. *God it is so cold!* He used the back of his glove to wipe the snow from his goggles. He looked at the tactical display, checking his location on the map. *Just north of Stepne.*

"Sergeant Waters, you see anyone yet? The airborne should be somewhere to our right," Larrabee asked his gunner.

"No sir."

Larrabee didn't respond. He looked at the display again. *Too bad light infantry units don't show on the map like vehicles do.*

"Guidons, guidons, Thunder Six, intel shows a BTG from the Sixth Tank Division is moving north to counterattack." Pacheco's voice on the radio focused Larrabee on the enemy icons populating on the tactical display. Larrabee traced his finger on the screen. *Oh, here they are.*

DING. The message inbox flashed a message. Larrabee clicked on it to open the message from Top.

> SIR, RECOMMEND YOU EXPEDITE YOUR TIE-IN EFFORTS AND RETURN TO THE CENTER OF THE TROOP. POSITIVE TIE-IN ON THE LEFT FLANK TIME NOW.

Larrabee sat back and thought a moment. *I need to know what the paratroopers see and compare it from our perspective first. Where are the tank platoons supposed to mass at? Oh yeah, near Koshmanivka. Yeah, they're already there.*

Larrabee keyed up his troop radio, "Guidons, continue mission. I'll finish linkup. Four-One, get observation on NAI1. Out."

"Six, Four-One, we have eyes on NAI1." Squeaky's platoon already had observation on the east side of Seleshchyna. How, Larrabee did not know. The vehicle icons seemed too far away.

"How is the snowstorm?" Larrabee asked.

"Six, Four-Four, pockets of heavy snow. Better as you go east."

Dill took the tank to the northwest corner of Stepne and left the streets to cut across the fields. The change in track sounds as the tank entered the snow refocused Larrabee on the tank. *Where are we?* Larrabee rose out of the hatch to look around. Waters swinging the turret over the left side to scan the south confused Larrabee. *This whole rotating perspective thing is annoying.* Larrabee turned to look where the tank was driving.

A flash and puff of snow from the trees ahead startled Larrabee. *What the— Oh! Missile!* Panicking, Larrabee keyed up the radio instead of just yelling to his crew, "Sagger, sagger!" *Too late!* Larrabee cringed as the missile rushed in and skipped up the front slope and detonated at the turret ring below him. Blackness swallowed Larrabee instantly.

Fifteen klicks east, Savvy stared at the tactical display in her Bradley. Larrabee's rushed radio traffic cut off before the explosion, but in her heart, she knew it was bad.

"Six, Five, say again?" Savvy radioed.

Silence.

"Six, Five, you okay?"

Silence.

"Four-Four, Five, you have visual on Six?" Savvy released her radio and spoke to her crew. "Seymour, turn around and haul ass back to Koshmanivka now."

"Five, Four-four, saw an explosion. Snow is thick, but LT has a section investigating."

"Roger, guidons, use caution. Ivan must have a CSOP out." Savvy rapidly spoke, using the acronym for the combat security outpost.

She switched channels to squadron. "Thunder X-ray, Lightning Five, contact missile south, out." Savvy immediately switched back to the troop radio channel. *I'm sure Top will take over reporting things up automatically.*

Savvy looked up at her vision blocks. Covered in icy snow again, the periscopes were impossible to see through. Savvy stood up and scraped them clear again. The cold wind on her face stung and the snow pelted her goggles. Shaking her head, Savvy dropped back into the protection of the turret.

"Five, Four-Four, his tank is stopped. No fire, but the gun is drooping over the side. I think they got hit from the west."

"Roger. Find Ivan," Savvy quickly answered and zoomed in the map on the L66 icon. She traced her finger west. The intersection of two tree lines caught her attention. She grabbed the grid coordinates and sent them to Lucas. "Five-One, Five, I just sent you a grid. Give me shake and bake."

"Roger!" the troop's fires platoon leader answered and Savvy knew they would have a round of high explosive and a round of white-phosphorous smoke from the 120mm mortar tracks outbound in a matter of just a couple minutes.

Time ticked by slowly, but the Bradley flew down the snow and icy road.

"Seymour, better slow down well before you get to that dike crossing the river. Remember that was super icy."

"Roger, ma'am." Seymour responded immediately by letting off the throttle.

"Five, Three-Four, contact tanks, PCs, south." Ratty's clipped radio traffic pulled Savvy's concentration from Larrabee's plight. A new red enemy icon appeared on the tactical display. Savvy clicked on it and saw Ratty's observation report of three T-90 tanks and seven BMP-3s moving north toward Kalynivka.

"I see your report. Continue to observe, break." Savvy let go of the radio and thought a moment. "First and Second, move south two klicks, on line, and engage as soon as you have targets."

"One-One, wilco."

"Two-One, moving."

Savvy stood up on the hatch. *They should be just off to the left. There!*

"Seymour, tuck in behind the middle of the tank platoons but hang back about two hundred meters."

"Roger." Seymour slowed the Bradley almost to a crawl before easing it across the icy ditch and into the field behind the tanks. Once on the snow, he accelerated into position.

Savvy turned and looked around. Two more Bradleys raced across the field to catch up. *Lucas and his B-Stinger. Good.* Savvy needed her fire support officer if the whole Russian BTG was aimed at the troop.

"Five, Four-Four, contact, troops west." Torres's radio report coincided with a new enemy squad icon west of L66. *Right where we dropped that fire mission.*

"Roger, Four-One, destroy that squad. Priority of fires will be Second."

"Wilco. We will maintain observation on NAI1 and attack with the rest of the platoon."

"Good hunting. Break." Savvy looked at the map before continuing. "Tanks, find us a good position to defend south."

Almost on cue, the tanks ahead spread out and found positions along a tree line. The lack of leaves left the tanks still visible. Perhaps there was an intervisibility line they found. Savvy hoped hard.

"Seymour, ease up between some tanks. I need to look south too."

Seymour said nothing, but slowly moved forward until Savvy told him she could see. A gap in the snowstorm offered a window to the southeast. *Nothing yet.* Savvy dropped down into the hatch to use the thermal sights. Nothing showed.

Sounds of Bradleys shooting in the west carried through the snow. Savvy watched the tactical display as two Bradleys from Squeaky's platoon parked on the edge of Stepne, while two others swung around the north. *Won't be much longer now. Maybe fifteen minutes. Squeaky knows what he's doing.*

"Five, Three-Four, update: the forward detachment is on south edge of Kalynivka. Column of platoons. Tanks in lead." Ratty's voice betrayed his excitement.

"Roger. Tanks engage at will." Savvy didn't feel like trying to orchestrate a volley without knowing the ability of the whole troop to see the battlefield. Swirling snow squalls would make this a close and more reflexive fight.

The crack of a cannon in the east was quickly followed by another. More followed and Savvy saw the flash of light from a cannon firing just beyond her vision. She scanned left.

"Gunner, sabot, PC!" Savvy sang out and spun the turret so her gunner, Sergeant Martin, could engage.

"Identified!"

"Fire and adjust!" Savvy unleashed Martin.

"On the way!" Martin called as he pressed the trigger and the 25mm auto-cannon fired in rapid mode. Savvy watched the tracers fly to the target and sparks sparkle on the BMP-3. She watched as it stopped moving and then burst into flames. Martin stopped shooting on his own. Savvy scanned the battlefield again. The tank on her right fired its cannon. The blast shook the loose snow off Savvy's Bradley.

"Five, Four-Four, slant six, engaged and destroyed the Russian squad. We have one WIA. Checking on Six now."

"Roger. Consolidate and then orient hasty defense south," Savvy replied. A moment later, she heard Top relay the information to squadron.

"Five, Three-Four, contact tanks, PCs south! Rest of the BTG two klicks behind!" Urgency flavored Ratty's accent.

"How many?" Savvy asked.

"Twenty-five tanks, maybe forty PC!" The sound of a Bradley's cannon carried over the radio as Ratty responded.

"Five-one, get us some artillery! Everyone, engage with everything. I think we are facing more than one BTG." Savvy's orders barely cleared her lips when the first sounds of cannons firing in the east crashed through the falling snow.

"PC!" Martin called out and immediately fired. Cannons barked from both the east and west. A flash of light in the south preceded the sinister high-velocity crack of an enemy round whizzing over.

"Back up!" Savvy looked over her shoulder. *Clear.* Seymour goosed the Bradley hard and it rumbled away from the trees.

"Forward up to the left!" Savvy called. In front of her, she could see four tanks rapidly firing their cannons, moving forward and back between engagements. Even before Seymour had them back in the trees, Martin resumed shooting. Fires glowed through the falling snow.

Russian artillery arrived without warning in the chaos, blasting frozen dirt and snow into the air. Trees splintered. Savvy pulled her hatch closed. The sound of shrapnel pinging off the armor unnerved Savvy, but the fight was committed. *What if we advance? Ivan won't expect that.*

"Tanks, Five, advance. Slow pace, but move forward out of the artillery and assault through the Russians."

"How fast?" Seth asked.

"Advance at ten miles per hour," Savvy responded.

A moment later, the tanks on both sides moved forward. The symphony of cannons and machine guns swelled. Savvy scanned intently for Russians still in the fight. Each vehicle not burning received more fire until it was. As they grew closer to the Russian lines, Martin switched to the coax to engage soldiers in the snow. Savvy looked to the sides. With her thermal viewer, she could see all the way to the ends of the tanks. One was missing. *Crap.*

"Five, Two-One, slant three, you want to advance through the town?"

Gene's question forced Savvy to look at the map. The Tahmlyk River valley was one solid string of houses in front of them. *We are moving fast enough I don't think Ivan had time to rally in the town. What to do... What to do...* Savvy's brain hurt.

"Assault through the town. Three-One, maintain observation on NAI2 and recon Mashivka and east. Four-One, maintain NAI1 and recon there west. Tanks, we assault south to the high ground a klick south."

Ding. Savvy's inbox had a flash message from Top.

6 IS WIA LITTER URGENT. YOU ARE COMMANDER NOW. 6G AND 6L KIA. 6D WIA.

Savvy swore under her breath. The weight of the world only crashed harder on her shoulders. *Step up. Thank you, Captain Trondfjell, for making me step into this role during training a few times. Okay. Continue mission.*

Savvy switched to the squadron radio. "Thunder Six, Lightning Five, over."

"Thunder X-ray, go for Six," a sergeant in the TOC answered the radio instead.

"I need Thunder Six actual." Savvy blew out a long breath.

"You good?" Martin asked without pulling away from his sights.

"Six is down," Savvy whispered.

"Lightning Five, Thunder Six." Pacheco's voice seemed reassuring. Savvy rehearsed her message before responding. *Fifteen Bradleys, seven Abrams remaining, commander is down and we are going to the south of Mashivka. Double check the graphics. Okay.*

"We are fifteen-slant-seven. Lightning Six is down. Acting commander now. Assaulting through the enemy to Phase Line Omaha. Over."

There was a pause on the radio before Pacheco answered, "Roger. Keep me posted. You got this. Out."

Savvy stared at the tactical display a moment, unsure how she should feel. Martin's cannon firing pulled her back to the immediate situation. Thoughts and emotions could come later.

Chapter 6

Holubivka, Ukraine – January 21, 0745 hrs

Molchalin pulled his gloves off and picked up the steaming teacup with shaky hands. The heater was barely keeping the chill out of the bunker. The metal walls of the shipping container transmitted the cold of the frozen soil outside. *Still, this bunker has never been hit. Yuri Kamaludinovich's idea was genius.* In August, they began construction of the bunker, hiding in plain sight. After rapidly digging trenches and placing the shipping containers in, they filled the trenches over quickly. To provide cover for the obvious disturbance of soil, Molchalin's chief of staff had the engineers construct vehicle positions over them. In two days, the engineers made the position appear ready to accept an air defense battalion that never occupied the position. Cables from the bunkers, buried four feet deep, led to radio antennas more than two kilometers away. Despite the safety, the comforts lagged.

"Sir." Major General Yuri Frosin knocked on the door. "The tank division's counterattack failed to break through. They encountered American Abrams and Bradleys south of Stepne."

"You expect that outcome, didn't you, Yuri Kamaludinovich?"

The chief of staff nodded. "They left their recce battalion screening the Vorskla and attacked without proper recon."

"A battalion can only be in one place at one time. Which is more important, screening the enemy where the division pulled out, or finding the enemy where you are attacking?"

Frosin pursed his lips and scratched his chin. "I would rather have good reconnaissance. I think I would consider leaving a BTG to screen. I know you will tell me they aren't trained for that mission though."

"Correct, but I share the sentiment."

"General, with the Sixth Tank Division defeated and the rest of the First GTA stuck defending at District's orders, that leaves only us to counterattack NATO's penetration of the Vorskla Line. I recommend we prepare a massed attack. We should also take the time to perform good reconnaissance."

"Thank you, Yuri." Molchalin offered a sad smile and a nod. *Yuri is correct, but will Colonel General Dronov allow me?*

"Would you like me to get the BTGs in motion?"

"Get the 138th Guards Motor Rifle Division ready. I want them to be able to rapidly strike north on my command. Have them send leaders to link up with the 27th Motor Rifle Division to gain intelligence. I can do that without violating my orders from District."

Frosin nodded and spun away.

Molchalin took another sip of the now-lukewarm tea. He looked at the cup and then chugged the rest of it. *No sense letting it get cold.* He set the cup down on his desk and grabbed his phone. From memory, he dialed the number for the 27th Guards' commander.

"Davit Anatolyevich," Molchalin greeted the major general, "give me an update."

"General, we are in position at Hupalivka, all six BTGs dispersed in hiding positions. The 404th has their recon company forward with the 6th Tank Division, tying in with their flank. General, the situation isn't good. The tank division attacked blindly in the snowstorm and took heavy losses. They expected to find the Yankees near Stepne, but found them as far south as Mashivka. They also reported finding them farther north. I'm unclear if they successfully penetrated the Yankee lines and then were thrown back, or if they aren't sure what and where they found."

Molchalin looked at his map. "Yuri, wait a moment." Molchalin shifted his focus to the computer and pulled up the intelligence update. He scanned it and took another twenty seconds to formulate his plan. "Davit, are you still there?"

"Yes, General. I'm here."

"Good. I want you to push your regimental recce detachments forward and find the Yankees' lines on an arch from Mashivka where the Sixth

Tank Division ends, to the east until you make contact with the Forty-Seventh Tank Division. Establish a line on an arch centered on Lyp'yanka, using one BTG. Have another BTG come alongside their right, centered on Lanna. We cannot afford to stumble forward again and find NATO moved farther south. You will attack at dawn tomorrow. District wants us to strike north once we break the enemy lines."

"I will make it so."

"Davit, this is important: If you find NATO already that far south, I want you to use maximum artillery and attack very carefully to gain those lines. It is imperative we maintain enough combat power to successfully attack. Don't get pulled into a meeting engagement prematurely. I don't want to attack without the 138th, but I am still working to get that permission."

"I understand."

"Be careful, Davit." Molchalin hung up and called Dronov next.

"Western Military District HQ, wait one." The voice on the other end annoyed Molchalin. His watch ticked loudly as he waited.

The voice returned. "Okay, go for HQ."

"This is Lieutenant General Molchalin, I need to speak with Colonel General Dronov."

"Wait."

Molchalin blew a breath out, watching it condensate on the metal walls.

"Victor Aleksandrovich. I'm glad you called. I need you to attack in the morning. The Sixth Tank Division attack weakened the enemy's south flank. Strike north into their rear."

"Sir, I knew you would want me to attack at dawn. I want to pull the 138th up so I can attack with two divisions."

"Are you serious? We've already assumed risk by pulling out of the Novi Sanzhary sector. Now you want to do the same in the Bilyky sector as well? Besides, you don't have time to pull the 138th up before morning."

"Yes, General. If I had my way, I would pull the Twenty-Fifth Guards Motor Rifle Division up as well, but I know you won't approve weakening the Kobelyaky sector."

"Victor, we have only identified one American corps attacking. They have a second, and then there are the Ukrainians. If you pull everyone out and leave the door to Dnipro open, you will lose this war and probably get us all killed."

"General, if we don't mass for our attack, it may well fail like the Sixth Tank's did."

"You don't understand. The American's most mobile corps is still not committed into their salient. If you pull out, they could quickly take Dnipro. Dnipro is just as strategically important as Kharkiv, if not more. Partisans have damaged the rails farther south."

"And if NATO takes Kharkiv and we don't have enough power to smash their flank, Dnipro becomes irrelevant. General, please let me use the 138th."

"Victor. No. For starters, the president wants this attack in the morning, not in two more days. But Victor, for the love of life, don't get your command destroyed without stopping NATO first." Dronov hung up abruptly.

Molchalin stared at the phone. A cough caught his attention and he looked toward the door. Frosin stood there.

"General Dronov is loud. I could hear that conversation from here." Frosin shook his head. "Higher seems frozen with fear of committing and yet fear of failing."

"Yes, Yuri. The eight o'clock update should be almost ready. I would like to have fresh information."

"It is in your inbox. We've identified the enemy units north of us. From west to east, the American 173rd Brigade, then a battalion of their 3rd Cavalry Regiment, then an unknown brigade of the 1st Armored Division. Two more brigades of that division are north, behind those three enemy units. 1st GTA reports the enemy armored division is oriented on a line north from Berestyn to Khrestyshche."

"That's more than the Twenty-Seventh Motor Rifles can handle. If we are to have any chance of success, we will need to prepare the battlefield carefully. Get the intelligence section focused on locating the enemy command posts. I will get with First GTA and coordinate a massive attack on enemy battalion and brigade headquarters. I suspect we can get higher to assist with farther away targets. The GRU might have something in the works already."

"Yes, sir. With luck, General Dronov will evaluate this intelligence update and allow us to use the 138th."

Molchalin nodded his agreement.

Frosin leaned in and lowered his voice. "District won't allow us to use whole divisions, but perhaps we could move a few BTGs closer. Then we would have more power available by the twenty-third. No way we could have them in place for the twenty-second."

"Hmmm... Perhaps. We can pull two from the 25th Guards Motor Rifle Division. Then pull the two farthest BTGs from the 138th. Then once General Dronov approves committing the 138th, I can reinforce it with the extra BTGs and have it massed in time for a coordinated attack. Then, if the 27th isn't too chewed up, we can have a chance."

"Yes, sir." Frosin nodded.

Molchalin steepled his hands and stared at the computer. Timing would be everything. Still, he worried. NATO and the Ukrainians were not Chechen insurgents. They would need some luck.

Smorodshchyna, Ukraine – January 21, 0800 hrs

Logan stared at Pacheco, sitting next to him in the plans vehicle of the TOC. For his part, Pacheco stared at the tactical display in front of him. A squeeze on Logan's shoulder led Logan to look up. Douglas returned Logan's glance with sad eyes.

Pacheco turned and looked at Logan. "How did Savvy sound to you? Think she can hold the troop a day?"

"She sounded okay. I trust her," Logan answered.

"Okay. I'll see who regiment has on deck and how fast we can get them to Lightning. In the meantime, does this change our plans?" Pacheco looked at Douglas.

"Sir, I think Lightning is still capable of executing the plan. We still haven't seen indicators of the Sixth Combined Arms Army moving yet."

"And then it all depends on which avenue of approach they follow." Pacheco raised his eyebrows, then nodded. "Okay, let me call Colonel Ollerich."

Pacheco got up and shuffled passed Douglas and opened the troop door. The bitter cold draft elicited an immediate shiver from all. Pacheco closed the door and Douglas took his seat.

"The plan to slice over a tank platoon from the adjacent troop might be complicated for Savvy," Douglas said after a sigh.

"She can handle the troop short tanks. I have confidence in that. Every exercise I made her instant commander was that way."

"And did you ever overload her with an additional maneuver element?" Douglas steepled his hands.

"No, sir." Logan sighed. "I'd like to know how my old tank crew is." Logan minimized the tactical display on his laptop and pulled up the administrative and logistics log. He ran his finger down until he found the entry:

> 0733: L/3/3—2X KIA, SGT WATERS, PFC CATRON. 2X WIA, CPT LARRABEE LITTER URGENT, SPC DILL AMBULATORY ROUTINE. L66 TANK PENDING EVAL. 3/L 1X WIA, PVT DUDLEY, AMBULATORY ROUTINE.

"Waters and Catron." Logan sighed. *Damn. Waters... Until Valhalla, my brother. You were a great gunner. Ah...at least Dill isn't hurt too bad. But Waters is gone. Gone. Catron gone.* Logan's jaw tightened until his teeth hurt. Memories of everything Waters had been there for flashed through his mind. Catron was a new addition to the troop. Still, Logan had gotten to know the kid from Cincinnati. *Wonder what happened. Not that I can change anything.*

Douglas leaned over to look at the screen. "Dill is ambulatory, routine. That's a good thing. I have grown fond of that soldier."

"Me too, sir. Me too. I wish I could see him, but that isn't likely."

"No, probably not. We have a fight on our hands. As soon as we see Ivan moving, we need to look hard at our plans again. For now, I'm gonna talk to the colonel about accelerating the rest of the squadron up on line with Lightning's new frontline trace."

"Roger that, sir." Logan offered a half smile to Douglas as the major got up and left the plans vehicle.

Logan put his head in his hands and closed his eyes. The flood of memories was powerful. Logan let the tears flow.

Next to him, the operations sergeant major quietly left Logan alone. The old timer knew the pain—he had been a fiery buck sergeant at Combat Outpost Keating and watched so many of his friends suffer and die during the longest day of his life.

Stepne, Ukraine – January 21, 0900 hrs

"Ma'am, if I catch you taking a picture of blood, I'm warning you, I'll punch you so hard your grandchildren will get a broken nose." Heydte's sudden harsh threat startled Kristyn.

"I'm sorry, what?" Kristyn blinked.

"These were my friends. Their painful last moments are private. Okay, ma'am?" Heydte looked away from the road long enough to stare Kristyn down.

"Frankly, it's important for the public to know the reality of war," Kristyn countered softly, sensing raw emotion was on the verge of exploding. "Or would you rather they don't know the cost? Don't you think the people back home should know what you've had to endure?"

Heydte glared at the road. "I wouldn't want my family to see me torn up and on the cover of the paper. Sounds like the enemy's propaganda."

"What makes news propaganda? Offering a slant on it, distorting the truth?" Kristyn countered. Heydte's face grew dark. She sensed he was still listening. "Dave, here is the thing I've learned. If I gloss over the cost, I provide propaganda to one side. If I overdo it, I provide propaganda to the other. You wouldn't want me to do either."

"And?"

"But if I provide blunt observations and write about the men and women living this reality, I remain between the two. I've learned that only the families and close friends, and people living in military communities have the slightest clue about the realities of war. I think the higher commanders understand that also. That's why I'm allowed to take pictures of anything, write of anyone. I just cannot publish names or pictures of the dead until the Department of Defense has properly notified the next of kin."

"Up there, they don't give a damn, but down here, these are guys we hang out with. Not just names. I know their families. You hear me?"

"Are they—um the, um—uh... still at the tank?"

"No. Top already collected them. We just gotta see if I can fix the tank. I know I can fix Running Bear's."

Kristyn's shoulder slumped in relief. Dead bodies always left a void in her heart.

"Dave, between me and you, I agree with you. My personal rules are to never publish a photo without asking permission from the person first. I can extend that to parts...blood of people."

"Okay, ma'am. I can live with that. Still. You've been warned." Heydte faced back to the road.

The light snow falling dusted over the tracks on the asphalt, but did nothing to cover the tracks in the deeper snow of the fields. Heydte slowed down and bounced across the field.

The tank looked so sad to Kristyn. The cannon was depressed all the way as if bowing to the lives of the men who ended inside it. Heydte pulled to a stop behind the tank and got out. Kristyn watched him walk around the tank, looking closely here and there. As Heydte climbed onto the tank, she got out of the truck and focused her camera on the downcast face. Heydte climbed to the top of the turret and peered in the hatch. Shaking his head, he carefully and slowly climbed down. He shuffled over to Kristyn.

"Thanks for just staying there. The skiff of snow on the tank doesn't hide much." Heydte gestured for her to get back in the truck. "We can't fix this tank."

"Oh, what now?"

"Squadron recovery will come and get it. They'll probably strip parts off of it and eventually, it will find its way back to a depot."

"It doesn't look that bad from here."

"The missile entered at the ring. The turret is probably welded to the hull now, and the race ring—the gears that turn the turret—is scattered all over inside. We can't fix that in the field."

"Oh." Kristyn climbed in and Heydte immediately turned the truck around and followed his tracks out of the field. "What's wrong with Running Bear's tank?"

"Sprocket's shot off. A pain to fix, but well within our parts and time available." Heydte's voice lacked any fiber or variation.

Kristyn looked over at Heydte. *He's numb to it all.*

"Does it get easier or harder with time?" she finally asked softly.

"Ma'am, it never gets easier. Maybe you get used to it. I don't know." Heydte paused and pushed his cheek out with his tongue. "During that first week, we couldn't take the time to examine, much less recover and fix some of our vehicles. Some of our guys that died, some...we couldn't even rescue from the flames. But I will tell you this, ma'am, that which has been seen can never, ever, be unseen."

"Amen to that," Kristyn bitterly agreed. She had seen enough horror from one crisis to another. Only a politician could brush the carnage under the rug and dismiss the price. *Hmm...is that why he didn't want to let me see the blood? Interesting. I won't be asking that. Sure not. Nope.*

Heydte broke the silence after a long pause. "The only answer is to just get on with it. Win the war as fast as possible, while avoiding taking unnecessary risks."

"How do you determine what unnecessary risk is?" Kristyn probed.

"Unnecessary is not paying attention to the battlefield. Not knowing where your protection is at all times. Ya know? Gotta be smart about how you tackle a repair job. Even in peacetime, this is a very dangerous occupation."

"Yes, I've read the stories of soldiers killed during training. Written some too."

"Anyway, we're almost there. If you don't mind, let me concentrate on the work I need to do."

Kristyn nodded and looked forward. Ahead, an Abrams sat behind a tree line, the track knocked off the wheels and the skirts ripped up. Several soldiers labored in the snow on the track.

Heydte parked the truck off to the side and quickly opened his roll-up doors.

"Impact wrench will speed that up."

"Yeah, bolts are just snapping," Running Bear hollered back.

"Have you prepped what's left of the sprocket?"

"No, not yet. I think the final drive is damaged also." Running Bear pointed at the sprocket. Kristyn looked at it as she got out of the truck. The sprocket was truly mangled and the track had gaping holes in it. She wasn't sure what a final drive was.

"Okay, well McBride is coming with the eighty-eight. Should be here any minute."

"Good. My platoon is on the other side of the valley. Need to get back up there with them." Running Bear nodded at Kristyn before turning and hollering at his crew, "Gomez and Hofi, let's punch the gun tube while we wait!"

"Roger, Sergeant!" two soldiers with their backs to him replied in unison before stopping their work on the track and climbing onto the tank.

Running Bear moved over to inspect the track. Heydte quickly had an air hose hooked up to an impact wrench and began removing bolts. Kristyn moved closer to watch.

"Running Bear, what is punching the gun tube?" Kristyn yelled over the hammering noise.

"Hi ma'am, it means cleaning the cannon. We use a long rod to pull a brush through the barrel." Running Bear paused and scratched his cheek. "I have no clue how it got the name punching though."

"I see. Don't forget our deal, Running Bear." Kristyn smiled. "What happened to your tank?"

"Sorry, Kristyn. T-90 almost missed. Gomez lost the fast draw, but he shot straighter." Running Bear shook his head. "It was a close shave."

"I'm glad it wasn't closer."

"Me too. Yeah."

"Want to tell me about it?" Kristyn blew on her hands and thrust them into her pockets. Gloves would be nice, but she didn't want to break the moment to get them from the truck.

"We shot up the enemy's lead element. They got in kinda close using a heavy band of snow. XO had us assault to get out of artillery. The follow-on Russians were closer than normal. Anyway, we didn't make it very far before getting hit by the T-90. The rest of the troop kept moving south and destroyed the Russian attack pretty thoroughly." Running Bear swung his hand at the tank. "They are now there, and we're here for a while."

Heydte interrupted, "Your track is shot. I'll have Baker steal one off six-six. I'll get you up by darkness, I promise."

Running Bear nodded and gave a thumbs-up. He then looked back at Kristyn. "I need to do some admin stuff."

"You going somewhere?" Kristyn asked back.

"My tank. I'm still the platoon sergeant, even if a few klicks away." Running Bear strode purposely toward his tank and swiftly climbed up. Kristyn watched as he dropped into his hatch.

"Hmph." Kristyn shook her head before fetching her gloves from the truck. As she pulled them on, she watched Gomez and Hofi punch the gun tube. Kristyn was fascinated as they pulled the brush out, unscrewed it, then tossed it to Running Bear who suddenly appeared in the hatch. The two ran the pole back up the gun tube. A moment later, they pulled the brush out again. This time, they disassembled the pole and put everything away.

When they walked away from the gun tube, Kristyn approached, careful to avoid getting whacked by the long pole as Hofi disassembled it.

"What's your name?"

"Specialist Hofi, ma'am."

"Call me Kristyn. Ma'am is my mother. How often you have to do that?" Kristyn pointed to the pole.

"Every time we shoot, we punch the tube first chance."

"I see. Where are you from?"

"Dude, can't you tell? Compton. I'm guessing you never been there."

Kristyn grinned. "No, didn't venture that way from Kabul or Benghazi."

Hofi laughed.

"When's the last time you heard from your family?"

"About a week ago. Mom and Pops are good about writing."

"You are fortunate to have that. If you could talk to them right now, what would you tell them?"

"Hmm." Hofi kicked the snow. "I'd say we will be good. Sergeant Running Bear is taking good care of us. But, damn, this place is cold."

"Yeah?" Kristyn raised a corner of her mouth, something she learned helped people continue talking.

"Yeah, dude. My folks met him when I first got to Carson. They seemed to like Sergeant. That was before I or they knew he was a certified badass."

"What makes a certified badass?"

"Well, for starters, have you seen him? And he is one of the Fiery Cross vets. Only Sergeant Hamasaki is more decorated than him—in the whole regiment. The dude can tank. I mean, he can *tank*. So, when we deployed, I knew I was in good hands. You should have seen Grizzly Bear that first week of the war. Fricking nuts, dude. Anyway, he will get us home if anyone can."

"Who's your new girlfriend?" A voice from behind carried a tone of youthful arrogance. Kristyn turned and saw Blucher walking over.

"Grease tube, shut up. Dude, grow up for once in your life." Hofi's eyes narrowed. "You don't seem to remember why you got busted and never got your rank back?"

Blucher ignored Hofi and came to a stop right in front of Kristyn and stuck his hand out. "I'm Theo. What's your name beautiful?"

Kristyn stifled a laugh; only her eyebrows danced to reveal her mirth. Hofi saved her from immediate response by elbowing Blucher in the ribs. Her eyes noticed Blucher's nametag.

"Blucher, you on Sergeant First Class Running Bear's tank crew?" Kristyn pulled a notebook from her pocket.

"Unfortunately." Hofi answered before Blucher could shift gears from his fizzled attempt at suaveness.

"How long have you two been together?"

"Two years. Running Bear keeps me because I'm the best driver in the troop." Blucher grinned.

"Or because he doesn't want to saddle a new sergeant or the LT with a problem child." Hofi spat on the snow and climbed up onto the tank.

"Seems to be some tension between you two." Kristyn pointed her pencil at Hofi, now climbing into his turret hatch.

"He thinks he is better than me. Whatever. He's just jealous."

The roar of the M88 repositioning ended the conversation and Kristyn watched it ease up to the Abram's mangled sprocket.

"Ma'am." Heydte strode over and gently pulled Kristyn's elbow. "Need to move out of the way. Can you sit back in the truck?"

"Of course." Kristyn immediately jogged to the truck. *What is going on?* She looked back and saw Heydte swiftly striding after her.

"Ma'am, I wanted to tell you, watch out for Private Blucher. Avoid him if at all possible." Heydte turned and began walking about to the tank before Kristyn could respond.

"Running Bear! We're gonna use the eighty-eight to rip the old sprocket off! Hang on and stay inside the tank!" Heydte's yelling carried over the sound of the revving engine.

Kristyn started for the truck again. *First warning from Dave about someone. Odd.* Kristyn scanned the area again. Blucher was now nowhere to be seen. She quickly opened the truck door and sat down and watched through the windshield. Heydte disappeared between the M88 and the Abrams before scrambling back to the front corner of the tank. He gave a thumbs-up and ducked.

Dark smoke poured from the M88's exhaust as it roared and lurched backward. The Abrams yanked as if a mere toy before a bang and several following clanks ripped through the air. Heydte got up, laughing. Kristyn could hear several others laughing and joking.

"You guys good? Running Bear?" Heydte called. Running Bear rose out of the hatch and shook his finger at Heydte before giving a thumbs-up.

Kristyn got out of the truck and waved to Heydte before approaching. He waved back. *Must be safe now.* Kristyn joined Heydte as the M88 moved away. Scrape marks scarred the front of the vehicle. Kristyn gaped at the sprocket, torn in half. Skips in the snow caught her eye and she followed the trail to see part of the sprocket a hundred feet away. *Gonna have to ask Heydte how that played into his unnecessary risk calculations.* A mechanic edged Kristyn out of the way to work. She returned to the truck and climbed in. A few minutes later, she typed happily on her article.

Chapter 7

Vatsi, Ukraine – January 21, 1400 hrs

"Sir, got a message from battalion." Burton tapped Michael's shoulder, waking him from his catnap. Michael squinted at his XO, glared, then finally responded.

"What?"

"We are to move to contact south until we reach Zavorsklo. LD in thirty minutes."

"Are you kidding me?" Michael rubbed his eyes as he grabbed his map. *Seriously? Just up and move forward without time to plan? Time to prepare targets? Someone is responsible for this. They better have a good excuse.* Michael found the town.

"Sir, I've got the graphics. And we have targets already planned," Burton offered.

Michael grabbed Burton's map and studied the graphics before handing him the other map. "Update my map. And have First Sergeant Kim round up the platoons. We must hustle."

Burton nodded and quickly moved out of the room Michael had commandeered for his own. The command post was in the kitchen of the small home. Michael muttered under his breath as he stuffed his belongings back into his rucksack. His shoulders still ached from the nearly nonstop movement. *Attack south. Don't rest. Just move a little further. Oh wait, move some more.* Michael shook his head in exhausted disgust. *Pull it together. Show no weakness.*

Michael paused and stood tall, taking a moment to breathe. *Better.* Michael finished packing his rucksack and resumed study of the map. The wooded terrain was pretty straightforward. A suspected minefield would protect their flank as they moved south to come on line with the cavalry. Michael wondered why the legs moved south early. Michael snorted. "Well, the real soldiers will march to the fight on our own feet."

"Yes sir?" Burton called from the kitchen, barely hearing Michael.

"Nothing. Where are the platoons? We need to get moving."

"Should all be here any minute, sir. They already have the warning order."

"Tell them to hurry up." Michael yelled back, "Oh, and is my radio battery charged up yet?"

"Almost, sir."

Michael formulated his plan while he impatiently waited. It would be a simple patrol south. The same order of march, the same formation had worked well so far and there was no reason to change it. Michael smiled. The hasty defense at Zavorsklo would just be the platoons filling in from the right to left as they arrived at the position. Michael was pretty sure the 6th Combined Arms Army would never try to push through their own minefields and the woods. No, they would attack farther east, where terrain favored armored vehicles.

Voices in the kitchen announced the arrival of the platoon leaders and platoon sergeants. *Showtime.* Michael composed his command presence and strode into the kitchen.

"Troopers, listen up!" Michael bellowed to gain their silence. He did a quick head count before continuing. "Time is short, so pay attention." Swiftly, Michael outlined his plan. Really, the plan was just and extension of the previous day. Only the destination was different. The platoons would find good defensive ground when they reached Zavorsklo. There were no questions. Michael dismissed everyone and pulled his radio from the charger and returned to his room to gear up. He did not notice Burton and Kim going outside with the platoon leaders and platoon sergeants to answer their questions in private.

Michael picked his gear of the floor and set it on the bed. Next, he pissed in the corner of the room. Satisfied, he adjusted his uniform and began the process of putting on all his gear. Last, Michael swung his rucksack onto his back and stomped into the kitchen.

"We ready?"

"Roger, sir," Kim answered. He had his ruck on his back and was ready to continue the walk south.

Michael swung the door open and stepped into the pale winter light. The sky was still overcast, but the snow had stopped. In exchange, the wind was much stronger, biting at Michael's skin.

Michael pulled his neck gaiter up and coughed. *This cold burns the lungs.* It was still warmer than last week, but the wind chill bothered Michael more. He squinted and waved his arm forward. As soon as he saw his soldiers begin their long slog, he too swung one foot in front of the other.

Artillery thundered in the distance. The woods were eerily quiet. Not even the birds chirped. No squirrels chattered. Loose powder snow muffled the steps. Michael's eyes grew heavy as the sun slipped lower on the southwestern horizon.

Without warning, the soldiers in front of Michael suddenly stopped. Michael blinked and realized his troops were taking cover. Belated, he flopped down.

"One-Six, what's your holdup?" Michael called on the radio.

"Bunkers ahead."

Michael craned his neck up to see across the snow and through the trees. He couldn't see anything. *Sure won't move up to the lead squad to see for myself though.* He sighed and looked at his watch. The clanking of metal caused him to roll over and watch the mortar squad setting up.

"Six, One-Six. Line of bunkers facing west. There's a cluster of three bunkers guarding their right flank. That cluster is right in our path."

"Well, are they occupied?" Michael rolled his eyes at 1st Platoon's lieutenant's half-assed radio report.

"Unknown."

"Fix that lack of information. Out." Michael pulled out his map and GPS. *Okay. We are exactly on course. These bunkers are supposed to be farther west.*

"Sir, should I move up to First Platoon?" Padilla came up in a crouch.

"Why would you do that? Second Lieutenant Cameron better be capable for a simple task." Michael glared at his FO.

"I was thinking, sir, I can get fires in support better up there."

"Second Lieutenant Padilla, your position is near me at all times. I don't know how many times we have gone over this and it's long past old." Michael spat the words out and rolled away.

"Roger, sir."

Michael watched as the squad ahead of him got to their feet and rushed forward, leaving their rucksacks in the snow. *Well, might as well get comfortable. They have to come back for those. If Ivan hasn't started shooting yet, nobody's home.* Michael rolled over to sit, leaning on his rucksack.

"Six, One-Seven, bunkers are empty. We will be ready to continue mission in a few."

Michael shook his head. "Roger. Hurry up."

Soldiers ran back through the snow, panting as they found their rucksacks and hoisted them on. Michael waited for the platoon to move out again before slowly getting to his feet. Once again, one foot slogged ahead of the other. He found himself alternating between daydreams and noticing the empty bunkers as they moved along through the trees east of them. When the last bunker faded into the woods behind Michael, the daydreams of a warm bed took full control of his brain.

The rippling explosion caught Michael off guard and his bladder sphincter took a momentary vacation. *Damn it!* Michael dove and buried his face into the snow.

Screams and frantic yelling echoed through the trees.

"Medic!" a voice carried over the chaos.

"Minefield!" another immediately countered. "We have a bunch of wounded in a minefield!"

Terror gripped Michael, stapling him to the ground. "Nobody move!" he yelled.

"One-Six, Six, give me a SITREP!"

"This is One-Six," the radio voice paused and groaned, "we are in some Bouncing Bettys. All of first squad is hit. I think most of Second Squad is down also. One-Seven is down and not answering."

"Pull yourself together. Do not let anyone move. There could be trip wires in the snow and those are area mines." Michael pulled his radio out and changed the channel to the battalion's. "Rock X-ray, Attack Six, contact minefield, area mines. We have a MASCAL. Send the sappers and medics."

Michael didn't wait for a response before switching back to his company radio. *First Sergeant Kim can handle the rest of the report.* "All platoons carefully check for trip wires around everyone. Get the minesweeper up here." *Which platoon has that thing anyway? Probably Third.*

Michael pulled his notebook out of his arm pocket. He ripped a page out and used it to gently brush the snow around him. Minutes ticked by and the calls of pain south of him quieted as he cleared a spot for him to take his rucksack off. *I doubt anyone else will be as careful. If they get me killed, I swear to God...*

Another band of snow moved in by the time a soldier brought the metal-detecting minesweeper to Michael's spot in the formation. The process of clearing a path through the middle of the company formation, then out to each soldier to be able to come in was painstaking.

Kim and the medics waited patiently behind the soldiers checking for mines. As soon as they passed Michael, he got to his feet and walked back through the formation. The desire to get away from the next blast tugged him farther and farther. He masked his purpose by stopping and looking over each paratrooper, pretending to inspect them.

"I would hope they've moved far enough forward of my ruck I can safely return," Michael whispered when he reached the end of the company. Self-discipline prevented him from tracing footsteps back to Poltava. *Just barely.*

Kim had the first several casualties near Michael's rucksack by the time he returned. The rumble of diesel engines announced the arrival of the battalion ambulances. Without any direction from Michael, his soldiers rose up and ferried litters down the formation and hauled their wounded buddies away. Michael pulled his notebook and busied himself, lest he think about how close he came to meeting death.

"Take it easy, sir." The voice of a medic behind Michael was clearly not addressing him and he looked over.

1st Platoon's leader lay in the snow, bloody from the waist down. Cameron shivered and nodded, eyes unfocused.

Michael got up and walked over. "Second Lieutenant Cameron, what happened?"

Cameron looked up slowly and tried to sit up. "Sorry sir, I can't get my legs to work. Permission to stay sitting?"

Michael crossed his arms. "Yes. What happened?"

"Bouncing Bettys or something. Must have been wired together in a large pattern. Not sure who tripped it, but the explosions surrounded the front half of the platoon." Cameron's face contorted in pain. "Jesus. Sergeant Medina must have died instantly, because he wouldn't answer at all, not moving. I think Gansler and Purcell did too. Yoho stopped answering us after about thirty minutes. Louth wasn't answering, but he was still alive when the medics got to him. Hope he makes it."

"You lost a whole fire team's worth."

Cameron slumped and nodded, then started counting on his fingers. "And another eight wounded. And me."

"A third of your platoon." Michael shook his head and looked off into the woods.

Cameron gulped and closed his eyes. Michael looked at Cameron before shaking his head again and turning back to his rucksack. He opened the notebook and wrote the names down and stared at his paperwork. When the litter bears returned to take Cameron back to the ambulance, Michael pretended not to notice.

A soft voice talking with soldiers as it approached pulled Michael out of his notebook. He looked up and saw the battalion commander coming down the path. Michael quickly stood up and brushed the snow off his shoulders and knees.

"Lieutenant Colonel Saint, good to see you." Michael forced a smile.

"Tough day." Saint's face was strained. He came closer before lowering his voice and asking, "You okay, Michael?"

"Of course, sir. We will be ready to move out to our objective shortly. As soon as the path through the minefield is cleared and the last of the casualties are moved back."

Saint nodded and narrowed his eyes. "Damn landmines. Not a Ruskie in three klicks, yet they've held our advance up a few hours. I really hate the toll the mines take on the locals."

"They are illegal for a reason, sir."

Saint snorted. "Ivan has never cared much for the law of warfare. Anyway, want to tell me about finding this minefield?"

"Yes, sir. This is not the one the S2 had on the intel graphics overlay. I confirmed and reconfirmed it."

"Yeah, it's a new one. Probably won't be the last."

"Hooah. We were advancing through the woods, First Platoon in the lead. They slid to the left of our axis of advance after the bunkers. Second Lieutenant Cameron took his platoon into the minefield. Must have been a daisy-chain job, because it was a single ripple. The lead three quarters of the platoon were in the kill zone."

"I saw Cameron as they loaded him. He has a long road ahead." Saint's eyes softened and he sighed. "The sappers think the minefield was mainly MON-90s, booby trapped to detonate when a bounding mine went off. They disarmed several OZM-72 bounding mines. One was tied into a MON-90. You know the MON-90, Michael?"

"Yes, sir. It's the Russians' beefy version of our Claymore command-detonated mine."

"It's a miracle, and a testament to Cameron's platoon being properly dispersed, that it isn't worse."

Michael looked blankly at Saint.

"We'll get through this. Every day we move forward is a day closer to defeating Russia and going home." Saint squeezed Michael's shoulder. "I want you to split the remains of First Platoon. Give half each to your other platoons. But make sure we take care of them. Survivor's guilt will be rough for this incident."

"Roger, I'll make it happen. We will reorganize on the move so we still reach our objective before midnight."

"Always the taskmaster, Michael. Carry on." Saint nodded and turned. Michael watched him head down the line, stopping to talk with several of the sergeants. *Okay, let's get moving.*

Koshmanivka, Ukraine – January 21, 1600 hrs

The Bradley rattled into the maintenance collection point without fanfare. Kristyn watched it stop in the field near Running Bear's tank. The ramp dropped and Savvy clambered out. She looked around and then made a beeline to Heydte. Intrigued, Kristyn pulled her gloves on and got out of the truck. She walked over and listened.

"How long until two-four is ready?" Savvy looked at Running Bear's tank.

"Another hour or two. Found more damage than expected. I had to steal a lot of parts from six-six."

"But definitely up in time for stand-to. Good. Think someone can look at my Brad? The TOW launcher wouldn't come up earlier."

"Of course."

"How are you holding up?"

"We are doing all right, ma'am. It's always best when the troops are busy following a close loss."

"Definitely has been a busy day."

"Sergeant Waters was popular with the mechanics. He always made an effort to check on them too."

"He was a great NCO. How are you holding up." Savvy put her hand on Heydte's shoulder.

"I'll be okay. Had a good talk with Running Bear earlier. Helped me a lot. Let me go get someone to look at your TOW launcher." Heydte nodded and walked off.

Kristyn hung back, waiting to see what Savvy would do. Savvy just stood there in the fading light and looked over at Kristyn. Savvy's chest rose and fell and Kristyn closed the distance.

"You look tired, Lieutenant."

"Call me Savvy, please." Savvy slowly nodded and slurred her words.

"You are tired. Got time to rest now?"

"Not really. Not sure I want to."

"You don't want to rest?" Kristyn lowered her voice.

Savvy shook her head. "I don't think I could sleep if I tried."

"What makes you say that?"

"With Captain Larrabee out, I now have to lead the troop. It's not that I don't want to lead them, I just feel insufficient and don't want to let them down."

"That's pretty heavy." Kristyn gently touched Savvy's arm. "I can't imagine what it's like to find yourself suddenly the one to answer everything."

"You take for granted having a commander. And we had a great one for over a year. Captain Trondfjell used to make me step up in training for a few hours, but jeez, this is different. This is real. We don't stop 'pretending' to be dead at the end of the exercise. Those killed by my mistakes are gone forever." Savvy paused. "I guess I understand why he needed a lot of alone time during those weeks before the war started."

"Savvy, who do you unburden your soul to? You do have someone?"

"I'm lucky. I can message my husband. Tye's also in the regiment. For some reason, I don't worry as much about him."

"You don't?"

"His unit is pretty smart about displacing after fire missions and keeping their local security. I bet they've taken the fewest casualties of any artillery battery in the whole theater."

"That's good to hear. I suppose a message is better than nothing, but not quite a hug."

"Ha, yeah. Well, those things will come soon enough."

"Kids?"

Savvy shook her head. "No, not yet. We aren't ready for that yet. What about you? You've seen enough war you must need to unload it yourself."

"Well, that is an occupational hazard of a combat reporter. Especially print. At least the film crews have a team to commiserate with."

"What about at home?"

"Home? Savvy, my parents died a decade ago and I've been single for as long."

"Oh, wow. I'm sorry about your parents. You must have been young."

Kristyn laughed. "You're too generous. I'm older than I look. I was out of college already. Mom and Dad died in a car wreck. Drunk driver going the wrong way on I-25. At least they died instantly. Unlike many of the soldiers I've met."

"You sound more like a warrior than a civilian. I gotta admit, I've never read any of your reports, at least not that I know of. I'm curious to see what your stories are like."

"The next one I'm ready to send off, you can read on my laptop."

"Deal. How is Sergeant Heydte taking care of you?"

"No complaints. He cares a lot about his troops."

"He's one of the best. Between him and Sergeant Running Bear and Top, the troops are well cared for. You get a chance to talk with Running Bear?"

"Sort of. He was distracted. I hope to get another chance."

"Running Bear doesn't open up to just anyone. Don't be offended. The only ones I know he will open up to are Heydte, Hamasaki, and Captain Trondfjell. I imagine his crew to some extent."

"He has one of the only original crews in the troop, right?"

"Correct. It is interesting the two remaining original crews are both led by heroes of Fiery Cross."

"Running Bear wouldn't like you using that word, *hero*."

Savvy grinned. "Neither would Hamasaki. Both would be offended. But that is the way real heroes are. Behind their back, I get away with it."

Kristyn laughed. "Well I won't rat you out."

"Thank you. I'd like to enjoy the respect of both. Tell you what, Kristyn, I'm gonna check in with you every day. I need to get to work though." Savvy patted Kristyn on the shoulder and slogged through the snow to her Bradley.

Kristyn smiled. *Something about warriors. They really do care about people on a level I've never seen back home.*

"Talking with the XO? You get any good information on what's next?" Blucher came up to Kristyn.

"The XO is good people. Your tank ready to go back to the fight?" Kristyn stiffened. *Something about this kid defies the others.*

"Oh, the tank? Yeah, soon. You know, the XO is shacked up with another lieutenant in the regiment."

"I think most people use the word *married*."

"Same thing. Most of the smoke show soldiers are. I still haven't figured out who Hamasaki is shacking with. Got my suspicions though. Maybe she was shacking with the old CO."

"Smoke show?"

"Hot. Duh."

"You seem mostly concerned about your fellow soldiers' love lives."

"A guy has to have something to think about if you can't enjoy any right now."

"A different theory."

"I'm surprised my sergeant hasn't tried with Hamasaki. Man, they would be badass. If I was him, I would have already. Of course, Hamasaki won't even look at a mere soldier. But Running Bear, yeah, he could. You'd think after that nasty divorce, he would want a hottie to move on with life with."

Kristyn blinked in the dark.

"Probably the only reason he hasn't made a pass. Too butt hurt still. You haven't been told the story? No? Juiciest tidbit in the troop. Trainwreck story. His ex divorced him after Fiery Cross and took the kids. Convinced the kids to tell the court he is dangerous and they didn't want him around. Him dangerous? All I saw was a blabbering pussy. So what if he fought in a war? Anyway, he doesn't talk about it because he sold his man card. Of course, his kids hate him. Gotta have swagger for kids to like you."

"What the hell are you doing, skid mark?" Hofi's voice hissed in the darkness with doppler effect. Kristyn barely had time to react before Hofi tackled Blucher and wrapped him into a chokehold. "What the hell? And you wonder why everyone calls you Three Lima? You worthless piece of goo. If Running Bear hears you, we're screwed. You want to trade Grizzly Bear for Sad Panda again? Now? You dumb exhaust sample!"

"Let me go! Can't wait to get out and away from you assholes," Blucher sputtered.

"You gotta survive this war to get out. Hasn't that registered? Our only chance is to keep Running Bear Grizzly Bear."

"I'm telling LT you assaulted me."

"And I'll tell him why. LT would find a way to nail you to the wall."

"Not like Running Bear will scalp me."

"Jesus, you and your mouth." Hofi rolled and slammed Blucher's face into the snow. "You obviously didn't learn your lesson from last year."

"Eff off."

"Blucher, listen to me very carefully. I won't tell anyone if you shut the hell up right now. But if you continue to risk our lives needlessly by breaking Grizzly Bear's heart again, I'll personally make your life hell. You want to repeat the Blondie's beatdown? Except maybe this time I'll actually break your knees."

"Why you gotta pick on me?"

"I treat people as they ask to be treated. You keep asking for an ass whupping with your actions." Hofi tightened his grip and ground Blucher's face into the frozen dirt, the snow now pushed out of the way.

"Ow, you're hurting me."

"I'm not playing, Three Lima. You got one chance."

"Fine. Fine. Ow. Fine."

"You fail your promise, I'll end you. Now go back to the driver's seat." Hofi released Blucher and hopped to his feet. He then offered his hand to Blucher. Blucher looked at it and rolled away. He scrambled to his feet, slipping and falling again. His second attempt was successful.

"Blucher, what happened to you?" Running Bear's voice carried in the dark.

"I slipped and fell, Sarge."

"You all right? Gotta be careful."

The sound of the driver's hatch swinging closed ended the conversation.

Hofi turned to Kristyn. "Sorry about that, ma'am."

"That was intense. Why do you call him Three Lima?"

"We call him that because Three Lima is the most expendable soldier in the platoon. The platoon sergeant's wingman's loader is the designated guy to take his gas mask off first and we see if he survives before we take ours off too. The only reason why Sergeant doesn't kick Blucher to the wing tank is because he won't pawn problems off onto others. He won't even ditch him to First Platoon. Says they have enough problems of their own because of all the new sergeants. Three Lima just runs his mouth nonstop. Doesn't even care if anyone listens."

"He does offer unsolicited gossip. What happened at Blondie's? You're referring to the Colorado Springs nightclub, right?"

"Yeah. He was mouthing off saying Hamasaki got her Navy Cross via unmentionable and unprofessional acts. I told him to shut up. He swung his beer bottle at me. Barely connected and then I taught him a lesson. The police arrested the dipwad. Captain Trondfjell took the case from the police and busted him down a rank. Anyway, feel free to tell the command I just tackled Blucher. It was worth it."

"Maybe I don't agree with the methods, but I appreciate your intervention."

"Right on, dude. Still, even a court martial would be worth it. We can't afford our tank commander losing focus right now. Three Lima just doesn't seem to understand that at all. A crew's lives are all in a single basket."

"Blucher gonna sulk and risk you all now?"

"No. The fool rarely holds on to it for longer than ten minutes. He is afraid of Sergeant enough to not run his mouth on the tank, but he doesn't notice who is around when he does run his mouth off the tank. Stuff gets back to Sergeant."

"Believe me, I won't be talking with Running Bear about this. If there was any truth in Blucher's story of the divorce, that's too horrible to want to talk about."

"Thank you. He's a good platoon daddy. I don't want to let him down. Sergeants don't come much better than Running Bear. Anyway, sorry you got stuck with Three Lima for a bit. I need to get back to work." Hofi jogged off before Kristyn could respond.

"Wow. Well, that just happened." She suddenly felt thirsty. *I wonder how fast my water would freeze outside of the truck's heat? Would I be able to earn Running Bear's trust? I can't believe what Blucher said about Running Bear's kids. What the hell did I just witness?*

Poltava, Ukraine – January 21, 2000 hrs

The roar of the jet turbine engines and rotors above Sam penetrated even the foam earplugs she stuffed into her ears. Despite the full moon, cloud cover lent darkness. Wind buffeted the large helicopter. Leaning forward, Sam could look through the doorway to the cockpit. Ahead, a dozen AH-64 Apache gunships from 1-10 Aviation cleared a path for the MH-47 Chinooks of Company C, 3-160 Special Operations Aviation Regiment to follow.

Conveniently, the massing Russian 6th Combined Arms Army south of the landing zone provided an opportunity for a sleight of hand. While the Chinooks deposited Sam and her fellow Rangers on the Oril floodplain near Zarichne, the Apaches would continue another ten klicks south and engage the lead elements of the Russian counterattack.

Sam smiled at her map. The LZ was a frozen pond near the river. Thick woods south of the LZ would be their rally point. The hills around the valley served to screen their landing from the air defenses around Pereshchepyne. Sam wondered if the valley and trees would protect the LZ from the ground blizzard sweeping across the farmland. Then the real work would begin.

The Chinook banked and hugged the ground. Sam recognized the shape of a Bradley on the hill overlooking the valley. *We just crossed the frontline trace. Enemy territory now.* They would be at the LZ in a couple minutes. At the back of the aircraft, the ramp opened and the Rangers prepared their gear to exit. The crew chief held up a finger: "One minute!"

The Chinook slowed and flared before settling down into the snow. Immediately, the Rangers got out of the canvas bench seats and ran out into the snow. Sam followed and flopped into the snow as soon as she was clear of the ramp. The Chinook quickly lifted off and roared away into the night.

Sam plucked her earplugs out and thrust them into her pocket. A wave of the arm, and the Rangers jogged through the shin-deep snow to the trees south of the pond. Once in the trees, they formed up into their platoons. Sam moved to the center of the rally point and found her company commander, Captain Greeley.

"Sir." Sam nodded and dropped to a knee in the snow and pulled out her map.

"You ready?" Greeley asked.

"Roger that. Thirty klicks in this snow is gonna be slower than expected."

"I'd like to get as much distance in tonight though. Once the wind dies down and the clouds clear, the full moon is going to be a problem."

Explosions in the distance carried through the wind in the pines. Sam stopped and listened carefully.

"That must be Task Force Tigershark."

"Yeah. Get some." Greeley grinned.

First Sergeant Slidell briskly walked up. "Sir, we are accounted for. Ready to move out."

"Thank you." Greeley made eye contact with the lead platoon leader and waved for him to move out. Without another word, the company stood and the long march east began.

Greeley moved out behind the lead platoon. Sam linked up with the weapons platoon and moved with them. Closer to the east edge of the woods, snowdrifts were deeper. Sam moved over to follow in the path of a Ranger ahead. In minutes, Sam was warm from the exertion of the march.

Ahead, the column stopped and Rangers took to a knee in the snow. Sam shook her head and moved forward. Ahead, Greeley consulted with the lead platoon over the map. Greeley looked back at Sam and waved for her to join.

"What do you think, XO, will the ice under the snow support us?"

"I would think so. The pond ice didn't break under the Chinooks."

"Okay, let's use the river as a trail. Should be less snowdrift to bust through."

"Concealment?" Sam asked, worried to be in the open.

"The banks are lined with these tall rushes. Most are still standing taller than us."

"Roger, sir." Sam looked at the map. The Oril River meandered all over the valley. *Old waterway.* Sam's mind flashed back to her military geography classes at West Point. The flat floodplain would have plenty of oxbows and holes they could use for cover in a fight. To the north, the tall hills overlooking the valley worried Sam. *Not that anywhere in the valley would be safer.*

Greeley nodded and waved the lead platoon forward. Silently, the Rangers got to their feet again and plodded forward. Sam waited until her place in the column caught up to her and then joined the march east.

Stepping from the deep snow onto the ice seemed easy enough. Much to Sam's relief, enough grit froze into the ice to reduce the risk of slipping. The wind howled in the trees on the hill and the rushes whispered. Sam's mind wandered. The silent anticipation reminded her of the long voyage to Fiery Cross Reef a lifetime ago. *We had a great team then. We have a great team now.* Sam smiled. *I wonder who we will find at this POW camp.*

The Rangers ahead of her pushing into the rushes on the bank pulled Sam's mind back. She pulled her map out. *Ah, cutting across the narrow necks. Yeah, the river would have added a few klicks easily.* The march was long enough, but the night would last.

Holubivka, Ukraine – January 21, 2300 hrs

The main room of the command post was tense. Nobody had slept more than three hours in two days. Molchalin walked over to the intelligence officer seat and put his hands on the younger officer's shoulders.

"What have you found, Colonel Beketov?"

"Sir, we pinpointed the command posts for six American units. The regimental and one battalion headquarters in the American Third Cavalry, and the brigade and three battalion headquarters in First Brigade of First Armored Division. We cross-referenced the callsigns on the radio intercepts with the data, then triangulated both. Our information is now six hours old, but we are confident the Americans don't suspect we were able to decipher this much. I have plotted the enemy command posts on the map." Beketov pointed to the room's large situation map on the wall.

"Good work." Molchalin moved to the map. "What time are the Spetsnaz hitting the enemy command structure?"

"They are synchronizing with our attack at first light," Frosin answered from his desk.

"Good. I want to have the BM-27s of the 27th Motor Rifles and the 138th Guards Motor Rifles to evenly hit all of the enemy command posts at 0700 hours. District is selecting targets for our tactical ballistic missiles. I want our drones to focus efforts on enemy artillery. The disruption of American command and control will help us, but the 27th Motor Rifles will need to exercise caution in their advance. I know District will authorize the 138th to attack sooner or later. I want to reserve enough strength in the 27th to join that attack."

"Yes, sir. Also, I confirmed with First GTA they are planning a holding attack to support us."

"Good. Good." Molchalin rubbed his eyes. "I am going to lay down for a few. Should anything happen, wake me. If not, wake me at four." *I need my brain functioning fully in the morning. This might be the most important attack of my life.*

Molchalin set his cot up and tossed his blankets out onto it. He took his boots off and carefully placed them under the cot before crawling under the blankets. Sleep came quickly.

Yosypivka, Ukraine – January 22, 0100 hrs

The metallic squeal of tracks carried on the wind. Sam stopped, cocked her head, and tried to pinpoint the direction. *Definitely more than one tank.* Sam's heart raced. A flurry of hand signals cascaded down the column and the Rangers broke into a jog. Sam rounded the bend of the river and saw the railroad bridge ahead. The column ran under the bridge and then dove into the rushes on the southside. Winded, Sam followed. In minutes, they moved into some scattered trees.

Greeley moved back on the column.

"Sam, we'll set a perimeter in these woods. Hopefully the Russians bypass us. Sounds like at least a dozen different vehicles."

"Sir, want to get a drone up?"

"No, I think the wind is too strong." Greeley paused to point the weapons platoon into position. Smoothly, the Rangers prepared their anti-armor weapons.

"Right. At least the ice let us avoid leaving tracks."

"Didn't think about that, but yes, I'm also thankful." Greeley pulled out his map. Sam leaned in to study it.

"Think these are part of the expected Russian counterattack toward Karlivka?" Sam traced her finger up what intel thought was the expected path of the Russian 6th Combined Arms Army.

"Seems too far east though. Though maybe this is a holding force?"

A barking dog interrupted Greeley. He looked up. A small farm compound was just a hundred meters away.

"Get down!" Sam hissed as a Russian tank followed the railroad out of the woods beyond the farm. She flopped down. The Rangers were to avoid contact at all costs. Now they would test nerves and discipline.

A T-90 followed the railroad toward the bridge. A trio of BMP-3s followed it. Sam sucked her breath in. *Please be complacent.* Sam looked at the vehicles over her rifle sights. No heads were visible in the hatches. *Too cold to want to be up.* Sam remembered frosty days at Fort Carson freezing her face while a Bradley platoon leader.

"I think we are far enough into their rear they aren't expecting to find a fight," Greeley whispered.

"Yeah, and they don't mix tanks with their scout elements. These dudes think the path is clear."

"But if we get up, they will see us for sure." Greeley rolled over and looked over at the weapons platoon. The Javelin gunners were ready.

Sam followed Greeley's gaze. The weapons platoon only had six missiles. *And you know we're gonna need those at the objective.* Sam frowned. A fight now would ruin the mission completely.

Another T-90 emerged from the far woods. More BMP-3s followed. Sam examined the vehicles through her sights. *The turrets are still. We might be okay.*

"Here comes some more." Greeley pointed.

"Gotta be at least a company. Maybe even a whole BTG. Bet they're using the railroad as a guide."

The growl of engines increased as the lead vehicles climbed onto the far bank.

"I guess the ice is thick enough," Greeley remarked as the Russians streamed north.

Sam didn't reply. She looked at her watch.

"Uh oh." Greeley's alarm caused Sam to look back at the railroad. A platoon of BMP-3s stopped near the farm. The dog barking increased in urgency.

Sam gripped her rifle tightly. *Oh man.* She looked at the Javelin gunners again. All three sat in the snow, missiles ready. Quickly Sam refocused on the BMP-3s. Sam crawled to the squad. *Where is the platoon leader?* Pausing to look at the farm, she saw a Russian soldier get out of a BMP. Sam hastened her crawl, snow sliding down the neck of her jacket.

"Easy men. Easy," Sam whispered as she reached the gunners. "We can't afford to start a fight!"

"Roger ma'am." The first gunner gritted his teeth.

Sam looked to the farm again. The Russian soldier was nowhere in sight. "Where did that Ivan go?"

"Behind the house."

Sam pulled her rifle up and aimed for the corner, just in case. The BMPs still had their turrets to the front. Perhaps the Russians were stretching their legs? The BMP engines rumbled as they idled, so hearing the Russian conversations was out of the question.

"Ma'am, I don't think they know we're here."

"Hooah, let's keep it that way." Sam's heart thumped heavily.

The crack of a rifle shot shattered the night. Sam gripped her rifle tightly. *That was an AK.* Sam looked to the sides, looking for any reaction from the Rangers. Nothing. *Good. Hmm, the barking ended. Don't tell me they shot the dog!*

"What are they doing?" the gunner whispered.

"Not sure. Steady." Sam shivered. The snow down her neck was freezing. Still, she lay in the snow and watched. Time passed slowly.

A loud yell in Russian carried over the wind. A metal hatch slammed. Another slammed, then the Russian returned from behind the house and climbed back into his BMP. A moment later, the engines growled and the BMP-3s rumbled northward.

Sam picked her head up higher and looked around. The CO was back on a knee, waving his arm and pointing east. *Time to go.* Sam watched the CO repeat his signal and got to her knee, relaying the signal down the line of Rangers. The weapons platoon leader rose to a knee from the other side of the Javelin gunners and also waved. In seconds, the squad leaders got the Rangers up and the company melted farther away from the farm. The going would be slow now there were Russian forces moving through the area. Sam looked at her map as she wove through the trees. *Twenty-two klicks to go. No way we will make it before dawn.* Sam traced their planned route. Two large open areas would be dangerous to cross, even in the dark, and the clock was ticking.

Chapter 8

Moscow, Russia – January 22, 0200 hrs

Voroshilov tossed three pills to the back of his mouth and swallowed. The bitter taste annoyed him. He poured some vodka into his glass and took a big gulp. Swishing the vodka helped the taste.

"You're making my headache worse, Andrey Vladimirovich." Voroshilov spoke to an empty room, staring at the situation map on his computer. *I've never had a headache this bad.* Voroshilov couldn't remember when it started, but it interfered with his ability to focus.

Voroshilov picked up his phone and called Popov. The phone rang several times before Popov answered.

"Heh, um, yes, President Voroshilov?"

"Took you long enough to answer. Were you sleeping or are you drunk?" Voroshilov sank back in his chair and closed his eyes, oblivious to his own words slurring.

"Asleep. I've been asleep for...two hours now. Maybe you should sleep too."

"When the nazis have attacked and penetrated your impenetrable lines? How can you sleep?"

"No sleep makes bad choices."

"And sleeping while the enemy advances will lead to surprises in the morning." Voroshilov stopped. Popov said nothing. "Popov, I suppose it is safe to assume, since you were sleeping, that you have no updates for me."

"No updates. Correct. We are attacking at seven. The drones will take off before that, as they and the artillery are synced. You might as well get some sleep until then."

"You are confident there is nothing more you can do to prepare the attack's success?"

"No, President Voroshilov."

A knock on the door interrupted the conversation. "Hold on, Popov. Yes?" Voroshilov yelled at the door.

"Sir, message from the communications center. Copies are going to the members of the security council." The messenger brought an envelope and laid it on the desk in front of Voroshilov. He snapped a salute and marched out of the room.

"Don't hang up." Voroshilov set the phone down and opened the letter. He read it twice before crumpling and throwing it at the door. "The unholy scum! Is this all a joke to them?"

"Sir?" Popov inquired.

"The West! Those arrogant nazis! How can they presume to *offer* for *us* to *give* back the very land we control as a condition of peace?"

"I'm confused. What exactly are you talking about?" Popov still hadn't received his message.

"The Chinese forwarded an offer from the West. They want us to give up all of our gains since last summer in exchange for recognition of our annexation of the Donbas and Crimea. Why don't they just ask for the Kaliningrad while they are at it!"

"Was that all of the message?"

"Oh, and the Ukraine joins NATO and there would be a DMZ. They are insane. Our troops are still dug in from Odesa back to Kharkiv. The nazis can't even *shell* the Black Sea from their positions. How can they dare to expect us to retreat, unbeaten from our strong fortifications and minefields?"

"We do have strong lines. NATO as yet has a very small salient."

"Don't I know! You! Instead of sleeping, you need to be focused on smashing those arrogant bastards! I want the nazis driven back to their side of the Vorskla by noon! Do you hear me?" Voroshilov's headache exploded in fury and veins popped out in blue rivers across his forehead.

"Yes, President Voroshilov."

"How can it be? You have made my head feel like NATO's salient is inside of it. Now go before you make me angry!" Voroshilov hung up and tossed the phone back onto the desk. "Why is it that I am the only one who sees how important destroying this attack is?"

The thought of his generals being unable to stop the attack bubbled to life. Voroshilov closed his eyes and rubbed his scalp with both hands. *Think.*

Ten minutes later, Voroshilov stopped his massaging and picked the phone up. He dialed the head of the military intelligence agency, the GRU.

"Kochetkov," the voice answered after just three rings.

"It's me, Boris."

"You sound rough, Nikolai."

"I could use a good sauna. And a victory."

"We all could. That is not why you are calling, is it?"

"No. Boris, I think we need to be careful. We have some operations rightfully remaining secret."

"Yes. NATO's attack has you worried. What are you wanting?"

"If anything should fall back into Western hands, we might have some difficulty with future international relations. I'll not have the same legacy as Germany after the Great Patriotic War. Nobody batted an eye at our camps because they stayed in our control."

"You are thinking of my camp at Pereshchepyne."

"NATO cannot capture it. They definitely cannot find what we have gained there."

"Moving it at this point would be incredibly difficult and impossible to hide. Remember, avoiding moving these assets was the point of the camp's location."

"I know. If it looks like NATO will capture it, liquidate it. Burn it. Blow it up. Dispose of all evidence."

"Of course. It would be a shame to lose the assets though."

"Yes, Boris. Don't do it prematurely. We still have time to counterattack and crush the NATO invaders. But Boris, if it fails tomorrow, the clock is probably ticking. Be ready to liquidate our assets by noon on the twenty-third. That is my deadline for the army to defeat the nazi attack."

"Yes, Nikolai. I will see to it."

"Good." Voroshilov hung up and closed his eyes again.

Smorodshchyna, Ukraine – January 22, 0700 hrs

Logan rubbed his eyes, feeling grit grind under his eyelids. He looked at his watch and glanced at the door of the armored vehicle. A moment later, it opened and frigid air rushed in.

"Brrrr." Douglas climbed through the door and pulled it closed.

"Sunrise in half an hour," Logan offered.

"Coldest part of the day will be over soon. But the day is gonna get hot in other ways." Douglas slid into a chair and rubbed his hands together.

"True. Ivan seems to sense our presence and his scouts are moving forward very slowly." Logan pointed to the Russian reported frontline trace south of Thunder Squadron's observation posts.

"This will be no rash action. Ivan will prep the battlefield first." Douglas leaned his head back and stared at the ceiling. "Logan, go to the XO's Bradley. He is putting together the next TOC jump. I'd like you to help him. Colonel Pacheco is gonna come in here momentarily anyway."

"Roger. Sir." Logan grabbed his helmet and gloves before ducking out the door. He was used to giving up his seat for the squadron commander to operations officer discussions.

The zero-degree air instantly brought all Logan's senses to full alert. The glow of the morning peeked between the Plans vehicle and the signals truck. Logan paused to look around. The tarp tied between the vehicles of the TOC blocked Logan's view of the sky. Curious, Logan squeezed between the vehicles. Overcast. With a shrug, Logan returned to the TOC and quickly opened the Bradley's troop hatch.

"Hi, Logan." Noyes nodded for Logan to grab a seat next to him. Across the compartment, the squadron signal officer, Captain Conner Upton, looked up from his laptop screen to smile a hello.

"Sir, Major Douglas said you wanted me to help with the TOC jump."

"I did. First Armored's attack bogged down some and with the Russian Sixth Combined Arms Army coming up from the south, Regiment is considering giving us a tank company so we can plan a mobile defense as part of our covering operation."

"Okay." Logan leaned closer to the map to study it.

"So, I want today's TOC jump to put us in the best spot to command and control with the additional company and the necessary depth."

"Logan," Conner interjected, "terrain is conducive for signals, so no limitations."

"I see." Logan traced his finger over the mass of blue icons cluttering the map on the highway through Karlivka. "Ivan's gonna want to sever this line. We gotta stop him south of it."

"Correct." Noyes pointed his finger to the town of Tahamlyts'ke. "I'm thinking about here. Thoughts?"

Logan sat back and scratched the stubble on his chin. *Ivan will probably pound the highway with artillery to sow confusion in our rear. Two thousand meters enough separation? Probably?* Logan made eye contact with Noyes before answering. "Sir, has anyone used that area as an assembly area yet? The area near checkpoint two-five-five?"

"I don't think so. With 1ID coming up online with 1AD, the trains have shifted closer to the interdivisional boundary and away from the flank."

"I think that spot is as good as any. Still, it would be good to advance our lines farther south. Another ten klicks of depth would let us string Ivan's neck out for a decisive blow."

"We can't do that just yet." Noyes shook his head.

"No?" Logan stared back.

"You know that POW camp you discussed with Andy a while back? Well, higher is afraid if we get too close, Ivan will execute our POWs."

"Well, what the hell? Let's push hard and get there before they can do that!" Logan snapped. *Seriously? How has this not been the plan from day one?*

"We've kept this from the digital airwaves for security, but there is something in motion already. We have to stay far enough away we don't accidentally push Russian combat units into the Pereshchepyne area." Noyes smiled at Logan. "Don't worry, we didn't fail the faith."

"Special Ops?" Logan asked.

Noyes nodded. "We are on standby to link up with them, if necessary, but it is unlikely. The infil went really well and the decoy mission put a huge dent in the 6CAA."

"Okay. Fair enough." Logan looked back at the map.

"Back to the here and now. Let's sequence this TOC jump." Noyes opened his laptop.

KABOOM!

The Bradley shook violently from the nearby explosion.

"Incoming! Driver, displace!" Noyes yelled over the sound of more explosions.

Logan fell out of his seat as the Bradley surged forward, engine roaring.

"Thunder X-ray, Thunder Five, displace to rally point alpha! Thunder Yankee, establish at rally point bravo." Noyes rapidly spoke into the radio hand mic as the Bradley took a sudden turn.

Another explosion rocked the Bradley and shrapnel pinged off the armor. Logan climbed back into the seat and hung on tight. Another sudden turn tossed Logan's butt out of the seat, but a death grip on the table kept him from flying to the floor again. The explosions faded into the distance. Noyes opened the turret door and climbed up. Logan quickly took Noyes' seat so he could see the command and control screen better. Logan pulled a headset on.

"You okay?" Logan asked Conner.

"Yeah. Ivan found us somehow. I even had our antennas remoted three hundred meters away." Conner frowned.

"Those were pretty large booms. I'm guessing at least 220mm rockets. They might have decided to saturate a huge area."

"I'll have to go back and salvage what I can in a bit. Looks like our BFT isn't updating everyone. The Plans track icon hasn't moved." Conner pointed at a lone icon remaining where the TOC had been.

Logan didn't reply. The alternate reason jumped to the forefront of his mind.

The radio interrupted Logan's dark thoughts. "Thunder Five, Thunder Nine, I've got the Yankee vehicles, but I don't have Six actual or Three actual. Over."

"Roger. Establish and then we can assess. Break." Noyes released the radio a moment before addressing the medical platoon leader. "Band-aid One, have an element meet us at rally point alpha. Out."

Logan used the intercom to speak to Noyes. "Sir, Colonel Pacheco and Major Douglas were in the plans track and its icon hasn't moved since we displaced."

"I know, Logan. I see that. We only have two tracks following us. I can't tell which ones." Up in the turret, Noyes was able to see the world around the speeding Bradley. "Logan, when we get to the rally point, I want you to stay in here and manage the squadron fight while I get the TOC sorted out."

"Roger, sir. I'll call up the contact to regiment." Logan quickly selected the regimental radio and reported.

The Bradley slowed as Noyes guided it into the rally point. A moment later, the Bradley stopped and Noyes quickly climbed out. Conner followed, leaving Logan alone. The computer dinged the arrival of a new combat message from Killer Troop.

> ENGAGED AND DESTROYED ENEMY COMBAT SECURITY DETACHMENT SOUTH OF FEDORIVKA. OBSERVED FORWARD DETACHMENT AND FOLLOWING BTG MOVING NORTH UP ORCHYK RIVER VALLEY.

Logan copied and pasted the message into the logbook. The red enemy icons appeared on the tactical map as the system refreshed data. *Only one of four expected BTGs.*

"Where are you guys?" Logan whispered. Logan opened the contact report from Killer Troop and tallied the enemy vehicles. The count matched an undersized BTG. *Patience, Logan. Patience.*

"Thunder X-ray, Ironhawk Five, contact tanks and PC south." The squadron radio crackled a moment before the new red icons appeared on the screen south of Kumy.

"Roger. Engage and report," Logan answered. He then opened the new reports and counted vehicles. *Ivan will hit Ironhawk squarely, right into the main engagement area. Perfect. Gonna hit Killer left of their center. Justin's got good troops though. Killer will be able to handle this attack.*

"Sapper One, Thunder X-ray," Logan radioed, "cease work and displace." There was no reason to risk the squadron's engineer platoon. The fighting positions they were digging for Ironhawk would help, but now Logan needed to protect the valuable asset.

"Wilco." The terse reply made Logan wonder if he waited too long for that decision.

Logan checked the time and made an entry in the logbook. This time, Logan added notes about his rationale for decision.

"Thunder X-ray, Lightning Seven, contact tanks and PC south." Top Harris's deep voice lifted Logan's spirits. *Oh, what a familiar voice can do.* "Twenty-seven BMP3 and ten T-90 moving northeast in NAI9 Over."

Logan studied the map. The new Russian formation would travel out of Lightning's area and hit Killer nearly center. *That means the fourth and final BTG of this attack has to be behind these three. Killer Troop is going to take the brunt. It's like Ivan knows where the seam between Killer and Ironhawk is.*

"Roger. Guidons, enemy main axis of advance north-northeast toward Fedorivka. Break." Logan released the radio and took a breath before continuing. "Lightning, disrupt Russian BTG in NAI9 with your mortars and Maddog's tubes. Hand targeting over to Killer Five-One when they reach your boundary, but continue to hammer with your mortars for Killer. Killer and Ironhawk, fight your engagement areas. Over."

Logan glanced at the regiment's instant chat feed. *Good.* The TAC was feeding information up to regiment and asking for air support. Distant booms announced the battle opening. Logan rubbed his hands together as a chill ran up his spine. More explosions joined. Logan wished he was back in a tank, watching the fight unfold with his own eyes. This waiting and waiting for radio updates was frustratingly slow.

"Thunder X-ray, Sapper One-One," the radio crackled.

"Thunder X-ray," Logan replied.

"We are clear of Ironhawk. Checking on the artillery impact area for casualties," the squadron's engineer platoon leader, First Lieutenant Gianola, reported.

"Roger." Logan set the hand mic down and scrutinized the tactical display. The plans track's icon still hadn't moved, though the engineer icons now gathered around it on the map. *Who all was in it still after I got out? Major Douglas. Probably Colonel Pacheco. Sergeant Major Jimenez. Specialist Poindexter was in the driver's seat. Sergeant Bezuidenhout was on guard in the hatch. I hope they are okay.* The thought failed to offer hope. Minutes ticked by.

"Thunder X-ray, Sapper One-One. Two KIA and three WIA here. The plans track is burning. We will link up with the medics to hand off the wounded and continue our mission."

"Thunder X-ray, roger." Logan answered a moment before the computer dinged with a message. It was Gianola.

THUNDER 6 IS KIA. THUNDER 3 IS WIA. DIDN'T WANT TO AIR THAT ON THE RADIO.

Logan slouched lower in his seat. *Colonel Pacheco is gone. Oh crap. How badly is Major Douglas hurt?* Focus faded as Logan's eyes watered. Logan bit his lip and glanced around. The driver and gunner were out of the vehicle, leaving solitude.

"Thunder X-ray, Killer Five, eleven-slant-eight, engaged and destroyed three T-90s and seven BMP3s. Enemy broke contact. Continuing to defend." Killer Troop's report interrupted Logan's grief. Logan glanced at the combat power tracking board and saw Killer Troop lost two Bradleys and one Abrams since their last report.

"Roger. Continue mission. Do you need anything?" Logan considered the tone of voice on the radio. Logan sensed tension in Killer Troop's XO, First Lieutenant Devin Schofield.

"Negative. Working CASEVAC and recovery. Are we still priority of fires?" Devin responded.

Logan thought a moment before answering, "Roger."

The troop door opened and Andy climbed in. "Logan."

"Andy. What do you know?"

"You heard about the colonel?"

"Yeah. You know more than I do?" Logan asked, pointing at the message from Gianola.

"Major Noyes got the report on the A&L net a couple minutes ago. Major Douglas is litter urgent, but he will live. Sergeant Major is better off, but won't be returning. Poindexter didn't make it. Sergeant Bez lost an arm."

"Damn." Logan's voice cracked.

"Yeah." Andy sat down. "We don't have time to be miserable. Ivan is still massing."

"Do you know why their attack fizzled? It doesn't look like they pressed Killer very hard."

"Not sure. Their main body didn't commit. My team is working on it."

"They will be back. If Ivan gives up on this counterattack, they give up on the Donets Pocket."

"And if they give up on the Donets Pocket, Logan, they give up on this war."

"That would be nice. I don't see how they can though. Gotta save face, you know."

"Yeah..." Andy sat back. "With the colonel down, Major Noyes has to step up, and with Major Douglas out, that makes you next in line."

"I'm sure regiment will have someone first. But yeah, we gotta step up to help the XO with those duties too now."

"Definitely. We keep working together to give him good plans and stay on top of operations; it will help him a lot."

"On that note, what do you think Ivan's next move is?" Logan changed the topic.

"He is gonna continue the counterattack. Maybe they spend some time to prep the battlefield more. Maybe more artillery and drones first."

"Figure that is the most likely? Timing?"

"If the 6CAA wanted, they could prep starting immediately and attack this afternoon. If they want to beef up their attack with the units farther south, maybe tomorrow. They could use artillery and drones to suppress us until then."

"Most dangerous. Yeah. I'd buy that."

"Logan, you held against multiple BTGs last summer. How many do you think we could hold now?"

"We had depth then. Now we don't. Maybe five. I think we are good on ammo for that much. Might need to shuffle resources around as the fight develops."

"Okay. I'll get back to work on what Ivan is going to do."

Logan nodded. Andy pushed himself out of the seat and climbed out of the Bradley. Logan returned his focus to the map and the combat power tracking board. The answers would come to him soon enough.

Ding. Logan saw it was a message from regiment.

> FLASH TRAFFIC: RUSSIAN DRONES AND LONG-RANGE ARTILLERY SYSTEMATICALLY TARGETING COMMAND AND CONTROL NODES. TAKE ALL NECESSARY PRECAUTIONS.

Logan grimly shook his head. *A dollar short and a day late.* Logan knew they had already done nearly every precaution he could think of, short of using runners only.

"Sapper One-One, Thunder X-ray." Logan keyed up the radio as he swiftly typed a message.

"Sapper One-One," Gianola immediately responded.

"Copy digital FRAGO." Logan clicked send as he spoke.

"Received. Wilco." Logan could visualize the engineer platoon leader reading the message.

> DIG TOC POSITIONS AT BEST AVAILIBLE SPOT VIC CHECKPOINT 255.

The next TOC jump would be to a dug-in position.

Holubivka, Ukraine – January 22, 1215 hrs

"Davit, how bad is it?" Molchalin answered his phone as soon as he saw the caller ID.

"General, not too bad. We were careful. As soon as it was apparent the enemy would not yield, we backed off."

"What are your losses? I need the truth."

"A total of seven tanks and fifteen BMPs. We are currently reorganizing BTGs to balance for tomorrow. Are we still on for tomorrow?"

"We have to keep the Kharkiv line open, so I'm sure we will attack. If we can't keep the rail line, you know what that will mean."

"Yes, General."

"Make sure you have ammo and fuel for tomorrow."

"I will."

"Okay, Davit, thank you for not destroying your division today." Molchalin hung up.

Molchalin got up and paced around his office. *If someone high up finds out how little we pushed the attack today, it might be hard to explain. But if tomorrow is successful, all will be forgiven.* He lit a cigarette and stood behind his desk, staring at the map. With nothing but a short butt left, Molchalin dropped it in his ash tray and picked up the phone.

This time, Dronov was quickly on the other end. "Victor, your attack this morning didn't even dent the enemy lines. Tell me the Twenty-Seventh Motor Rifles remains a division we can use tomorrow."

"Yes, sir. The Twenty-Seventh remains combat effective. But they are not strong enough to break the enemy alone."

"I agree. We will have to attack again. We have no choice."

"What news from the rest of the district?"

"An American helicopter landing outside of Kharkiv cut the rail line. Kiselyov reports it is a whole infantry brigade. Additional landings nearly surround the Fourth Guards Tank Division. They can still retreat north and Kiselyov is having them fall back to the border while they still can. What's left of them."

Molchalin whistled.

"Yes. Kiselyov is moving his headquarters because the enemy is nearly in his yard. They will use the forward bunkers at Bryansk."

"Long move. How long before he is reestablished?"

"He is commanding from his BTR while en route. Kiselyov promises to be up and running by midnight."

"Hope he's careful."

"Yes. Victor, I need an updated assessment of your supplies. District cannot supply you anymore. I'm working to get Southern to provide supplies, but General Lipilin wants control of your army first."

"He wants Golovko's job." Molchalin's disgust oozed.

"I'm sure he does. Perhaps even Popov's." Dronov coughed. "If your attack tomorrow fails, he might just get his wishes by default."

"Allow me to use all my divisions and it will not fail."

"There is no time to bring up the 25th Guards. But use the 138th and the 27th Motor Rifle Divisions."

"Sir, if this attack fails, then what? We have no more options. I must make the attack strong enough. I can't get the Twenty-Fifth Guards in place in time for a dawn attack, but let's delay until we can. I can attack at thirteen hundred and smash north with enough power to break the enemy flank."

Dronov stayed quiet and Molchalin waited patiently.

"Victor, there is weather moving in tomorrow. More importantly, President Voroshilov chose noon tomorrow as a decision point. I will ask him if we can delay the attack, but you must be prepared to attack sooner."

"I can attack with the 27th in lead with the 25th Guards as the follow-on force and have the 138th Guards widen the shoulders to the west. If, sir, you allow me to control the 47th Guards Tank Division's attack in support."

"I need to think on that. The Forty-Seventh is weakened. It might not be able to offer much."

"General, with the blizzard coming in tomorrow, the Yankees won't make much progress either. Let's take the opportunity to make a stronger attack. The storm can protect us from enemy drones too. I can have all three divisions ready by noon."

"I said, let me think on it. Victor, plan your attack well with the troops you have. Two divisions. Now, I must go." Dronov hung up.

Molchalin shrugged. There was much for the staff to do.

Two hours later, Dronov called back. "Victor, you will attack at noon. You will attack with both the 138th and 27th. You can have two BTGs from the 47th to attack from the east to hold the enemy. I will allow the 25th to follow in support. Once you break the enemy lines, cut north to Chutove to sever the enemy supply lines to Kharkiv. Use the blizzard to protect your forces from enemy drone and helicopters."

"Yes, General." Molchalin's shoulders relaxed in relief.

"Victor, plan it well. Execute it well. We will not have anything left if you fail." Dronov hung up without waiting for a response, leaving Molchalin feeling hopeful for the first time in two days.

Koshmanivka, Ukraine – January 22, 1445 hrs

Kristyn woke to soft knocking on the truck door. She squinted and saw Savvy standing outside. Kristyn rubbed her eyes and opened the door.

"Hey Kristyn, I was wondering if you wanted to ride with me to check on the platoons? I've got space in the back of my Brad."

"Yeah. Let me grab my camera and notebook." Adrenaline blasted away the post-nap fog. *Finally! A chance to see more than just the same mechanics.*

Savvy led the way to her Bradley and pointed Kristyn to a seat in the back. Pezo handed her a headset, letting her listen to the vehicle crew and radio chatter. The Bradley lurched and rocked for several minutes before coming to a stop.

"I'll be here maybe fifteen minutes or more, Kristyn. Feel free to stretch your legs around the platoon, just listen to their concerns regarding security and safety."

"Thank you. Which platoon is this?"

"Second Platoon, one of our tank platoons."

"Thank you." Kristyn removed the headset and pulled her neck gaiter up as the ramp dropped. Savvy appeared from the turret and they ducked out into the weak afternoon sunlight.

"Ma'am, I meant to ask you," Running Bear greeted Savvy, "you still want all the XO stuff sent to you or do you have someone designated to cover down on that?"

"I'll keep taking it. Only a matter of time before we get a new captain. I'm gonna have a chat with your LT. How is he doing in your opinion?"

"LT is doing well. Platoon is doing well."

"Good. And you? Close one yesterday."

"It worked out. I'm good."

"Want to show Kristyn around while I talk with your LT? Thanks, Sergeant." Savvy gave a small wave and trudged off to a tank parked a couple hundred meters away.

"Kristyn." Running Bear nodded to her.

"Good to see you. This is the farthest I've seen you from your tank." Kristyn pointed to his tank fifty meters up the hill.

"I walked down to catch the XO. Sometimes it's best to talk with leaders out of earshot of the troops."

"Makes sense to me. You can speak more freely."

"Yes." Running Bear made no movement toward the tank. Kristyn wondered if he suspected the incident with Blucher.

"You have work to do?" Kristyn canted her head.

"No, I'm caught up."

"Yeah?"

"It helps to have a good and experienced LT." Running Bear nodded. "Lieutenant Sinclair has been our platoon leader since before the war started. He has done well. Both wingmen are solid. Black and Meigs are replacements, but they are good tankers. Makes my job a lot easier."

"Easier, but never easy?"

"Nothing in this business is easy. But some things can be very, very hard."

"Such as?" Kristyn quietly asked.

"The family shares the sacrifice with the soldier."

Kristyn frowned. "They do."

"Yes. My old wingman, Staff Sergeant Eric Zimmer, and I had been in the same company for six years. We made it through Fiery Cross. Back in the day, we would take our families fishing together. But he took an artillery round through the roof in July. Now Jenna and the boys must go on without him." Running Bear trailed off, his eyes clouding.

"I can't imagine." Kristyn closed her eyes. It had been so long since she had a boyfriend, and without kids, there was no way for her to fathom such grief. She was aware of that.

"It is hard. There are days when the grief stabs you in the gut and twists. When your heart is so broken the dawn never comes." Running Bear's words were barely more than a whisper.

"You lost someone very dear to you." Kristyn felt pain in her own heart watching this warrior soften.

Running Bear nodded.

Kristyn quietly leaned forward, wishing she could comfort Running Bear, but unsure how. *I'll just be a human and listen then.* Kristyn felt her heart slowly thumping, slowly softening. As she struggled between a reporter's inquisitive mission and the compassion of a human, Running Bear composed himself. He straightened, seeming to grow an inch. His face hardened and the watering of the eyes ceased. In two blinks, Running Bear merely looked cold.

"All soldiers sacrifice more than people think." His voice returned to a normal volume and pitch.

"Truth. Don't have to spend all that much time with soldiers to see that."

"Perhaps you see it. Not sure many civilians would."

"To be fair, Running Bear, I'm not sure I fit in the civilian category cleanly any more. I'm no soldier, but what I've seen, shared, felt, has slowly eroded any sense of belonging with other civilians. Like humanity's no-mans-land."

"What changed you?"

"If I had to pin a single event, the fall of Kabul. I'm not sure if it was Abbey Gate. Or watching people fall from taking-off airplanes. But maybe it was just years of watching death randomly and abruptly snuff out some promising young life. I don't know." Kristyn shook her hand as if she had slammed it in a door.

"You get it," Running Bear announced.

Kristyn looked him in the eyes and smiled. "One way to put it." Warmth welled inside her chest as Running Bear smiled back.

"Not everyone gets it. Not everyone is strong enough to handle the burden of war's hell."

"That sounds like a personal observation."

"You could say that, Kristyn."

"If and when you are ready to share, I would listen."

Kristyn enjoyed Running Bear's double take.

Running Bear looked at the horizon, letting silence engulf them. Kristyn looked south too. *I'll let him make the next move.*

"Kristyn, you've been doing this a long time."

"Fifteen years."

"Almost as long as I've been in the Army. You've learned some things you can't share with just anyone?"

"Oh man, yeah. It seems like those who haven't seen it themselves can't fathom what resides in our memories."

"Right?"

Kristyn snorted. "And so you have to be careful who you can let in on your darkest thoughts."

"Lest you break them." Running Bear nodded.

"Honestly, I've never known anyone I could share it all with. You soldiers are lucky in that sense. The collective nature of the unit gives you friends with similar experiences."

"Perhaps. Not quite as easy as that though. Are there no other combat reporters you can do the same with?"

"Meh, none that I want to. It's a small pool really."

"I didn't know that."

"For that, I'm happy to be embedded this go around."

"Feels like home?" Running Bear now turned to Kristyn, meeting her eyes.

"Yeah. I do feel at home right now."

"Well, I'd appreciate if you turned the thermostat up. You forget to pay the utility bill or something?" Running Bear grinned.

Kristyn swatted his arm and shook her head, trying to not grin stupidly.

"Looks like the XO is done. I better go check on my LT." Running Bear started to walk away before stopping and turning around. "Thanks for the talk, Kristyn."

"Of course." Kristyn waved and then headed for the Bradley. Time to go. *Running Bear bottles up. Big time. Do you blame him? But he almost trusted me. Almost.*

Chapter 9

Somivka, Ukraine – January 22, 1730 hrs

The last colors drained from the western horizon as the Rangers stirred in their patrol base. The forced rest had rejuvenated Sam and her fellow Rangers. Even the temperatures had been warmer than the last month. Distant rumbles of artillery provided focus as Rangers watched for approaching danger. The woods in the bend of the Oril River were pretty far from the beaten path though.

"Well, eight and a half klicks." Greeley stretched and nodded at the company leadership.

"I think these rushes will conceal us from that missile battery on the hill." Sam pointed toward a hill in the distance.

"And those Ivans are gonna be more focused on the sky than the valley below," Greeley added. The Rangers would follow the river again. To the south, a BTR-82 and its squad of Russian infantry was just three klicks away, across a field of grass. The river would let the Rangers slip behind the Russians guarding the north end of the minefields. Once past the BTR, the going would be easier. The Oril valley became wooded again all the way to the objective rally point.

"True. Wonder how things are going up north." Sam adjusted her gear as she mused. The advantages of radio silence were worth the ignorance of the events around. The company radio operator set up the satellite radio to listen. Battalion would broadcast coded messages if something important changed. Nothing all day was a good sign. As far as the world knew, the Ranger company was doing nothing.

"The artillery rumbles haven't gone away, so I would say the Russian counterattack failed." Greeley stopped working on his rucksack to answer. "Well, we need to be at the objective in just six hours. Better get moving."

Sam didn't reply, throwing her rucksack over her head and onto her back. She stood tall and cinched her shoulder straps tight. "Let's move out." Sam nodded to Greeley and moved along the patrol base perimeter, making sure everyone was ready. The company first sergeant did the same in the opposite direction. They met up on the far side of the triangle and high-fived. Sam grinned and found her place with the weapons platoon.

Silently, the Rangers moved out of the woods and onto the river ice. The river was narrow in places and the file hugged the rushes on the banks. The moonlight was bright on the fresh snow. Even without her night vision goggles, Sam could easily pick out soldiers moving at the front of the column. *Thank God for these tall rushes. The final approach to the objective will be a challenge though.*

The moon swung south, high in the sky. The cloudless sky allowed Sam to see billions of stars through her night vision goggles. It was amazing how many more there were than she had thought as a kid. *Truly infinite.* Sam smiled. The joy of a night march was the quiet time to think. Tonight, with a fight just hours away, Sam found her memory going back to Fiery Cross Reef. *What a battle that had been. We were good. And lucky. Well, this is a great company. Rangers lead the way!*

The file turned out of the river and into dark woods. Sam checked her watch. They were making great time. Unless something changed, they would reach the objective rally point by 2300 hours. *Good.* The snow was not as deep in these woods. Perhaps the heavy bands missed this area.

Greeley drifted back along the file, checking in with each Ranger in the company. "How are you doing?" he whispered to Sam.

"Good. We are making great time."

"That we are. I was thinking..." Greeley paused. "I was thinking as bright as it is, a local counterattack won't wait long. The MLRS we have on standby won't be much use against armor moving fast."

"No, and those BTR-82s have thermal sights. They don't need daylight," Sam agreed.

"I want you to get our anti-armor ambushes ready sooner than later."

Sam thought a moment. The security teams on each end would include a fire team and one Javelin team. The third Javelin team was with the support by fire. Each rifle squad carried one AT-4 for this mission. *The assault team will need at least three though.* "Let's pull First and Second Platoons' Carl Gustavs and attach those to the security elements. Collect the AT-4s from Second and Third and give to the security teams. They can ambush with those and save the Javelins for whatever lingers out of range. It's not like we should use the Gustavs on the objective since Ivan could have prisoners in any of the buildings."

"Except the water tower bunker. Yeah. I like that, Sam. Third can keep their Gustav for that bunker."

"Figure what, one platoon counterattack initially?"

"About all they can muster locally. But the wild card is if Ivan has another unit passing through. And I'm sure Ivan will unleash artillery as soon as they know they don't have anyone left on the objective." Greeley grew quiet. Sam trudged through the snow alongside. Finally, Greeley nodded and drifted back to the next Ranger. Sam quietly planned her new variation on their plan.

Sam's watch showed 2248 hours as she stepped into the objective rally point, hidden in woods north of the objective. Faces now strained with focus. It would be game time soon. While Greeley and the platoon leaders departed for their leaders' recon of the objective, Sam kept the company busy. Rangers removed the mortar round they carried and added it to the stack of ammunition next to the mortar squad. The mortar squad, with three tubes, was planning to nail three targets simultaneously. Now they verified their position and laid in for their barrage.

"How we looking, Sergeant?" Sam asked the mortar squad leader.

He looked at the readout on the ballistic computer and gave a thumbs-up. "We are set. I'll re-verify a few more times though. Hardly any wind to affect the rounds."

"Right on." Sam gave the sergeant a pat on the shoulder and headed over to the security element. First Sergeant Slidell met her there.

"XO, don't forget to touch up your face paint," Slidell whispered.

"As soon as I check the ammo redistribution." Sam was almost done. *Amazing what a hive of activity waiting can be.*

Slidell inspected the security element Rangers, while Sam focused on counting the AT-4s. In a few moments, Sam was satisfied and returned to her rucksack in the middle of the triangle of Rangers. She pulled off her gloves and fished her camo paint compact out of her arm pocket and rubbed the paint to warm it. Even in the pocket, the paint hardened too much to apply. *Stinking cold.* Sam's fingers were stiff before she finished wiping more paint on her face. With a swipe of her fingers on her uniform, Sam thrust her gloves back on and put the compact away.

Greeley and the platoon leaders returned and split up. Little clusters of whispering Rangers dotted the patrol base. Greeley and Slidell met up at Sam's ruck.

"Okay, intel was spot on for defenses. The shack north of the farm is empty. The north wall is destroyed so you can see in it. Sam, the security teams have good spots. The best place for you to coordinate is from the assault position because you can see all the avenues of approach from there."

"Sweet. I'll be First Sergeant's battle buddy." Sam nodded at Slidell.

"Right. Still gonna have the snipers engage the water tower position first, and the mortars fire at the same time. Breach in the northeast corner. Questions?"

"Any signs of minefields?" Slidell asked first.

"No. There are vehicle tracks in the fields."

"Small miracles," Sam exhaled.

"Right. Let's go." Greeley got up and waved to the platoon leaders.

Three minutes later, Sam stepped back into the moonlight. Most of the company was ahead of her. Across the river and through a matted grass plain, Sam silently scanned the horizon for trouble. To her surprise, she wasn't able to see the tall building or water tower over the trees. *Greeley plotted a good route.* Back in another small wood, darkness embraced the Rangers. *The canal is beyond and then we are there.* Sam's pulse quickened.

Out of the wood Sam saw Rangers sliding down the slick canal bank. In the distance, the far security team followed the canal west. *Hell yeah.*

Even after more than a year with First Batt, Sam still got excited watching the Rangers on final approach to the objective, knowing extreme violence of action was coming.

In a few minutes, the support by fire position was ready, perched on the canal's south bank. Sam picked up her pace with the rest of the company as they scrambled out of the canal and moved into the comforting trees. Where they could see the bright moonlight beyond the south edge of the woods, the Rangers massed in the snow. Ahead Sam saw Greeley on a knee, checking his watch. Sam and Slidell selected a thick tree trunk to use as cover. Sam checked her watch also. 0023 hours. *Seven minutes to spare.*

Slidell noticed. "We made our hit time. The Air Force and long-range artillery SEAD mission at zero one hundred is gonna keep Ivan busy."

Sam pursed her lips and nodded. "Let's hope the POWs are able to move on their own to the LZ."

"If not, it's just outside the wire. We can carry every one of them out by zero one thirty."

"And you know the Night Stalkers won't be late." Sam half smiled.

Seconds oozed by. In the north, distant artillery pounded. Some dogs in Pereshchepyne barked in reply. Nearby, a Ranger stifled a cough. Sam looked at her watch again. Slidell caught her eye. He nodded. Sam took a long breath and steadily blew it out. *Just a little bit longer.*

Crack! Three sniper rifles fired as one. A split second later, Sam heard the thud of the mortars firing. The flash and boom of the mortars bursting on the objective carried through the trees. The angry chatter of machine guns joined the symphony. In the crisp air, even the suppressed weapons seemed overly loud.

"Breach." The first call on the radio crackled in Sam's earpiece. From the front of the Rangers massed in the trees, a squad bounded forward. Sam got up and ran to the edge of the woods where she could observe the battle and the approaches from town. Avoiding detection no longer mattered. Sam flopped down behind a tree trunk and looked across the road. Tracers scissored into the objective from the support by fire on the canal. None returned back. The breach team reached the fence and two Rangers hung a detcord charge on the chain-link fence.

"Fire in the hole!" The yell of the squad leader carried across the din and the squad darted back to the trees. *Boom!* The explosion was hardly more impressive than the mortars impacting the roof of the main building.

"Shift fire, assaulting!" Greeley radioed. There was a pause before the tracers converged on the four-story building and a squad of Rangers rushed forward from the trees. Sam focused on the objective. A light came on in the small administrative building near the breach. A Russian came around the south corner of the building and Sam brought her rifle over. Before she could align her sights, a smattering of rifle fire cut the Russian down.

The first squad through the wire quickly stacked on the corner of the administrative building. More squads rushed across the field to the breach. Rifle fire from the mill seemed feeble compared to the avalanche of firepower from the Rangers. Sam swung her head to check the approaches from town. *Clear. Stay that way.* Sam looked back at the objective. The squad stacked on the administrative building was gone. Sam knew they had entered the building.

"Lift fire!" Greeley's command ended the machine gun chorus. Sam watched a squad disappear around the corner and head for the mill building. More squads continued to flow through the breach. A machine gun team set up near the breach and opened fire on a shed in the southeast corner. The fight was now in the hands of the two platoons assaulting the compound.

The ferocity of gunshots muted as the fight moved inside the buildings. The following silence hung like a shroud.

"Savage Five, Savage Two-Seven. Objective secure. Confirmed package. Savage Six is down."

"Roger. Actions on the objective," Sam answered and looked at Slidell. "Let's go."

Slidell shook his head. Greeley had been by Slidell's side for a year. "Let's hope he is just wounded."

Sam and Slidell got up and ran across the field to the breach. A moment later, she was at the doorway to the main building. A Ranger guarded the doorway and waved them in.

"First Sergeant, let me know when we have full accountability."

"Roger that, ma'am." Slidell gave a curt nod and peeled off to establish the company casualty collection point in a side room.

Sam turned and nearly ran into a Ranger. It was First Lieutenant Conner Davis, 1st Platoon's leader.

"Ma'am, the outbuildings are clear. I've got a fire team on each corner of the compound and a squad on the roof."

"Good. Casualties?"

"Two wounded. Both ambulatory."

"Good work. Conner, find Sergeant Yates and have him establish the command post in this room. As soon as I understand our situation, I'll have further guidance." Sam touched Conner's shoulder and turned and followed the bellowing voices from Second Platoon deeper in the building. She bounded up the stairs three at a time.

"Lieutenant Pike!" Sam yelled.

"Third floor!" a voice answered.

Sam continued up the stairs and found 2nd Platoon's Leader coming down the hallway.

"Ma'am." 1st Lieutenant Tim Pike paused.

"Sitrep?" Sam asked.

"Building secure. One KIA, two WIA. Plus Captain Greeley KIA. Still counting the POWs and Russians. Our POWs look rough." Tim frowned.

"What do you mean?"

"They have been starved. Sick. Uniforms in tatters." Tim spit in disgust. "Ivan clearly didn't care about their well-being."

"Awesome. Glad we came then. Give me a count as soon as you have it." Sam turned and continued up the stairs to the roof. The cold night air was refreshing after the flurry of movement. Rangers lined the parapet, scanning for trouble beyond the fields. *Wow, what a view.* Sam turned and looked north. *Time to consolidate.*

"Five, Seven, gonna rotate by platoons to get rucks." Slidell was already thinking the same thing.

"Roger. Break." Sam thought for a moment. "Three-one, is that bridge clear and passable?"

3rd Platoon's west security team was just 150 meters from a small farm bridge.

"Roger."

"Seven, see if we can get a Russian truck running and use it to get the rucks." Sam pointed down at the collection of Russian cargo trucks in the yard below. That Slidell was inside and wouldn't be able to see her pointing didn't matter.

"On it."

A streak of light in the north flashed up from the ground into the sky. Several more followed. *The SEAD mission!* Distant booms cracked the night.

Sam turned from the parapet and went back down the stairs. She found Yates in the temporary command post.

"Ma'am, we are accounted for. Two KIA, four WIA. We rescued one hundred and seventy-seven. Maybe fifty or so won't be able to move very far though. Oh, and forty-one dead Ivans. No EPWs."

"Thank you. You report up to Batt yet?"

Yates shook his head side to side.

"Okay. The satellite retrans set up?"

"Roger."

"Thank you. Good work." Sam gave Yates a thumbs-up and pulled her radio out to switch to the correct frequency. She then pulled out her notebook and flipped to a dogeared page. Carefully, Sam found the correct codes.

"Venom X-ray, Savage Five, Kansas. Bananas one-seven-seven, monkey zero. Over." *Primary LZ, 177 POWs rescued and no Russian prisoners taken.*

"Acknowledged. Charlie-mike." The radio crackled after a couple-second delay. *No change to mission.*

Yates scribbled in his notebook as the reply came. He checked the time and announced it as he wrote it down. "0113 hours."

The coughing of a cold diesel engine stopped Sam's response. She listened as the truck slowly came to life. A second truck joined it. Sam smiled. "Sweet."

"Ma'am." Tim entered the room. "I've got Lieutenant Colonel Holcome."

Sam stood straight as a haggard man shuffled in behind Tim. Sam thrust her hand out. "Captain Gentry. We never leave a fallen comrade behind, sir."

Tears welled in Holcome's eyes as he shook Sam's hand. "Thank you. We are eternally grateful. What is the plan from here, Captain?"

"Birds will pick us all up from here in about fifteen minutes. The LZ is the field. From there to Poltava and get your people some medical attention." Sam rested her hands on the butt of her rifle hanging from the sling.

"None of us have coats. Some won't last long at all in the cold." Holcome's sunken eyes and thin uniform hanging like a tent conveyed the point well enough.

"Right. We will do what we can and wait to the last minute to move outside. Do you know how many there are supposed to be here?" Sam's question seemed to slap Holcome in the face.

"We once had over two hundred here. Everyone is either an officer or some specialty MOS." Holcome shivered. "I don't know where they took those who died."

"I can't imagine, sir. Do you know if there is another camp in town?"

"No. At least we haven't heard the guards mention it."

"Okay. Sir, if you can get your people organized into chalks of thirty, that would be very helpful." Sam turned to Tim. "Tim, let's make sure we thoroughly check the Russian documents in the compound for indications of another camp."

"Moving." Tim nodded and left the room. Holcome shuffled out also. Sam put her hands on top of her helmet and thought.

"We are missing about seventy?" Yates murmured.

"Yeah. But is that because they already died, or because Ivan has them stashed elsewhere?" Sam blew out a breath to clear her mind. *If there is another camp, it's not right now's problem.* "Okay, we have much to do and time is running low." Sam and Yates refocused on the mission.

Ryas'ke, Ukraine – January 23, 0100 hrs

Captain Vladimir Ivanov pulled heavily on his cigarette, allowing the tobacco to steady his trembling hands. Life was so fragile. He sighed as he blew the smoke out, adding to the thick haze inside his command vehicle. The map in front of him was so obvious. *NATO is paving the way for a penetration raid. I cannot let them!*

"Captain, should we move again?" The driver interrupted his thought.

"No, we are safe here. We must be patient. We must have courage," Ivanov chided with a smile. It wasn't worth trying to explain what his plan was to this simpleton draftee. When the NATO jets started their targeting of air defense radars thirty minutes ago, Ivanov ordered his Pantsir battery to switch the radars to standby and relocate. The result was satisfying. All four launchers remained alive. *Too bad the colonel isn't alive to see this. If only he had listened to me.* Ivanov took another drag. *Stay mobile. Stay alive.* His ideas on how to defeat the agile NATO "wild weasels" in their counter-SAM efforts flew in the face of doctrine. Now, as the sole surviving air defense officer in the division, Ivanov was able to regroup the SAMs into his own concept. Squads with Verba shoulder-launched missiles served as pickets, providing early warning and disruptive attacks. Ivanov's Pantsirs would take turns using their radars once targets developed. They would control the missiles from the other launchers before quickly turning off their radars and rapidly displacing. A new launcher would take over. Ivanov kept his three Sosna-R launchers, with their zero-emission systems, as an ambush for the main approach up the Oril River valley. The terrain was too obvious.

"What are we waiting for?" the driver asked, more bored than interested.

"Ah, NATO's actions tonight hint at a raid, perhaps even an airborne envelopment operation. This is no bombing raid. Their weasels have hung around too long for that." Ivanov was able to monitor the information from the Russian integrated air defense system. Even with the nearest radars going offline, others farther back could provide information.

Ivanov took one last pull on his stubby cigarette before pulling a new one out. He lit the new cigarette and ground the old butt under his boot. It would be a long night. The map again regained Ivanov's study. Across the vehicle, his driver stared at him. Time passed slowly. Too slowly.

"I'm going to piss." Ivanov set down his map and opened the door. Smoke curled out into the crisp night. Ivanov shivered in delight at the refreshing winter air. *Such lovely moonlight tonight. So beautiful.* Ivanov paused to soak in the view overlooking the Oril valley. A few minutes later, his bladder reminded him why he was out of the command vehicle. With a sigh, Ivanov unbuttoned his fly and relief flowed.

"Captain! Something is happening in Pereshchepyne!" the driver yelled, hanging half out of the door.

"What?"

"Enemy infantry attacked on the north side. Division is preparing a counterattack and we are to provide protection."

"Are there enemy vehicles?"

"No, sir."

"Quick! Then there will be helicopters coming to support or retrieve them!" Ivanov ran back to the vehicle without even buttoning his fly.

Breathless, Ivanov sat back in his seat and pulled the map into his lap. The radio crackled with more reports. He listened a moment and turned to his driver. "I thought you said our division was going to counterattack."

"Sir, um, yes."

"Wrong. The Forty-Seventh Guards will, not us. We are just supposed to deny enemy air in support of them. *Our* division is still focused on tomorrow's attack into the Yankees' flank," Ivanov corrected. *Stupid draftee. This is hardly the bakery he came from. Why couldn't I get some Siberians with at least a sense of the hunt?* Ivanov lit another cigarette. *Yes, the enemy will fly right over us. We just have to wait and ambush them.* He thinly smiled.

"What time is it?" the driver asked to change the subject.

"You tell me what the clock says." Ivanov rolled his eyes.

"Oh."

"We will not have to wait much—"

"Many helicopters inbound," the radio interrupted Ivanov. "Eight American Apaches and eight Chinooks!"

"Squads, engage the Apaches," Ivanov replied. In the west, Ivanov's Verba squads began battle. They were his old battery before yesterday's forced promotion. The gunners were well trained under Ivanov's ways. It was why they had as many kills as any SAM battery in the entire Russian army. *About...now...*

"Shorty, they are coming to you. Low in the valley. We got two Apaches."

Ivanov smiled and traced his finger over the map. *Bad luck for NATO. They are coming right down the security line. Three squads will get to engage! And what will their reaction be? Curve east? No, they will want to avoid high ground where so many SAM systems like to be. They will come right to me.* Ivanov was certain NATO knew roughly where the Buk-M battalions were located. NATO had tried too hard to smash it with long-range rockets and wild weasels. Not to mention BMP and tank gunners also enjoyed shooting at the dreaded gunships and some fifty tanks and BMPs held the ridge just north of Ivanov.

Shorty came up on the radio a few minutes later. "We damaged one Apache and killed a Chinook. The Americans are angry now."

Ivanov snorted. Americans would be liberal with return firepower now. Shorty might have casualties in his platoon, but Ivanov could deal with that later. The fight was on. Ivanov looked at his watch. The helicopters would reach his ambush in just three more minutes. The third squad destroyed one more Apache before the enemy turned east.

"Steady. Stand by," Ivanov radioed. In the night, the sound of rotors carried. Ivanov could imagine his Pantsir and Sosna-R launchers hiding on the east side of buildings, ready to ambush the passing helicopters.

"Now!" The roar of an Apache nearby urged Ivanov into action.

The flash of missiles and auto-cannons danced shadows through the vision blocks of Ivanov's command track. Missiles and cannon fire reached back from the sky. An explosion in the sky east of Ivanov resulted in a falling fireball. *A Chinook?* More flashes in the sky indicated other helicopters hit. The ground shook as an explosion nearby marked the demise of one of Ivanov's Pantsir launchers.

"Jets inbound!" the radio crackled.

"Displace if possible!" Ivanov replied. Time to survive the enemy's counter moves.

"Us too?" the driver asked.

"No, we didn't shoot and are well hidden. We stay."

From across the valley, two missiles rose higher into the sky and arced west. Missiles streaked back in return. Several more explosions rocked the night before the chaos subsided.

"All batteries, report." Ivanov pulled out a new cigarette after setting his radio down. He sucked in vigorously before slowly blowing out the smoke. Across the vehicle, his driver furiously took notes as the batteries checked in. For the loss of one Pantsir and one Sosna-R, Ivanov's battalion destroyed six Apaches, four Chinooks, and one F-16. Now it was time to reload, regroup, and reposition. It would not be worth trying to target the helicopters on their way out, if the enemy was foolish enough to retrace their path. With surprise gone, it was too dangerous to continue the fight.

Chapter 10

Pereshchepyne, Ukraine – January 23, 0130 hrs

The thump of rotor blades carried in the icy air before the radio chirped in Sam's earpiece.

"Savage Five, Dagger One-Five, ambushed on infil, only have four birds."

"How far are the downed birds? Can we push to them?"

"Negative, twenty-plus klicks. We are working the downed aircraft contingency. ETA to LZ now three mikes."

Sam spun to face west, searching for the Night Stalkers' helicopters before replying. "Roger." *What else can I say? Four birds?* Sam turned and looked at Slidell a moment before snapping into action. "First Sergeant, we'll send rescues and casualties only."

"Roger ma'am. They are pretty light so we can cram them all and be okay." Slidell turned and yelled across the snow-covered field. "Four chalks—get them even!"

A flurry of movement followed as the Rangers helped reorganize the shivering POWs. An Apache buzzed the field and settled down low behind the woods, watching town. Four Chinooks followed, flared, and created a ground blizzard as they settled down in the field.

"Go!" Sam yelled as the snow cleared. She moved to where she could watch the haggard POWs load into the Chinooks. Slidell followed. "Top, we can't stay here. The Russians will attack soon, artillery, then troops."

"Agreed, ma'am."

Out of the corner of her eye, Sam saw the platoon leaders and platoon sergeants jog to her. *Everyone knows our situation dictates a new plan.* Sam pulled out her map and studied. "We have two options. One, we head north, the way we came, through the woods. We exfil until we meet friendlies. Two, we go south into the city. We lose our access to the exfil route, but we can fight better in urban terrain."

"Those woods aren't big enough to hide long."

"You're right. We gotta move into the city. Hold until we have a new exfil plan."

"They are loaded. We sure can't stay here. I vote for the urban fight," Slidell announced a second before the helicopters pulled pitch and lifted into the sky. The silence following descended rapidly.

"Okay, listen up. Ivan is gonna respond. Probably with vigor. If we stay here, they can easily pound us with artillery. The mill is an obvious landmark. We are going to move into town. There we have the advantage. The enemy concentration is on the east end. They have that MIC on the western approaches, but nothing in the western suburbs. That is where we are going. Lieutenant Trevino, Third Platoon is lead. I want us to take any RPGs and SAMs we found here. Questions? No? Let's move."

"Ma'am, you want to tell Batt?" Yates asked as the leaders dispersed.

"Not yet, displace from the objective first, then security, then comms." Sam put her ruck on. Her mind raced. *They won't try choppers again. It will have to be 3rd ACR. How fast can they get that plan moving? How fast can Ivan react? What if we try to exfil on foot? Will our footprints in the snow betray us?*

"Tanks!" The yell froze Sam's blood. Before she could give orders, the pop and swoosh of a Javelin responded. The security element never gave up their mission in the chaos. A second Javelin followed as Rangers took cover in the snow. Sam followed the flash west and watched a pair of BTR-82s explode.

"Bound by platoon! Weapons, send a Javelin team with each platoon's movement!"

A third BTR came around the western woods and another Javelin raced out and ended it in a thunderclap.

"Move! Move! Move!" Slidell's voice urged the Rangers. Sam got up and dashed forward with the lead platoon. The houses of Pereshchepyne were a kilometer away. Sparse woods cut that distance in half to the south. 3rd Platoon reached the woods and took positions facing west.

Sam took a knee and looked back. 1st Platoon followed, angling to her left. *That is our biggest threat. The east.* Without woods to screen, two kilometers of open field offered a panoramic view of the city. Platoon reached the woods and a moment later, 2nd Platoon rose and ran south. They passed through the woods and Sam joined them.

Sam's lungs burned and sweat dripped down her back as they crossed an icy pond. She slipped and went down hard. A Ranger stopped and pulled her back onto her feet. They ran on. Tall rushes hid them from the houses. Onward she crashed through the rushes and popped out the south edge and found herself in a garden. A dark house loomed. A squad burst into the house and a muffled "Clear" echoed inside. Sam stopped and watched as the platoon took positions. The Javelin gunner faced back to the northeast, missile ready.

"Tim, we are going to move farther south. We'll make Ivan have to find us." Sam grabbed 2nd Platoon's leader by the shoulder and pointed. "Central patrol base with squad ambushes around the approaches."

"Roger, ma'am." Tim pulled his map out and stabbed a gloved finger at a cluster of buildings three streets in. "Here?"

Sam nodded. Tim flashed a thumbs-up. Sam looked at the sky. The moon was getting low, casting long shadows in the night. Morning was coming soon. *I want us set before sunrise.*

Fifteen minutes later, the rest of the company reached the safety of the houses. Sam grabbed each platoon leader and detailed their mission. As she talked with the last platoon, the flash and booms of heavy artillery erupted at the mill. She stopped and watched the barrage. *Thought so.* Connor whistled as the smoke and dust billowed into the sky over the POW camp.

"Right, time to go." Sam waved her Rangers forward.

Connor moved with his platoon and Sam joined him. They crossed the street at a jog and slipped through the gardens between houses. They reached another street and crossed quickly. Ahead, a Ranger waved them to a house. Closer, Sam saw it was Slidell. Sam let him count her into the patrol base before stopping behind him.

"All accounted for. Yates should have the comms link up by now."

"Thank you, First Sergeant. We have any ambushes out yet?"

"Yes, two on the street south of us."

"Good. How are we on our ammo?"

"We still have three Javelins, nine AT-4s, eleven Gustav rounds, thirty-one mortar rounds, and about two hundred rounds per machine gun team. Good on the rifles, 40mm grenades, and SAWs."

"Okay. Have Yates get our position and status to Batt. I am going to check all our ambush positions. Figure we have at least twenty-four hours before the cavalry comes. Once we come into contact again, we need to capture weapons and ammo. Update the actions on the objectives for the platoons, effective immediately."

Tahamlyts'ke, Ukraine – January 23, 0715 hrs

Inside the Bradley's troop compartment, Logan squirmed in the seat to return blood flow to his legs. *How long have I been awake now?* Logan studied his watch, trying to count the hours. The loss of a quarter of the TOC wrecked the already-strained staffing rotation. The adrenaline long wore off and the MRE at midnight did little to supplant the minimal rest.

Noyes's computer dinging captured Logan's attention. Logan was now using a spare laptop and using the space next to the XO's seat.

"Well, saw that coming," Noyes whispered.

"Sir?"

"The Russian attacks on TOCs yesterday took a toll. No replacement for either Colonel Pacheco or Major Douglas any time soon. Russian Spetsnaz even hit corps."

Logan blinked and stared at Noyes. Noyes's face was devoid of any hint of emotion. Logan cricked his neck. "We still have a good staff and I trust you sir."

"Thanks, Logan. I do my best not to let you or any of our troopers down."

"I know."

Noyes looked up at the tactical display. "Hmmm...regiment's LNO section is coming our way. Wonder if it's new comsec or a change in mission."

Logan pondered the icon moving on the map. "Not sure."

Noyes dropped the conversation and resumed working at his laptop. Logan watched a moment before staring back at his own. *What was I working on? Hmm... I'll write Erin until I remember.*

Sweet Erin,

I love you so much! I wish I could hold you tight. The last day has been hard. LTC Pacheco got hit yesterday and MAJ Douglas too. We are having to all step up and work harder now. I hope staff duty in peacetime is less all-consuming than this.

We are making good progress, and so far, Ivan hasn't been able to stop us. We have some weather moving in that might though. I'm optimistic we will break the trapped Ukrainians in the Donets free and then the Russians will have no choice but pull out. This war could be over quickly if we do this right.

I'm glad you aren't still here. These are lousy flying conditions. Between the Russian SAMs and the weather, I'd be very nervous to lose you. Have a beer for me tonight and let my family know I'm still alive and well.

Love you so much!

Love,
Your Logan

The door opened and the pale winter morning light flooded the dark compartment.

"Sir, Remington Six is here."

"What?" Noyes quickly grabbed his helmet before shoving Logan out of the way and out the door. Logan barely grabbed his own helmet before getting out the door, Noyes still pushing him forward.

"Colonel Ollerich," Logan greeted the regiment commander suddenly in front of him.

"Logan." Ollerich shook Logan's hand as Noyes stepped next to Logan. "Ben."

Noyes shook Ollerich's hand and responded, "Sir. Wasn't expecting you."

"It's intentional. Trying to keep this meeting secret." Ollerich turned and gestured for Noyes and Logan to follow him as he walked toward the nearby field. "Lieutenant General Evans is en route."

"W-w-what?" Noyes stammered. "Why?"

"We have a mission for you. This one is a hand delivery type."

Noyes nodded. "Okay. Roger sir."

"While we wait, Logan, can you give us a few minutes." Ollerich gently put his arm around Noyes and kept walking forward. Logan stopped and watched from a distance. *Probably wants to see how Noyes is holding up.* Logan watched the two talk, unable to hear the words and finding himself drifting off in a daydream.

The sound of a Black Hawk interrupted Logan's thoughts of Erin. Soon Logan was able to pick out the different rotor sounds of Apache gunships also. Half a minute later, the Black Hawk barely cleared the trees on the north side of the field and settled down. As the wheels touched down, two soldiers jumped down into the snow. The Black Hawk quickly took off and circled back north. As quiet returned, the two got back onto their feet and strode toward Ollerich and Noyes. Logan recognized Evans.

"Got somewhere we can talk?" Evans asked.

"Yes, General. We can use one of our TOC tracks," Noyes answered and led the group to the TOC. Logan jogged ahead to clear everyone out of the HHC track, the designated meeting room. Logan watched Evans, Ollerich, and Noyes climb in and then stood in the cold.

Andy came up beside Logan. "Heard the corps commander just showed up."

"Nothing gets by you, does it?" Logan smiled at Andy.

"He say anything to explain this sudden meeting?"

"No." Logan stamped his feet in the snow. "I probably should get back to work though."

Andy nodded and the two crossed the small area between the TOC tracks and climbed back into their respective tracks. Logan barely had time to log back into his laptop when the door opened.

"Logan, General Evans wants to talk with you." Noyes gestured over his shoulder with his chin.

Logan nodded and climbed back out. Butterflies churned in his stomach. Noyes gestured for Logan to go into the HHC track first and followed Logan in.

Evans sat in the back corner next to Ollerich.

"Logan, how are you?" Evans held out his hand to Logan.

"Fine, General." Logan warily shook it. Generals didn't just come talk to captains.

"Major Noyes and Colonel Ollerich both hold you in high regard."

"Yes, General?" Logan replied as he sat down, stealing a glance at Ollerich. The colonel smiled back.

"I have a mission that needs the right person. We agreed you are that person." Evans leaned forward.

Logan's heart jumped and he pulled his notebook out of his pocket. Evans didn't let up before continuing.

"You will take a task force to Pereshchepyne and link up with some Rangers cut off behind Russian lines. They may have some rescued POWs with them. Once you link up with them, you will return, leaving none behind. Can you handle this mission?"

"General, a task force?" Logan asked, confused why the squadron wasn't getting the mission as a unit.

"Correct. Colonel Ollerich is giving you two task-organized teams, plus a few additional resources."

"Roger, General. But why me instead of just giving the mission to our squadron?" Logan looked back and forth at Evans, Ollerich, and Noyes.

"It's complicated, Logan." Evans shook his head. "We know the Russians are going to counterattack with pretty much everything they can this afternoon, evening, and possibly into the morning. We also believe they will attack the Rangers in Pereshchepyne as part of that. I can't pull Thunder Squadron from the flank and slash southeast with it. Ivan's been too good at reading our mail and will exploit a change in our dispositions. But that in itself creates the opportunity to deceive Ivan. You following?"

"Roger, General." Logan still wasn't quite sure where this was going.

"Captain Trondfjell, you are now the commander of Task Force Thunderbolt. Your callsign will be Bolt Six. Your two teams will be Ace and Battle. Your enablers will be Certain."

"Uh, General, what unit is that?" Logan asked as he took notes.

"I'm honoring ol' Abrams himself. These were my first assignment's callsigns back in the day. 4-37 Armor. These callsigns on the air will confuse Russian intel into believing we have another battalion. It might slow them down some."

"Yes, sir. Who are my real units though?" Logan looked around, his mind reeling.

"Logan, I'm giving you Lightning Troop, part of Killer Troop and the sappers. We are getting a tank company from First Armored to back fill Thunder Squadron. We don't have time to wait for shuffling units," Ollerich answered. "You gotta remember you aren't back to being Lightning's commander. That is Lieutenant Kraemer's role."

"Yes, sir. Savvy will be Ace Six."

"Good, Logan. Killer's XO, Lieutenant Schofield, will command your other team. Devin will be Battle Six."

"Logan," Evans interrupted, "it is essential you move fast. You are taking the breaching elements from your squadron's engineers so you can in-stride breach any obstacles. The sapper squads, the bridges and ABVs."

"Roger, General." Logan nodded. "Do I have any graphics? An axis of advance?"

Evans shook his head. "My staff wanted to give it, but I trust the man on the ground. This is why having the right person matters. We did scrape together some radio nets for you to use. We don't have time to fix the BFT identifiers, so you gotta have those all off, or the gig is up. Can you handle that?"

"Roger. I've fought without the digital C2 systems."

"Good. Logan, I want you to LD no later than ten hundred hours. You have to cut through enemy lines before their afternoon attack hits. If you penetrate fast enough, they might lose track of you or decide to bypass you." Evan thrust his hand out. "If you have questions, Colonel Ollerich and Major Noyes will best answer them. Good luck."

Logan shook his hand and the general quickly got up and left.

"Logan, here is your task organization and assigned callsigns." Noyes handed Logan a scrap of paper.

Logan read it. *Savvy has both Lightning tank platoons and the scouts of Third Platoon. Devin would bring one of Killer's tank platoons and get the other scout platoon from Lightning and the sapper platoon. Okay. Lightning's fires platoon and part of the distro platoon round out the task force.*

"What about medical and recovery?" Logan asked.

"Use Lightning's medics and M88. Don't take any trucks. Travel light. If you can't recover a broken-down vehicle, destroy it and keep moving."

"Umm..." Logan pulled out the map. "Looks doable on a single ammo unit of fire and fuel loads. I'm not comfortable with a single eighty-eight and only Lightning's medics. I'd like another medic track from the medical platoon and another eighty-eight."

Ollerich looked at Noyes and shrugged.

"I can give you another medic track and squad, but I don't know if I can spare another M88." Noyes announced after looking at the ceiling.

"I'd like to have Sergeant Heydte then. A single recovery vehicle for a task force is gonna make us prioritize. I need Heydte's expertise."

"Fair. Okay. He can fall in with your distro platoon element. But I want the rest of Lightning's mechanics to help us get Killer and Ironhawk's damaged vehicles back in the fight."

"I assume I won't be able to send casualties back until we all return?" Logan looked to Noyes, then Ollerich.

"Correct," Ollerich answered. "Logan, you are going to report on the regiment net to me. Remember you are another battalion task force. And I think we forgot to mention it—the Rangers are roughly two hundred soldiers and their contact info is on that paper. Point of contact is Savage Five. You will contact them on your net."

"Oh, Logan, take Colonel Pacheco's tank and crew. I can't spare you any staff on your mission, but we will help you plan it. I'm sending the LNO sections out to start your units moving and get them on your radio net. We'll assemble them a klick south of here." Noyes smiled at Logan. "You are the right man for the job. Make us proud."

Logan nodded. "Okay, sir. This is what I'm thinking for a concept of operation." Logan quickly outlined his plan. A few modifications, and he was ready. Logan looked at his watch. 0833 hours.

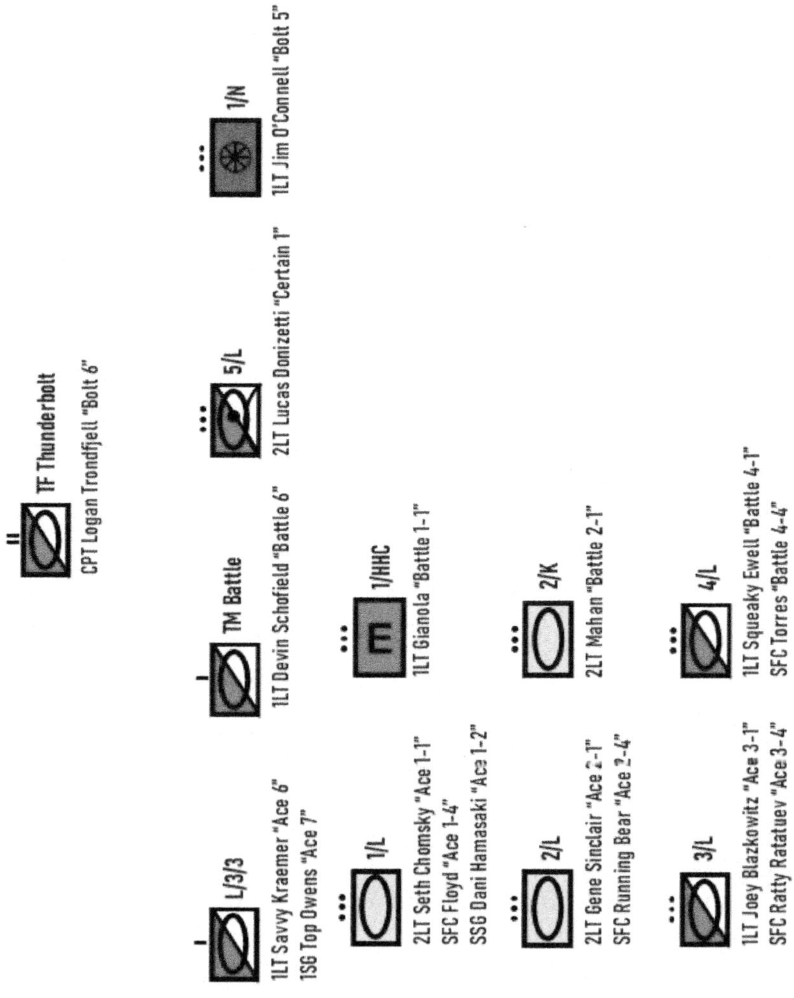
TF Thunderbolt
CPT Logan Trondfjell "Bolt 6"
TM Battle
1LT Devin Schofield "Battle 6"
5/L
2LT Lucas Donizetti "Certain 1"
1/N
1LT Jim O'Connell "Bolt 5"
L/3/3
1LT Savvy Kraemer "Ace 6"
1SG Top Owens "Ace 7"
1/L
2LT Seth Chomsky "Ace 1-1"
SFC Floyd "Ace 1-4"
SSG Dani Hamasaki "Ace 1-2"
E
1/HHC
1LT Gianola "Battle 1-1"
2/L
2LT Gene Sinclair "Ace 2-1"
SFC Running Bear "Ace 2-4"
2/K
2LT Mahan "Battle 2-1"
3/L
1LT Joey Blazkowitz "Ace 3-1"
SFC Ratty Ratatuev "Ace 3-4"
4/L
1LT Squeaky Ewell "Battle 4-1"
SFC Torres "Battle 4-4"

Bryansk, Russia – January 23, 0830 hrs

The Mi-24P Hind helicopter gunship banked steeply around the field before settling down, blowing snow in all directions. Before the wheels took the full weight of the huge helicopter, Dronov opened the door and jumped out. His chief of staff, aide, and security team hastily followed. With every footstep closer to the entrance to the command bunker, Dronov's frown hardened. Behind him, the Hind returned to the sky and thundered away.

"Attention!" the guard barked as he opened the door into the operations room. Chairs scraped on the concrete floor as officers rose to their feet.

"Keep working!" Dronov snapped, ignoring their looks as he stomped to Kiselyov's side office. Opening the door himself, Dronov found Kiselyov standing rigidly behind his desk.

"General Dronov, good to see you." Kiselyov's eyes were gray and dull and his voice empty.

"Mikhail." Dronov shut the door behind himself. "Oh Mikhail, you have let me down."

Kiselyov said nothing.

Dronov moved around the desk and sat on top of it next to Kiselyov. He crossed his arms and looked at his feet a moment. "I just heard NATO linked up with the Ukrainian forces in the Donets Pocket."

"Yes, General, Chuhuiv fell two hours ago and the counterattack failed to regain the bluffs overlooking the river. The Americans are moving very quickly. The Seventy-Sixth Airborne Division lost over a thousand casualties trying to break the enemy. Heavy artillery, we believe from the American's Third Infantry Division, pounded the attack. Now, I don't have forces to counter the enemy."

"I thought it was enemy airborne infantry, not mechanized forces at Chuhuiv. Were you mistaken?" Dronov tilted his head to the side and glared.

"No, General. It was airborne infantry. They arrived by helicopter. Before we could begin our counterattack, the enemy moved artillery from another division up. It was artillery from two separate divisions that eviscerated our own infantry."

Dronov pulled his pack of cigarettes out of his tunic and tapped two out. He handed Kiselyov one. "Mikhail, do you know what this means?"

Kiselyov nodded and lit both cigarettes with trembling hands.

"I don't think I can save you. I don't think even Popov can save you. Golovko and Kochetkov both suggested the president has you shot for cowardice." Dronov sighed and put his arm around Kiselyov. "I will take care of your family...if I survive."

"I don't know what I could have done differently."

"Everything now hinges on Victor's attack. Perhaps I can delay any rash action until then. Victor's successful attack might save you."

The desk phone rang and both stopped and looked at it. Dronov nodded and Kiselyov answered.

"General Kiselyov." He listened a moment and then handed the phone to Dronov. "It's Golovko."

Dronov took the phone. "Yes, General?"

"Tagir, I know you are about to lead your counterattack into the Yankee right flank, but we have a situation."

"I'm listening."

"This comes straight from Voroshilov and is a no-fail mission. There is a GRU camp at Pereshchepyne. The Yankees took it early this morning with a helicopter assault. We believe the enemy is still there. You must destroy them. All of them. No prisoners. No survivors. None."

"None? General?"

"Correct. Tagir, I want you to smash them today. Before the enemy can escape. Ensure you block their retreat before you attack."

"If they came by helicopter, they are on foot now and won't get far."

"Don't underestimate them. We are confident they are elite special operations forces. Use the First Guards Tank Army units south of the enemy salient. If you must pull units from the counterattack to complete this mission, then do so."

"General, I need every BTG I have for the counterattack, or it might not be strong enough to collapse the enemy salient."

"Then delay the counterattack. President Voroshilov is adamant this camp is more important. There is more at stake than I have time to explain."

"Confirming you want me to delay the Sixth Combined Army's counterattack and pull units to find and destroy the enemy force at Pereshchepyne?" Dronov was surprised.

"Correct. Make it happen today. Call me back when you have details."

"Yes, General Golovko."

Golovko hung up. Dronov handed the phone back to Kiselyov.

Kiselyov tapped the phone in his hand before returning the handset to the cradle. "General, the Forty-Seventh only has one BTG left. We had to consolidate the last two after a brisk engagement during the night."

"Why didn't you tell me?"

"I told Victor. My artillery and air defenses are still potent, so I gave him direct control of those units to make up the loss of the BTG."

"Hmm."

"General, I'm doing everything I can to make things better."

"I know, I know, Mikhail. Today, it just isn't enough. I'm sorry."

Kiselyov hung his head, letting the cigarette slowly burn, trembling in his lips.

Dronov pulled one last puff before stabbing his cigarette out on the desk.

"General, how much time do I have?" Kiselyov whispered.

"Perhaps a few hours. I'll try to delay as long as I can." Dronov grabbed Kiselyov's shoulders with both hands. "For an old friend, Mihail Aleksandrovich, it is the least I can do. I trust you to use your time wisely."

Kiselyov embraced Dronov and then stepped back, straightening his uniform. "Sir, allow me to lead my army."

Dronov nodded.

Kiselyov marched to the door and opened it. "General Pyataev! Staff, orders!"

Dronov slowly closed the office door and sat down at Kiselyov's desk. There was no reason to move. He would be leading the district from this bunker until the new 1st Guards Tank Army commander was ready to fill the pending void.

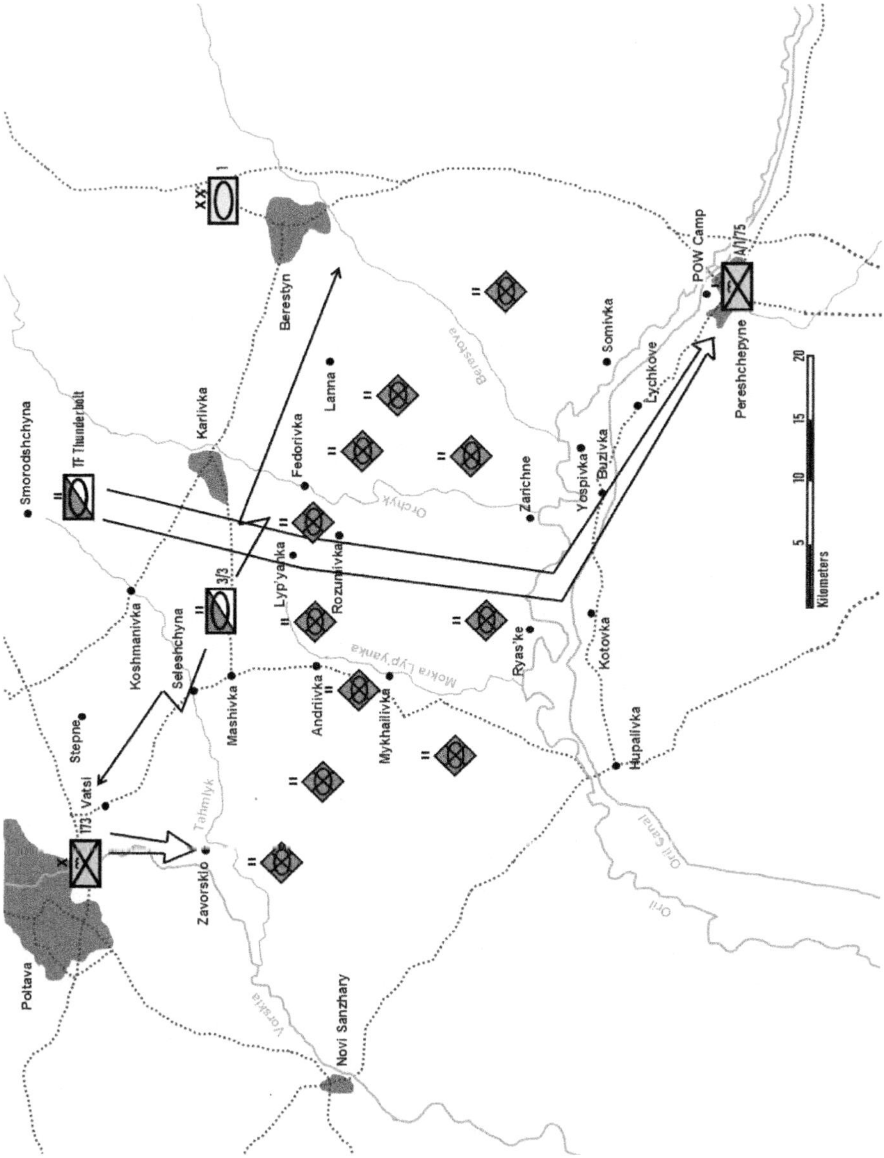

Chapter 11

Tahamlyts'ke, Ukraine – January 23, 0915 hrs

The wooded valley between fallow fields was a hive of frantic activity as Logan guided his tank into his task force's assembly area. The task force did not look that much bigger than Lightning Troop had been at full strength. *It's really just two extra platoons, but I only have to manage three elements. Well, four.* On the far end, Logan saw the ammo and fuel trucks from the distro platoon topping off the vehicles.

"Brown, how are we on fuel?" Logan asked his driver.

"Sir, we are good. Fronts are full and the rear is like ninety percent."

"Drop me off here, then top off anyway," Logan replied.

Brown stopped the tank and Logan dismounted with his map board. Savvy waved and tapped the soldier she was talking to. The two walked over. Logan recognized the other as Devin.

"Savvy, Devin, good to see you."

Savvy beamed. "Sir, happy to have you in command."

"Sir, honored to work for you." Devin held his hand out to Logan.

"Gonna have to stay flexible. This is a very hastily planned op. Well, welcome to Task Force Thunderbolt." Logan shook Devin's hand and patted Savvy on the shoulder.

Devin turned to business. "We should be ready to roll in maybe twenty minutes."

"Okay. We got time for a face-to-face. Wanna round up all the platoon leaders and platoon sergeants? Please be quick."

Savvy keyed up her radio. Devin stepped a few feet away and did the same. Logan waited for the two to finish their radio traffic.

"Okay..." Logan held up his map board. "Did you get copies of my graphics?"

"Roger, sir," Savvy answered. Devin nodded.

"Good. As soon as everyone is here, I'll brief the plan quickly. Do either of you have any questions before they get here?"

"Yeah, I understand my fires platoon is directly under your control?" Savvy asked first.

"Correct. And Lucas will also control the three distro platoon trucks. Mainly make sure they stay safe."

"Sir," Devin chimed in, "I saw Lieutenant O'Connell with those trucks. Jim said he's coming with us."

"Correct. But I'm having him be my staff instead of being a platoon leader. Jim will be Bolt X-ray."

"Okay, that makes sense."

"If we have to breach an obstacle, how are you envisioning that?" Devin asked.

"Devin, Battle Troop will have to provide your own SBF and breach element. Once you have the breach complete, I'll have Ace Troop assault through. If it takes more than your two maneuver platoons to suppress the enemy, I don't want to breach there. But, now Savvy, you will be lead element, and I want to bypass if at all possible. A breach could take too long."

"But you think we will?" Savvy asked.

"Pereshchepyne is a major Russian logistical hub. It will have defenses. We identified an entire Russian air defense regiment around it. There is an anti-tank ditch on the west side of town. I'm pretty confident we will have no choice. Intel shows the Russian motorized rifle company defending the western approaches has not left positions to join the counterattacks. It has ten BTR-82s and possibly three T-90s. That is what we would have to breach into."

"Not so bad," Devin commented.

"Right. Keep in mind, we expect the Russians to attack the Rangers with a Forty-Seventh Guards Tank Division BTG from the northeast and a Twenty-Seventh Motorized Rifle Division BTG from the south. In addition to all this, we are cutting through the Russian counterattack.

Okay?" Logan paused to see both nod. "Devin, I want your maneuver platoons in a company echelon right. We'll tuck our fires and the trucks in tight."

"Won't the Russians do a local counterattack when we rupture their front lines?" Devin asked.

Logan nodded. *Devin is sharp.* "Correct. I want us all to quickly burst through together and keep moving south fast and hard. I'd like them to counterattack into an empty field. Your sapper platoon will be responsible for rear security. Our S2, Captain Baldwin, is pretty good at understanding Ivan and believes if we hit hard right now, they won't expect it and will have a delayed reaction. They know we know they're massing for a major counterattack."

"As long as we don't smash into their massed forces?" Savvy wryly asked.

"Correct. They have three BTG massed east of the Orchyk River. Those are from the 27th Motorized Division. There are another four BTG from the 138th Guards MRD west of the Mokra Lyp'yanka River. Those are the two strongest forces the 6CAA has, but their 25th Guards Motor Rifle Division is moving north behind them. In the middle, two BTG from the 27th MRD are up front, and one south of the Oril. That one south of the Oril is supposed to hit the Rangers. The two north of it are reshuffling after the fizzled attack earlier. They are weak. We'll pierce them."

"Lot of Ivans."

"We aren't fighting them all. We pierce hard and fast. Don't forget we have three batteries of artillery supporting our breakthrough. The blizzard is supposed to hit around noon. That will add confusion and hopefully cover our tracks. Lots of chaos to go around, so let's harness it."

Devin quietly nodded. Logan watched, waiting for more questions. He had enough of his own to sort through. Before anyone spoke up again, the platoon leaders gathered. Logan noted the time. 0937. *Cutting it close.*

"Listen up, we have just twenty minutes to LD. First of all, everyone give me a thumbs-up or down on your BFTs being off." Logan waited until he saw all thumbs-up. "I want you to personally verify every single vehicle. Okay? When you call up REDCON-1, that means you completed your verification." Logan saw heads nodding. Quickly he covered his plan and the Russian situation in as much detail as he could. There was no time for questions. *Commander's intent and end state will carry the day.*

Heydte's truck bouncing to a stop next to the M88 caught Logan's attention. Heydte's voice carried across the assembly area as he yelled to the M88 crew. Someone Logan didn't recognize got out of the truck's other door and took photos with a professional-looking camera.

"Savvy, who is that?" Logan pointed.

"The embedded reporter, Kristyn Rhodes."

Devin's jaw dropped. "Gotta be kidding me. This is an urgent and secret mission and we are dragging a reporter?"

"Right?" Logan shook his head. *What do I do about her?*

"Not like we can kick her out here and hope Ivan's counterattack misses her." Savvy crossed her arms and scowled.

"Well. I don't know." Logan opened his notebook at his task organization.

"Sir," Savvy said, tucking her chin, "we bring her. No time to punt her off. She hasn't been a problem for Lightning Troop."

"She been riding with Sergeant Heydte this whole time?"

Savvy nodded. "You know, perhaps if we are picking up guys rescued from an illicit POW camp, maybe a reporter to see that firsthand is worth the headache to you."

"I don't know. We don't have time to figure this out." Logan waved his hand to dismiss the conversation. Savvy nodded yet again.

"Sir," Savvy announced, "It's zero nine fifty. Roll time."

"Let's mount up and roll. Don't forget to verify the BFTs. Move." Logan nodded.

Jim remained behind as the others scattered to their platoons. "Sir, where do you want me at?"

"You have your gun truck?" Logan asked.

Jim nodded.

"Form up with the distro platoon trucks then. Tuck in near the fires platoon."

"Roger sir." Jim nodded and swiftly turned. He returned to his truck at a jog.

Logan watched him go, then climbed up the sprocket of his tank. The engine was already running. With the fluidity of an old hand, Logan dropped into the commander's hatch and switched to his vehicle helmet.

"Game time men." Logan adjusted the boom microphone.

"Sabot loaded, sabot indexed," Staff Sergeant Litsky growled. Litsky was the squadron's Abrams master gunner, but had never fired a round in vain. The squadron commander's tank wasn't supposed to get involved in firefights.

"Roger that, Sergeant. Sherr, is your loader's two-forty locked and loaded?"

Sherr ducked his head and yanked the charging handle of his machine gun. "Now it is."

"Okay." Logan switched to the radio. "Guidons, Bolt Six, report REDCON-1. Over."

A long pause gave Logan time to look around at his task force. A few vehicles moved into lines. Logan turned his gaze to the sky. The overcast seemed to get closer to the ground.

"Bolt Six, Ace Six, REDCON-1." Savvy's voice seemed out of place with the new callsign.

"Battle Six, REDCON-1," Devin called a moment later.

"Certain One, REDCON-1." Lucas and the fires platoon was next.

"Bolt Six, Bolt X-ray, task force ready."

"Guidons, Bolt Six, execute." Logan released the radio.

"Hey Brown, I want you to follow behind Ace Seven's track. You see it off to our left?"

"Roger, sir. I see it."

"Thanks." Logan checked his watch as Savvy's troop moved out of the assembly area, spreading out into a troop wedge formation. Logan quietly watched and Brown drove forward as soon as he saw Top Harris's M1283 armored personnel carrier surge forward. Devin's troop also moved out of the assembly area.

Logan switched to the regimental radio net. "Remington X-ray, Bolt Six, LD."

"Bolt Six, Remington Six, roger. Good luck. Keep me informed. Out," Ollerich answered for the regimental TOC.

Litsky broke the tank crew's silence. "Looks like we got away with it. Sherr, pay up when we stop."

"What was that?" Logan asked.

"We bet if Ivan would notice Lightning pulling off the line."

"Well, we are rolling right back through, so we'll find out. But this simplifies the operation. Passage of lines is dangerous enough when well planned." Logan explained Killer Troop would fill the line back in after Logan's task force was beyond.

The whine of the engine and rattle of tracks resumed its solo reign as the crew withdrew into their duties. Logan studied his map board. Time passed slowly.

The distant crack of a cannon echoed across the field. Another followed it. Silence. Logan drummed his gloved fingers on his map board. "Come on. Report it."

Logan slowly counted, trying to force patience.

"Bolt Six, Ace Six, contact PC and troops south. Out," the radio chirped.

Logan pulled the cap off a marker, ready to write the report. He started by noting the time.

"Bolt Six, Ace Seven, engaged and destroyed one BMP and five troops at grid x-ray-victor-three-niner-five-one-seven-one-six-four. Negative casualties or damage. Charlie-mike."

"Roger." Logan plotted the enemy position. *Ivan's combat security outpost on the west side. Did they get the alarm out first? Time will tell.* Logan listened as Jim relayed the report to regiment. Logan yearned for the invaluable situational awareness BFT provided.

A flash of light in the south caught Logan's attention. A boom followed.

"Bolt Six, Ace Six, contact troops south! They are fighting from buildings in Dmytrivka and Lyp'yanka." Savvy's excited voice came rapidly on the heels of more explosions.

"Certain One, Bolt Six, get fires on those positions. Break." Logan paused. "Ace Six, can you bypass?"

"Negative! Enemy dug in on the hills either side."

Logan swore. "Brown, get me up to the front. I need to see what's going on."

Brown goosed the accelerator and the tank churned south, throwing a rooster tail of snow high in the air. They passed Top Harris and Logan pointed Brown to the right of an Abrams firing down the slope into the valley villages.

Light and smoke flashed on the ridge beyond.

"Missile! Coax on the way!" Litsky hollered. The cannon breach dropped nearly to the floor as Litsky ranged the enemy well beyond normal machine gun range. The machine gun clattered as he fired back.

"Driver, sagger drill!" Logan yelled as he grabbed the handles. Brown responded by swerving the tank left, then right. Logan found the enemy position with his fifty-caliber sights and joined the shooting. The swerves kept throwing his aim off. The missile continued in, a growing orange eclipse. Brown swerved right again, then turned back to front before dodging right once more. The missile zipped by just left of the tank.

"Find us some cover! The trees to the left!" Logan saw another Abrams head for the same trees.

"Identified PC!" Litsky's cry changed Logan's focus.

"Fire and adjust!" Logan replied as he saw outline of a flat vehicle roof and missile launcher in Litsky's sights.

"Up!" Sherr slapped the arming lever up and braced against the wall.

"On the way!" Litsky fired the cannon and it snapped back, spitting the aft-cap out and to the floor. Snow sucked up by the muzzle blast obscured Logan's view for a moment as Brown charged the tank through.

"Got 'em!" Litsky celebrated as Sherr reloaded the cannon.

Logan could now see the flashes of Russian weapons firing up the slope from the villages. *Where are their tanks and PCs?* All of Ace Troop now lined the north side of the valley, firing rapidly at the Russian infantry in town. Ripping linen announced the arrival of 155mm artillery from the north. Logan watched as explosions threw snow and frozen dirt high into the air.

"Battle Six, Bolt Six, come up on our right and suppress the enemy vicinity Dmytrivka. Ace Six, once they are established, assault through Lyp'yanka and the ridge south. Gain fires into the Rozumivka valley."

A chorus of acknowledgement followed.

Logan switched radio to the regiment. "Remington Six, Bolt Six, attacking Russian infantry positions vicinity Lyp'yanka, break." Logan stopped his transmission to target a group of Russians sprinting to a new building. He hit two with his machine gun. Litsky continued shooting with his machine gun. "Remington Six, Bolt Six, continuing, request Thunder provides drone recon assistance on our flanks. Over."

"Roger. Remember you have a task force to fight, not just your tank. You can't afford to get hit." Ollerich's rebuke stung Logan. *I gotta see what is going on though! How can he armchair this?* Logan shook his head.

More artillery impacted on the ridge beyond Lyp'yanka. Logan looked north. Devin's tanks and scouts came online to the west, adding their firepower to the fight. Russian fire from the villages dwindled. A new string of explosions rippled around Ace Troop as Russian artillery impacted.

"Observing artillery..." Top Harris calmly reported the impacts.

"You want me to follow when they attack forward?" Brown asked.

"Negative. Stay put. We are out of the impact area," Logan answered.

Logan looked left. *Come on. Go for it, Savvy.* Logan took a breath. *Finally.* Farther east, Abrams assaulted in pairs down the slope to the town.

"Bolt Six, Ace Seven, assaulting." Harris reported what Logan already saw. Tracers flew in all directions as the tanks stopped on the edge of town and pounded Russian positions. Bradleys raced down the slope and moved into the village. Logan watched the tanks follow and all disappeared between the houses. Logan looked back to the right. Devin's troops continued shooting at the Russians. New artillery joined their efforts.

"We got them." Logan smiled. On the far side of the valley, Russian soldiers fled up the slope in small groups, chased by merciless machine gun fire. None made it to the top.

"Bolt Six, Ace Six, cleared a path through Lyp'yanka. Continuing up the ridge."

"Roger, press them hard." Logan watched seven tanks emerge from the south side of the village and slowly move up the slope. Flashes and puffs of snow punctuated their steady advance, the cannon cracks echoing across the valley. The Abrams moved beyond the crest of the ridge and out of view. More cannon fire in the south carried back north.

"Bolt Six, Ace Seven, engaging tanks and PCs vicinity Rozumivka. Appears to be a maintenance collection point."

"Roger, do you need resources?" Logan noted the time as he scribbled the report on his map board.

"Negative."

"Roger, continue and report. Break." Logan looked back to his west. "Certain One, increase fires on the Russian positions in this valley so Battle can assault south. We need to get moving."

"Bolt Six, Certain One, wilco."

"Ace Six, expedite clearing the town so I can pass Battle and Certain through," Logan called to Savvy.

"Roger. Working on it," Savvy snapped back.

Logan keyed up the radio but changed his mind and released it without responding. Logan looked at his watch again. Time was flying too fast. *It's probably gonna take another half hour to clear the town enough to pass everyone through. And that means we are gonna eat a counterattack. Damn.* Logan stared at his map and considered how the Russians would counterattack. He might be able to deal with it if he could consolidate on the far ridge first.

Moscow, Russia – January 23, 1000 hrs

The pain was relentless. Voroshilov rubbed his head with closed eyes, slumped in his chair at the head of the table. The rest of the security council watching quietly. Voroshilov could feel their judging, their thoughts of deposing him to take the reins of the nation.

"What is the update on Kharkiv?" Voroshilov asked with closed eyes.

"The enemy corridor to the Donets Pocket is too wide to choke it off at Kharkiv," Popov answered. "All of our hopes are on the counterattack from the south. General Dronov is forward to ensure the success."

"President Voroshilov, I have reports of a new NATO attack on the south salient sector," Kochetkov added, knowing Popov probably hadn't had time to review the same information. "At least a battalion in strength, and an unknown enemy unit at that."

"A single battalion will falter in the face of a two-division attack." Popov scowled at Kochetkov.

"It is still concerning. We thought they would concentrate all of their efforts toward the Donets." Alexey Zusko, the head of the FSB, quipped.

"You promised me last year the West would not protect the Ukraine!" Voroshilov's anger snapped. "You promised me the West would not be ready to attack for another two weeks!"

"Correction, I promised their cavalry division would not be in place to attack for another two weeks." Zusko smiled. Semantics were his favorite.

"Could this new attack be that cavalry division?" Golubev asked, leaning forward.

"No." Kochetkov leaned back in his chair.

Voroshilov held out his hand to quiet everyone. His nostrils flared with each breath.

"Are you okay, my old friend? Perhaps the doctor could help." Kochetkov waved to an orderly to bring some tea.

"I'm fine. A doctor cannot fix the situation in the Ukraine." Voroshilov shook his head. "Your concern is appreciated, Boris."

"I don't know it worth our time to discuss the front until we have updates from the counterattack. Shall we turn our attention to other matters for now?" Zubkov quietly suggested, pointing to the agenda sheet.

"This will not help the president's headache any," Zusko countered.

"We must make sacrifices. Continue." Voroshilov opened his eyes and glared at his prime minister.

Zubkov nodded. "Let's talk about the home front then. FSB."

Zusko cleared his throat and put his glasses down on the table before briefing. "Western propaganda is having a stronger impact on our citizens than it should. My agents have arrested more than one thousand people since the NATO attack. The unrest continues despite our arrests."

"What are the agitators claiming?" Golubev interrupted.

"It varies a little. The high casualties are a common theme, a surprising one. I do not know how this week's casualty figures have leaked. Twenty thousand in a few days is high, but hardly on par with the Great Patriotic War. There seems to be an undercurrent of energy around the notion we cannot win this war. Rumors NATO is vastly stronger. Rumors we will see NATO troops on our soil. Rumors we soon will not have ground forces to stop NATO."

"That will not happen. If one NATO private steps foot on our soil, we will flatten his homeland!" Voroshilov slapped his hand on the desk. He winced in pain as if the slap hit his own head. Voroshilov lowered his voice. "We must win this war."

"Western propaganda persists despite our efforts to block it. Several internet sources published stories and maps showing NATO will sweep to the Sea of Azov, completely trapping nine-tenths of our ground forces. Those at this table understand there is a grain of truth to the possibility," Golubev weighed in. "I've seen the information firsthand."

"You," Voroshilov said, pointing his finger at Popov, "will ensure that cannot happen."

"I assure you, my president, that the brave soldiers, at every level, are doing their utmost for Russia." Popov crossed his arms and glared back.

"Ukraine on its own, we defeated and could have destroyed, President Voroshilov, but we are now fighting the combined might of the West. We are outnumbered at the front, something Russia has not previously experienced. Partisans and terrorists have sabotaged our supply lines to the southern front. Not a single train has made it across the Dnipro in nearly two weeks. We cannot use barges or our navy to supply because NATO submarines keep destroying anything we sail into the Black Sea. Perhaps, we should give some discussion to the offer forwarded by the Chinese. Nikolai, think." Golubev leaned forward over and put his hand on Voroshilov's arm. "We are still in a position of strength."

"When did my deputy become a defeatist? Igor, don't tell me you have fallen prey to the same propaganda scourge!" Voroshilov shook his arm away. The movement spiked the headache and Voroshilov put both hands to his forehead and closed his eyes.

"Are you sure you are feeling all right? This NATO attack has taken a heavy toll on you." Zusko pursed his lips before continuing. "There are rumors, President Voroshilov, that we cannot have peace without a change of leadership."

Voroshilov looked up and stared at Zusko. Distrust of the FSB always ran deep in Russia.

"That is what the agitators are saying. Of course, we all disagree." Zusko smiled and deflected the discussion. "We have been arresting agitators as fast as possible, but new ones spring up immediately in their void. I've dispatched two thousand officers to Saint Petersburg in anticipation of the protest tonight."

Kochetkov raised his cup of tea. "What of the protests in Volgograd? Do you have troops there too?"

"We think it will be more manageable for the two hundred troops there."

"The families of the airborne troops are planning a vigil in Pskov. What is the tone going to be?" Zusko turned to Golovko.

"Alexey, how should I know? I haven't been to Pskov in weeks. Nor can I ask Major General Ugarin, since he died alongside so many of his troops yesterday. The airborne forces have fought valiantly and I would expect their families would honor their memory."

"Nikolai, perhaps we should reorganize our forces to allow them to more effectively stop the NATO attack," Golubev said.

"What are you suggesting?" Golovko's hackles raised and his eyebrows lowered.

"Perhaps we should assign the remainder of the airborne to the Western Military District and everything south of the enemy penetration to the Southern Military District."

"Preposterous. Dronov wouldn't command the respect of the airborne and giving Lipilin command of nearly the entire army isn't a prudent option," Golovko growled.

"Lipilin couldn't do worse than you have," Zusko slyly added, enjoying the general squirming.

"Says the man who assured us many falsehoods."

"Careful, General Golovko," Zusko retorted.

"Enough," Zubkov interrupted, looking to Voroshilov for support and seeing nothing but a deeply red face. "Comrades, bickering will not improve our situation. This is how I see things: First, NATO is clearly strong and with Ukraine, will likely surround and trap our army against the Black Sea. Second, without ground forces, we have no hope to keep—much less control—the populace in the occupied areas. Third, this peace proposal forwarded by the Chinese is fair and accomplishes some of our war objectives. International recognition of our claims to the Donbas and Crimea? That has lasting value for the future. That will give us more credibility and respect with the world. Lastly, if we delay until NATO completes their encirclement, Western peace offers will be less and less valuable to us."

Voroshilov looked up through his hands and shook his head. "Nobody will dictate terms to us. We have enough nuclear weapons to end their regimes permanently."

"You cannot use nuclear weapons if NATO doesn't cross into Russia! I will not see us rashly act and cause the destruction of our own cities and people." Golubev raised his voice.

Voroshilov slowly spoke. "The Crimea... Donetsk... Luhansk *are* Russia."

"Parts, yes. We annexed the areas we controlled before July. Still, the amount of partisan activity in those areas makes me wonder how Russian they truly are. I'm not prepared to see all of true Russia perish in a nuclear holocaust for them. But if we accept these peace terms, we avoid all that and we would not have problems with that distinction in the future."

"We still control a third of the Ukraine. They can pry it out of my dead hands," Voroshilov retorted, pushing his chair back. Without a word, he left the room.

"Andrey," Golubev said, turning to Popov, "man to man, what are the chances of this afternoon's attack?"

"Well, perhaps fifty-fifty at best. General Molchalin is a strong leader and a careful planner. Mistakes were made earlier that limit our chances. General Dronov should have consolidated a strong counterattack force immediately instead of piecemealing the First Guards Tank Army at the enemy."

"We had to retain forces to counter the possibility of the American airborne corps attacking elsewhere, so General Dronov needed to use a smaller portion of his forces," Golovko countered.

"Still, it would be prudent of us to consider a future. How do we end the war while we are still winning?" Golubev paused and looked at Kochetkov. "Boris, you have been Nikolai's friend a long time. Perhaps you could help him understand and come to a decision before it is too late."

"You put me in a difficult spot. But I agree Nikolai doesn't seem to see the situation for what it is. With the FSB help, and truth from the Ministry of Defense, we can fix that."

"It is important for Russia. Oh, and Andrey, make sure we don't have a strategic rocket trigger the end of us all. Such a decision must be the collective will of this council."

"That, we are all in agreement on." Popov spoke for the room, seeing nearly every head nod.

Chapter 12

Pereshchepyne, Ukraine - January 23, 1100 hrs

Sam unzipped her jacket. *So warm.* Sam studied the snow outside the house windows. While the sky had clouded over rapidly in the last hours, the warmth of earlier sunlight had glistened the surfaces as temperatures reached up to thirty-two degrees. She looked at her watch again.

"Ivan sure is taking his sweet time," Slidell remarked. Both expected a Russian ground attack to hit hours ago, but they hadn't even had any probing attacks yet.

"They don't know where we went," Sam offered. Deep in her heart, she knew the Russians had to at least have an idea.

"Maybe something up north has Ivan pinned?"

"That would be nice." Sam's tone conveyed skepticism. *I wish Captain Greeley was still alive.* Sam had prepared their ambush positions as best she could, but there was much to think about and the very lives of the whole company now hinged on her decisions.

Sam looked at Slidell and saw his eyes narrow and a sad sideways pull on his mouth. Sam blankly stared back.

"You are doing great, ma'am. We have a good position."

"You a mind reader?" Sam half smiled.

"I've seen that look before. It's hard to step up in such circumstances. You aren't alone in your thoughts, but you aren't on an island. We've a good team and together we will prevail."

"Think we should have tried to exfil on foot?"

"That's a hard call. No way we would have gotten far enough before dawn. You know the Russians have to be carefully clearing those woods. Maybe that's why Ivan's late for breakfast? Maybe Ivan decides to just burn the woods out with a TOS. Lots of maybes. You make decisions on what you know at the time. Let the maybes go."

"Thanks, Top."

The radio crackled and both stopped to listen. "Savage Five, Venom Three, prepare to copy."

Yates picked up the hand mic and answered. "Go for Savage Five."

"Relief force attacked at ten hundred from vicinity Objective Wild. Your point of contact is Bolt Six on net foxtrot-three-five-five. We are also monitoring that net. Intel shows a BTG from Forty-Seventh Guards Tank Division is moving into Pereshchepyne from the northeast. Potentially another BTG will attack from the south later. Air is black—I say again, air is black. Severe weather moving in. I've got a battery of MLRS dedicated to your fire support. Good luck. Over."

"Acknowledged," Yates replied as he continued to scribble the message in his notebook.

"Well, Top, thoughts?" Sam looked at her first sergeant.

"First, the relief force has to be from the ACR. Figure they have to fight their way here. Could be several hours before linkup. Might be too far away to raise on FM. Doubt they have our TACSAT net. Second, the Russians will probably beat them here. A whole BTG? Lot of tanks. Lot of BMPs. Lot of Ivans." Slidell looked at the map. "Figure they're gonna use recon first. Probably investigate the POW camp first. That was our last known location."

"Guards division means T-90s and BMP-3s. Bet on a battery of TOS and a battery of 155mm artillery. And Grads."

"Lot of firepower. They will want to find us and use it all."

"Then we stay mobile. We take the fight to them."

"What are you thinking, ma'am?" Slidell turned the map to face Sam.

"Let's push squads east and north across town. Ivan will send patrols down the streets to find us. We ambush as far out as possible and displace. But instead of displacing rearward every time, we circle around for another attack if possible. Need to have the west-end ambushes still though. Ivan might swing around from the POW camp on the west. If we find stationary targets, we use the MLRS to hit those. If possible."

"Makes sense. Push up to here?" Slidell traced his finger on the map.

"Yes. Also, I figure it will take Ivan five minutes to get his artillery onto us, so Yates"—Sam pointed to him—"every time we have troops in contact, start a timer for four minutes."

"Roger that."

"I like this plan. I'll get the platoons." Slidell nodded and turned for the door. Sam pulled out her notebook and furiously finalized her thoughts into a formal plan.

Thirty minutes later, the platoons had their orders and troops were in motion. Sam tapped her fingers on her rifle as she evaluated the situation for the umpteenth time. *Figure at least twelve hours before linkup with the cavalry. We can last that long. Yeah. They lasted all day and night in Mogadishu. Granted, this is a little different.* Sam pursed her lips and looked out the window again. The clouds were darker and moving faster now. *Storm is getting closer. That will help us, but slow the cavalry.*

"Top, the more I think on it, the more likely contact with Ivan is in the east. I'm gonna move that direction."

"Roger. What time do you want to start trying to make contact with the cavalry?" Slidell nodded toward the northwest. "Yates, did you get the radio net for the relief unit written down correctly?"

"Roger, First Sergeant."

"Good. Ma'am, when do you want to start radio checks?"

"Have a radio on their net. We'll hear them first. Vehicle radios transmit farther. I'd rather not chance the Russians eavesdropping and prematurely pinpointing station locations on that net too." Sam paused. "I'm not sure who Bolt is actually. When I left Carson, they were just standing up Third Cav. I remember B Troop was Bandit."

"We'll find out soon enough."

"True. Okay, I'm off." Sam nodded, shouldered her rifle, and went out the door. Outside, the gray sky and lack of wind matched her mood. *The literal calm before the storm.* Sam saw Trevino and some of his soldiers moving east. She jogged over to them.

"Ma'am." Trevino nodded as he continued moving from house to house.

"Let's hunt." Sam fell into line at the end. Distant artillery muffled in the distance.

Trevino held up his open hand, indicating a stop. Sam moved up next to him.

"First squad found a BMP hiding in the apartment complex ahead."

"Just one?" Sam looked at her map.

"Correct." Trevino whispered to his radio, "Second, probe around the left. If this BMP is alone in the complex, we'll destroy it and move your way."

Sam couldn't hear the reply in Trevino's radio earpiece. She would be patient and let Trevino lead his platoon. In her own earpiece, she heard Trevino's platoon sergeant update the command post. Sam looked at her watch, looked at the sky, then watched Trevino.

"Roger. I'm coming." Trevino suddenly spoke into his radio. He turned and looked at Sam. "Ma'am, Second Squad found two more BMPs." Trevino jerked his head to the north.

Sam nodded and followed the platoon leader as he darted between some houses. As they rounded a corner, Sam peered around Trevino to look up at the apartment building that dominated the street.

"One, two, three." Trevino counted before sprinting across the packed snow covering the street. Sam and the other soldiers followed. A moment later, they burst into a building. The hallway was dark, punctuated by shafts of light coming from apartment doors. Trevino swiftly moved down the hallway. Sam fingered the safety switch of her rifle as she glanced in the open doors. *Someone looted thoroughly here. How long have the residents been gone?*

Trevino stopped and whispered, "Friendlies coming in."

A hushed reply: "Come in."

Trevino ducked into an apartment. One of his soldiers nodded and gestured to another room. Trevino and Sam entered it.

"Sir, across the square—you see them backed into that courtyard?"

Sam followed the arm point of the squad leader. Two BMP-3s idled. A group of Russian soldiers gathered in a cluster between the two armored vehicles.

"Seems like they're trying to hide from the air. Think they're having an order brief?"

"Makes sense," Trevino whispered. "Okay, on my command I want you to engage. RPGs for the BMPs. I'm gonna take Third around to the northwest and assault. If any Ivans survive your initial shooting, they're gonna go into that building. If that happens, it will make things hard on us. When I order to break contact, we rally in the blue house west of here."

"Roger."

Trevino gently popped the squad leader in the shoulder with a fist and left the room. Sam followed.

Trevino spoke as he strode down the hallway. "Ma'am, gonna have First take out that lone BMP and then I'll use Third to assault."

"Okay. Just remember those BMPs can explode spectacularly."

"Right."

Trevino glanced left and right out the door before running north to another building. Sam saw movement as Third Squad came out of the building. Trevino pointed north and the squad immediately moved out at a swift walk. They cut between two apartment buildings and circled around to the east.

"Quietly, boys," the squad leader whispered as they stacked up on the doorway.

Sam watched with pride as they silently flowed in the door. Only the sounds of cold boot soles on linoleum marked their progress. Sam and Trevino followed them in.

"Trevino." Sam grabbed Trevino's kit to stop him.

"Did you recon north of us? Security?"

"Shit. No." Trevino whispered forcefully, "Third, hold up."

The soldiers stopped and the squad leader came to Trevino.

"Have two soldiers secure our north flank."

The squad leader grabbed two soldiers and went the other direction in the hallway.

"Sorry, ma'am." Trevino shook his head.

"Shake it off. We work together as a team and we will be okay."

Three minutes later, the squad leader returned. "Street is clear."

Trevino flashed a thumbs-up and the squad resumed its movement through the building. Sam could hear the BMP's diesel engine idling and

Russian voices. The lead Ranger stopped and held up his hand, fingers in a V. *See them.*

"On my command. Three. Two. One," Trevino whispered into his radio. "Fire."

The crashing explosion just outside the building reverberated in the hallway. Rifle and SAW fire from Second Squad joined the explosion. Suddenly the lead Ranger fired his rifle into the doorway.

"Frag out!" Another Ranger tossed a grenade through the door. Both ducked back from the doorway. The grenade exploded and screams of pain followed.

"Lift fire!" Trevino shouted into the radio. He paused then yelled out, "Assaulting!"

The first four Rangers flowed through the doorway, shooting as they exited the hallway into the apartment. "Clear!"

The rest of them followed in. Sam saw two Rangers shooting through the broken-out window. Flames crackled from the closest BMP.

"Through the window!" Trevino moved up and looked in all directions before raking the frame of the window with his rifle barrel. Broken glass tinkled on the floor. Without a glance back, Trevino swung his leg up and hopped out. Two Rangers followed before Sam was able to see past them.

"It's still alive!" one yelled as he leaned around the burning BMP. Another rushed past. Sam jumped through the window. The crack of the BMP's cannon stunned her. The explosion of its shot knocked rubble into the courtyard from where Second Squad had shot from.

"The back door!" Trevino pointed at the BMP's troop hatch, cracked open. Sam pulled a grenade out and pulled the pin.

"Frag out!" Sam rushed the BMP and tossed the grenade through the hatch. In a scramble, everyone darted to the far side of the burning BMP. The *crump* of the grenade seemed muted, but light smoke wisped out of the troop hatch. Trevino rushed the BMP and flung the door open. Sam and another Ranger were close behind. Movement in the smoke caught Sam's eye and she fired several times at it. The movement stopped.

"Grab that RPG and machine gun!"

Trevino leaned in and pulled the RPG out and handed it to one of his Rangers. Next, he grabbed the PKM machine gun laying on the floor.

"The ammo!" Sam took the machine gun and passed it to another Ranger. Trevino pulled out a pair of ammo cans.

"Let's get out of here."

The flames from the other BMP spread down the sides as it ate at the explosive reactive armor.

"Go!"

"Third, fall back!" the squad leader yelled.

One by one, the Rangers climbed back in the window. Inside, they moved down the hallway.

"First and Second, report." Trevino spoke into his radio. He listened before turning to Sam, "Second has two WIA. The other BMP is destroyed."

"Can they move?" Sam pulled her map out as they reached the hallway exit and stopped.

"A fire team will get them back. The rest of the squad will join me at the rally point."

"Okay." Sam looked at her watch. Six minutes since the shooting started. Time to get moving.

"After we consolidate at the rally point, I want you to take your platoon north and link up with Second Platoon."

"Roger." Trevino nodded and with the wave of his arm, the squad moved outside. The wind was now rustling the tree branches and snow fell.

Kharkiv, Ukraine - January 23, 1215 hrs

The Mi-24 Hind hustled south at maximum speed, barely ten feet above the ground. In the passenger area, Kiselyov watched trees and buildings flash by. Ahead, smoke and dust rose as Russian artillery pounded suspected NATO positions to allow the Hind to get past the enemy front lines. Each bank of the Hind tossed Kiselyov's stomach acid into his throat.

Highrise buildings flashed by as the Hind buzzed through the streets of Kharkiv. *These pilots are fearless.* Turns came in rapid succession, tossing Kiselyov back and forth in his seat. Across the compartment, the helicopter's sergeant grinned. Loud pops erupted from the helicopter as it launched flares. Kiselyov shuddered, knowing a pilot would only use flares if they detected a missile launch. He pushed the thought down. *I'm a dead man anyway.*

A fiery death failed to arrive. The Hind sped on, now cruising down a valley. Two minutes later, the Hind slowed and climbed higher, allowing Kiselyov to see beyond the trees next to the river. Without seeing landmarks or a map, he knew they were nearly to Peryomais'kyi and the headquarters bunker of the 47th Guards Tank Division. The Hind flared and settled down in a field. As the helicopter settled down on its wheel's, the sergeant opened the door and Kiselyov scrambled out.

"General Kiselyov!" A waving hand from a tree line accompanied the yell as the Hind took off.

"Ah!" Kiselyov recognized the division commander, Major General Evgeny Boyarsky.

"We need to hurry. NATO artillery seems to chase the helicopters." Boyarsky gestured to a command BTR. Kiselyov jogged over and the two climbed in. Before the door closed, the BTR bounced across the field.

"You beat the storm." Boyarsky shook Kiselyov's hand.

"Barely. There were some squalls of snow to help us get through the enemy's lines. What is the update from Pereshchepyne?"

"The enemy seems to be everywhere in the city. Patrols into the city took heavy casualties in ambushes near the water tower. The lead company oriented on that, but then were ambushed farther north, near the city park. Major Agranov hammered the area with artillery and then attacked. They found no enemy, but then enemy infantry attacked and destroyed his mortar battery near the river. It is very confused. The enemy is elusive."

"And what of the camp?"

"Nothing but burning rubble. I hit it with a whole load from a TOS and added a howitzer battery-ten for good measure. Nothing could have survived that, General."

"Did you check for bodies?"

"Yes, we found our troops, but no enemy and no prisoners. But of course, we have not sorted through the remains of the mill."

"What is the status of Major Agranov's BTG?"

"Still combat capable."

"Evgeny, have you linked up with the BTG from the Twenty-Seventh MRD?"

"Not yet. It sounds like there is some chaos within the Sixth Combined Arms Army right now."

"Okay. Start pulling together another BTG from your troops. I must have more troops." Kiselyov wagged his finger and pulled out his phone. He chose a number and called.

"Mikhail, I heard you were not at your command post," Molchalin answered without pleasantries.

"Yes, I'm coordinating the Pereshchepyne attack from the front."

"Ah, I was worried it was something different. Tell me, what is going on with District? General Dronov wants me to attack two opposite directions."

"I know. This camp in Pereshchepyne is the distraction we worried it would become. Only worse."

"Yes. Mikhail, it is the last thing I need. This weather is complicating my attack and NATO is hitting the Twenty-Seventh MRD with a spoiling attack. I had to pull the BTG I was going to send to Pereshchepyne to plug the line. But then Dronov insists I countermand that order. It seems like this camp suddenly is more important than winning the war."

"Victor, winning the war, your attack is more important than Dronov understands, I fear. I sense panic in Moscow."

"Perhaps we can work together and achieve both."

"That is why I came south. I can personally coordinate the attack in Pereshchepyne and let you focus on the counterattack."

"Deal. Is there any way you can achieve your mission without using my BTG from the Twenty-Seventh Motor Rifles?"

"No, Victor. I need a BTG. I need someone to seal the south and west. My BTG in the city is not strong enough to do everything. I need to pull it back and regroup. I am scraping together another BTG from the Forty-Seventh Guards Tank Division."

"I can't spare anything from the Twenty-Seventh, especially without the Forty-Seventh attacking to pin the enemy on the river at Berestyn. The BTG is attacking to plug the line as we speak. I cannot pull them back now."

"Okay. What do we have available?"

"There is a motorized rifle company guarding the western approaches to the city. They are under the command of the supply depot. Also, there might be some tanks and BMPs at the repair depot. I will order Colonel Ogoltsov to give you anything that can fight."

"What about the Twenty-Fifth Guards Motor Rifle Division? Could they spare a BTG?"

"Yes, perhaps. I could divert a BTG, but it won't reach Pereshchepyne until after dark. You don't want to attack in the dark with an ad hoc force, not with all the minefields in the area."

"So dawn tomorrow? That won't work. I will see what I can scrape together here then."

"Ah, Mikhail, I need to go." Radio traffic in the background reminded Kiselyov his friend was in the midst of the only attack that could restore his fate.

"Good luck, Victor." Kiselyov hung up and looked at Boyarsky. "Give me anything you have that can drive and fight. Even if they are just platoons, I will forge them into a BTG. Let's go to Pereshchepyne and see what we can assemble there too. Have your troops rally at the supply depot east of town."

Chapter 13

Abramivka, Ukraine – January 23, 1300 hrs

Running Bear shivered as the wind shifted and drafts flowed down his neck. The falling snow—now stinging icy crystals, pelting his face with gusto—dropped visibility to just a hundred meters. Even the thermal sights failed to see far in the storm.

"Guidons, Ace Six, tighten it up."

Savvy's voice over the radio caused Running Bear to look each direction. Staff Sergeant Meigs's tank was barely visible on the right. To his left, Gene's tank was a little closer and easier to see.

"Four, Three, I still have First Platoon on my wing. This storm sure got bad fast," Meigs called on the platoon radio.

"Roger. Keep an eye out for them."

Running Bear sat back down to get out of the wind. Even though the advance was slow, too slow for Running Bear's taste, the wind chill was surprising.

"What do you think, Sergeant, you think Ivan will counterattack?" Gomez asked without pulling away from the gunner's sights.

"Yeah, we took too long to consolidate after breaking through the Russian lines."

"What was the holdup?" Hofi said.

"They had to get one-three hooked up to the eighty-eight. We can't leave it behind with just the track and idler wheel shot off."

"Can it still fight?"

"If it was my tank, hell yeah. I bet McBride hooked up to tow it backward so the tank could cover their rear. They can operate the turret with aux power easy enough."

"Suck to be in a fight like that." Hofi shivered. "Getting colder."

"Yeah. Well now first is short a tank, so we gotta be ready to help them."

"How? We can barely see our wingman."

"You know what I mean, Hofi. Just watch your sector. Probably don't have to worry too much about the sky. Drones won't fly in this."

Hofi let the matter drop. Running Bear rechecked the map before rising up to look around again. Somewhere off to the right, beyond First Platoon, was Battle Troop, probably with the engineers following behind, maybe even directly behind First Platoon. To the left was the platoon leader's section and the Bradleys of Third Platoon.

"Identified tank!" Gomez's cry pulled Running Bear's focus down the gun tube. The storm obscured the enemy.

"Up!" Hofi followed without waiting for a proper command. Running Bear dropped down to look at the sights. A T-90 filled the sights. *Too close!*

"Fire!"

"On the way!" Gomez fired the cannon and Running Bear saw the sizzling sparks fly a moment before the T-90 exploded. The turret flew high out of the sights before crashing back down. Oblivious to the spectacle, Hofi loaded another sabot into the cannon.

"Target, cease fire." Running Bear scanned urgently with his thermal viewer. A flash and cannon crack from the right hinted at more Russians. Running Bear keyed up his radio. "Ace Six, Two-Four, contact tanks south. Out."

Another crack on the right. Out of the corner of his eye, Running Bear saw Meigs's tank fire at a target even farther right.

"Six, One-Four, multiple tanks and PCs. Recommend hasty defense." First Platoon had more in front of them. More cannons and auto-cannons echoed on the wind.

"Driver, kick it up. Get me even with Sergeant Meigs." Running Bear's voice stayed low and steady.

"Roger that, Sergeant."

The radio crackled again: "Guidons, Ace Six, tanks come up online with First. Third, echelon and extend. Watch our flank! I'm working on getting fires."

Running Bear keyed up the radio to respond, "Two-Four, wilco." Even as he spoke, Gene gave orders on the platoon net. Only an experienced warrior could multitask radio traffic on two nets, all while fighting a vehicle. In less than one minute, Running Bear and Meigs were even with the frontline trace of First Platoon. Ahead, Russian armored vehicles materialized out of the blowing snow. The deadly game of whack-a-mole consumed Running Bear's attention.

A supersonic crack sucked the snow off the top of the turret as a T-90 barely missed. *There!* Running Bear grabbed control of the turret from his joystick and slung it to the right.

"Gunner, sabot, tank!" Running Bear spit out the words as he released a button on the joystick and gave Gomez control.

"Identified!"

"Up!" Hofi shoved the round home with a fist and slapped the arming lever.

Running Bear glanced over to verify Hofi was clear. "Fire!"

"On the way!" the breach snapped back.

As if released by the starting pistol, Hofi slapped the arming lever down and opened the ammo door.

"Target!" Wind cleared the snow cloud in front of the tank and Running Bear saw the T-90 veer to the side, its gun tube drooping. "Cease fire."

Running Bear scanned for more targets as Hofi finished reloading the cannon. The cacophony of high-velocity cannons on the right continued.

A glow on the right caused Running Bear to look away from his thermal viewer. Somebody was burning in First Platoon.

"Ace Six, One-Four, slant two. LT's tank is burning. Can we get Second to cover?"

"One-Four, Two-Four, we are coming," Running Bear interrupted before Savvy could respond. He released the radio and spoke on the intercom, "Driver, back up hard!"

Blucher responded instantly, throwing rooster tails of snow up in front of the tank.

Running Bear switched to the platoon radio. "One, Four, I'll extend beyond our right. Three, slide right a couple hundred meters."

A new voice called on the company radio, "I can't! I can't get my hatch open and nobody in the turret will respond!"

A puzzled silence engulfed Running Bear's tank before Hofi spoke. "I think that was Maxwell. In First Platoon."

"Watch out!" Running Bear saw a First Platoon tank suddenly back up before cutting diagonally toward the burning tank. "Driver, come up on the right side of the burning tank. Stay a hundred meters away though. Go!"

"PC!" Gomez called as a BMP-3 charged forward.

"Up!" Hofi didn't wait for Running Bear.

Running Bear mentally measured the angle between the BMP-3 and the First Platoon tank blocking for its burning wingman. *Clear.* "Fire!"

Gomez fired. The BMP-3 slowed to a stop, flames licking out of the front slope. A new BMP-3 appeared to the left. Before Running Bear could open his mouth, the First Platoon tank fired and the BMP-3 exploded.

"Troops!" Gomez didn't wait for a command and fired the coax machine gun. Red tracers disappeared in the storm.

Running Bear switched from the thermal viewer to his fifty-caliber machine gun and joined Gomez in the hunt for Russian infantry.

"Holy shit! Sergeant Hamasaki just climbed in the burning tank!" Hofi called as he unlocked his machine gun.

Running Bear glanced over, unable to see past Hofi's bulk. Another BMP-3 appeared in Running Bear's sights. "Gunner, sabot, PC!"

"Identified!"

Hofi jumped down from his hatch and armed the cannon. "Up!"

"Fire, fire MPAT!" Running Bear ordered.

Once again, Gomez fired the cannon and Hofi pulled an MPAT round to reload the cannon. Four seconds later, the cannon was ready for a new target. Bullets smacked against the tank's armor as unseen Russian soldiers fired back blindly. Hofi peeked out of his hatch.

"The turret is slowly moving!"

"Whose turret?" Running Bear snapped before looking over. Now Hofi was low enough Running Bear could see over to the burning tank. The turret slowly moved as someone inside was manually turning it. The flames from the engine deck now were distinct from those rising out of the bags in the bustle rack. The blocking tank busily fired its coax and fifty caliber at targets in front of it. "Keep an eye on them!"

Running Bear returned his attention to his sights. A T-90 loomed into view. Gomez saw it at the same time. This time, the MPAT round hit the tank and there was a spectacular flash of light on the front of the turret, but the T-90 fired back. The bang of the glancing blow off the front slope echoed and dust and snow shook into the cordite-laced air inside. Hofi slammed a sabot round home and Gomez fired again. This time, the T-90's turret rocketed up into the air. The falling turret ungracefully bounced off the burning hull and slid in front.

Running Bear rose up to check the tank. In the corner of his eye, he saw the burning First Platoon tank now had the gun over the burning back deck, the only turret position allowing the driver to escape through it.

A new boom reverberated in the tank as frozen dirt and snow leapt into the air behind the tank. A second boom followed.

"Incoming!" Running Bear pulled his hatch down. Russian artillery pounded the field just behind them. Shrapnel pinged off the armor.

"Hope we killed their FO," Hofi grumped.

Running Bear quickly scanned the battlefield, seeing no enemy vehicles with signs of life. "Well, Hofi, they're probably blind. They're looking into the blowing snow too." He finished just in time to see Hamasaki appear out of the burning tank's hatch and pull a soldier up by the straps on his back. Another *boom* and Hamasaki tumbled back into the turret. *Dani!* Hamasaki reappeared and finished pulling the soldier up. The soldier quickly rolled off the turret and fell to the ground. Dani leaned over the edge and pointed toward her tank. The whipping wind carried her yells away and Running Bear could only guess at what she told the soldier.

Another explosion shook his tank. Running Bear popped his hatch open and rose up. "Get out of there, Dani!"

Dani seemed not to hear and scrambled back inside the burning tank hatch. Flames now roared from the back deck. A moment later, she pushed the dead weight of another soldier up out of the hatch. The soldier slumped over on top of the turret. Dani followed and pushed it over the edge.

"Ace Seven, Two-Four, First Platoon has at least two litter urgent, prepare to copy grid." Running Bear verified his location and relayed the information to Top Harris, as he watched Dani drop back into the tank once more.

"Dammit, Dani!" Running Bear thrust his hatch fully open and started to climb out.

"PC!" Gomez's call froze Running Bear half out of the hatch. Squinting into the storm, Running Bear couldn't see anything. He swore and dropped back into the hatch. The enemy BMP-3 appeared on the screen for his sights.

"Fire and adjust!"

Gomez fired. The BMP-3 exploded.

"Target, I'm gonna—" Running Bear stopped as two more BMP-3s appeared. "Cease fire, PC on the right!" Running Bear shook his head in frustration. *Too many Ivans to go help Dani. Dammit!*

A T-90 and three more BMP-3s appeared. The burning and still derelicts collecting served to hide the new Russians arriving at the battle. Running Bear found himself studying each vehicle, eating at time.

"Sergeant Hamasaki is climbing back on her own tank now." Hofi pointed through the snow.

Running Bear looked over. Dani's Nomex was orange and stained dark on her arms and legs. "Where did the casualties go?"

"There are three about twenty meters behind the burning tank."

"Okay. Driver, back up and slide us farther right."

The crew became silent as they repositioned the tank. The new angle into the killing zone offered more enemy soldiers to shoot at.

"Guidons, Ace Six, friendly artillery splash." Savvy's voice reminded Running Bear there was a whole task force alongside. The ripping linen sound of 155mm rounds passed overhead and flashes winked in the sights as high explosives churned the killing zone.

"Hofi, how we looking on rounds?"

Hofi opened the ammo door and counted before responding, "Got five sabot and four MPAT."

"Thanks." Running Bear turned his attention to the rest of the platoon, compiling a complete status report to pass up. Hofi passed the time by chucking spent 120mm aft caps out of the turret. By the time the artillery faded out, Running Bear reported the platoon's situation to Top Harris.

Five hundred meters west, Logan surveyed the battlefield through his thermal viewer. The loss of one Abrams and one Bradley seemed miraculous compared to the nearly forty burning hulks in front. Still, time was burning quickly.

"Guidons, Bolt Six, report," Logan radioed, ready to write down the reports.

"Bolt Six, Ace Six, nine-slant-six. We need to cross level ammo. Over." Savvy reported her nine Bradleys and six Abrams ready to fight. Logan knew she wasn't counting the tank in tow with the M88.

"Bolt Six, Battle Six, eight-slant-four. We could use it too." Devin sounded calm.

"Bolt Six, Certain One, no change, ready to roll," Lucas answered last.

Logan finished writing and scratched his chin scruff before radioing, "I want to keep pushing. We need to clear the main battle area. We can't stay here any longer because the main Russian counterattack is coming. Let's go."

"Ace Six, moving."

Logan looked left and right, watching his task force resume its southward slog. "Brown, take us to the left. Guide on the burning Abrams."

Brown said nothing as he put the tank in gear and cruised over. Top Harris and the medics loaded three soldiers into an armored ambulance. Logan saw Heydte's tool truck bounce over. Heydte stopped the truck and got out to talk with Top. Logan watched as Heydte talked with Top a moment before getting back in his truck. Top jogged over to Logan's tank and climbed up.

"That makes three KIA and five WIA, plus one WIA still in the fight." Top gestured south toward the tanks' tracks.

"Who is still in the fight?" Logan yelled over the wind.

"Staff Sergeant Hamasaki, sir. Maxwell says she took shrapnel or a bullet before she got to him."

"She did what?"

"Sir, Maxwell radioed he couldn't get out of the burning tank and Hamasaki ran over and manually traversed the turret to get him out through the hole."

"You're kidding. Jeez. But she's still in the fight?"

"Yeah, she went back to her tank and I didn't know she was wounded until Maxwell told me." Top shrugged.

"Well, when we get a chance, dig into it." Logan made a mental note.

Top nodded and scampered down off the tank.

"Okay, Brown, let's move out. Follow the tracks south until we catch up with our tanks. Same deal—follow about three hundred meters behind the lead tank."

"Roger, sir," Brown replied.

"Hey sir, doesn't Sergeant Hamasaki know these tanks can blow up when they catch fire?" Litsky asked.

"Believe me, she knows. She's seen more than most. Her own tank cooked off at Fiery Cross. I was there too. I *know* she knows." Logan paused. "And Fiery Cross claimed another catastrophic kill. The explosion knocked out the whole crew. They were never the same again. Then last summer, we had two other tanks cook off their ammo. Yeah, Dani knows better."

"Jesus," Litsky whispered. The tank rattled south, devoid of further conversation. Only Jim updating regiment on the radio kept them company.

Chapter 14

Holubivka, Ukraine – January 23, 1400 hrs

Even underground, the wind shrieking carried over the din of a command post at its busiest.

"General Molchalin!" Beketov raised his hand and waved for Molchalin to come to the intelligence desk.

"What do you have, Colonel?"

"We are getting some signal intelligence on the enemy spoiling attack. We haven't been able to find their data signature yet, but audio captures gave us some callsigns. This is a new unit, most likely a battalion, I believe."

"New? Who, where? How?" Molchalin leaned on the desk to look at the computer screen in front of Beketov.

"They are reporting to the enemy Third Cavalry Regiment. The new unit callsign is Bolt. We isolated new radio nets, with callsigns Ace, Battle, and Certain. There may be more, I don't know. We don't have this unit in our database, but naming convention indicates a battalion."

"Fantastic. A phantom enemy battalion just smashed a hole in the Twenty-Seventh MRD, and you have no idea who they are."

"I'm sorry, General. Internet search isn't very helpful either. I found a document that had all four callsigns, but it's dated."

"Go on."

Beketov retracted his neck into his shoulders. "Fourth Battalion, Thirty-Seventh Armor. Our records show the unit was disbanded in the 1990s."

"That isn't helpful. Is it possible an enemy battalion just changed their callsigns?"

"I don't think so. Well, at least, all of the enemy battalions we have been tracking are still active on the radio."

"Hmph. What do you know about this new enemy battalion?"

"We know they have Abrams and Bradleys, so it is either an armored or mechanized infantry battalion."

"Keep working on what other surprises we will find. If the enemy has a new battalion, is it possible there is a whole brigade we don't know about? Get me the information as soon as you have it, Colonel."

"Yes, General."

Molchalin stood upright and stretched his back. He looked at his watch. *Where is my update on the attack?* He walked around to the operations map and stared at it.

"General..." Frosin cleared his throat. "The attack is delayed still. The 27th MRD is still sorting out the situation at Lyp'yanka. The blizzard has reduced visibility significantly, so it has been difficult. We don't dare have the 138th attack alone."

"When will we be ready? Even the president is watching this attack."

"Perhaps in another thirty minutes."

"Do we have enough ammunition to begin the barrage now and keep it going until then?"

"If we use the reserves."

"Do it. I want artillery on the enemy now, so I can tell higher we have begun. And push the recce patrols forward. Have them be aggressive."

"Yes, General, I will make it happen."

Molchalin nodded his head and closed his eyes. The radio crackling the news of the barrage initiation brought a smile to his face. *Once in motion, the attack will prevail.* He looked at his watch. *Just two hours of daylight left.*

The storm howled, masking the distant thunder of artillery, though Molchalin could sense the powerful barrage.

"General," Frosin called, radio in hand, "the artillery is switching to their secondary targets in the Karlivka area. The line at Lyp'yanka is now plugged. The BTG did not encounter any enemy on the road from Buzivka up the Orchyk River valley to Fedorivka. They've reestablished contact with the troops defending Dmytrivka."

"Good. What of the Americans?"

"The storm is too bad to tell. Blowing snow already covers the battlefield and we cannot find the tracks to see in which direction they retreated."

Molchalin swiftly crossed the room to Frosin and put his hand on the chief of staff's shoulder and whispered, "You assume they retreated."

"The American's know we are coming. They stand nothing to gain with a single battalion penetration. Focus on our own attack. Deny the enemy the distraction they hoped for."

"You are correct. Push our divisions forward."

Frosin nodded and snapped his fingers for the staff to resume their efforts. Molchalin watched a few minutes before returning to his office to brew some tea. The kettle slowly rose to a boil, giving Molchalin time to think. Once steam rose, he poured the water into his cup and dunked his teabag in. Clutching the cup in both hands, he returned to the operations room. Reports slowly came in.

"General, the 138th reports severe enemy artillery. They are losing tanks and BMPs rapidly and they haven't even found the American front line." Frosin put a pointer on the map at Mashivka.

"They must push through!"

"Yes, General." Frosin turned and talked on the radio.

Molchalin took a sip. *Would I be more effective farther forward? Perhaps at one of the division command posts?*

"General, a report from the Twenty-Seventh."

"Go on."

"Their lead BTG struck the enemy near Karlivka and was stopped. They are pushing the rest forward, but are having trouble staying on course in the snow."

"Tell them to do better. Get my BTR ready! I'll help the Twenty-Seventh find their compass."

Molchalin returned to his office and pulled his coat and hat on. The ten minutes waiting for the BTR to come seemed like eternity. The snowstorm was stronger than Molchalin expected. The bunker did much for hiding the full fury of the wind. He leaned into the wind and staggered to the BTR. Inside, the cold armor sucked the warmth from his legs.

"Driver, take me to Kotovka and the Twenty-Seventh MRD command post!" Molchalin peered through the vision ports, straining for landmarks in the storm. The BTR surged forward.

Reports crackled on the radio, darkening Molchalin's mood. The Americans were pounding the 138th Guards with massed artillery. Two whole BTGs would never reach the American lines. He called his command post. "Colonel Beketov, what enemy artillery are we facing?"

"General, indications are we are seeing the artillery battalions from at least three brigades, plus the artillery brigade of the American First Armored Division. The rocket artillery hitting the 138th is likely Ukrainian. Radar tracked the flight paths from near Novi Sanzhary. At least their drones can't fly in this storm."

"Give General Frosin the best targets for counter-battery. We need to silence the enemy artillery immediately." Molchalin ended his radio call and looked at his map. The counterattack would only succeed in cutting NATO's salient if he broke through with at least six BTGs still in the fight. *And that is just to cut north to the bridgeheads. It doesn't count units to parry the countermoves.*

The BTR slowed and made a turn.

"Driver, do you know where you are?" Molchalin yelled over the engine, seeing they were now cutting across a field.

"Yes, General. We are just east of Novopetrivka. We have to go cross country to avoid our minefields. We will be to the Twenty-Seventh Command Post in another fifteen minutes."

Molchalin sat back in his seat and attempted to relax. The attack was now nearly an hour behind schedule and floundering. Relaxation was an impossible goal. The BTR's engine growled as Molchalin closed his eyes and cleared his mind. The BTR lurched to a stop.

A major opened the door and Molchalin tumbled out into the wind and snow. A few feet away was the command truck for the Twenty-Seventh MRD. Molchalin quickly entered.

"Attention!" The staff fell silent and turned toward him.

"Carry on." Molchalin moved away from the door and into the crowded and busy mobile command post.

"Lieutenant General Molchalin, welcome."

"Davit, give me an update."

"Ah. The weather is making the attack nearly impossible. We are attacking into the wind, and snow blinds our vehicles. The crews must stop frequently to clear the snow from the gunners' sights and the driver's vision blocks."

"NATO is fighting the same weather too. This attack must succeed. You must break the enemy lines."

"No, General, they have the wind at their back. The snow isn't plastering against their sights. With their excellent thermals, they can engage us long before our own thermal sights can make out the shapes through the ice and snow crust."

"Damn it. Davit, come with me."

Molchalin stomped out of the warm command post and back into the storm. Davit followed, tugging his collar up.

"Davit, the fate of the war hinges on your attack. You cannot fail. If you fail, the repercussions will be far and deep."

"General, you are placing me in an impossible position. If this attack cannot fail, then we need to modify our plan so that it can succeed." Davit rubbed his face after pleading his case.

Molchalin looked at Davit, then stepped away from the shelter of the vehicles. The full fury of the wind forced him to lean heavily. Slowly, Molchalin turned in a circle, experiencing the icy snow pelting him. Facing northeast was impossible to keep his eyes open.

"Davit, order your troops to stop their attack. Pull them back to regroup. We will turn our attack toward Poltava so the wind is blowing across us and we can see. Hurry, get your stop order out before we lose another BTG. I will tell the 138th the same. We must be quick to get our attack back underway. Hurry!" Molchalin clapped his gloves together and jogged to his BTR. Grabbing the radio, he radioed his orders to the rest of his combined arms army and staff.

Ten kilometers west of Novi Sanzhary, a Ukrainian rocket artillery battery hastily plotted the coordinates from the signal intelligence unit. Opportunities to bag co-located enemy headquarters were rare.

Stepanivka, Ukraine – January 23, 1430 hrs

Two kilometers north of town, Logan hunched in his seat, trying to stay out of the wind. As Task Force Thunderbolt reached the bluffs overlooking the Oril River and dropped into the valley, the shelter from the wind was most welcome. Even better, the forest hid the task force further. Logan still had doubts they had escaped Russian attention.

"Bolt Six, Ace Six, the river ice is broken. Looks like artillery hit earlier. Break." Savvy's voice on the radio conveyed no surprise. "We found a crossing point."

Logan uncapped his map pen and wrote down the grid as Savvy gave it.

"Acknowledged. Battle Six, bridge the river and secure the far side. Give us enough room and check on the bridge over the canal at Kotovka."

"Roger."

Logan looked west, impatiently waiting to see the armored assault bridge rumble through the formation. A few minutes later, the sapper platoon moved past Logan, their bridge layer following their Bradleys.

"It's a good thing the storm is keeping everyone hunkered down." Litsky broke the silence in the tank.

"For many reasons. Which are you thinking of?"

"That bridge deploying will be a big tall flag telling Ivan where we are."

"We don't have a choice."

Litski didn't respond. Logan studied his map. The rest of Battle Troop rattled by.

"Hey, Brown, follow Battle's last tank down to the river. We will follow behind them and then find a good spot on the south bank."

"Yes, sir." Brown put the Abrams in gear and followed the line of tanks through the forest. Logan stood up into the hatch. The storm seemed to swallow the sound. He smiled.

A few moments later, they reached the edge of the woods. The bridge layer already had the bridge up and extending across the Oril River. Logan watched as the bridge straightened out and lowered to the ground. The launcher, an Abrams chassis, backed away and pulled to the side.

"Bolt Six, Battle Six, touchdown," Devin called on the radio as a Bradley from the sapper platoon rumbled across the bridge to the far side. Then, all of Battle Troop flowed to the bridge. Once across the bridge, they fanned out.

Without waiting for Logan's word, Brown followed. Logan's heart pounded as they lined up on the bridge. In all his training and time, Logan had never crossed one. The tread paths looked narrow and it seemed the slightest mistake by the driver would topple the tank into the icy water below. Brown carefully lined up and charged across the bridge, giving Logan little time to worry.

Logan turned and saw Savvy's vehicles following.

The incoming rockets gave no warning. Large explosions ripped through the storm south of Logan. Instinctively, he dropped down and pulled the hatch closed. Through the vision blocks, he watched an explosion hit a house and toss debris into the wind. *Odd. They seem to be coming from the west. Friendly fire!*

Logan quickly changed to the regimental radio. "Remington X-ray, Bolt Six, observing artillery impacting at checkpoint two-five-niner. Possible friendly fire!"

"Roger." The terse reply annoyed Logan.

"Make it stop!" Logan released the radio and swore. He switched to the task force radio. "Guidons, Bolt Six, push east out of the impact area."

Logan looked around through his vision blocks as Brown sped the tank east. Logan counted three vehicles failing to move. Brown sped across the frozen marsh next to the river. An oxbow pond suddenly appeared and they crashed down onto the ice and skidded across before slamming into the steep far bank.

"Sorry." Brown switched to reverse and backed away from the bank.

"Everyone okay? Driver, come right. The bank isn't as steep over there."

"Roger." Brown slowly drove up the bank. He saw other Abrams and headed toward them. Logan looked around and tried to count vehicles, giving up as they passed in and out of vision as they raced through a village. Finally, the Abrams ahead slowed and took positions along a canal.

"Driver, stop a couple hundred meters back from that platoon."

As soon as Brown stopped the tank, Logan plotted their new location on his map.

"Where are we?" Litsky asked, traversing the turret left and right.

"Between Kovpakivka and Buzivka," Logan answered.

"I don't know those towns, sir."

"Right. We are about twenty klicks northeast of Pereshchepyne."

"Gotcha." Litsky returned his focus to his sights.

"Bolt X-ray, Ace Seven, negative damage, negative casualties. Ready to Charlie-mike." Top's report to Lieutenant O'Connell elicited a sigh of relief from Logan.

"Roger. Battle, sitrep?" Jim called on the radio.

"Battle Six, stand by. We have damage and casualties, yes." Devin's reply was choppy.

"Ace, have your mechanics and medics assist Battle. Battle, give me that update as soon as you have it. Out."

Logan looked at his watch and wrote a note on the side of his map board.

West of Novi Sanzhary, the Ukrainian rocket artillery battery noted their miscalculation and adjusted before firing the second half of their barrage, oblivious to the chaos they caused.

Kotovka, Ukraine – January 23, 1500 hrs

"General, artillery!" the BTR driver screamed as he started the motor.

"Obviously!" Molchalin yelled back. He looked out the small vision block and saw smoke drifting past on the wind. The snow failed to mask the stench of buildings burning. "I think we dodged it. It appears to be on the other side of town."

The command phone rang. Molchalin looked at it, seeing it was his command bunker. He calmly answered. "Yes?"

"General, this is Colonel Beketov. I have fresh SIGINT triangulation putting enemy radio traffic at Kotovka! They are dangerously close to you!"

"Where, exactly?" Molchalin carefully scanned the world through the vision blocks.

"The grid is approximately two hundred meters north of the east canal bridge." Beketov spoke rapidly. He knew where the 27th Motor Rifle Division command post was set up on the east edge of town. "They cannot be more than seven hundred meters away from you!"

"Are you certain of the grid plot?" Molchalin asked gently.

"Yes. I verified it. The triangulation team is excellent. I trust them."

"Colonel, I'm watching enemy artillery thrash the very location we are talking about. Perhaps the enemy has deceived us."

"We're working to decipher the enemy transmission. Perhaps they are observing and controlling the artillery. It would be prudent for you to take precautions."

"Don't worry, Colonel. I will. Keep me updated." Molchalin hung up, leaving his phone on the seat. *Hmm....* He opened the troop door and climbed back out into the storm, nearly running into Davit.

"General, enemy artillery is impacting just outside down. My security detachment recommends we move."

"Davit, do they see any enemy vehicles or soldiers?"

"Negative."

"How is your security deployed?"

"The squads are in buildings. Their BTRs are hidden. Drones are our biggest threat."

"My intelligence officer reports enemy radio transmissions right over th—" Molchalin pointed northeast, cut short by the arrival of a new barrage. The first explosion seemed to rip the very air out of his lungs.

Black smoke cruised past Molchalin's vision. *Why is it going downward?* He blinked and turned his head, discovering snow up to his nose. *Why am I laying in the snow?* Molchalin took a labored breath. Next, he lifted his head and looked around. His command BTR was toppled on its side and flames roared from the engine compartment. The 27th MRD command post truck was also burning. *Artillery?*

"Anybody here?" Molchalin coughed, trying to yell.

The wind shrieked in reply.

Molchalin sat up and tried to get to his feet. His left hand refused to push off the ground. He looked at his arm, noticing the coat was ripped and blood dripped into the snow. *Of course.* He took a moment to examine his legs, straightening and flexing them one at a time. Satisfied, Molchalin slowly got to his feet. His head swam. *One step at a time.* Another deep breath. Darkness closed in and Molchalin felt himself falling.

"Oh good, he is still with us." The voice in the fog woke Molchalin. As his eyes regained focus, he saw a metal ceiling a few feet above him. The hum of a diesel engine competed with the ringing in his ears. "General, can you hear me?"

Molchalin look for the voice, seeing a face next to him.

"What...where...where am I?"

"We are in my BTR, driving to your command bunker at Holubivka."

"Who are you?"

"Senior Lieutenant Usik, General. My platoon was guarding the division command post."

"What happened?" Molchalin tried to sit up, but Usik held him down.

"Please, General, remain still. You have wounds on your head and arm." Molchalin relaxed and Usik released his grip. "Enemy artillery struck the command post."

"What of the command group?"

Usik shook his head. "General Kostyuk died shortly after I found him. He and you were the only ones outside the command post when it was hit."

"No... Davit..." Tears welled up in Molchalin's eyes. He gritted his teeth to compose himself.

"General, the surgeon is waiting for us at the command bunker. It is safer than trying to get to the field hospital at Pereshchepyne."

"What? Why?" Molchalin slowly remembered something was going on there.

"Enemy infantry are reportedly in the city itself, and one of my squads possibly saw enemy tanks on the north edge of Kotovka, heading east."

"Enemy tanks here?"

"Possibly. It was a fleeting glimpse through the storm and artillery. But I don't want to risk it, General." Usik frowned.

"I must regain my grasp on the situation." Molchalin groaned as the BTR hit a bump and pain erupted in his head. Through the pain, he listened to Usik and the BTR driver discussing where they were. *So tired.* Slowly, he drifted back into darkness.

Chapter 15

Pereshchepyne, Ukraine – January 23, 1545 hrs

Darkness closed in early in the worsening storm. Kiselyov's mood matched. *So much time wasted trying to piece together a BTG.* He rode in the passenger seat of a Tigr armored truck. The ride was smooth on the freeway. In a moment, they were over the river and canal bridges. The driver slowed and gingerly took the icy exit. From the elevated roadway, the supply depot should have stretched out across the view. Instead, heavy blowing snow limited Kiselyov's sight to the first row of vehicles.

"Are they following?" Kiselyov asked his driver.

The driver glanced in the side mirror. "Yes, General. They are."

"Good." Kiselyov wondered what the driver's name was, but it seemed silly to learn it just to take it to the grave in the next day or so. *I hope my family is spared.*

The driver pulled up to a command van. Kiselyov opened the door and the wind nearly ripped it out of his hands. Carefully, he got out and forced the door closed. He composed himself and marched into the command van.

The colonel sitting in a chair facing the door looked up and studied the rank insignia on Kiselyov's jacket a moment before snapping to attention. "Sir!" A puzzled look flashed on the colonel's face.

"Colonel Ogoltsov, I'm Lieutenant General Kiselyov. You will offer me all available vehicles and crews in your depot."

"Sir, General Molchalin notified me you would come. By all available vehicles, do you mean anything that can move, or just those able to shoot as well?"

"Naturally, that which can shoot and move would be ideal." Kiselyov attempted to stifle his sarcasm. "Crews are also helpful. Unless you've made the tanks robotic."

"Ah. Unfortunately, that is beyond our depot's capabilities. We merely repair and match up replacement soldiers."

"How many of these conscripts have seen the vehicles you assign them to, much less learned how to operate them?"

"You know how it is, general. We do our best to train them here before we forward them to the divisions."

"Of course. What do you have to offer?"

"We have a mixed bag." Ogoltsov looked at a chalkboard next to his desk, "I've got five T-80s, three T-90s, seven BMP-3s, one Khrizantema tank destroyer, and two BTR-82s. There are no squads for the infantry vehicles."

"Thank you. Any officers or contract soldiers?"

Ogoltsov shook his head.

Kiselyov pulled a notebook from his jacket pocket and took notes. He quietly returned the notebook to his jacket and looked up at Ogoltsov. "Have these replacements join the end of my column and follow us into town."

Kiselyov's phone rang. He pulled it out of his pocket and looked at the screen. *Dronov.*

"This is General Kiselyov."

"Mikhail, you are overdue for an update by an hour. I was wondering if you were ambushed en route."

"No, General Dronov. The weather is terrible. I just got to the depot and collected reinforcements. Such as they are." Kiselyov looked at Ogoltsov who shrugged.

"What does your force consist of now?"

"Sir, I will reinforce Major Agranov's BTG with five T-80s and seven BMP-3s. My other BTG now has nine T-90s, twenty-three BMP-3s, and now, one Khrizantema and two BTR-82s."

"What regiment is that one from? Who is leading the BTG?" Dronov asked intently.

"Well, it's a collection from nearly every regiment. A platoon here, a platoon there. I've got it organized into three companies. One is led by a captain, one by a senior lieutenant, and one by a junior lieutenant who learned to shave last week."

"And who is leading the BTG?"

"I have no choice, General. I must do it myself. It's a helluva a lot smaller than the tank regiment I took into Grozny. I can handle it and controlling Major Agranov."

"President Voroshilov wants to know when you will complete your mission. Soon?"

"We are heading out now."

"Good. It is vital you hurry. We have indications an American battalion attacked through General Molchalin's assault and was last plotted south of the Oril."

"Say that again, General?" Kiselyov sucked in a breath.

"An American battalion may have penetrated as far south as the Oril. *May have.* There is some uncertainty as the enemy also blasted the hell out of the same location with their own artillery."

"What is generating this intelligence? Signals? GRU?" Kiselyov saw a map on the wall and walked over to it.

"Signals. Our last ping was about twenty minutes ago at Kotovka. The enemy also destroyed the Twenty-Seventh Motor Rifle's command post."

"So likely legitimate information."

"Perhaps not. It was artillery that got the command post. The survivors said nothing of ground troops. Oh, Mikhail, there is one more thing..." Dronov paused.

"Yes, General?"

"Victor was hit. I don't know how bad. The security detachment is taking him to his bunker for the surgeon."

Kiselyov sucked his breath in hard. He let it out slowly and gritted his teeth.

"I'm sorry, Mikhail. I know you were close. I will share any updates I have with you."

"Thank you. If you talk to Victor, wish him a speedy recovery."

"I will. Now Mikhail, go destroy the enemy in Pereshchepyne. The president is adamant we leave zero survivors. Zero witnesses."

"Yes, General."

Dronov hung up on Kiselyov.

"Good luck, General." Ogoltsov offered his hand to Kiselyov.

"You too." Kiselyov shook hands and briskly walked out the door.

The drive into the city took just two minutes. Kiselyov found Agranov waiting for him in front of a school on the east side of the stream. Agranov snapped a salute as Kiselyov got out of the Tigr.

"I have hot tea inside, General." Agranov held the schoolhouse door open.

Kiselyov poured a cup of tea and held it in both hands. "What is your situation?"

"The enemy fights like a ghost. They hit and run. There seems to be no pattern to their attacks. They have not crossed the stream ever. We have them contained on the north and east. I've got two infantry companies blocking the east and a third blocking at the canal. My reserve tank platoon, Tunguska platoon, and my anti-tank platoon are blocking the north, where they can use the field for standoff. The Americans can't have that many more Javelin missiles, but they have been using RPGs against us. Perhaps captured ones."

"How is your ammunition supply?"

"I'm low on rockets for the TOS. Each launcher only has a few. My howitzers have a half load still."

"Save the TOS until we identify an enemy troop concentration."

"Yes, General."

"I will take my BTG and close the western approaches. There should still be a company defending toward the west. I need to link up with its company commander. I don't even have a unit name or radio channel."

"Want us to attack?"

"No, keep up pressure with artillery when the enemy surfaces. I want to seal off the escape routes before we squeeze. Await my command."

Kiselyov downed his tea and returned to the storm. He walked down the column until he reached the first replacement T-90. He waved for the crew to come down. All three soldiers quickly got out. They could see Kiselyov's rank.

"Who here has fired the cannon before?" He looked at the crew.

None moved.

"Who was trained to fire the cannon?"

"I have, General." A private raised his hand.

Kiselyov pointed to the other private that had climbed out of the turret. "You will report to the schoolhouse and see if Major Agranov needs another tanker. This is now my tank. Now load up."

Kiselyov climbed up onto the T-90 and lowered himself into the tank commander's position with familiar ease. The privates scrambled in.

"Driver, move out. Stop at the school. I need to get something from my bag."

The tank engine growled as the driver jerkily headed down the street and stopped next to the Tigr, and Kiselyov hopped down and retrieved his bag from it. Back on top of the turret, Kiselyov pulled a faded and stained leather jacket with sheepskin lining out of the bag and changed.

"Once more into battle, my old friend," Kiselyov whispered as he popped the collar up to block the wind. He placed his uniform jacket back into the bag and hung the strap around the radio antenna.

Kiselyov turned and waved for the column to follow. "Okay, driver, move out and take a left. We are going south out and around town."

Buzivka, Ukraine – January 23, 1600 hrs

Logan shivered as he climbed into the back of Savvy's Bradley. His eyes adjusted to the blue lights. Savvy sat in the turret door. Jim and Devin hunched forward in the seats, studying the map. Lucas rested his eyes, his head flopped backward.

"Is Top Harris joining us?" Logan asked as he sat next to Devin.

Lucas opened his eyes and sat up straight. Savvy nodded. "Any minute."

Logan nodded and opened his notebook and map board.

The troop door opened and Top climbed in, chased by swirling snow. "Sir, we are ready to move again. We are abandoning one Bradley and one bridge layer. Sergeant Heydte dropped thermite grenades on both. Casualties are stable."

"Thank you. Sergeant Heydte was able to fix the tank from Battle?"

Top nodded.

"Where did you put Roston and the two sappers?"

"The body bags are on one of the distro platoon trucks."

Logan looked around the room for reaction. There were none. Only distant looks returned. Two of the dead were from the bridge layer that took a direct hit. Specialist Roston was from Squeaky Ewell's platoon, now assigned to Battle.

"We were lucky. Those had to have been BM-30 or MLRS rockets. Thank God they weren't cluster munitions," Lucas whispered.

"Sometimes luck is all that matters." Logan patted his old fires platoon leader on the shoulder. "Now, I think we've penetrated okay, but if they send reinforcements this way, they will likely come on the roads. We go cross country from here. Savvy, your troop will be in front. Cut south over the canal before turning southeast. I want your far-left flank at least two thousand meters from the Lychkove highway. Devin, your troop will follow two thousand meters behind Ace. I want the trains tucked in tight behind Battle. Lucas, I want your fires platoon with me, right behind Ace. Once we are rolling, I want radio silence. The only exception is to report enemy obstacles or units."

"Who has rear security?" Top asked.

"Battle has it."

"Yes, sir." Devin nodded.

"Sir," Savvy said, leaning forward and turning her map to face Logan, "taking a route like this, where do you think we will encounter the Russian western defensive obstacles?"

"Ivan didn't show much originality with the obstacles on the Vorskla. Figure they will be a thousand meters west of the arc we've plotted for their fighting positions. Minefields don't show up well on satellite photos. The tank ditches you see plotted on the intel overlay is from those photos though. That answer your question, Savvy?"

"But we don't know how completely the minefields wrap around the city."

"No clue." Logan paused and saw everyone looking intently back at him. "That being said, we are deep into their rear. Ivan will have them marked or fenced for their own safety. Look for red signs on trees, posts, or wire."

"And hope the snow hasn't drifted over them," Savvy quipped.

"Right." Logan jerked his head at Savvy. "What is your formation?"

"Wedge, tanks in the center. Figure we will transition to bounding overwatch about five klicks from the minefield."

"Good. Devin?"

"Kinda a triangle. I'll have the sappers in front and center. Tank platoon will be on the right flank in echelon right. Scout platoon will be on left, with a section across our rear behind the trains."

"That will work. When we get to the minefields, Savvy, identify a place to breach it, while attritting any Russians overwatching it. We will bring Devin's troop up. Devin, you will establish the SBF and breach with the sappers. We then assault Savvy's troop through. Devin, when you establish the SBF, leave one section of Bradleys to protect our rear. Once we are through the minefield, I'll contact the Rangers and we can plan the linkup with them from the far side. Understood?"

"Yes, sir." Savvy flashed a thumbs-up.

"Any questions?" Logan looked around. Everyone shook their head. "Let's roll."

The Bradley ramp dropped and they jogged through the blowing snow to their own vehicles. In five minutes, the task force was moving again.

Pereshchepyne, Ukraine – January 23, 1715 hrs

"Anything?" Sam didn't wait to shut the door before unleashing her anxiety.

Slidell frowned. "Nothing, ma'am."

Sam sighed and slid her helmet off and dropped it onto the table.

"A couple times earlier, I thought maybe I heard something, but not strong enough to make it out. Could have been the storm too," Yates offered.

"What about from Batt? They relay an update?" Sam remembered the answer as soon as the question escaped her lips. Last update was over an hour ago and the relief force was more than twenty kilometers away.

Yate shook his head.

"Next radio check with Batt, confirm the radio net and callsigns for the relief force."

"Hooah, ma'am."

Artillery rumbled in the distance.

"Ivan's renovating part of town again." Slidell grinned. "They still haven't got us figured out yet."

Sam laughed. "Ivan's like a drunk heavyweight thrashing around the bar. Dangerous, but easy to avoid."

Yates and Slidell laughed with Sam. Silence fell.

Yates shifted in his chair after a few minutes. "Gotta a question for both of you."

"Go." Sam looked him in the eyes.

"What do you think is next? After we return to base."

Sam closed her eyes and pondered before returning her gaze. "Well, at the big-picture level, once we break through to the Donets Pocket, we will probably swing south to the sea. Then the whole Russian army is trapped and only the bridge between the Crimea and Russia is left to supply it. I would think our next mission will either be related to helping cut the Crimea line of communication, or maybe seizing the nuke power plant so the Russians can't destroy it."

"Would they do that?" Yates's eyes grew big.

"Of course. I could see them nuking Kyiv the moment we cross out of the Donets Pocket into Luhansk." Slidell crossed his arms.

"Why?"

"While most of the world doesn't recognize Russia annexing Crimea, Donetsk, and Luhansk last summer, Russia sees those as part of the motherland. If we are on Russian soil and the Russian army appears to be unable to do anything about it, it's high risk of them popping a nuke."

Slidell rubbed his neck before continuing. "The war is approaching the most dangerous phase, Sergeant."

"Could we preemptively destroy the Russian nukes?"

"No, Yates, not a chance. There are too many. They have some in bunkers and some constantly moving around on big trucks and some in submarines. An attack on one would likely lead Voroshilov to launch all the remaining nukes."

"And goodbye world."

"Correct."

"Surely someone is trying to avoid that. To stop it." Yates grew pale.

Slidell leaned forward. "Better believe our president and the other national leaders are doing what they can. The best way to avoid it is to offramp the war before it gets there."

"Such a motivating talk." Yates shook his head. "Let's change the subject. What's the first thing you do when we get home?"

"Hot shower," Sam answered first.

"Do we smell that bad?" Slidell sniffed his collar. "I've smelled worse."

"The operative word was *hot*."

Yates grinned and his eyes twinkled. Sam made a face at him. *I know where your mind is.* Sam shook the thought off. *The price of being in a male-dominated world.*

"Ma'am." Slidell turned to Sam. "What time do we want to start trying to make radio contact? I know you didn't want to earlier, but it's getting late."

"Let's be patient. Ivan hasn't been very aggressive this afternoon. That will change at some point, I'm sure."

"If we have to hoof it out of this city on our own, I'd like to get going before dawn. We don't want to be here when the sun comes up."

"I know, First Sergeant, I know. Tell you what, if we haven't heard anything by twenty-two hundred, we start trying every thirty minutes. And if we don't have contact at all by midnight, we consolidate and break out on our own." Sam pointed on the map. "We exfil west and north."

"Fair 'nuff."

Zavorsklo, Ukraine – January 23, 1800 hrs

Michael's teeth chattered, despite being wrapped in his sleeping bag. *Why did we choose the only house in town without a fireplace for my command post?* Michael listened to the storm rage outside. In the next room, Burton and Kim chatted, obviously unaware Michael was trying to sleep.

"I feel bad for Bravo and Charlie Companies," Burton commented.

"They at least have their backs to the wind, but those woods have to be miserable," Kim agreed.

"Good positions though."

Michael thought about the battalion's battle position, holding the shoulders of the great salient. Large clearings offered beautiful fields of fire and the road south out of Zavorsklo was easy to mass weapons on. The anti-tank company to his left flank covered the wide open Tahamlyk River valley. *River. Ha. What a joke. Just like everything else in this miserable frozen wasteland.*

The radio in the next room beeped. "X-ray, Three-Seven, we have unarmed men coming up the road."

"Roger. Enemy, or civilian?" Burton answered the radio.

"Pretty sure enemy. No weapons—okay, a bunch just put their hands up. I think they are surrendering."

"Follow the SOP and keep us posted."

The roar of the wind covered the silence. Michael listened from his room. Time passed slowly, too slowly for Michael.

"X-ray, Three-Seven! Chalk up eight Russian EPWs. They told us they were sent forward to see if we would shoot. The rest of their comrades are planning on following suite in a few if there were no shots."

"Good news. Get a count of how many we are expecting and keep your guard up."

"Roger, we are doing that. Three-Two is sending a team with them to the CCP."

"Roger. Out." Burton loudly dropped the radio hand mic on the table. "Well, how about that?"

"Gotta be a good sign. First Russians we've seen since the minefield and they are surrendering."

"Maybe, just maybe..." Burton laughed.

"X-ray, Three-Seven, here they come. Looks like about fifty so far."

"Roger."

A chair scraped and Kim announced, "I'm heading that way. I'll have to grab another squad to guard them."

Michael unzipped his sleeping bag. *Fifty!* He quickly pulled his boots out and jammed his feet in. By the time he was fully presentable, the official count was seventy-one Russians. Michael darted into the other room, causing Burton to startle as he was writing in the notebook.

Michael grabbed the battalion radio. "Rock X-ray, Attack Six, I just captured seventy-one Russians. I need to send my EPWs back to you. Can you have the MPs come get my prisoners?"

"Roger. We will relay to Bayonet Main the request for the MPs."

"Attack Six, out." Michael grinned. *Ivan is throwing in the towel! I should get a picture in front of them for my future desk.* Michael looked down at Burton just in time to catch a head jiggle and chest puff. Burton looked up, caught Michael's look, and deflated. Michael decided he could ignore it.

"I'm gonna lay eyes on the EPWs. First Lieutenant Burton, you have the command post. I'll be at the CCP. What is the security situation at the CCP?"

"We didn't patrol the immediate area much since the whole battalion moved through those woods behind it. I'd be shocked if there are any Ivans lingering."

"Okay." Michael went back to his room. "Better throw on a few more layers for the trek up the street." He hurriedly added his waffle sweater and coat. He tucked his neck gaiter to his goggles and left the warmth of the building smiling.

Outside, the wind screamed straight down the street. The pelting snow hammered his goggles and took his breath away. Drifts lined both sides of the street. A few houses later, Michael stopped. "Where's the path to the collection point?" The chemlite marking the path beginning was nowhere in sight, even with the aid of night vision goggles. *Well, the*

Russians are giving up. They won't ambush me if I just follow the street. Michael leaned into the storm and pushed into the wind. The crossroads beckoned. *A minute more before I turn out of the wind.* The open field beyond was covered in deep snow. Drifts fingered across the road from the few trees along.

Boom! The flash of light below preceded the feeling of flight.

The voices yelling seemed so far away and distorted. "Medic!"

Michael lifted his head off the ground. The snow around him was blackened and a red stain spread from his legs. *Landmine.* "Medic." His voice cracked.

"Sir, put your tourniquet on!" a voice called from a building. "I've sent for the metal detector and medics."

Michael groaned and tried to sit up. *I don't want to know.* Waves of pain assaulted his brain. "Send the medics now! Don't wait for the...the..." Michael dropped his head back to the ground. Bile rose in his throat. He turned his head and gagged.

"Hang in there, sir!" a voice screamed from downwind.

Michael squirmed enough to see a medic carefully following his steps up the street. "Hurry!"

"Put your tourniquet on your left leg! Now, sir, now!"

Michael tried to sit up, and gave up as soon as a new wave of pain flared. Michael raised his hand a few inches off the ground and let it drop. "Aaaaahhhhhhh."

The medic reached Michael and dropped to his knees and roughly ripped Michael's pants open. Michael closed his eyes and grit his teeth.

A second voice interrupted Michael's descent into the darkness. "Let's get him stabilized while they check for other mines."

The darkness rose swiftly and swallowed Michael. He wouldn't be aware of his surroundings for another seventy-five hours.

Lychkove, Ukraine – January 23, 2000 hrs

"Why are we going so slow?" Brown asked. The tank sat idling under the cluster of poplar trees waving in the wind. They had been stationary nearly fifteen minutes.

"We are getting close to the minefield. We can't afford to stumble into it. Wire can be hard to detect until you are right up on it. In this wind, the signs might be horizontal and also hard to spot." Logan sighed. "Believe me, I'm ready to move too."

Logan used his commander's thermal viewer to watch a platoon of tanks slowly bound forward to the next tree line. He recognized the familiar extra container bolted onto a bustle rack, marking Running Bear's tank. *Second Platoon. God, I miss commanding Lightning Troop.* Logan rubbed the back of his neck as he watched.

Suddenly, Running Bear's tank pivoted right and the cannon swung over and lowered. The flash of the machine gun firing was hidden by the storm, but the tracers digging into the snow near the tank showed.

Another Abrams fired its cannon at a target far beyond Logan's vision. A second Abrams fired.

"Bolt Six, Ace Seven, contact troops, PCs east." The radio crackled for the first time since they left Buzivka.

"Roger, engage and develop the enemy positions." Logan replied, "Driver, mo—disregard."

"Sir?" Brown asked.

"I almost forgot to be patient."

Litsky grinned. "Don't want another ass chewing from Remington Six?"

"Right?" Logan smiled a moment. "Okay, focus."

"Bolt Six, Ace Seven, still seven-slant-seven, engaged and destroyed a missile team point blank and a BTR. Identified the minefield. Break for grid."

Logan used Top's pause to prepare to copy the grid. Top added grids for the enemy missile team and BTR. Logan noticed the BTR aligned with the exact position intel provided ahead of time. *Good.*

"Ace, slide a platoon north and engage any targets you find. Prepare to assault through. Once Battle begins their SBF, pull that platoon back to your assault position. Stay on the fringe of detection range. Battle, breacher up. Everyone, expect incoming artillery in about five minutes."

Logan found himself pumping his body back and forth in excitement. *Bread and butter of the armored corps.* "Go time." Logan's whisper caused Sherr to pump a fist and grin.

The storm still raged. Out of the hatch, Logan could barely see north east, and even across the wind, visibility was less than a hundred meters. Looking down wind, he could see almost three hundred meters.

"Well, the storm will help with our obscuration efforts." Logan sat back down out of the storm and pulled his hatch down.

The flurry of activity on the radio seemed loud after hours of silence. Ace called in contact reports of BTRs and a tank they engaged at long range. Battle reported establishing their support by fire position and Lucas aired his mortars firing to suppress and obscure the breach site.

"Okay, Brown, take us up next to the sappers. I'll observe the breach from there."

Brown goosed the tank forward and bounded across the field to the next tree line, pulling up next to the sappers' Bradley section. Logan could finally see across the field toward the enemy positions. Mortars exploding on a distant tree line guided his study of the enemy.

"Looks like that near line of trees was intentionally thinned. Must be the enemy kill sack," Litsky remarked as he scanned for targets.

"Yeah, I think I can see the minefield along the far edge of those trees." Logan used his thermal viewer.

"Bolt Six, Battle Six, kickoff!" Devin's radio call caused Logan to scan over until he saw the sapper's armored breach vehicle, an Abrams without a cannon. Instead, the ABV had a mine plow on front and carried two mine-clearing line charges where the ammo compartment would be. The ABV charged forward out into the field, slowing to nearly a stop when it reached the thinned trees. The ABV dropped its mine plow and then pushed forward slowly as one of the MCLIC launchers raised up. Logan held his breath as the ABV stopped and immediately the rocket flew up and away at a steep angle. In his thermals, Logan could see the explosive line charge trailing out behind it. The rocket ran out of fuel and the line fell to the ground like a snake.

BOOM! The flash of light and shockwave momentarily paused the blizzard, while simultaneously sucking snow and dirt into the air and hiding the ABV.

The sapper's other ABV charged forward, the Bradleys following.

"Bolt Six, Battle Six, first down!"

"Roger. Ace, prepare to assault!" Logan looked over his shoulder and saw Savvy's Abrams and Bradleys massing behind him.

"Go! Go! Go!" Logan yelled, watching the first ABV emerge from the dust and snow, pushing forward.

A flash of light and wobbling flare speeding across the field from the far trees caught Logan's attention.

"Gunner, MPAT, missile team!" Logan pressed the designate button, slinging the turret to align Litsky's sights with his thermal viewer.

"Cannot identify!" Litsky missed the flash and nothing stood out as a target.

"Hit the tree in the center of your reticle!"

"Identified!"

Sherr slapped the cannon arming lever. "Up!"

"Fire!" Logan snapped.

"On the way!" Litsky fired and the breach snapped. Logan watched their cannon round zip across the field and explode on the tree. The tree toppled over.

"Cease fire!" Logan called, watching 25mm rounds from Battle's Bradleys ripple across the same spot. Each flash was equivalent to a hand grenade exploding.

"Did the missile hit?" Litsky asked.

"Don't know."

Almost as if in sync, the radio crackled, "Bolt Six, they got the ABV. The second is taking over."

"Roger. Hammer that far tree line. Assume Ivan's got more missiles."

Logan swore as Devin acknowledged the order.

"Gotta be a Spriggan," Litsky commented.

"Likely." The AT-14 Spriggan, known as a 9M113 Kornet by the Russians, was a potent anti-tank missile. "At least the storm will limit how many of them can engage. They gotta be using them to cover the huge arc. Remember they only have a company covering nearly twenty klicks of minefield."

Logan turned his attention back to the breach. The first ABV burned fiercely. The second ABV stopped some twenty meters behind it and fired a MCLIC off to the right of the other ABV. As soon as the charge exploded, the ABV rapidly pushed forward into the dust and snow."

"Bolt Six, Battle Six, second down."

Logan watched as sappers spilled out of the back of the Bradleys and quickly set up flags to mark the breach lane. They quickly loaded back up and the Bradleys moved into the lane to the burning ABV. More flags set up and one sapper tried to approach the burning ABV but was driven back by the flames. Logan shook his head. Two young soldiers were gone and they wouldn't be able to recover the bodies to bring back with them.

"Bolt Six, Battle Six, third down." Devin's call told Logan what he couldn't see. The second ABV safely exited the far side of the minefield. The sappers' Bradleys quickly moved through the lane to the far side. The snow and dust cleared enough that Logan could see the sappers setting flags up and the Bradleys taking positions to either side.

"Bolt Six, Battle Six, touchdown!" Pride swelled in Devin's voice.

"Great work. Ace, assault, assault, assault! On the objective, orient fires north and east!" Logan called and twisted in his seat. Behind him, Savvy's troopers already crowded forward. A moment later, the Abrams surged forward in a column, racing for the breach. In just a minute, the lead Abrams reached the first set of flags.

"Battle, Bolt Six, lift fire! Once Ace is through the lane, assault and orient east and south. Certain One, cease fire and displace!" Logan's face flushed with blood surging in his veins. "Go!"

Chapter 16

Pereshchepyne, Ukraine – January 23, 2045 hrs

The massive explosion carried even upwind to the edge of Pereshchepyne. Kiselyov could barely make out the cannon cracks and mortars over the storm.

"What was that?" the driver asked.

"Either a massive bomb, unlikely, or a mine-clearing charge, more likely," Kiselyov remarked. The Russians had their own versions of MCLICs and he had used them in Chechnya.

"The Americans are here?"

"Probably." Kiselyov looked at the notes he had written on the turret wall. "Shit. I don't have the radio channel for the company guarding the minefields."

Kiselyov tapped his pen on the wall while he thought. *I dropped off Senior Lieutenant Goryachev's conscript company on the south side and Captain Konnov's troops block the west edge of the city. That leaves me Lieutenant Zhugan's half company. Not enough to counterattack with. Or is it? No.*

Kiselyov keyed up his radio. "Agranov, give me Toropov's company of tanks from the north side of town. Have them stay wide to avoid enemy missiles from the city. They will meet me at the pig farm."

"Yes, General."

"Have your howitzers cease firing into the city and prepare to take a fire mission from me. I am going to find the enemy west of us and destroy them with a counterattack. I want Babushkin and Toropov to switch to my BTG's radio channel."

"Right away."

Kiselyov changed channels to his own BTG's. "Zhugan, follow me to the pig farm. Konnov, send me your tank platoon."

"Zhugan moving." The lieutenant sounded even younger than he looked to Kiselyov.

"Konnov moving."

Kiselyov opened his hatch and looked across the wind in time to see Zhugan's tanks back away from the houses and then turn to follow him. *Twelve tanks and a few extra infantry vehicles. It will do.* He looked at his map again. A finger of woods pointed southwest from the corner of town. *Hmm...* "Zhugan! I want your tanks to follow me. Take your infantry vehicles and follow the woods southwest until you get to Svichanivka. Be careful and report what you find while I mass our tanks."

"Zhugan understands."

"Driver, hurry to the pig farm. When we get there, I will have you point our tank south. Make sure you aren't pointed at a building."

"Kiselyov, this is Toropov on your radio." A new voice joined the conversation.

"Toropov, we are going to attack south along the minefields as soon as you are here. Everyone will guide off my tank in the center on line. Hurry."

"Yes, sir. I will have the Tunguskas and the anti-tank platoon follow behind us."

"Good."

Kiselyov wiped the snow from his vision blocks and sat back down out of the wind. His driver cut across a field to the highway and turned west. *At least this kid can read a map and think some.* Ahead, the pig barns on the left side of the highway closed into view. The driver slowed and turned. The tracks slipped and the tank skid across the icy blacktop until smashing into a drift on the edge. The driver swore and gunned the engine to churn through the drift.

"Stop to the left of this barn. We need to stay close enough to the road the others can find us." Kiselyov turned and saw Zhugan's T-90 slowing to make the turn. He stood and waved his arms out, directing them to come alongside. They formed up on his left. The next platoon of T-90s came on the right. Each tank was just twenty meters away from its neighbors. In the dark, they were mere shadows.

"Kiselyov, Zhugan here. I lost a BTR. Enemy tanks facing east at Svichanivka. Awaiting your command."

"Wait for my attack, then attack as the enemy turns to face my tanks. Keep low in that valley."

"Zhugan understands."

Kiselyov looked at his watch. There was still time to complete the mission before midnight. He looked up just in time to see Toropov lead his tanks into view. Kiselyov waited until the sounds of engines revving and tracks squeaking ended.

Kiselyov keyed up his radio. "Forward."

Just two thousand meters southwest, hidden by the single-street village of Malokozyrschchyna, Running Bear scanned the field east of his tank. After racing through the breach lane, Savvy had Running Bear's platoon fan out to the northeast, while the scouts of 3rd Platoon came up on the left to watch the north. 1st Platoon came alongside on the right.

"Sergeant, can we scrape the ice off my sights again?" Gomez asked from the gunner's position.

"Hofi, hop to it. Be quick." Running Bear snapped his fingers at his loader.

Hofi disconnected his helmet and scampered up, scraper already in hand. Quickly, Hofi chiseled the ice off the gunner's sights and turned his attention to the commander's thermal viewer. He looked at Running Bear and pointed at the front slope. Running Bear nodded and Hofi slid to the front slope and cleaned Blucher's vision blocks. In just a minute, Hofi was plugged back in, shivering and patting the snow off his uniform.

"Brrr."

"Thank you, jerk," Blucher called.

Hofi grinned. "You're welcome, ass hat."

Running Bear shook his head.

"What's the plan now?" Hofi asked, looking at Running Bear.

"Well, Lieutenant Kraemer thinks there's another BTR platoon, possibly the enemy's reserves, between us and the city. Once the task force is all on this side of the minefield, we will attack to edge of the city and make contact with the Rangers."

"Gotcha."

The crack of a cannon to the north stopped the conversation. Running Bear spun his thermal viewer to face the threat and Gomez scanned faster.

"Got it!" Kiselyov's gunner yelled in delight as the cannon reloaded. In the thermal viewer, flames licked up the front of a Bradley.

"Tank!" Kiselyov grabbed the turret controls and aligned the sights on an Abrams facing left. He pulled the trigger. Sparks showered into the wind from the back of the Abrams.

The tank slid sideways into a ditch. The driver tried to correct and ended up driving down the deep slope. A clump of trees blocked Kiselyov's view of the battle. A tank on his right exploded in a thunderclap.

"We're gonna die!" the gunner screamed as a T-90 in front of them exploded and the turret fell in their path. Kiselyov's tank slammed to a stop as it collided with the turret.

"Shut up! My gun! Driver, get to the end of this ditch and quickly turn south again! We will use the railroad tracks to protect us some!"

The driver said nothing but backed away from the fallen turret and climbed the slope around it. He accelerated to the ramp out of the ditch.

"Easy. Driver. Don't crash." Kiselyov spun the turret to face south.

The tank slowed and then came around the corner. The driver accelerated. An Abrams loomed into view, firing at a different T-90. Kiselyov fired. The cannon round exploded on the front of the Abrams turret.

"Driver, stop! Back up!" Kiselyov yelled. The cannon jerked down as the tank slid to a stop. The driver ground the gears and the tank lurched backward, dropping down into the ditch again. Kiselyov counted the raging infernos marking destroyed T-90s, counting all but three of his tanks. "It's duel time. Driver, you must do exactly as I say, or we die."

"Yes, General."

The gunner said nothing but stared with bug eyes and trembling lips.

"Driver, we are going to go back west in this ditch. From there we go back into the town. We can use the houses to hide our attacks. Go."

"Switch to manual!" Running Bear yelled, hitting the over pressurization system to clear the smoke from the turret. The smell of hot hydraulic oil stung his nose. At his knees, Gomez shifted his body to the manual wheels to turn the turret.

"Driver, back up!" Running Bear barked. "Okay, forward and come up on the left of Meig's tank! Hofi, you good?"

"Roger!" Hofi wiped hot oil from his face. "That was close!"

"No shit!" Blucher yelled.

"Shut up! Focus!"

"Tank! Driver, stop. Come right a touch!"

Blucher stopped and held the right to pivot.

"Driver, stop!"

"Identified!" Gomez yelled as the T-80 entered his sights.

"Up!" Hofi plastered himself against the wall.

"Fire!"

"Hang on... On the way!" Gomez fired and the T-80 erupted.

"Target! Driver, move up again to the left!" Running Bear yelled. He spun his thermal viewer to look for the rest of the Bradleys. Only the three destroyed ones remained forward near the trees. He spun the viewer back north. *Thank God for electric drive on this puppy!* "Where did you go? You little rat."

"One-Four, we are degraded but fighting. Still got more tanks up this way," Running Bear called on the platoon radio net.

"Roger. We got enemy to the east also. Can you hold?" Gene's voice on the radio sounded oddly calm.

"Yes." Running Bear cut himself off, "Driver stop. Let's use Meigs tank as a shield."

Hofi stared at Running Bear a moment before finishing loading the cannon.

"Hey, I see three guys survived. They are under their tank," Blucher called out.

"Okay. We gotta fight how we gotta fight." Running Bear scanned back and forth quickly with his thermal viewer. Movement caught his eye. A T-80 was slinking behind the railroad tracks.

"Gunner, sabot, choke tank! Driver, come forward and right."

"Roger. I see it in my thermal viewer!" Blucher yelled, goosing the tank forward.

"Steady, on! Got it Gomez?"

"Roger!"

"Up!"

"Fire!"

"On the way!" Gomez fired and the sabot penetrator zipped into the base of the T-80's cannon. The cannon drooped.

"Re-engage!"

Hofi scrambled even faster to reload the cannon. The second shot exploded the T-80.

"Driver, back up. Hold your right! Straight!"

The tank raced backward.

"Driver stop! Go hard right, then fast to the corner of the field!"

A cannon crack on the right reminded Running Bear there was enemy to the east.

"Crap. Blucher, hold up. We gotta stay on the flank. Back it up and we will go a ways down the tree line."

The flash of a cannon firing in the north preceded an explosion on the machine gun mount.

"Driver, stop!"

"Tank!" Gomez yelled, spinning the traverse wheel.

"Up!"

"Stand by... Fire!"

The tank settled and Gomez made a slight adjustment to his aim.

"On the way!"

The shot skipped off the frozen field and up into the T-90. Flames licked out of an open hatch.

"Driver, back up and hold the right. Go! Go! Go!" Running Bear let the tank run south in the open field a few hundred meters before stopping it. "Now forward and to the left, go another two hundred meters left of that burning Bradley."

Kiselyov's tank raced between houses in the ditch before climbing out and to the west.

"Driver, go to the end of the houses and slowly approach so I can check the far flank." Kiselyov was unaware he was in a race for position. An exploding tank southeast of them lit up the snow. *I'm the last one fighting.*

"Okay, careful." Kiselyov carefully scanned the south and east until he saw a burning Bradley. "Back up. I want to find a spot where the houses will hide our outline."

Kiselyov waited as the driver backed away from the corner.

"How-how-how about that gap to the left?" the driver stammered.

"Yes. Stop between the houses. Slowly, driver, slowly."

Kiselyov carefully scanned, noting the Abrams he hit in the side. Next was a Bradley. It did not seem to be dead, nor obviously alive.

"Driver, stop." Kiselyov waited for the tank to stop and fired. His shot struck the Bradley at the base of the turret. Sparks flew. "Nobody survives that."

The autoloader shoved a new anti-tank round into the breach. Kiselyov patiently waited for it to finish. "Okay, driver, slowly forward."

The burning Bradley in the west pulled into view. *Yes! Time to assault forward!* "Driver, give it everything. Go south to those trees!" The fires of the burning tanks lit up the world enough to allow the driver to clearly see beyond the railroad tracks.

"Tank! Blucher, come right! It's moving fast!"

"Moving!" Blucher pivoted the tank right. Frozen clumps of dirt popped in the tracks.

"Up!"

"Steady, Blucher, I got him!" Gomez yelled. "On the way!"

Gomez fired. The sabot's tracer zipped in front of the T-90 and disappeared into a house.

"Re-engage!"

The T-90 veered right and the cannon spun rapidly toward them. The flash of the T-90's cannon barely beat the crack of the enemy round passing under the tank. The T-90 now charged straight at them, the cannon jumping up as the autoloader fed it again.

"Up!" Hofi won the race.

"Fire!"

"On the way!"

Gomez's second shot struck the T-90 in the driver's hatch and the turret launched into the air as the tank exploded.

"Target! Good shot. Jeez." Running Bear patted Gomez on the shoulder. "Okay, let's see what else comes out of that town."

Running Bear let the thermal viewer linger on the burning T-90, watching a coat flutter down in the wind before catching on a tree branch. *Did that blow off the poor Ivan wearing it?*

"Four, One, sitrep?" Gene called on the radio.

"One, Four, negative contact at this time. Destroyed one more T-90. I count a total of twelve destroyed tanks north of us."

"Roger. We've killed five PCs east of us also. Six wants us to push up to the last tree line before the city. We are going to swing north to check your work on those tanks as we bound forward. First Platoon is covering."

"Roger." Running Bear popped out of the hatch to survey the damage to the tank. His sponson box was shattered and ripped apart. The fifty-caliber mount was pocked and inoperable. He could only imagine how the rest of the tank would look if he climbed out.

"Hofi, get up here and man your machine gun. We are gonna drive through the Russian tanks."

"Roger, Sergeant."

"I see LT and Sergeant Black's tanks," Blucher called out.

"See 'em. Okay, move out and come up on their left."

The tank slowly moved forward, cutting through snowdrifts as it closed in on the clump of trees. Running Bear watched the other Abrams cut to the right.

"Stay left of the trees." Running Bear leaned to the right, looking past the damaged machine gun. A coat hanging in the tree caught his attention and he remembered how it got there. "Hey, come right some more. I want to grab that coat."

Blucher eased over and slowed as he came under the coat. Running Bear reached up and yanked the coat out of the trees and dropped it down into the turret.

"Dude, I don't see any live bait at all." Hofi looked back and forth with his night vision goggles. Not a body stirred in the field.

"Okay, Blucher, catch up with the LT and hang on his left." Running Bear ducked down into the turret. He looked at the coat, noticing the rank. *Holy shit. We killed a two-star general.*

Running Bear switched to his company radio. "Seven, Two-Four, I just collected a coat from a Russian tank. Rank is a Russian lieutenant general. Two stars in a line like their generals."

"Roger. Hang on to it. When we get a chance, I'll have Three-Four read the name."

Chapter 17

Pereshchepyne, Ukraine – January 23, 2130 hrs

The small kitchen buzzed with excitement; the Rangers gathered around the radio on the table. Sam had a map out and was marking locations called out over the Task Force Thunderbolt radio. Hope was so tangible.

"What do you think, ma'am, things calmed down enough for us to jump onto the net?" Slidell nodded toward the radio.

Sam nodded. "I'll give it a try now." Sam picked up the radio hand mic and pressed the transmit button. "Bolt X-ray, Savage Five, radio check. Over." Sam released it and waited.

"Last station, Bolt X-ray, say again." The voice sounded hesitant.

"Bolt X-ray, Savage Five, radio check, over."

"Savage Five, Bolt X-ray, loud and clear. Stand by. Out."

Sam looked up at Slidell. He smiled but canted his head. "At least we can talk."

The radio beeped. "Savage Five, Bolt Six, we are closing in on you. Need your exact situation. Over."

"That voice sounds so familiar," Sam whispered, looking at the map.

"Think they want eight-digit grids of every squad? That will take forever to transmit," Yates asked, furiously writing grids down for every blue mark on the map.

"No, armored forces don't work that way. They might prove me wrong on this one. Let me try something," Sam answered before keying up the radio again. "Bolt Six, Savage Five, we are scattered. All positions are east of the six-niner-point-seven easting. I say again, east. Also, we are inside of the outermost streets."

"Roger. We are closing in on you, currently at the six-six easting. What is your enemy situation? We just penetrated the minefields and destroyed part of a BTG."

"Bolt Six, Ivan has a MIC south of the outskirts, a thousand meters out. At least one MIC is defending the east side along the stream cutting north-south. There was another tank or MIC north of town, but we can't see very well that direction now. Break." Sam took a breath and composed her thoughts. "Continuing, they have been actively targeting us with tube artillery the last few hours but they have not shown any forward patrolling. Over."

"Acknowledged. Any obstacles within the town?"

"The east half has a lot of rubble. No known minefields. The swamp north of us has broken ice from artillery."

"Roger. Savage Five, do you have a recommended linkup point and route?"

Sam looked at Slidell then back at the map and drew her finger along the railroad spur that cut into the middle of the western end of town. Slidell nodded back.

"Bolt Six, prepare to copy grids." Sam smiled and quickly wrote down the grids describing the route. After a pause, Sam radioed them.

"Savage Five, Bolt Six, route works for us. Fire control status for us will be weapons tight against troops and weapons free against vehicles. You shall be weapons hold for vehicle targets. Once my vehicles stop at the linkup point, have someone give us a close recognition signal before coming out to the vehicle."

"Wilco. Close signal will be three IR chemlites tossed in the street and an IR lasso."

"If we make enemy contact with vehicles, we will engage. You keep hunkered down while we engage. If the enemy makes contact using troops, you will control the fight. We can assist at your command. Once we are completely linked up, I will take control of the fight. Acknowledge."

Sam again looked around the room, waiting for thumbs-up from her leadership team. "Bolt Six, Savage Five, acknowledged. We are awaiting your move. Over."

"Ace Six, Bolt Six, did you copy all?"

"Roger."

"Execute. Out."

The radio fell silent and Sam grinned up at Slidell. "This is happening."

"We're gonna make it." Slidell grinned back. "Okay, let's get this plan out to the platoons."

"Yes. I want you to take care of that. I'm heading to the linkup point. Yates, relay to Batt we made radio linkup with Bolt."

"Hooah, ma'am."

Sam grabbed her rifle and headed for the door. At the door, she pulled her night vision goggles down into place and stepped out into the storm. The wind sucked the warmth away rapidly. Sam caught her breath and then jogged west through the snowy backyards. Ten houses down, she paused in the shadows and softly called, "Bad."

"Avalanche," a voice countered from a window.

"Friendly coming in."

"Come in."

Sam walked to the door, nodding to the window as she passed. Inside, she found Conner and one of his squads. "Lieutenant Davis, have your reserve squad come to the linkup point with us. We gotta be quick. Weapons and ammo."

Conner yelled, "Go time!"

A chorus of voices in the house responded and the squad materialized in the room. Conner pointed to the door and the squad quickly moved out. Conner stopped and turned to Sam. "How are we getting our rucks?"

"Once we linkup, we can deal with the logistics. Linkup is dangerous enough. One thing at a time." Sam pushed Conner forward.

The storm howled through the trees and electrical wires. Sam now had enough adrenaline to shrug off the chill. She followed the squad as they moved through the back yards. At the end of the block, they turned north. The trees and houses sheltered the Rangers enough to hear the swish of clothing rubbing and the click of weapons on plastic from time to time. Every few minutes, Sam had to rub the snow and ice off her night vision goggles.

"This house." Conner's whisper carried on the wind to Sam. Sam watched with pride as the Rangers smoothly stacked on the door. A relay of arm squeezes moved up the stack and they flowed into the building. Sam followed them in, checking the view from the windows. The house overlooked a sparsely treed drainage between the industrial section and the neighborhood. The linkup location was secure.

"What is taking them so long?" Connor whispered to Sam.

"Ivan is out there also. An ambush right now would wreck the linkup."

"They have tanks."

"And many things can kill a tank. We lost every single tank at Fiery Cross. Patience, Conner."

"Hooah."

A cannon cracked in the distance, followed by an explosion to the north. The Rangers collectively flinched and those at windows facing north shifted around the room to see into the storm.

"What was that?" Conner leaned close to Sam. She shrugged and held a hand up. *Wait.*

Sam's earpiece finally crackled. "Bolt X-ray, Ace Seven, engaged and destroyed a T-90 west of town." She pulled out her map and plotted the location when the grid followed on the radio. Sam looked at Conner. "Our tanks killed a Russian vehicle. Gonna be slow going. Patience."

Conner nodded. More cannon cracks and explosions punctuated the night. The T-90 was not alone, but the other Russians seemed to try to hide from the slowly advancing Task Force Thunderbolt.

Time slowly passed. The endless snow limited vision and the howling wind negated the Rangers' ability to hear the advancing Abrams and Bradleys. Only imagination could fill the void. Sam looked at her watch. 2237 hours. *This is taking way longer than I expected.*

The Abrams materialized out of the storm, creeping down the street. The turret swung back and forth.

"Quick, the chemlites!" Sam shouted.

Conner already had the chemlites unwrapped and staying warm inside his coat sleeve. He ripped his glove off and tugged them out, snapping them. The soft light lit up the room before Conner opened the door and threw them in the street. "The wind is too strong!"

Sam looked and saw the chemlites barely halfway to the garden gate. She rushed out into the yard and picked up the chemlites, underhand throwing them into the street. This time, they made it. Sam looked up and saw the Abram's fifty-caliber machine gun swing toward her. *They see me!* Sam let go of her rifle and raised her hands up to slowly wave. The Abrams stopped moving.

"What about the IR lasso?" Conner called from the door.

"You do it! I'm not moving my weapon with a machine gun pointing at my face!" Sam yelled over the wind.

Inside the house, out of sight of the tank, Conner activated his rifle's infrared aiming laser and drew circles on the fence across the street.

Sam slowly grabbed her radio. "Bolt Six, Savage Five, in visual contact with one of your Abrams. Confirm linkup."

"Stand by."

Sam's heart raced, waiting impatiently. Finally, she watched the tank's machine gun swing away and then go up and down as if nodding. Sam's shoulders slumped in relief.

"Savage Five, Bolt Six, your team may approach the tank."

"Wilco." Sam grinned and slowly walked into the street.

A second tank appeared and moved past her, stopping at the intersection. A third tank followed, though the turret did not move like the others.

The stopped tank commander stood up in the hatch and waved for Sam to come up. Sam grabbed the handles and hoisted herself onto the front slope. She nearly slipped on the ice. Gingerly, she crossed to the turret and climbed up.

"Hi. We sure are glad to see you," Sam yelled over the wind.

"Glad we made it. I'm Lieutenant Sinclair. Looking for Savage Five so we can complete linkup of forces."

Sam shook Gene's hand. "I'm Savage Five. Captain Gentry."

"Roger, ma'am." Gene dropped down into the turret and Sam heard him talking on the radio. He popped up a moment later. "My commander will be here in a sec. She'll stop her Bradley here and coordinate with you. I gotta move with my platoon up some more."

"Thank you, Lieutenant." Sam smiled and slid back down the front of the tank. Once on the ground, Sam leaned on the yard gate. The Abrams moved up and disappeared into the storm. The familiar whine of the jet turbine engine made Sam smile even bigger.

Breakthrough at Kharkiv

(BBC) Poltava, January 23 - BREAKING NEWS. NATO forces took the strategic city of Kharkiv and broke through to the Donets Pocket. For the first time since July, supply trucks brought food and ammunition to the 20,000 Ukrainian soldiers fighting in the pocket. In a decisive moment, Western forces tightened the noose on the bulk of the Russian army in Ukraine. Only a 300-kilometer-wide corridor connects the southern front Russian soldiers with their homeland.

NATO forces have advanced 200 kilometers in just three days to reach the Donets Pocket. The Russian minefields and anti-tank ditches along the frontlines did little to slow our armoured forces. Soldiers from the 20th Armoured Brigade cheered from the hatches of their Challenger main battle tanks as they liberated the city of Berestyn, waving to our reporters. Morale amongst the soldiers is high. A tank driver pointed out this pace would see them at the Sea of Azov in just a week's time.

Tanks and armoured vehicles bearing the markings of the British 1st Armoured Division crossed into Ukraine yesterday on trains heading east. In Hamburg, more American armor unloaded and marshalled onto eastbound trains. These two divisions will increase NATO forces in Ukraine by more than 15 percent. The fresh troops will allow the offensive to retain momentum.

Ukrainian soldiers from the Donets Pocket celebrated as fresh troops cleared Russian forces out of their positions along the Donets River bluffs. One Ukrainian commander took the time to talk with our reporter. "The enemy never understood the Donets Pocket," Major Lelechko explained over his map. "Our glorious soldiers trapped six Russian airborne divisions into holding us here. We disrupted the enemy's ability to move deeper into Ukraine last summer and they fell prey to our mobile defenses and drones."

Russian forces seem powerless to stop the NATO and Ukrainian combined might. Army spokesperson Colonel Bryne spoke to the press earlier. "The Russian 1st Guards Tank Army no longer exists. In three days, it has lost over six hundred tanks and armored vehicles. This was the Russians' most powerful army, though their performance was unimpressive." The Ukrainian daily update put the Russian losses at over 30,000 soldiers killed, wounded, or captured since the offensive began.

Despite the sweeping battlefield successes, the war remains a grave threat. Royal United Services Institute analyst James Simons explained that with the destruction of the Russian army, Voroshilov will look to other military capabilities to stop NATO and Ukrainian advances. The Russian navy, neutralized and unable to leave port, offers nothing. The Russian air force has not been able to achieve air superiority over the battlefield. Strategic raids have done little to the Ukrainian or NATO logistics, morale, or industry. The only source of untapped Russian military might is the Russian nuclear arsenal. While the war has been in stalemate and far from Russian soil, the spectre of nuclear weapons has been of little worry. The war carrying to the very border increases the risk.

The Foreign Office expressed hope Russia would recognize the need for peace without turning to nuclear war. Sources spoke of urgent negotiations, brokered by the Chinese. The Chinese remain Voroshilov's most important ally and offer the best hope for bringing Voroshilov to the bargaining table. Diplomats continue efforts to reach a peace in snowy Davos.

Chapter 18

Moscow, Russia – January 23, 2300 hrs

"President Voroshilov, it is time for us to be frank." Golubev broke the silence that accompanied the members of the security council taking their seats around the table.

"Yes. Minister Popov, begin your update." Voroshilov's voice was hoarse and his eyes deeply sunken.

The council exchanged nervous side glances, each trying to remember the last time Voroshilov used their titles. The late-night meeting was bad enough without ominous title use.

Popov cleared his throat. "Yes, President. The counterattack has failed. The Sixth Combined Arms Army bravely fought into the storm and suffered severe losses. I fear it will not be able to defend the line, much less mount another attack."

"Worthless lazy whores!" Voroshilov exploded. His headache ratcheted up several levels of pain. He blinked his eyes to purge the tears welling. "I want their commander arrested. I want his head. I want his family arrested!"

"Sir, the commander was wounded leading from the front. The attack faltered *after* he was incapacitated."

Voroshilov snorted. "A true hero. Fine, let him be... But I want blood!"

"President—" Golovko interjected, Voroshilov cutting him off.

"General, do not fail me. You are on the brink of arrest yourself. I will have those responsible pay the price. This all is the fault..." Voroshilov held his hand out to silence any attempt to interrupt his faltering train of thought. "This is the fault of the commander of the First Guards Tank

Army. Arrest him! He allowed the nazis to penetrate our lines in the first place!" Voroshilov snapped his fingers at Zusko.

Everyone shuddered at the unleashing of the FSB. Where would the arrests end?

"President Voroshilov," Golovko softly interrupted, "the commander of the Guards Tank Army, Lieutenant General Kiselyov, went missing near Pereshchepyne and is presumed dead. He was personally leading the attack on the enemy raiders at the GRU's prison camp. General Dronov's last communication with Kiselyov was Kiselyov beginning his attack. He reported an enemy mechanized battalion had reached the city."

"So Dronov is overseeing two epic failures? I want *him,* worthless whore Dronov, arrested immediately! Alexey Igorevich, why are you just sitting there?"

Golovko looked at Zusko, raising an eyebrow. Zusko held up his phone and showed he was texting instructions to his FSB subordinates. Golovko turned to Voroshilov. "General Dronov is coping with the loss of both of his army commanders at the front. It is not so easy to pick up the reins from afar, especially since both army leaders were on the south side of the NATO attack."

"Arrest him..." Voroshilov stopped and took a gulping breath. "His failure cannot stand." He glared at Golovko and nodded to Zusko.

"My men are on their way now," Zusko answered.

"Shall I continue?" Popov asked, eager to change the topic, though the next was sure to go as poorly.

Voroshilov snapped his head back toward Popov. He glared, took a breath, then nodded.

"The NATO bridgehead to the Donets Pocket now is from the Berestova River to the Merla River, more than fifty kilometers wide. Only our long-range rockets can span their salient. The 76th Air Assault Division in that sector of the pocket was destroyed. We might be able to scrape together a BTG or two from the remnants that escaped northeast across the border. Of the 1st Guards Tank Army, only two BTGs from the 4th Tank Division remain combat capable. We do not have status of the BTG General Kiselyov was leading at Pereshchepyne. Of the 6th Combined Arms Army, the 138th Guards Motor Rifles and the 27th Motor

Rifles were nearly completely destroyed. The 25th Guards have three BTGs. They are only combat formations between the Dnipro River and the Lyman sector."

Voroshilov let out a loud groan, pausing Popov. Popov looked down at his notes and then locked eyes with Voroshilov. Voroshilov's eyes appeared unfocused and bloodshot. The hair on the back of Popov's neck stood up.

"Continuing, President Voroshilov, our air forces have been unable to establish parity over the battlefield in this weather and our SAMs took a severe beating last night, leaving the front vulnerable to NATO air attack. So far, they have not come near our border. We still have our integrated network along our national border.

"In the south, synchronized partisan attacks struck our ammo dump at Kherson. The dump is a total loss. The fuel dump at Dnipro was also hit and burning. The civilian fire brigades are doing their best to extinguish the flames and save the refinery. The rail bridges across the Dnipro River also came under attack. All were damaged. Only one at Dnipro city remains useable. This is now the third day in a row we have been unable to move supplies forward to the Southern Military District forces west of the river. As you know, the Crimea bridge is destroyed completely now. The Southern Military District has perhaps enough supplies for forty-eight hours, possibly seventy-two if they are thrifty."

"How, how could you let this happen?" Voroshilov hissed.

Popov ignored the sting and continued after puffing his chest out, "GRU sources have confirmed the American First Cavalry Division's equipment arrived in Hamburg and is unloading. Their troops are already in Germany and we can expect them at the front within three to five days. Additionally, the British are deploying another division, using ferries across the English Channel. We could see the lead brigade at the front in two days."

Popov paused, watching Voroshilov's face flash red. "And finally, there is no change to the situation for our navy or strategic forces."

Voroshilov's nostrils flared. "Boris Borisovich, is this news true?"

The head of the GRU shifted in his seat. "Yes. We still have not identified the new enemy battalion at Pereshchepyne. It is concerning because it could indicate yet another NATO brigade or even division escaped our agents and technological monitoring. We believe it is American though, and certain it does not belong to their cavalry division."

Voroshilov shook his head before returning his gaze to Popov. "And what, pray do tell, is...is standing between the nazis and Moscow...right at this moment?"

"The two divisions of the 20th Combined Arms Army cover the Bryansk and Kursk front. We could abandon the eastern end of the Donets Pocket and move the 106th Airborne and 7th Airborne Divisions to the Belgorod sector."

"Four Divisions?" Voroshilov stood, knocking his chair over. "Four divisions to cover more than eight hundred kilometers? Are you insane?"

"Perhaps, my president and old friend..." Golubev paused to let Voroshilov's chest to slow its heaving. "Perhaps we should strongly consider the peace proposal."

"No!" Voroshilov shook his fist. "We still control a full third of the Ukraine! I will not give it back after all I have done to give it to our people!"

"At the moment, yes. It sounds like our control is in jeopardy and we don't have the means to stop the West from erasing our gains since July."

"Oh, but we do. Our strategic forces are the strongest in the world. Nobody can stop us!" Voroshilov waved his hands above his head, the veins in his forehead popping. He stopped waving and cradled his head in his hands, gripping his hair between fingers.

"I will not see you destroy our country!" Popov screamed back. "If you use a nuclear bomb, NATO will use one on us, then Dead Hand unleashes all of ours and NATO responds the same. Anyone who survives the fire will merely die from radiation poisoning. Everyone from Kaliningrad to Novosibirsk. Perhaps some of the Siberians deep in the taiga would escape."

"Mind your place, Minister Popov!" Voroshilov rounded the table and grabbed Popov by the collar. "You are dismissed! Someone send in...send in, commander of my strategic rocket forces! Bring Colonel General Ognev...now!"

"Get control of yourself, Nikolai!" Popov tried to pull Voroshilov's hands from his collars.

Voroshilov tightened his grip and shook Popov. "Get me Ognev! We will nuke Kyiv and Kharkiv right now and end this! The West will back down!"

"Nikolai, no!" Golubev yelled, rising from his chair and tugging on Voroshilov's shoulders.

"Old friend! Think of our country!" Kochetkov forced himself between Popov and Voroshilov, breaking the grip. Voroshilov spun to the edge of the room, panting heavily.

"You are turning on me also? Boris, we are...friends!" Voroshilov bent over at the waist, pointing his finger at Kochetkov. His vision closed in as the pain in his head rocketed to new heights.

"And we always will remain friends. You are not yourself."

Voroshilov put his hands on his knees and backed against the wall. "Arrrggggghhhhh!" Voroshilov lowered his head and closed his eyes.

"President Voroshilov..." Zusko came around the table. "I must tell you, the FSB strongly advises you do not escalate to nuclear weapons, even on the battlefield. The West has repeatedly proven more defiant than expected this last year. It is a risk that will burn us all."

Voroshilov lifted his head up and glared around the room. *The GRU betrayed me. The FSB betrayed me. The military has failed me.*

"The peace offer is fair enough. We achieve many of our goals with it." Zubkov ventured for the first time in the conversation. The prime minister hesitated to risk.

"The peace offer is, the offer is..." Voroshilov's chest heaved as he struggled to catch his breath. "...is, is an insult."

"The offer gains us much of our war objectives. It avoids nuclear escalation." Golubev leaned forward, offering his hand to Voroshilov. Voroshilov slapped the hand away.

"Nikolai, something is wrong. You look about to faint." Kochetkov's voice softened.

"Don't change...subject. You...lack the...spine...commit... Launch the..." Voroshilov panted, wagging his head.

"Nikolai, no," Kochetkov urged. He turned and pointed at an aide. "Summon the medical team."

Voroshilov pushed off his knees and rushed to the map display. "We will nuke Kyiv and Kharkiv. Immediately." He slapped his hand onto the display, shaking the flat screen TV.

"No." Popov straightened his collars and stood taller.

"You will... My orders...immediately, Minister!" Voroshilov's yell cracked. His face was now a deep purple. He wobbled, his feet staggering to remain upright. His hand grasped the TV, the knuckles blanching on purple hands.

"No."

"You!" Voroshilov gasped. "You... Will... You will...arrest."

"President Voroshilov, are you okay? I will not order a nuclear strike. Especially when you seem ill," Popov called across the table.

"Yes! Do...it...imm—" Voroshilov's eyes turned gray and he toppled to the floor, his head striking the marble with a sickening *thwack*. Blood flowed from his nose.

Silence and shock gripped the room. The ticking of the grandfather clock in the corner counted the passing of time.

Kochetkov was the first to move, rushing forward. "Nikolai! Someone call the doctor!" Kochetkov rolled Voroshilov onto his back and leaned close to his face. "He's not breathing!"

Golovko rushed forward and dropped to his knees. Immediately the old general began chest compressions. Blood now trickled out of Voroshilov's mouth and nose.

"Look at his eyes." Zubkov leaned over, pointing at the lifeless gray eyes. The prime minister gagged and turned away.

"Make room!" a medic yelled as he entered the room. Everyone but Golovko moved back. The old general held his post until the medic pushed him back and took over chest compressions. Another medic arrived. The security council moved to the far side of the room as more responders took over the scene.

Golubev pulled Zubkov and Popov over. "I've seen that look before. We must face the possibility our leader is incapacitated at best."

"Agreed. We should wait and know for certain though," Zubkov cautioned.

"Nikolai may have pushed himself too hard. Perhaps we have also found our nation's limit." Popov lowered his voice. "The Chinese proposal is worthy of our consideration. Think of it. International recognition of the Crimea and Donbas. We have been pariahs since 2014. Now is our opportunity to end that. Your yacht even could come home."

Golubev snorted. "My yacht means nothing if the Rodina is nuked into oblivion. I fear short of our strategic rockets, we are out of options for continuing the war."

"I could try to reposition the Southern Military District forces for one last counterattack, but it is risky. Should that attack fail, we would have zero armed forces to defend our interests. Our allies in Africa and the Middle East would abandon us in favor of having Chinese troops assist them. Our place on the world stage would become a corner booth." Popov finished and pulled his lips tight at the corners.

"Clear!" The medic's yell stopped all conversations and the room watched as they manually shocked Voroshilov's now naked chest.

"Epinephrine!" The doctor filled the syringe and quickly administered it.

"Get me the ETA of that ambulance!" the president's doctor snapped at the medics.

"Less than five minutes."

The CPR continued. For the entire two-minute round, the room quietly watched.

The automatic emergency defibrillator announced in a metallic voice, "Stand back. Analyzing heart rhythm."

The medics pulled away. "No shock advised."

"Shit. More epinephrine! Override the shock." The doctor frantically drew another dose into the syringe as a medic manually shocked Voroshilov's gray and blood-smeared body.

The council watched the medics resume CPR.

"This was no heart attack." The doctor turned to face the cowed council. "Was the president complaining of anything before he fell?"

"He has had a bad headache for several days," Kochetkov answered.

"I wish he had come to me! If it was an aneurism, I could have addressed it before it ruptured." The doctor's voice was barely audible across the room.

The medics continued CPR until the defibrillator announced no shock advised.

"He isn't coming back." The doctor hung his head. "Keep trying, men. He is our president."

"The president is dead," Zusko announced quietly to the security council. "We should move to another room and take action in private."

Golubev gestured to the door. "My office down the hall."

The council filed into the office, filling every seat and some leaning on the walls.

"Gentlemen, Prime Minister Zubkov is now our leader," Golubev announced in a clear voice.

"That is our constitution's mandate." Popov nodded his head.

"Has someone notified Nikolai's wife?" Zubkov deflected the conversation.

"Yes." Zusko raised his hand.

"Good. He is still a man." Zubkov grimaced. "And now we face our future."

"President Voroshilov has been a loose cannon and I would suggest he was on the brink of destroying everything we love," Popov growled.

"Dmitry," Golubev began, "We have an opportunity suddenly. We have an opportunity to immediately end this war. Without Nikolai, we can rationally discuss our options. I fear rational thought left his brain when the headaches began."

"What are you saying?" Zubkov turned to Golubev.

"How could Voroshilov end the war he started with anything less than his stated outcome? He would never back down, and that became obvious this week. How were we going to be able to end the war while we still hold some bargaining chips? We would have had to remove our president. A coup? A civil war? The options were horrifying. But think, now that he is dead, we can end *his* war."

"Igor has a point," Zusko offered. "We just looked into the brink. I'm sure we all had the same sick feeling. But with Nikolai's natural, perhaps timely, passing, we can avoid that."

"We've already lost a half-million soldiers. If we end the war tonight, that stops." Golubev paused and looked around the room, "We can have our Beijing embassy relay the acceptance. We can have a senior commander at the front initiate an immediate ceasefire."

"Let's discuss the terms offered," Zubkov directed.

"Yes. Item one, Ukraine gets NATO membership and EU membership." Popov held out a finger. "NATO is already fighting alongside Ukraine since day one. They already are de facto members. Really, this term is nothing new for us to face."

"I agree." Zusko nodded.

"Me too," Golubev added. Heads around the room nodded.

"Okay. Item two." Zubkov pointed to Popov.

"Item two is we gain international recognition of annexing Crimea and the Donbas breakaways from 2014."

"That is where our borders were prior to last July. We would be giving back tens of thousands of square kilometers we bought in blood," Golovko tossed out halfheartedly.

"Yes, but we took on sanctions in 2014. Sanctions that would only escalate in time. Since July, the West has successfully badgered all but the poorest of our allies to avoid trade with us. Our economy is weakened. We could see serious effects in another two years," Golubev countered. "International recognition restores our status among the world."

"I think it is wise to consider our place on the world stage. If we become too weak and too isolated, we will allow China to dominate us," Popov added hastily, "China's domination would be insufferable."

"Such recognition would also mean the West would never attack our naval base at Sevastopol ever again. It becomes as safe for our fleet as the Kola. The Black Sea becomes ours. Our radar and missiles can see everything from the Crimea."

Kochetkov tossed out another aspect: "I hate to give up our control of the lower Dnipro. The Ukrainians will be able to regain port access. Our boys fought so hard to gain that."

"To a sea we utterly control. Remember how the cargo ships avoided the Black Sea last summer just from the threat of war? Rumors we will sink ships would prevent anything from leaving Ukrainian ports." Popov glared at the GRU head.

"Is the international recognition worth more than the land we control without such recognition?" Zubkov asked, looking around the room. Several nodded. Some looked blankly back.

Golubev cleared his throat. "I say yes. I say the recognition and the restoration of status on the world stage allows a future beyond a hermit regime like Pyongyang."

"True. Yes." Popov nodded.

"Then yes to item two. What was item three?"

"A DMZ. Three kilometers on their side and three on our side of the border."

"Whatever. We mine the hell out of it and NATO can't and won't cross it." Golovko smirked.

"As long as the DMZ includes all drones. Then they can't even see across it. Six kilometers is good. I don't think this point is worth debating. In the grand scheme it has no permanent effects on us."

"If it makes the Ukraine come to the table, then fine. Whatever." Popov waved his hand dismissively.

Zusko grinned. "We just had the most meaningful conversation about ending Voroshilov's war that we've had in months."

"Nikolai has been my friend for many, many years. But you are right, he has been the obstacle to discussing the future," Kochetkov replied.

"Perhaps we check with the doctor before we get too excited." Zubkov wagged his finger. "Everyone stay put. I'll be right back."

Zubkov strode out of the room without waiting for a response.

"If Nikolai hadn't blown an aneurism, I was prepared to discuss alternate means for a leadership change. Risk of nuclear war is unacceptable for this situation." Zusko shrugged.

"It would have been hard on the country. His popularity was wavering. His control on the military fading. But the last coup was a disaster overall." Popov's bushy white eyebrows wagged up and down.

Golovko suddenly broke into nervous laughter. "Does this mean we all won't be arrested and shot?"

Zusko laughed.

"General Golovko has a point, though. We do need a scapegoat to hang failure on." Golubev sternly looked at Golovko.

"Perhaps President Voroshilov was correct in his assessment of competence in our chain of command." Popov cleared his throat. "Some are perhaps overly hasty. The enemy always gets a vote in war. I would agree that General Dronov failed the Rodina miserably."

Several nodded, but nobody spoke up. Zubkov returned, holding the door open and announcing, "The doctor pronounced President Voroshilov's time of death at thirteen minutes after midnight."

"We must inform the country." Golubev stood and walked to Zubkov. "You are now our leader until we can hold emergency elections."

"My first directive is to contact the Chinese. I want Voroshilov's war ended. I want a senior field commander to contact the Western forces and ask for an immediate ceasefire until a formal treaty is signed. I want us to contact an American unit and not a Ukrainian unit."

"I will make that happen. The best sector for that would be the Pereshchepyne sector. The Sixth Combined Arms Army headquarters bunker is near there. I would trust Lieutenant General Molchalin…or Major General Frosin to secure a ceasefire."

"Quickly. Before the front changes enough the West changes their mind."

"Once we get that in motion, perhaps we should discuss some other necessary leadership changes." Golubev's eyes narrowed and he put his arm around Zubkov. "Let's take a short walk."

Zubkov nodded. He also shared the concern. The two walked side by side down the hallway, the security detail discreetly keeping a distance.

"Igor," Zubkov started when they were far enough from the others, "for our nation to get a clean start, I believe we must remove those whom pushed this war on us and those whose shortcomings allowed the West leverage over us."

"The West will not trust our sudden change of heart with merely Nikolai's removal. They know Andrey Popov was an architect of Nikolai's war, even if it was Nikolai's personal crusade. Yet, I don't think that arresting Andrey is the proper move."

"Do you think Andrey would quietly step down?"

"Dmitry, the man turns eighty in May. He would do what is right. Especially if the alternative is arrest. But I think you should suggest retiring first, and word it as *retire*, instead of *resign*."

"Seems fair."

"General Dronov must go," Golubev bluntly assessed. "General Golovko too."

"I got the impression both were too hesitant to take decisive action to counter the NATO attack. Dronov though..." Zubkov paused. "...is most responsible for the defeat of his armies. Zusko has shared information with me. Information not even Golovko knows. This stays between you and me."

"Oh?" Golubev's eyebrows raised.

"Dronov restrained and then fed his units piecemeal into the meat grinder instead of following our army's doctrine. Had he followed doctrine, perhaps we would be celebrating the destruction of over a hundred thousand western troops."

"Nothing escapes the FSB. I'm surprised we haven't heard of this from Andrey or Boris."

Zubkov smiled. "Why would we? Dronov and Kiselyov were Andrey's protégés. He was grooming them. He wanted Dronov to replace Golovko and Kiselyov to move up to the all-important Western Military District. The GRU said nothing because they belong to Andrey, even though Boris has a place on the council. The GRU provided enough failures this last year Boris knew he was at risk of arrest himself. Boris needed to focus his briefings on the enemy."

"One might argue Dronov is an enemy of the state."

"And shall be treated accordingly." Zubkov was growing into his new role. "Golovko shall go, but perhaps resignation instead of death is more appropriate."

"I applaud your decisiveness."

"We still have one important matter to decide. Who can we trust to secure a ceasefire?"

"I'll be damned if General Lipilin does it. I don't trust that man's ambition." Golubev waved his hand. "Anything that gives him relevance is one step closer to him leading a coup."

Zubkov laughed. "I share your worries. Come, let's go ask Golovko who is left we can trust."

The two briskly returned to the council. The office was full of many different phone and side conversations. All grew quiet with Zubkov's return.

"General Golovko, who do we have immediately available at the front we can trust to secure the ceasefire?"

"Prime Minister Zubkov, the best man for that is General Molchalin."

"He was wounded, no?" Golubev countered.

"Yes, while you were out, I received an update on his condition. He reported back to duty leading his army. He is weakened and bandaged, but I trust no one more."

"I will call him personally." Zubkov turned to Golubev. "Will you handle what we discussed? Thank you. I will be in my office bringing an end to Voroshilov's war."

Chapter 19

Pereshchepyne, Ukraine – January 23, 2300 hrs

"Savage Five, Savage Seven, you want to start pulling everyone back to the rally point?" Sam's radio earpiece crackled.

"Negative, I'm still waiting on linkup with the relief force commander. I think this is the commander coming now." Sam saw a Bradley ease down the street to her. The last ten minutes had taken forever. The tanks had discovered Russian armor nearby and engaged them before the commander moved into town. *Perhaps we can plan from inside the Bradley, out of the wind and snow.* Sam loved being an elite Ranger, but she missed some of the comforts of the mechanized infantry.

The Bradley pulled to the side of the street and came to a stop just past Sam's gate. The ramp dropped and a soldier waved Sam in. Without hesitation, Sam scrambled in. The ramp immediately closed.

The turret door opened and Sam noted the rank and name on the body armor of the soldier who dropped down out of the turret. "Hi, Lieutenant, I'm Captain Gentry." Sam offered her hand.

"Lieutenant Kraemer. XO, well, acting troop commander." Savvy shook hands and nodded to the map displayed on the wall of the troop compartment.

"Glad you're here. Are you Bolt Six?" Sam noted there were no vehicle icons on the tactical display.

"No, ma'am. I'm Ace Six. Bolt Six is the task force commander. He's coming here too. While we wait, can you show me where your troops are? We want to consolidate into the town, without a fratricide incident."

"Definitely." Sam pulled her blue map pen out of a pocket and plotted the Ranger squad positions. Sam switched to her red pen. "LT, there are

Russians on the east side of town, and on the north. Our patrols have sometimes attacked and sometimes just noted locations. Trying to keep Ivan on his toes and out of our hair. The last couple hours, Ivan has been content to pound the city with artillery, probably 152mm."

"How many casualties do you have?" Savvy asked, her notebook out.

"Two KIA, three litter, and seven ambulatory. My casualty collection point is next to my company command post." Sam leaned forward and tapped her finger on the map.

The ramp opened, interrupting. Logan and Devin squeezed in and the ramp closed.

"Small world! I knew that voice was familiar!" Sam leaned forward and hugged Logan.

"Indeed, Sam. Good to see you!" Logan grinned and then looked at Savvy and Devin. "We were lieutenants together at Fiery Cross. This is one badass infantry officer."

Devin's eyes flashed with recognition and Savvy nodded, piecing the puzzle together.

"What unit are you with? Never heard of Bolt. That short for Thunderbolt?"

Logan grinned. "I'm with Third ACR. Bolt is actually a fictitious task force. With the Russians sending a whole combined arms army toward us, we needed to convince Ivan we've got more than we actually have. Definitely didn't want them to know we thinned our lines to attack south."

"How are things going up north?"

"We broke through to the Donets Pocket and the Russian counterattack fizzled. Okay, Sam, what is your situation and how would you like to pull your troops back in for loading up?"

Sam pointed at the map and quickly explained the situation. "Logan, I think it will be least risky to have your troops establish a perimeter here in the west end of the city. I'll co-locate a control point and count my Rangers in at it. We can slip away from Ivan unnoticed on foot. What is your plan for getting us back north?"

"It's less than ideal, especially with the storm, but it's what we had immediately available. We have some PLS with empty flat racks. We will expand our formation out so you won't take direct fire."

Sam's face fell. "No chance we can fit in the Bradleys?"

"If it was just a couple squads, yeah, but not your whole company."

"Logan, there's a thermometer at the house we're using as a command post. The temp is ten below and falling. This wind takes the wind chill down to minus forty. By morning, it could be minus sixty, and that isn't counting the wind from the vehicle movement."

"Frostbite in minutes." Logan scrunched his mouth to the side and scratched his cheek. "We will need to create some shelter on the flat racks. It will delay our LD from here, but you're right—the risk of frostbite requires us to take action."

"Sir, we could probably find something in the industrial area just west of here and manufacture something," Savvy offered.

"Some wood and nails. Maybe we can find some blankets and such to pile on the flat racks and get your troops off the cold metal. We can use tarps to cover the shelters," Logan agreed.

"We could live with that." Sam nodded.

"Okay," Logan said, drawing a circle around the western industrial area of Pereshchepyne. "Devin, you have the west half, Savvy the east half. Savvy and Sam, you will be responsible for pulling the Rangers into the perimeter. Devin, I want the sappers to help the distro platoon with construction. Find a warehouse or something to work out of the weather and conceal our activities. Sam, we have two medic tracks. You want to take them to get your casualties?"

"Roger." Savvy nodded as she scribbled instructions in her notebook.

"Yes, sir." Devin turned to the ramp to open the door.

"Where will your command post be?" Sam asked Logan.

"Next to our construction area. I'll get a grid out once we choose the spot."

"Okay."

"Let's move. I want us REDCON-1 by sunrise." Logan turned toward the driver. "Open the ramp."

The ramp dropped. Logan and Devin scrambled out into the storm.

"Logan, if you have the medics meet me here, I'll send my squad here with them to the casualty collection point," Sam yelled.

Logan turned back and flashed a thumbs-up.

Sam turned to Savvy. "I'll stay with you, that okay?"

"Of course, ma'am. Let me get my troop perimeter established, then we can move to the entrance point. Do you have any troops inside this circle?" Savvy pointed at the circle Logan put on the map.

"Not after my squad here takes the medics out."

"That simplifies things. I want my scouts to clear our interior before we do anything else."

"Smart move, Lieutenant. We haven't patrolled the industrial area yet."

"We destroyed some Russian BTRs and BMPs in the neighborhood just west of it. We gotta be careful, even though we didn't find any Ivan infantry with those vehicles. Maybe they didn't have any squads left."

"The Russians on the east side of the city have squads. We've probably killed around thirty or forty Ivans since dawn." Sam looked at her watch. "Okay, let's get troops in motion."

Holubivka, Ukraine – January 24, 0030 hrs

Molchalin opened his eyes to the dim light of his office. Sitting across the desk, he recognized the familiar outline of Frosin. "Ah, Yuri, how long have I been asleep?"

"About three hours. You needed the rest. The blizzard is still severe. Our troops are trying to organize into a defensive line north of the Oril. What's left of them."

"Any enemy activity while I was out?"

"The enemy broke through to Pereshchepyne, penetrating the western obstacles. The BTG we assembled from the depot east of the city counterattacked. They failed and the enemy is somewhere in the city. Colonel Ogoltsov is getting reports from the last remaining officer. Enemy tanks are in the city. Their thermal sights must be better at seeing through the snowstorm because we are losing vehicles to cannon fire without seeing the enemy. The remaining troops have backed off until the storm isn't blowing in their faces. On the north side, the BTG from the Forty-Seventh Guards Tank is preparing a final attack with what's left of them. Now that General Kiselyov isn't on the radio anymore, a Major Agranov is providing us information through Colonel Ogoltsov."

Molchalin held up his hand and shook his head. "No, we need to stop wasting units attacking blindly at what is clearly a superior enemy force."

The desk phone rang. Molchalin picked it up without looking at the caller ID. "General Molchalin."

"Victor Aleksandrovich, this is Prime Minister Dmitry Zubkov. I understand you are wounded."

Molchalin hesitated, shooting Frosin a puzzled look. "Yes, Prime Minister Zubkov, I was, but I will survive."

"I am glad to hear you will recover. May you recover quickly and fully. Now, General, are you sitting down?"

"Yes."

"General, President Voroshilov died tonight. He collapsed during our meeting and died quickly, perhaps a heart attack."

Molchalin blinked.

"General," Zubkov continued, "our nation does not have time to grieve right now. The war is in a fluid and precarious state."

"Yes, I know."

"I'm sure. I know your attack to stop the NATO thrust failed this evening. I do not blame you personally for the failure. Nobody here in Moscow does."

"Prime Minister Zubkov, I assure you my chief of staff, my headquarters staff, my troops all did their best. Given the circumstances, all were heroic and diligent in their duties."

"Relax, Victor. Nobody is suggesting otherwise. At least within your command. Now, General, as the leader of our nation, I have a duty for you."

Molchalin pressed the speaker phone button and motioned for Frosin to come closer, while holding a finger to his lips. Frosin nodded and came forward.

"Victor, where is the closest enemy unit? The closest to you right now."

"Pereshchepyne. There is an American task force there."

"Americans, good." Zubkov's sigh was audible over the phone. "General, we are going to end the war. We have peace terms that are beneficial to our nation. It is important for us to end the fighting immediately, while we still retain a positional advantage at the front."

Molchalin held his breath, unsure what to say.

"Yes, Victor. I agree." Zubkov paused again. "I know you are wounded, but I understand you are able to still perform your duties. I now need you to contact the American forces and secure an immediate ceasefire. Only through radios at the front can we quickly end the fighting."

"Yes, Prime Minister. Have all nations agreed to the peace terms?"

"I don't know. We just relayed through the Chinese we are accepting the terms proposed by the Americans. Because the terms originated from the Americans, it is important you arrange for the ceasefire with them."

"This weather will make this difficult," Molchalin cautioned.

"Waiting out the storm is unacceptable. I'm told it could last another twelve to eighteen hours. I want a ceasefire in place before dawn."

"I will immediately get on this."

"Good. Victor, there is no one else I trust with this mission. As soon as you have a confirmed ceasefire, I want you to directly report to me."

"I need to inform General Dronov of my actions."

"Ah, there is no need. He will not be available to discuss anything with you. For that matter, I have Defense Minister Popov and General Golovko in my office, so directly report to me, and me only. I want updates from your staff every thirty minutes until we have the ceasefire in place."

"Yes, sir."

"Now go fulfill your duty to the nation." Zubkov hung up.

Molchalin looked up into Frosin's eyes. Words escaped both and tears formed. Molchalin wiped his eyes and smiled. "We may yet live to see our families."

"We still have the touchy task of contacting the Americans."

Molchalin frowned and nodded. "In the storm and dark, a white flag won't work. I fear their tanks will shoot first and ask questions later."

"Someone will need to approach walking. Someone completely unarmed. A small flag of truce will work." Frosin nodded and zipped his coat up.

"I forbid you from taking that duty, Yuri. I need you at the command post to keep Moscow informed."

"Yes, General. It occurs to me this weather will prevent the Americans from being able to fly someone of appropriate rank to negotiate with."

Molchalin snorted. "After the successes of my tactical air defense units, they wouldn't dare fly in any weather. Americans have lieutenant colonels leading battalions. There will be one of those in Pereshchepyne and my ego can handle discussing strategic matters with a field grade officer. I'm sure the Americans will be in radio contact with higher ranks quickly."

"True. I can ensure we have our jammers off. Let's not let anything slow bringing an end to the bloodshed."

Molchalin smiled. "Yes. Let's end this. Now, I need someone we can trust to arrange my approach under flag of truce. I don't want to approach in a Tigr unless we confirm the Americans will allow me to approach alive."

"Colonel Beketov would be my suggestion. He speaks fluent English and is a quick thinker under pressure."

"Okay. Though we are within mortar range of the enemy here, we should move up to a closer position before we send him into the storm." Molchalin stood and pulled a coat on. Frosin helped zip it over the arm sling.

"I don't think your hat will fit over your bandaged head. Perhaps we can arrange to have negotiations indoors." Frosin turned and hollered to the staff operations room, "Colonel Beketov, come here please!"

"Coming!"

Molchalin waited patiently for Beketov to enter and snap to attention. "Colonel Beketov, we have instructions from Moscow to arrange a ceasefire immediately."

Beketov's jaw flapped open and his eyes widened.

"Yes, you will have the honor and duty to approach the American forces under flag of truce. You will carry a radio and call me when you have secured permission for my Tigr to approach."

"Yes, sir!" Beketov smiled briefly. "How am I going to approach without getting shot?"

"If you drive up, they will shoot your vehicle without hesitation. You have no choice but to approach on foot and unarmed," Frosin answered. "You will want to bundle up and borrow some goggles."

"Yes, sir." Beketov nodded.

"We will drive closer though. While you get ready for a walk in the blizzard, General Frosin will confirm the American positions and the positions of our forward forces between us and Pereshchepyne. Now, unless you have questions, go get ready."

Beketov snapped his heels and saluted. As soon as Molchalin returned the salute, Beketov spun and marched out of the room.

"Yuri, have the staff ready a Tigr and assign someone you trust with your life to verify no weapons and a white flag is flying."

Frosin nodded and hurried out of the office. Molchalin watched him go before pulling his desk open and pulling a flask out. *Zyr, Mikhail's favorite. I was saving this for toasting my old friend after the war.* Molchalin studied the flask. The crest of the 81st Motor Rifle Regiment was stamped into the metal. *Mikhail gave it to me after the battle of Grozny. Ah, Mikhail. I know you went out in glory.* Molchalin sighed and slipped the flask into his pocket. With another sigh, Molchalin leaned back in his chair and let his mind slip away.

"General, the truck is ready." Frosin appeared in the doorway. "Are you okay?"

Molchalin looked up. "Yes. The pain is manageable. We are ready?"

Frosin nodded. "Colonel Beketov is already in the truck."

"Good." Molchalin stood slowly and pulled a mitten on his lone hand.

"Also, I confirmed the Americans are on the west end of the city. We will approach up a small road that leads north to them from our positions near the Oleksandriya train platform. The company commander is now the senior officer in his BTG. Senior Lieutenant Goryachev is expecting us."

"A senior lieutenant? We are truly at the end of our means."

"General, this ceasefire cannot come fast enough."

"Indeed, Yuri. Indeed. Have you confirmed that all our units, including what's left of the Forty-Seventh Guard Tanks, has stopped firing all weapons except in self-defense?"

"I did. Also, all units understand they cannot fire artillery without your express permission."

"Good. The last thing we need is the Americans to suspect a trap or something sinister."

Frosin held his hand out to Molchalin. "Good luck, sir. I'll see you when you return."

"Yes, and don't forget to call Moscow top and bottom of the hour. It might take us a couple hours at least to secure the ceasefire."

Molchalin didn't wait for Frosin to answer and carefully walked to the bunker exit. The world spun on him and stars floated. *Careful, Victor. You must have lost more blood than you thought.* He snorted. *Or need some water.*

A guard opened the bunker door and snow swirled in with a slap of icy wind. The Tigr waited, engine running, just a few feet from the door. Molchalin strode as erectly as possible to the waiting vehicle. The driver opened the door for Molchalin and offered to help him up. Molchalin ignored the offer and carefully pulled himself in. The driver closed the door and ran around the vehicle to his own door.

"Okay, Sergeant, let's go."

"Yes, General." The driver put the armored truck into gear and crunched through the snow.

"Colonel Beketov." Molchalin looked over his shoulder, not quite able to see his intelligence officer behind him.

"Yes, General?"

"You will serve as my interpreter once you have arranged for my approach. Do not let them separate us. Tell them you are the interpreter if they try."

"Yes, sir."

"Be careful. You must not fail to secure my safe approach."

"Yes, sir."

Molchalin looked forward. *Beketov is going to have a miserable walk into the wind.* The storm gust rocked the truck and the snow pelted the windshield as they slowly drove north. The frontline was less than ten kilometers away. After several minutes, they came to a BMP-3 parked blocking the highway. A soldier waved for them to follow from the commander's hatch.

"Follow him," Molchalin instructed, even as the sergeant turned the Tigr to follow.

The BMP-3 headed west across snow filled wheat stubble. It cut through a gap in some trees and down into a shallow drainage. Snow drifts as high as the BMP threated to stop the Tigr, but the sergeant expertly stayed in the tracks from the BMP and followed it out the other side of the trees. The BMP turned north, cutting across a field. A row of trees appeared and the BMP stopped. Molchalin could see a gap in the trees ahead. The soldier climbed down from the BMP and slogged through the snow to the Tigr.

"General, Senior Lieutenant Goryachev. There is a road from that gap north to the American positions. As long as you follow the trees lining the road, you will stay on path." The lieutenant saluted.

"Colonel, did you hear that?"

"Yes, General."

"Good luck. I await your radio call."

Beketov got out of the Tigr. Molchalin watched as Goryachev briefed Beketov, then saluted. Beketov looked back at Molchalin one last time through his goggles, then pulled a scarf up to cover his face. He picked up his small flag pole, the white flag flapping wildly, and trudged north. In a few minutes, Beketov was out of view.

Chapter 20

Pereshchepyne, Ukraine – January 24, 0200 hrs

Wind whistled through small holes in the shed roof. The cold at least was tolerable out of the wind. Logan leaned on Jim's truck, doubling as the task force TOC. On the other side of the large shed, soldiers worked to build frames on the flat racks.

"Sir, got a minute?" Savvy called as she approached behind Logan.

"Sure." Logan turned and saw Running Bear and Ratatuev accompanying Savvy. Running Bear carried a bundled-up jacket.

"Ratty, how is your platoon?" Logan asked. Third Platoon had lost half its Brads and eleven casualties since leaving friendly lines.

Ratty nodded then tilted his head to the side. "Hanging in there. I'd feel better if we could fly our wounded out, or even send them back now."

Logan grimaced. "Me too. Is anyone in danger of not surviving long enough?"

Ratty shook his head.

"We're here, sir, because Running Bear found something after the Russian's counterattack at the minefield breach." Ratty changed the subject.

Logan looked at Running Bear who shook the jacket out. The Russian lettering and rank immediately caught Logan's attention. "That's a general."

"The jacket is of Lieutenant General Kiselyov. Heard of him?" Ratty pointed at the jacket.

"That is General Kiselyov's jacket?" Logan asked, eyebrows raising.

Ratty nodded.

"Kiselyov is the commander of the Russian First Guards Tank Army. Where did you get that?"

"It was caught up in a tree where the Russian tanks attacked us. It had to have come from one of the tanks we destroyed. Not sure which one." Running Bear handed the jacket to Logan.

"What is a general doing leading a local counterattack?" Logan asked the jacket. "I need to call this in."

Running Bear looked at Ratty and put his arm around him as Logan turned to grab the radio hand mic. Logan quickly radioed the information to regiment. Logan put the hand mic down and returned to the group. "Well, that should spice up the night. Good find."

"It was a tough fight. Ivan had some veterans in that tank company." Running Bear's voice was flat.

A door slammed and Logan looked over, seeing Heydte and Kristyn walking over.

"I completely forgot about her, Savvy," Logan whispered.

Savvy shrugged. "She hasn't been in the way."

"Good to hear that, at least." Logan looked at the reporter. *I hope she isn't expecting to talk to me right now.*

"Sir, ma'am," Heydte called as he approached.

"Sergeant Heydte, I hope you come with good news." Logan smiled. *I probably need to be civil with the civilian.* "Hi, ma'am, I'm Captain Trondfjell."

"Kristyn Rhodes." Kristyn shook Logan's hand with a firm grip.

"Sir." Heydte waited for Logan to finish the handshake. "I'm actually here with good news for Running Bear."

"Well do your thing. Don't mind me listening though." Logan took one step back.

"Running Bear, your tank wasn't fully penetrated. The hit broke a wire connection and a hydraulic line from shock. I was able to fix it and you are back in the fight. Ma'am," Heydte said, turning to Savvy, "L13 is back up and running. This frees up the M88. Do you want me to see if one of the Bradleys from Third Platoon is worth trying to salvage, or keep the recovery vehicle available?"

"Ratty?" Savvy turned to the platoon sergeant. "You know better than any of us."

Ratty sadly shook his head. "Sergeant Valenti's Brad was burning. Sergeant Buchanan's has a hole through the engine into the turret and Hayes's TOW missiles exploded and destroyed the turret."

Logan knew Staff Sergeant Hayes and his gunner Sergeant Tatum both perished instantly. The platoon would need rebuilding when they returned to friendly lines. Logan put his hand on Ratty's shoulder and squeezed. Ratty's head dropped.

"The M88 remains available then," Savvy declared quietly.

"We may yet need it." Logan watched everyone's shoulders sag slightly. "I mean, if it keeps storming like this, the trucks might have trouble getting through snowdrifts. I want the M88 to travel with the trucks."

Heydte's head jerked up. "Yeah, the drifts."

Logan caught Heydte's eyes and saw the mechanic didn't fully believe. *Well, of course. He's been here since the beginning of the war.*

"Ivan's lack of artillery right now makes me think they are pausing in preparation of another attack." Savvy pointed at the engineers building the shelter frames. "It'd be nice if they hurried."

"I know. I'm trying to be patient and not get in the way. Besides, the last Rangers still haven't counted in yet," Logan replied.

"True." Savvy held up a hand to her ear and listened to her radio. Everyone watched. Savvy tossed her head. "Sir, we've got a lone guy walking toward our positions from the south. Coming up the farm road. He looks unarmed and appears he's flying a flag."

"How far are the Russian positions that direction?"

"Not sure, at least three thousand meters. We can't see them. That's the distance to the farthest trees we can see," Running Bear answered. It was his platoon's sector.

"I'm intrigued." Logan raised his eyebrows. "Savvy, you have a scout ready to intercept this lone Ivan?"

Savvy nodded. "How do you know it's an Ivan?"

"No Ukrainian civilian would be dumb enough to walk into a blizzard on a battlefield. Going into the wind too. I mean, would you be out in this storm without a really good reason?"

"I have a good reason and I don't want to be out in it," Heydte quipped.

"Amen, brother." Running Bear patted Heydte's body armor. "I better head down there. They say how far out this guy is?"

"About two klicks. I'm heading back to my command post," Savvy answered. She, Ratty, and Running Bear briskly walked away.

"Captain," Kristyn began, watching them leave, "mind if I hang out with you and chat a bit?"

Logan studied her. "If you're looking for an interview, I'm not really in a mindset for that right now."

Kristyn laughed gently. "No, no. See, I'm unarmed. No notepad, no camera." She flashed her disarming smile. "I've heard a lot about you and it would be nice to meet the person the troops hold so highly."

"Well, flattery won't get you anywhere. That being said, I don't mind a chat. We're at a point where I don't think I can make anything happen any faster."

"You mean the building of shelter for the Rangers? Captain Trondfjell?"

"You may call me Logan, but yes, building the shelter. The last Rangers reaching our perimeter. The troops preparing for the movement north. Competent and motivated troops don't need micromanaging."

"I see why they like you so much, Logan. Where are you from?"

"Longmont, Colorado."

"I've been there. Beautiful city. Very friendly people. I'm guessing there is an interesting story there."

Logan closed his eyes. *Fat chance.* "Longmont seems a long way from home and off the beaten path. How has your time with Sergeant Heydte been?"

"Eye-opening. Dave is quite the character and incredibly competent. Lightning Troop has some very interesting leaders and I've enjoyed getting to know them," Kristyn immediately responded, though her eyes flashed. *She suspects I questioned her honesty.*

Logan nodded. "Good people make a good unit."

"I've heard stories about last July and I've heard stories about Fiery Cross. How does the current fight compare with those?"

Logan leaned against the hood of the truck and pulled his water out. He took a sip and thought before answering. "The fight is not as desperate. At least it doesn't feel that way. The cold is harder though. This blizzard is a major factor."

"The blizzard? How does it factor?"

"Well, if you look into the wind, you can't see as well and snow builds against the sights and such. Makes it hard to know what's in the northeast. So, as we move back north, our right flank is more vulnerable and we know there are Russian forces that direction. It's because of the windchill that we are stationary here, building shelter, instead of already heading out under the cover of darkness."

"I see. You prefer fighting at night?"

Logan nodded again. "I suppose you don't see as much at night though."

Kristyn smiled and shook her head. "Not really. It's okay. I trust your troops to keep me as safe as I'm gonna be."

"Well, ma'am, we can't prevent everything possible."

"Please, call me Kristyn. I'm not *that* old yet."

"Okay."

"I understand that war isn't safe for anyone, and I don't expect you to guarantee my safety. But I don't think too much about the possibilities and their probabilities."

"Yeah, those can eat you up. You can see it when soldiers do get stuck thinking of those too much."

Kristyn nodded. "How does this fight compare to others for you personally?"

"Hmm. I think... Well, it's different in that I'm leading the task force and so I'm removed some from the immediacy of the fight. Before, last summer, I found myself having to shoot and fight the tank as much as controlling the whole troop. Now, I'm controlling the whole task force. There is an added command level between the trigger pullers and me."

"You sound like you might not like that as much." Kristyn tilted her head.

"It's different." Logan sighed. "The price of moving onward and upward."

"Speaking of, I'm amazed you, a captain, are trusted with leading a battalion-size force on a mission this important."

"Don't kid yourself too much, Kristyn. This task force is not much bigger than my troop was last summer. Most are the very same troops I commanded just a few weeks ago. As far as being trusted with the mission, I don't know who else they would have used. The regiment is short on higher-ranking officers. I think it was more a matter of who was immediately available."

"I've heard speculation contrary to that line of logic." Kristyn leaned against the vehicle near Logan, facing the opposite direction. She leaned her head back, looking at Logan.

Logan looked her in the eye. "I wouldn't believe everything Sergeant Heydte says." Logan turned away and watched the soldiers building shelters.

"Seems like the front is ruptured wide open. What do you think will happen now?"

"We will defeat Russia. Their army is done. From here, we will attack south. No way they can stop us. Their army trapped west of us will run low on supplies quickly and then they are done-done."

"That would be nice."

Logan nodded. "Eh, I try not to get too far ahead of things. I know this war will end soon. I just hope it does without getting stupid."

"You mean nukes."

Logan gritted his teeth and locked eyes. "Yeah."

"I hope so too, Logan. So much."

"Moving on." Logan crossed his arms. He used the quiet pause to think through his plans for the return movement, making sure he hadn't forgotten anything.

"Yes." Kristyn shuddered. "What is your favorite place you've been?"

"Vienna," Logan answered quickly, blushing.

"When were you there?"

Logan glanced at Kristyn and realized she noted his blush.

"On leave at Christmas."

"Sounds lovely."

"Oh, it was." Logan blushed again, shaking his head. "You don't need to hear about it though."

Kristyn laughed. "Not a kiss and tell type of guy, are you?"

Logan turned beet red and shook his head.

"Well, I won't pry. But good for you. Good for her too. Wife?"

Logan shook his head and blew out a breath. "No, my girlfriend."

"You have a picture?"

Logan pulled a Ziplock baggie out of his jacket pocket. "Erin." He didn't open the bag, but smoothed it so Kristyn could see the picture Logan and Erin took in a photo booth they found in Vienna.

"She is beautiful. You make a good couple."

"She is. You have a family back home?" Logan asked his first question about Kristyn.

She shook her head. Logan nodded.

Kristyn slowly spoke, "My profession has made it hard for relationships. I've rarely met anyone worth wishing things could be different."

Logan looked over at Kristyn. *She's pretty enough, I'm sure she's had many men try. How many of my soldiers tried since she joined us?* Logan smothered the smirk. *Soldiers will be soldiers.* "How have the task force troops treated you?"

"Good. Very professional, the ones I've chatted with. You have some great people."

"I'll second that. Who has been the most interesting to talk with so far?"

"Well, I'll say that Sergeant Dave Heydte has been very entertaining and educational. I think the one I've found most interesting is Sergeant Running Bear."

"Running Bear and I go way back. He is a great man and a great warrior. I'm glad you've gotten to talk with him."

"I hope to talk with him more. He really is fascinating and a genuine good person." Logan looked over at Kristyn, but she had her head turned away, watching the soldiers.

"Sir," Jim said, leaning out of the truck, "the Rangers are all in and accounted for."

"Thank you, Jim. Relay that up to regiment, will you?"

"Roger, sir." Jim disappeared back into the truck.

Logan looked over at the shelter construction. After a few minutes he nodded to Kristyn. "Probably another hour or so left."

Kristyn looked at her watch. "We leave at three thirty then?"

Logan shook his head. "No, it will take a little longer to get everyone situated. I'm thinking closer to five. That will put the rising sun behind us as we approach the likely Russian positions north of the Oril."

Kristyn nodded.

"Sir." Jim got out of the truck. "Radio for you. Ace Six."

"Excuse me." Logan went around and sat in Jim's seat, enjoying the warm cushion. "Bolt Six."

"Bolt Six, Ace Six. That dude finally arrived with a white flag. Break."

Logan mentally focused.

"It's a Russian colonel. He speaks English and says he has orders from Moscow to negotiate an immediate ceasefire. Theater-wide ceasefire."

Logan gawked at the radio hand mic, then put it back to his ear. "Confirming the Russians want to negotiate a ceasefire."

"Roger. He's asked for the highest-ranking officer available."

"He seem legit?" Logan asked, his mind reeling.

"Roger. He says he is to secure safe passage for his boss, Lieutenant General Molchalin, to cross lines and negotiate."

Logan remembered that name. *Commander of the Sixth Combined Arms Army. Hmmm… We possibly killed the commander of the First Guards Tank Army. That does make him the ranking Ivan around.*

"Bolt Six, Ace Six, what do you want to do?"

"Ask him what sort of entourage this General Molchalin is bringing. Tell them it can't be more than a single unarmed vehicle and no more than three people. And tell him the weather prevents flying in anyone of similar rank."

Logan released the radio and looked at Jim and Kristyn. "Holy shit. Can this be for real?"

The radio crackled, "Bolt Six, he says that is fine. The Russian says they don't want to wait for the storm to end."

"Okay. Stand by." Logan drummed his fingers on the dashboard. "Jim, if this is legit, this might mean the end of the fighting. It could mean we don't have to risk the fight back north. Thoughts?"

"Sir, I agree. Probably want to take some efforts to make sure it isn't a ruse. Hope they aren't offended we don't have a general available."

"I know. I know." Logan keyed up the radio. "Ace Six, tell them to have General Molchalin approach on the same road. The vehicle needs to have its headlights on and no weapons. The vehicle will stop fifty meters short of the outskirts. I want scouts to search them and the vehicle. Then I want to bring them here in the back of a Bradley. No phones, no radios, et cetera allowed. We will use a different house so they don't see our work on the shelters. If talks break down, we keep them and take them back with us. I want Three-Four here to translate for me. Get an ETA on their general."

"Ace Six, wilco."

Logan shook his head. "This is surreal. We need to document this. Every second of it. Jim, do we have something we can record with?"

"Roger, we have cell phones. The cameras can still record even on airplane mode."

"Get me two officers to do that. I want a backup recorder." Logan turned to Kristyn. "Kristyn, can you cover this? I suddenly am thankful to have a reporter with me."

"Are you kidding? Yes! If this is for real, this is huge. I'll go get my stuff."

"Bolt Six, Ace Six, ETA fifteen minutes."

"Roger, let's move. Break, Savage Five, can I borrow you and a fire team of your Rangers for intimidation?"

"Roger."

"Ace Six, have the scout section that escorts the general to our negotiation room stay with us the entire time also."

"Roger."

Logan put down the radio and jumped to his feet, pacing. "What am I missing? Jim?"

"Better tell regiment."

"Oh man. Yes. Jeez." Logan turned red and sat quickly back down. He grabbed the hand mic for the regiment radio net. "Remington Six, Bolt Six. Flash traffic."

"Remington X-ray, go ahead."

"Negative, I need Remington Six *actual* immediately." Logan rolled his eyes.

"Stand by."

Logan drummed on the dash again, his leg twitching in excitement. "Come on, come on."

"Bolt Six, Remington Six. What's your traffic?" The colonel sounded annoyed.

"A Russian approached under flag of truce. Russian Lieutenant General Molchalin is en route to my location to ask for an immediate ceasefire. Over."

"What is the ETA?" Now the colonel didn't sound annoyed at all. *Funny how that works.*

"About fifteen mikes. The Russian said they are not willing to wait for a higher-ranking officer."

"You sure about that? That doesn't jive."

"Relaying what the Russian colonel said. He said Moscow doesn't want to wait."

"You have another linguist to verify your translation?"

Logan fought irritation welling. "The Russian speaks English and Ace Three-Four is fluent in Russian."

"Okay. Bolt Six, stand by. Out."

Logan let go of the radio. "He doesn't believe it, does he?"

Jim shrugged. Logan shook his head. "Okay, Jim, get me Devin. I want the office next door cleared out and lit up, like yesterday, even it if means cracking a hundred chemlites."

Jim nodded and snapped into action.

Logan chuckled. "Well, that rumor will fly as fast as lightning across the regiment."

"Talking to yourself?" Kristyn asked, having approached while Logan was distracted. She was now armed with her camera, a video camera on a tripod, and her notebook. She was now wearing a navy-blue parka and had her press credentials on a lanyard around her neck.

"Yeah. We're gonna do this next door. You can walk over with me in a moment."

"God, I hope this is for real and this works."

"Me too, Kristyn."

"Guidons, Guidons, Remington Six, clear the net of all traffic. All radio traffic will move to the A and L net immediately. Break," the radio interrupted. "Bolt Six, stand by for Victory Six."

"Bolt Six, standing by," Logan answered.

"Who's that?" Kristyn asked.

"Victory is the Fifth Corps callsign. Lieutenant General Evans. I guess we got higher's attention."

"Bolt Six, Victory Six on Remington primary." Logan recognized Evan's voice.

"Bolt Six."

"What are your instincts on this?"

"Probably legit. Worth finding out. Told them we can't get a general flown in with the blizzard. The reply was they don't want to wait."

"Roger. Bolt Six, I trusted you with your mission, I will trust you with this action. Know I'm on this net for you until further notice."

"Roger. Sir, what are my boundaries?"

"Accept a ceasefire as long as it doesn't require any concessions from us."

"Confirming I can say we will stop further advances?"

"Correct. Remember, a ceasefire is a temporary agreement between armies in the field. You are not negotiating a peace treaty."

"Roger. Am I negotiating on behalf of Ukrainian and other NATO forces?"

"Yes. I confirmed that with Combined Joint Headquarters."

"Roger." Logan took a deep breath, his heart threatening to pound out of his chest.

"Bolt Six, I have faith in you. I will be standing by on this net. Out."

Chapter 21

Pereshchepyne, Ukraine – January 24, 0345 hrs

Logan stood up and took his helmet off, rubbing his hair. He poured some water on his hand and rubbed it on his face. Logan looked in the truck mirror. *I look rough. No time to do anything about it.*

Sam and Savvy burst into the shed and jogged up.

"Sir," Savvy said between breaths, "ready next door."

"Logan, you good?" Sam asked in a low voice.

Logan nodded. "Yeah, I think so. I can't believe I'm about to negotiate on behalf of the United States of America and her allies. I'm just a captain."

"I think you will do fine. Logan, remember reading *A Message to Garcia* for Captain Jansen when we were in Darwin?"

Logan nodded. "No way he somehow foresaw this."

"No, but the message is rather poignant right now."

"This is still nuts."

Sam grinned at Logan and cuffed his shoulder. "Just don't screw up!"

Logan grinned.

Sam looked at Kristyn and frowned. "Ma'am, you will not take any photos with my Rangers in them. I will need to inspect your camera afterward to verify compliance. OPSEC matters to us."

"Of course." Kristyn turned away from Sam and Logan saw her roll her eyes.

"Thank you." Sam nodded. "I'm heading over to the room."

Logan noticed Jim's driver, who had managed to stay out of everything by sitting in the back seat. "You have the TOC. I am going over to the room also. Kristyn, you ready?"

The driver nodded and moved up to the front seat.

"Let's go." Logan gestured for Kristyn to walk with him. Logan's mind raced as he walked. He thought through everything the Russians might say, everything he might have to say. *I'm sure I won't have guessed any of that correctly.* Logan's thoughts returned to the immediate as he stepped into the blizzard. The walk to the main office building of the industrial site seemed much shorter than he remembered earlier. Logan barely noticed the cold.

Lights were on in the office as soldiers finished pushing furniture around, placing a large table in the middle of the room and placing several chairs around it.

"I know we used our own lights in the shed. Are these ours also?" Logan asked Devin.

Devin nodded. "My Bradley is powering these. Sergeant Heydte helped me wire into this room's electrical circuit."

"Let's get some backup lights, just in case."

"I've got some battery camp lanterns in that bag." Devin pointed the corner.

"Good." Logan looked around the room. "I guess this will do."

Sam huddled in the corner with her Rangers, giving instructions. Logan moved over to listen.

"Remember, be the quiet professional. Let your weapons hang on their slings and stand at ease. Ivans will be unarmed. We are here to remind them we are badasses."

Savvy came in the room. "They just arrived at the perimeter. The colonel from earlier, the general, and a captain who is the aide are coming in. The Russian driver will stay with my men in the Bradley and the Russians' radio."

"What?" Logan was puzzled. "What's with the radio?"

"They said they are instructed to radio the ceasefire without delay to their units. They seem a bit urgent. They wanted to bring the radio in with them. I'm worried about it being a bomb or tracking device."

"It's a risk we take. They know they aren't meeting with a general, so I don't think they are hoping to create a leadership vacuum." Logan paused. "Tell them we'll let them use it if we come to an agreement."

"Roger." Savvy stepped out of the room to talk on the radio.

Logan looked around the room as everyone took their places. Logan pointed at a chair facing the door. "I'll sit there. I want Ratty next to me. The three Russians will have these chairs closest to the door. Everyone listen up!" He raised his voice over all the discussions in the room and hallway. "When they get here, we will display the professionalism of the regiment and our nation. We will be polite. We will observe military courtesies. Nobody speaks unless spoken to and I give you the nod. Captain Gentry, I'm having second thoughts. Let's have your Rangers flank the door in the hallway. Can you be behind the Russians, where we can make eye contact and you can give me hand signals? Thank you."

"Can I be free to roam the room with my camera?" Kristyn asked, raising her hand.

Logan scanned the room. "I'd rather not have a distraction. Can you choose a single spot? Where are you setting up the video camera?"

"In this corner. I want it to capture the Russians entering and it will get both sides. I can stand over on this end of the table."

"Okay. Devin, have our video team so one is capturing from each side of the table."

"Roger, sir. I will place another phone in the middle of the table to capture audio." Devin smiled and flashed a thumbs-up.

"I suppose it's too late to get some flags. Oh well." Logan rotated his shoulders and neck.

The squeak of a Bradley's track and the roar of the engine as the Bradley made the corner into the complex stopped Logan.

"Sir, they're here," Savvy called from the hallway.

"Okay. I'm gonna meet them at the door to the building. If any juicy intel comes our way, step out to relay to higher." Logan marched to the door. Behind him, Kristyn and Devin followed with cameras in hands. Logan checked the time. *0405. This has to be the earliest morning ceasefire negotiation in history.*

Logan wiped his sweaty hands on his pants. *Show time.* Russian voices carried in through the open door.

"Squadron, Attention!" Logan called as the Russians entered the building. As one, the Americans snapped to attention. Logan picked out General Molchalin and stepped forward to him, saluting. "Lieutenant

General Molchalin, welcome. I am the task force commander, Captain Trondfjell."

Ratty immediately translated Logan's words into Russian as Logan studied Molchalin's bandaged head and arm.

"Captain? I speak English." Molchalin returned Logan's salute. "Though Colonel Beketov has better mastery of the language. I've brought him in case our discussion requires it."

"As you wish, General. If you will follow me, we will talk in here." Logan pointed to the office room before walking in. *Relax. Relax, Logan.* Behind, Logan heard the Russians speaking among themselves. Logan gestured for the Russians to take their seats and moved toward his.

"Ratty, what were they saying?" Logan whispered.

"They commented we must have as bad of leadership losses as them if you are the commander."

Logan nodded.

Beketov helped Molchalin remove his coat and hung it on the chair. Molchalin gingerly sat down.

Logan watched and sat down in his own chair. Only the scrape of chairs broke the silence as everyone took their places. Logan opened his notebook sitting on the table and uncapped his pen. He looked over at Molchalin.

Molchalin cleared his throat. "Captain, before we begin, I must start by telling you President Voroshilov died this night. Prime Minister Zubkov is leading the country, in accordance with our constitution."

"I was not aware. My condolences, General." Logan flashed his eyes at Savvy. He stifled the smile at her enormous eyes as she slipped out of the room and down the hallway. *Yet another bombshell to hand higher.*

Logan folded his hands over the notebook and waited. *Your move, Ivan.*

Molchalin looked at Beketov and his aide before looking at Logan and then over at Kristyn, just in time to watch her snap a picture.

"General, we have a member of the free press with us. Journalist Ms. Kristyn Rhodes."

"I see. Captain, I am here on behalf of the Russian Federation armed forces to discuss a ceasefire. Whom do you speak on behalf of?"

Logan gazed directly into Molchalin's eyes. "General, I am authorized to negotiate on behalf of all armed forces fighting in Ukraine."

"A mere captain speaks on behalf of NATO and Ukraine?"

"General," Logan said, forcing a smile, "your urgency and the weather limit in-person presence of higher-ranking officials. Are you wishing to delay this discussion?"

"No, Captain. If you speak with authority, the rank is immaterial." Molchalin smiled back.

Logan watched Beketov shift uneasily in his chair. *He doesn't agree.*

"In that case, General, what is your request?"

Molchalin sat up straighter. "Captain, I ask your forces for an immediate and total ceasefire. I ask for all forces to freeze the frontlines, with no further advances. I ask for all naval forces to avoid further contact."

Logan wrote the itemized request down in his notebook, using the delay to gather his thoughts. Finished, he looked up at Molchalin. "To what end is this request?"

"Prime Minister Zubkov, on behalf of my nation, has accepted the peace terms offered by the United States through the Chinese. As you might know, such intermediaries can take time. We wish to avoid any further unnecessary bloodshed awaiting the communiques."

"General, I understand you wish for the ceasefire in support of permanent peace negotiations," Logan summarized, hoping Molchalin would continue his offer.

"Correct, Captain. We all have lost far too many of our nations' youth."

"General, it is my concern you will use a ceasefire to reposition forces for the purpose of renewed fighting from better positioning."

Molchalin blinked. Logan focused on maintaining a poker face. *He didn't think a captain could think of that.* Molchalin looked at Beketov, who shrugged. "Captain, I assure you, that is not our intent. I propose a term of the agreement shall limit the movement of combat formations. Would that alleviate your concern?"

"Yes, General. I must point out the front lines east of the Dnipro River are non-contiguous. As you know, my task force penetrated your lines and you now have only fragments of formations scattered in my rear areas. We need to ensure there are no incidents as units require supplies. Particularly in this difficult weather."

Molchalin frowned and pulled his aide and Beketov in close, whispering.

Logan leaned toward Ratty, who listened a moment before softly telling Logan, "They are discussing what they want to do about the line between the Vorskla and the Donets. The colonel doesn't want to concede anything. The captain suggested they withdraw all their forces below the Oril."

Molchalin made a little wave with his hand, causing Beketov and his aide to stop and sit back in their chairs. "Captain, for the sake of simplicity of supplying food and fuel to my men, given the harsh winter, I propose to pull my forces south of your salient to a line generally described as the Oril River Canal to Izyum. The frontline along the Russian–Ukrainian national border to Belarus, and the frontlines west of the Dnipro River, shall remain static."

"General, I will have someone bring us a map so you can draw your proposed line." Logan waved his hand at Sam. She nodded and stepped out of the room. "And to clarify, this line is the ceasefire line; this is not anticipated to be the permanent peace treaty line of demarcation."

"Correct, Captain."

"We should establish a means for us to communicate via radio, for the purposes of clarifying intentions in the coming days. Movements of combat formations must be communicated ahead of time."

"Yes, my aide will write a radio frequency down that we can talk, without encryptions by either party."

"That would work. Ah, the map is here." Logan waited for Sam to place it on the table, a large-scale map without any graphics on it. Logan handed Molchalin a red map pen. Molchalin bent over the map and drew the line slowly and carefully.

"I only drew the sector we are discussing adjusting the front line. The other sectors can remain as they are."

"I agree to the terms so far, but I propose we maintain the city of Pereshchepyne as a meeting place. My task force will remain here for the time being, despite being south of the canal. I do not wish to stumble into any minefields. I ask your forces carefully mark all minefields and provide maps of them."

"Very well, Captain. We would like the ceasefire to go into effect immediately." Molchalin leaned forward and made the change to the line on the map.

"Me too. We should set a time, though. How does zero seven hundred hours this morning work?"

Molchalin looked at his watch. "That is soon enough, but enough time to transmit across the battlefield."

"General, I wrote the terms down as we discussed. If you would please review them and confirm I have them correct." Logan turned his notebook to Molchalin and waited for the general to read it.

"You have them as I understand the terms."

Logan signed and printed his name under the signature. He offered his pen to Molchalin to sign as well. Excitement bubbled up in his chest as the pen wiggled across the paper.

"Ah, this is good." Molchalin sighed. "Allow our staffs to share this with our forces and you and I can talk, soldier to soldier."

Logan stood and extended his hand across the table. Molchalin took it and pumped vigorously. A smile broke across Molchalin's face. Logan offered his hand next to Beketov, who politely but cautiously accepted. Molchalin's aide already stepped back from the table.

"Sergeant Ratatuev, will you escort them to their radios?" Logan carefully pulled the page out of the notebook and turned to Devin. "Get this relayed to higher immediately. Also, take the map. Turn on the tactical data router and get photos of this, and some photos you took during the discussion, sent up immediately."

Devin nodded. In a moment, the room was empty for Logan and Molchalin. Molchalin came around the table and sat in the chair next to Logan. Logan retook his seat. He noticed Kristyn in the hallway, taking pictures of the two.

"Captain, do you have a given name?"

"Logan, General."

Molchalin nodded and pulled the flask out of his pocket. "Logan, it takes politicians to start wars, but it takes soldiers to stop them. Doesn't it?"

"It is the soldiers who pay the price," Logan replied, dodging the question. "You were wounded recently?" Logan pointed to Molchalin's bandages.

"Yes. Artillery at Kotovka. I will heal."

"We passed through Kotovka yesterday."

Molchalin shook his head, then smiled before raising the flask. "I've been carrying this with me, waiting to toast the end of the war with my good friend. Now, General Kiselyov is dead, but I find myself the one arranging a ceasefire to end the war that took him. Logan, I would be honored if you would join me." Molchalin uncapped the flask and took a swig before offering it to Logan.

Logan took the flask and stared at it. *Ah, what the hell. Rules be damned. I'll not offend the general.* "To the end of fighting." Logan took a swig. The vodka was smooth and slightly sweet and citrusy. Logan handed the flask back.

"Yes. May it be the end of all wars, but we soldiers know better." Molchalin ran his finger over the crest stamped into the stainless steel. "My friend gave this to me shortly after the battle of Grozny. It was a thank you."

Logan nodded, watching tears form in Molchalin's eyes. Logan thought of the soldiers he had lost and felt his eyes misting up. "General, you said your friend was General Kiselyov. You're referring to Lieutenant General Kiselyov?"

"Yes." Molchalin's eyes watered heavily.

Logan keyed up his radio. "Ace Six, Bolt Six, can you bring me the Russian jacket?"

"Roger."

Logan saw Molchalin's eyebrows raise. "General, last night, we found a jacket on the battlefield, hanging on a tree branch. I believe it might have been your friend's."

"But nobody was wearing this jacket?"

"No, General."

"Then Mikhail found a tank to take into battle." Molchalin smiled. "He always kept his old tanker's leather handy. Decorum prevented him from wearing it outside of a tank."

Running Bear entered the room and handed the jacket to Logan. Logan showed the name and rank to Molchalin, offering the jacket.

Molchalin's chin quivered and he gingerly picked the jacket up and ran his bandaged hand over the name. "Mila will be grateful to have this." Molchalin picked his own coat off the chair and wrapped it around Kiselyov's.

"General." Running Bear stood at attention. "You should know General Kiselyov fought like a warrior."

Logan clasped his hands in front, fighting his own eyes watering. With the nod of a head, he let Running Bear leave.

Molchalin carefully folded the jackets over his arm and looked in Logan's eyes. "Logan, how long have you been at the front? You've seen your share of death and despair, haven't you?"

"Today is day 195 of this war for me. We were here before your forces invaded last July."

"You were? Where did you fight?"

"We started south of Synel'nykove, got cut off at Pavlohrad, then broke out to Kobelyaky via Dnipro during the initial week. After that, we moved around a lot."

"That was these troops?" Molchalin's eyes lit up as if he knew something.

Logan nodded. "That was us."

"Your battalion's attack wrecked my 138th Guards Motor Rifle Division last July southeast of Kobelyaky."

Logan smiled. "It was just my troop, uh, company size, not a battalion."

"And your task force now, how long ago did you lose your colonel?"

"Two days ago, before we attacked south from the Koshmanivka area."

"Before you broke my lines. That also was your troops?"

Logan nodded.

"Ah." Molchalin wagged his flask and took another sip. "That explains why your generals allow a captain to speak on their behalf in something so important as this ceasefire."

"It isn't me. It's the troopers. These are the best armored warriors I've ever served with." Logan smiled. *Well, maybe Captain Jansen is better.*

"It is a small consolation to know my divisions were defeated here on the banks of the Oril by some of the best my nation has ever encountered."

"I appreciate the praise and will relay that to the troops. Thank you, General."

"I will call you on the radio at noon and refine plans for movements. I think we can let the storm blow out. Noon is soon enough." Molchalin stood and nodded to Logan before walking into the hallway. Logan followed.

"Sir," Devin said, coming down the hallway, "I've got confirmation on the ceasefire. All forces, including the Ukrainians, will execute the ceasefire at zero seven hundred."

Logan made a fist and raised it to his chest. *We did it!*

"Logan, I hope we never fight again." Molchalin saluted.

Logan returned the salute and nodded.

Molchalin dropped his salute and climbed into the waiting Bradley. Beketov yelled over the motor. "The order just went out from Moscow. The fighting ends officially at seven local."

Logan grinned. "Okay, take them back to their Tigr." Logan turned back to the door. The hallway now crowded with the troop commanders and many of the other leaders within the task force.

"Everyone gather around and listen," Logan called as he checked his radio to make sure it was on the task force net. "Guidons, Guidons, Bolt Six, the ceasefire goes into full effect at zero seven hundred hours. Well done. You've accomplished our mission and then some." Logan paused, hearing yelling carrying on the wind. "Before we get too carried away in celebration, we must maintain security. It will take time for every Russian soldier to get the word. I do not want a mistake costing anyone their life at this point. Get full accountability of troops and equipment. Leaders' call at zero seven thirty. Out."

Chapter 22

Washington, DC – January 23, 2200 hrs

"Madam President, it is official," the US European Commander announced on the video screen on the wall of the Situation Room. Cheering erupted.

Tribolet let the cheers carry a few minutes before shushing the room. "General, what time is it in Ukraine? How long until the ceasefire starts?"

"It's five in the morning. Two hours to go."

"Do you foresee any issues?"

"No, Madam President. All NATO forces and the Ukrainian forces are already celebrating."

Tribolet smiled. "You know, General, when you told me a random captain was handling the ceasefire negotiations, I had my doubts. I'm glad this captain proved me wrong, but I'm annoyed you made me suffer the worry."

"Madam President, the blizzard prevented the Fifth Corps commander, General Evans, from being able to fly down and handle it himself. Not even a closer division commander could get through the storm. We chose to accept the Russian overtures at the time and place they chose, instead of risking the situation changing and the Russians changing their mind. A bird in the hand, they say."

"Well, have General Evans follow up as soon as the weather allows. Now, I'll let you go." Tribolet ended the video chat.

"Good thing we pressured Lytvyn ahead of time." Simons flashed her smile at Arnold.

"And you all have delivered what we promised last summer. We've ended the war in time for the primaries." Tribolet beamed. Her approval rating would go up as they carefully leaked how instrumental she was in getting everyone to agree to a peace terms. "Director Surles, have we been able to confirm Voroshilov is dead and how?"

"Russian state media announced the death already, stating a suspected brain aneurism," Surles answered.

"A brain aneurism of the nine-millimeter variety?" Arnold smirked.

"We will find out." Surles returned a snarky smile. "If many others died in Moscow tonight, I would say yes."

"Do you want to call the Russians directly then?" Simons asked, looking at Tribolet.

Tribolet nodded. The room grew deathly quiet as they waited for the connection.

"This is Prime Minister Zubkov," the voice on the phone answered after three minutes.

"President Kayla Tribolet here. We are pleased you have accepted our peace offer and took the initiative to implement a ceasefire on the front."

"It is good to end Voroshilov's war. We are happy to have safely found an outlet that avoided catastrophic consequences."

Nervous looks shot around the Situation Room. Tribolet sat back. "Indeed, there has been enough suffering."

Surles wrote on a piece of paper and held it up for Tribolet to see. *Voroshilov's war?*

"Do you have more information on what happened to President Voroshilov?" Tribolet asked.

"His health has been suffering this week. The doctor believes he suffered a ruptured aneurism."

"I see. Well, you did not waste any time moving forward on our offer, did you, Prime Minister?"

"We had the opportunity we have been waiting for." Zubkov paused. "We will have elections soon and of course we will need to finalize a peace treaty. Can you ensure President Lytvyn will fully participate? I propose the three of us meet in Geneva in person. With the right people, we can close the book on Voroshilov's war."

"Perhaps we can meet next Monday. With the ceasefire in place, we can take a breath and get the right people in the right place for successful negotiations."

"That would be sufficient. Goodbye." Zubkov hung up.

DeBever whistled. "I guess you and I are going to Switzerland."

"Interesting Zubkov called it Voroshilov's war twice." Surles leaned forward. "I think they feel cornered."

"Get me all the information you can. Perhaps we can squeeze a touch harder for Lytvyn."

"Or we just take the peace and run. The voters might get sticker shock when the casualty reports come out, and they will come out very soon," Arnold cautioned.

"Do you have those yet?" Tribolet blinked.

"Madam President, remember the media keeps comparing this offense to Operation Desert Storm, even though we are currently in a much more formidable fight." Arnold lowered his voice, "This week's reports are still not fully in and verified, but we are looking at a total now of about seven thousand killed or missing since July 13."

"And now it's over." Tribolet snapped her fingers at an orderly. "Bring in the champagne."

Ceasefire in Ukraine

(New York Times) Pereshchepyne, January 24 - BREAKING NEWS. Russian forces unexpectedly negotiated an immediate ceasefire in Ukraine. The ceasefire covers the entire theater of operations and all parties, going into effect at 7:00 AM local time. The ceasefire is the prelude to a formal peace treaty, ending the seven-month war. Russian forces announced the death of President Voroshilov, succeeded by Prime

Minister Zubkov. Zubkov directed his generals to obtain an immediate ceasefire.

The Russian move caught NATO leaders off guard as Russian Lieutenant General Victor Molchalin arrived at the advanced American Task Force Thunderbolt positions to negotiate in person. A blizzard prevented any Western generals from reaching the negotiations in Pereshchepyne. The highest-ranking American available, Captain Logan Trondfjell, negotiated on behalf of Ukrainian and NATO forces. Ukrainian-NATO Combined Joint Headquarters delegated full authority to Trondfjell via the radio as the Russian delegation arrived at his unit command post in Pereshchepyne. Molchalin and Trondfjell reached an agreement before dawn.

In a twist of fate, Trondfjell and his forces were among the first Americans to fight in Ukraine, having arrived as part of the Global Response Force in June of last year. It is only fitting the soldiers who sacrificed the longest oversaw the ending of bloodshed and suffering.

```
The jubilation among the soldiers at the frontline cannot be overstated. These soldiers have lost many close friends and faced the constant threat of painful and gruesome death. Many carry scars and fresh wounds from their own close calls. For them, peace is holy and is most welcomed. Hope for a formal treaty and a return home is widespread.
```

Pereshchepyne, Ukraine – January 24, 0900 hrs

Running Bear rested his eyes, slumped against the turret wall. Relief mixed with sorrow, joy, anger, and loneliness in a volatile mix. His crew sensed it and joined the celebration with the other soldiers of the platoon.

"I thought I would find you here." Kristyn's voice startled Running Bear, though his reaction was sluggish. He opened his eyes and looked up. She was squatting next to his hatch.

"Come on down." Running Bear sat up and pointed at the loader's seat.

"Thank you." Kristyn lowered herself into the turret and sat down. She smiled.

Running Bear stared at her. *I don't want to do an interview right now.* He sighed.

"Me too." Kristyn shook her head.

"Huh?" Running Bear blinked. "Reading my thoughts?"

"No, not really. I was just thinking I'm drained. You know? Utterly spent. God, what a wild twenty-four hours." Kristyn pulled off her hat and gloves before running her fingers through her hair.

"No kidding. I'm still a little shocked how suddenly this war came to an end. Struggling to figure out what I should be doing."

"I just sent off my article on the ceasefire negotiations. AP and Reuters must be pissed they missed it and a no-name got solo coverage." Kristyn put her hat and gloves back on. "Your tank is pretty chilly."

"Close the hatch if you want. It will eliminate the draft." Running Bear pointed at the hatch. He smiled as he watched Kristyn study the locking mechanism. After a few seconds, she figured it out and pulled the loader's hatch closed. "Figured that out pretty easily, didn't you?"

"Especially brain dead."

"You've never struck me as brain dead." Running Bear tugged his collar up tighter as he shivered. *Why are you here? Why am I glad you are?*

"I feel brain dead." Kristyn leaned back in the seat, the same stance Running Bear saw every loader eventually mold into. He watched her breath frost on the turret ceiling and smiled.

"My family calls this the Moon When the Trees Crack from the Cold. Some call it the Moon When There is Frost in the Tepee." Running Bear pointed at the icy crystals growing above Kristyn. She looked up and then gazed across the tank.

"I'd call it the moon of fingers too stiff to type."

Running Bear took a few breaths, watching his breath join the frost. "I'm gonna make some coffee. Want some?"

"Only if it isn't inconveniencing you."

"I've got enough hot water in my thermos for a couple and you can use the lid cup. I'll use my actual coffee cup." Running Bear held up his travel mug. "It's crappy MRE instant coffee. I ran out of the good stuff two days ago."

Kristyn snorted. "I'm not expecting anything fancy here."

Running Bear chuckled as he pulled two packets of MRE coffee and a hot chocolate packet out. "It's better as a mocha."

"You're the chef."

"Or barista?" Running Bear asked without looking up from his careful pouring of powder into the cups. Steam rose thickly as Running Bear unscrewed the inner cap and poured the water into the cups, swirling each. He handed Kristyn her cup before raising his own, enveloping his face in steam.

"I don't know why I'm here," Kristyn abruptly stated, though she made no effort to get up.

"Well, you're welcome to stay and talk." Running Bear took a sip. "I don't know why I said that."

"It's okay. I know what you mean." Kristyn smiled after taking a sip.

"You do? Cause I don't." Running Bear looked away.

Kristyn shrugged.

Running Bear let the silence hang as he drank his coffee. In the sub-zero temperatures, it cooled rapidly. Kristyn seemed to sense his desire for quiet and said nothing as she emptied her cup. Twice she met his gaze and Running Bear felt they managed to communicate whole worlds without a word.

"Instant coffee leaves much to be desired, doesn't it," Running Bear announced after finishing his coffee.

"A generous way of putting it. Tell you what, when you get home, I'll treat you to a better cup of coffee. I'll come to Colorado." Kristyn looked into Running Bear's eyes. He searched them, trying to decipher her.

"Deal." Running Bear nodded once. *I hope I didn't just agree to becoming the subject of a new article.*

"I see that look." Kristyn canted her head and shook her finger. "It will be a cup of coffee and talk. No work. Friend to friend? Man to woman? Not sure how to describe what I'm envisioning. Screw it. You and me. Just us as us. Wow, hard to believe I wordsmith for a living. Anyway, I'll find us a hole-in-the-wall coffee shop back in Colorado Springs."

"Sure."

Kristyn handed the cup back, then pulled her cell phone out of her pocket. "Will you put your phone number and email in please? Be a lot easier than me having to dig it up the hard way. Which I *am* capable of. I'll send you an email with my phone number."

Running Bear grinned and shook his head. *Somehow, I don't doubt that.* He entered his information.

"Thank you for the coffee and chance to clear my mind. I need to get back to work. These in-depth articles I've been working on will quickly lose their relevance." Kristyn opened the loaders hatch and quickly departed.

"Well, Jonny-Boy," Running Bear whispered to himself when he was confident Kristyn was gone, "you survived another war. The kids might hate me, but Lady Luck loves me." He patted the tank's turret wall. "Love you too."

Two hours later, the wind was still strong and driving snow across the steppes, but the clouds moved on, revealing a brilliant blue sky. Logan stood in the lee of a house, watching a pair of Black Hawk medical evacuation helicopters take off from the field.

"Any minute now," Logan whispered to himself. He looked over at the three Bradleys idling. The sixty-below-zero wind chill meant using vehicles was necessary even for distances of half a kilometer.

A new pair of rotors beating carried in the wind and Logan strained his eyes to pick them out in the sky. With the ceasefire, the helicopters now flew at a thousand feet. *There*. Logan watched as the Black Hawks circled the field twice before setting down. Unlike previous flights, these shut their rotors off.

"I guess they are staying a while," Savvy remarked. "Good thing we have an alternate LZ for the birds coming for the Rangers."

Logan looked over. "Looks that way. Not excited about hosting."

Savvy laughed. "You've never been one to mingle with the rank."

The doors on the Black Hawks opened. Evans, Ollerich, and Noyes all hopped out and trudged across the field. Others Logan didn't recognize followed.

"And just when you thought behind enemy lines was far enough from the flagpole." Logan giggled at his own joke before stepping out into the wind to greet them.

"Brave Rifles, General." Logan snapped his best salute.

Evans returned it. "Lead the way. I hope you have somewhere warm."

Logan led the group to the waiting Bradleys.

"Join me." Evan grabbed Logan's shoulder as he got into a Bradley. Logan followed him in. "You have quite the collection of destroyed Russian armor around you. Looks like Ivan's already falling back."

"Sir?" Logan looked across as the Bradley churned through the snow to the office building.

"We saw columns of Russian vehicles heading east to Highway 105. Looks like they don't have anything between you and the rest of the corps. This General Molchalin is a man of his word."

Logan nodded.

"Tell me how it went down."

Logan described the ceasefire negotiation. Evans asked questions periodically. The Bradley reached the office and Logan gave a tour before he finished his story. The room seemed different to Logan. Now, it seemed brighter. Perhaps it was the daylight. Perhaps it was the lifting of the storm. Perhaps it was the promise of peace.

"Logan, you did well. Beyond the shadow of a doubt, you were the right man at the right place. Proud of you." Evan shook Logan's hand before turning to his aide. "Let me know when the Russian delegation is on its way."

Logan stood patiently.

"You look ready for a nap," Noyes whispered to him.

"Better believe it, sir."

"As soon as you introduce General Molchalin, sneak out and get some rest."

"Roger, sir." Logan's mind drifted off. Somehow, Molchalin's second arrival and introductions faded into the blur that became the rest of the day. Logan's last memorable thought was remembering the early-morning negotiations, wondering if it would be the highlight of his life.

Epilogue

Colorado Springs, Colorado – May 22, 1745 hrs

Logan pulled his SUV into a parallel parking space a block away, happy to find a spot even this close on a beautiful Thursday night. Laughter and kids playing carried up the block from the neighborhood park.

"Hope they were able to score the gazebo tables for our food." Logan glanced at Erin before rolling up the windows.

"Somehow, I know they did." Erin smiled and got out. Logan pulled a cooler out of the back seat and pushed the door closed with his butt.

"Oh yeah? The girl who flew in this afternoon knows?" Logan had picked Erin up at the airport just after lunchtime.

"Oh, a birdy told me."

Logan grinned and walked down the sidewalk.

They rounded the corner and Logan spied Top grilling next to the gazebo. Top was wearing blue jeans and the company T-shirt Logan had bought everyone before Ukraine. Top waved at Logan.

"Welcome, sir!" the baritone voice boomed.

"Got the potato salad and some pop. Not sure who will drink those though!" Logan hefted the cooler up.

"Come and set up! Captain Haag, good to see you again!" Top wiped his hands on his jeans and came over to shake Erin's hand. "You look a lot better than last time I saw you."

Erin looked at her shorts and blouse and grinned. "Yeah, last time I was smeared in blood and couldn't walk."

"Top, how did you score the gazebo?" Logan shook hands with his old first sergeant.

"Easy. She took care of the quartering party." Top pointed to Kristyn, who waved as she pulled a beer out of another cooler.

"Good to see you. A long way from Johannesburg. You aren't on assignment, are you?" Logan asked, setting the cooler down.

Kristyn held up the beer. "Pfft, no. I'm staying in that apartment." She turned and pointed at an apartment building across the park.

"You are?"

"Thought I could try spending some time back in my native country for a bit."

"How did you get stuck with quartering party duty?" Logan still didn't understand. *Why are you here?*

"Well, Jonny told me about the party and I invited myself, but then offered to come early and get the gazebo as a preemptive apology. I had to test his claim I was always welcome around the troop." Kristyn cracked open the beer and took a sip.

"Jonny, huh?" Logan raised his eyebrows and whispered to Erin, "Running Bear."

"It gets a rise out of him." Kristyn laughed. "But it's not for the faint of heart."

"Captain's here!" Savvy yelled, pushing through the small crowd. She saw Erin and diverted, embracing her old friend.

"Hi, Savvy!"

"Welcome home!" Savvy beamed. Logan noticed Savvy's glance at Erin's left hand. Savvy made a pouting face at Logan and he responded by sticking his tongue out.

"Sir, glad you made it." Gene came up next, a beer in each hand. He handed one each to Logan and Savvy.

"Is your CO coming?" Logan asked, looking around the crowd.

"The CO? He was here for about thirty minutes, but said this should be for the combat veterans, not the replacements that came after the fighting ended."

"Well, I guess that's his prerogative." Logan opened his beer and took a sip.

"He did arrange for a van to get everyone home." Savvy added, "And we confirmed with the police nobody's car will get towed if left overnight."

"Well then."

"Make a hole!" Running Bear's voice parted the crowd. He came across the field with Heydte, carrying a massive cooler. The two set it in the shade of a tree next to the gazebo.

"Sir, you remember the night before the Russians came storming into Ukraine? You wouldn't let us help pay for the paint. Well, we'll be offended if you don't accept a beer from us." Running Bear pointed at Erin and waved. "We had a little help gathering intel on your favorite beers, and even a few whiskeys."

Logan laughed and gave Running Bear a hug. "I appreciate it. Well, I brought something for you in this cooler." Logan turned and pulled an Arizona green tea and slid it into a tall can cozy. Running Bear grinned and accepted the drink.

"I can nurse this awhile and be able to get out with just one beer on the day."

"If you need another Arizona, I've got a few more in the car for you."

"I've got some in the apartment too. Oh, did you hear?" Running Bear lowered his voice as he pointed to the apartment complex.

"No?" Logan wasn't sure what to expect.

"I came down on orders." Running Bear frowned. "To effin' Fort Bragg, or whatever they're changing the name to."

"Oh...for the new M10 Booker battalion. Good thing you did airborne schooling when you were eighteen."

"Yeah, I gotta worry about breaking a hip at my age." Running Bear rolled his eyes and smiled. "But I gotta deal with the airborne Ranger mafia."

"That is probably why they chose you, beyond already having passed jump school. There can't be more than a handful of Ranger-tabbed tankers in the whole Army, not enough to fill a battalion. But you have a very distinguished combat record. I'd say that's better than a tab."

"That makes sense." Running Bear's eyes had a fire in the flint.

"Oh?"

"Dani got the same orders."

"Interesting. Is branch rounding up every Silver Star and higher recipient to faceoff with the tabs? So much for asking people where they want to go next."

Savvy came up and Running Bear dropped the subject. "Sir, think you will be teaching by the time I get to the schoolhouse?"

"Probably. I doubt they will let me be your instructor though. But you better look me up when you get there."

"I will, especially on weekends that Erin is up from her captain's course."

Logan laughed. "You've been her friend longer, but I think I've been closer."

Erin giggled. "Better stuff a steak in your mouth before you end up eating your foot." She plucked a juicy T-bone out of a steaming pan and plopped it on a plate.

Logan grinned and blew a kiss before loading up a plate of his own. Logan and Erin moved out into the grass and plopped down to eat.

"Is that Dani?" Erin pointed out at the soldiers playing soccer. One had a beer in her hand.

"Oh my God. Yes. What is she doing?"

"Hamasaki challenged the younger soldiers to a game of soccer. Erin, she might be as good as you are. To make it fair, she has to play with a beer in hand." Savvy laughed.

"Fair?" Logan shook his head as Dani kicked a rocket to the upper corner. Beer splashed as she threw her hands up in victory. Dani looked over and saw them. With a wave to the game, she loped across the field and slid down next to Erin.

"Ma'am! How is the leg?"

"Healed up nicely, but I'll have an early warning on weather changes from now on. How is yours, Dani?"

Dani looked at her legs. The new skin was unnaturally light, contrasting with her dark olive skin. She shrugged. "I was lucky it didn't get too tight before I got active enough. Still struggle with my left forearm though. Doc thinks it's nerve damage that's holding up a full recovery there."

Erin grabbed Dani's right hand and squeezed it. "Doesn't seem to slow you much."

"Yeah, can't let it define me. Still, I got real lucky my wool scarf protected me from the fire as well as it did from the blizzard." Dani smiled.

"Dani is the definition of tough." Logan raised his beer to salute her.

"I gotta ask, though, which is more intimidating to men? Your Navy Cross or battle scars?" Erin leaned over and whispered.

"Scars. The few who know about the award, well, I just won't date them."

Erin grinned and flashed a knowing look at Logan.

Logan winked and shook his head to Erin. *No, don't tell her.* Logan still hadn't heard back on the Medal of Honor recommendation he put in for her rescue of soldiers from the burning Abrams. *I still can't believe she hid those burns until after the ceasefire was obviously working.* He didn't want to jinx the award by saying anything to anyone. Anyone other than Erin, of course.

Logan enjoyed watching the soldiers relax and soak in the evening sun. Many had come up to say hello and introduce family, girlfriends and boyfriends. His food was quite cold by the time he finished it.

Savvy climbed onto a bench and clicked her ring on her beer bottle. "Troopers of Lightning Troop! Gather around and grab your drink. I have a toast to make." Savvy waited as several had to grab something fresh from the cooler.

Logan nodded to Savvy's husband, Tye, who raised his beer in salute.

"Y'all take your time. Sheesh." Savvy shook her head as everyone finally seemed to be ready. "Troopers, today we raise our drinks in toast, much because of someone who gave us all his everything. Without him, too many of us would be having this toast in Fiddler's Green with those we lost. From pushing us hard before the war, to thinking outside the box, even spending his own money, to having the stones to negotiate with a two-star Ivan to end the war right-the-hell-now. We were all fortunate to serve with Captain Logan Trondfjell. Sir, they broke the mold after you. Here is a toast to the original Lightning Six."

"To Lightning Six!" The collective toast turned heads from a soccer practice on the other side of the park.

Logan wiped a tear from his eye. "Kind words, Savvy."

"Speech! Speech!" Squeaky started the chant.

Savvy held out her hand and pulled Logan up onto the bench. Logan looked over at Erin. Her smile boosted his courage to find something to say. Logan looked around, recognizing so many faces, including the family members of the troopers.

"Lightning Troop, you mean the world to me. Leaning into the fight alongside you was an incredible honor. No kidding, you are some of the finest armored warriors to ever climb into a fighting vehicle or on a horse. You know, that stormy day in Pereshchepyne, I was worried the Russians would be offended only a lowly captain was available to take their...frankly, their surrender. I could see the one Russian colonel was angry and I could see them backing out at the slightest provocation. But they were more desperate than that.

"Anyway, after we signed the deal and shook hands, the Russian General—Molchalin was his name—asked about our experience in the war. When I told him we started near Pavlohrad and then fought to Kobelyaky, he remarked our *battalion* had wrecked one of his divisions. I told General Molchalin it was just our single troop—you all—and he replied, 'That explains why your generals allow a captain to speak on their behalf in something so important as this ceasefire.' Praise from the enemy...well, that is the hardest to earn. So here is to you. Here is to those who toast us from Fiddler's Green."

Logan raised his beer high, then took a sip. Beer had never tasted better than in this moment. Logan was doubtful it would ever be again.

Glossary

ABV: Armored Breach Vehicle; a M1 chassis with a mine plow and a pair of MCLIC launchers instead of a cannon

ACR: Armored Cavalry Regiment

AGS-30: Russian automatic grenade launcher

AH-64 Apache: US attack helicopter, with a crew of two, armed with a 30mm auto-cannon, Hellfire missiles, and rockets

AMPV: Armored Multi-Purpose Vehicle; a tracked armored vehicle with versions for troop transport, command posts, medical, or mortar carrier purposes; looks similar to a M2A3 Bradley without a turret

AT-4: M136 disposable anti-tank rocket, 84mm

Auto-cannon: A cannon that fires like a machine gun

Battalion: Military organization comprising of multiple companies and a headquarters staff. US Army battalions are often referred to in shorthand, i.e., 1-503 Infantry for 1st Battalion, 503rd Airborne Infantry Regiment

Battery: Military organization the size of a company, comprising of field artillery or air defense artillery

BFT: Blue Force Tracker, a radio-transmitted data system that allows friendly "blue" forces to see each other's locations and pass information messages

BM-27 Uragan: A Russian multiple rocket launch system, firing 220mm rockets

BMP-3: Russian armored infantry fighting vehicle, with a crew of three and six passengers, armed with a 100mm cannon, a 30mm auto-cannon, and a 7.62mm coax machine gun. The cannon can fire anti-tank guided missiles

Brigade: Military organization comprising of multiple battalions or squadrons and a headquarters staff. In the US Army, the battalions or squadrons come from different regiments

BTG: Battalion Tactical Group, the primary unit of action for the Russians, task organized for a specific mission as a combined arms force

BTR-82: Russian eight-wheeled armored infantry fighting vehicle, with a crew of three and seven passengers, armed with a 30mm auto-cannon

C2: Command and Control

CAA: Combined Arms Army; a Russian unit comprising of multiple divisions and a headquarters staff.

Carl Gustav: An 84mm recoilless rifle, capable of firing a variety of ammunition types

CASEVAC: A method of evacuating casualties using non-standard vehicles or aircraft

CCP: Casualty Collection Point

CH-47 Chinook: US troop and cargo helicopter, with a crew of four and capable of carrying thirty-three passengers or twelve tons of cargo

Coax: A machine gun mounted coaxially with the main gun of an armored vehicle and part of the integrated fire control system

Company: Military organization comprising of multiple platoons and a small headquarters element

DMZ: Demilitarized Zone

Drone Defender: A soldier portable electronic warfare system for jamming and downing drones

EPW: Enemy prisoner of war

First Sergeant: The senior sergeant in a company, focused on the personnel and their needs

FO: Artillery forward observer

FRAGO: Fragmentary order, a partial order that modifies an existing operations order

FSB: Russian Federal Security Service; the replacement of the Soviet Union KGB, similar to the CIA

GRU: Russian Main Directorate of the General Staff; Russia's military intelligence agency

GTA: Guards Tank Army; a more powerful and better trained Russian combined arms army

HHC: Headquarters Company; the formation the battalion or higher staff and specialty platoons belong to

IR: Infared

Javelin: FGM-148 anti-tank guided missile, a fire-and-forget top attack missile

Khrizantema: Russian anti-tank guided missile system mounted on a BMP-3 chassis, with a crew of three; NATO calls it an AT-15 Springer

M1280 JLTV: Joint Light Tactical Vehicle, an armored 4x4 truck with multiple configurations

KIA: Killed in Action

LD: Line of Departure; the time and place an attack begins

LNO: Liaison officer

LOGPAC: Military term for a resupply operation, or logistics package, for an armored force, including fuel, food, ammo, and any other supply needs

LZ: Landing Zone

M1A2 Abrams: The US main battle tank, with a crew of four and a 120mm cannon, a .50 caliber machine gun, and two M240 machine guns

M240: A 7.62mm caliber belt-fed machine gun. Variants include infantry and vehicle weapon systems versions

M249 SAW: Squad Automatic Weapon; a 5.56mm caliber belt or magazine-fed machine gun

M2A3 Bradley: The US infantry fighting vehicle, with a crew of three, capable of carrying seven infantry, armed with a 25mm auto-cannon, a two-missile TOW launcher, and a M240 machine gun

M88A2 Hercules: A large armored vehicle for recovering tanks and armored vehicles, with a crew of three; has an A-frame crane and a dozer spade

MANPAD: Man-portable surface-to-air missile

MASCAL: Mass casualty event

MCLIC: Mine-Clearing Line Charge; a long explosive charge pulled out by a rocket before detonating to blast landmines out of a path

Mi-24 Hind: A Russian designed and manufactured troop-carrying gunship helicopter, with a crew of three and eight passengers, armed with a 30mm auto-cannon, rockets, and missiles.

MIC: Russian mechanized infantry company, usually ten BMP-3s or BTR-82s and reinforced with three tanks

MLRS: M270 Multiple Launch Rocket System, a US made long-range rocket artillery launcher

MPAT: Multi-purpose anti-tank 120mm cannon round designed to explode on impact or with a proximity fuse

MRD: Russian Motorized Rifle Division, comprising of six to nine BTGs, a headquarters, and various supporting subunits when at full strength

MRE: Meal Ready to Eat, a US field ration

NAI: Named Area of Interest; a graphic control measure used to focus reconnaissance efforts

OPSEC: Operational security

Orlan: Russian observation UAS; the drone is roughly three meters in wingspan

Pantsir: Russian truck mounted surface-to-air and auto-cannon system; NATO calls it SA-22 Greyhound

PC: Personnel carrier, an armored vehicle that is not a tank and carries troops

PKM: A Russian made 7.62mm belt-fed machine gun.

Platoon: A military organization comprising multiple squads and a small headquarters element

PLS: Palletized Loading System; American large supply truck

Raven: US small UAS

Red Air: Enemy aircraft over the battlefield

REDCON: Readiness condition. REDCON-1 means everything on and loaded, ready to move immediately

Regiment: Military organization comprising of multiple battalions or squadrons and a headquarters staff.

RPG: Rocket-propelled grenade, a bazooka

S2: Staff intelligence section of a battalion or brigade

S3: Operations section of a battalion or brigade

Sabot: A solid, non-explosive anti-tank round that relies on kinetic energy to penetrate armor. The penetrator is much smaller in diameter than the bore of the cannon and stabilized inside the barrel by discarding sabots (French for *shoe*)

SAM: Surface-to-air missile

SBF: Support by Fire; a position and task for a unit to establish a base of fire to allow another unit to maneuver on the enemy

SEAD: Suppression of Enemy Air Defenses; a combination of electronic warfare, artillery, and attack aircraft targeting enemy SAMs.

SIGINT: Signal Intelligence, information gathered from detecting enemy transmissions

SOP: Standard operating procedures

SP: Start Point; the beginning of a route

Sosna-R: BMP chassis mounted Russian SAM launcher; NATO calls it SA-25

Spetsnaz: Russian special operations forces, focused on deep strike reconnaissance and raids on critical military nodes

Squad: A military organization comprising of five to thirteen soldiers on average

Squadron: Military organization the size of a battalion, comprised of cavalry troops. US Army squadrons use the same shorthand as battalions

Stinger: FIM-92 man-portable (MANPAD) surface-to-air missile

T-80: Russian-made main battle tank with a crew of three and armed with a 125mm cannon and 12.7mm and 7.62mm machine guns. The cannon can fire anti-tank guided missiles in addition to cannon rounds. The tank has a jet turbine engine, similar to the M1A2 Abrams engine

T-90: Russian-made main battle tank with a crew of three and armed with a 125mm cannon and 12.7mm and 7.62mm machine guns. The cannon can fire anti-tank guided missiles in addition to cannon rounds

TACSAT: Tactical satellite communications

TF: Task Force, a battalion-size organization with elements of multiple battalions, tailored for a specific mission

Tigr: Russian 4x4 armored vehicle; similar to the JTLV

TOC: Tactical Operations Center, the command post where a commander and staff monitors and controls the fight

TOS: A Russian artillery system that launches thermobaric rockets, mounted on a tank chassis; thermobaric warheads use aerosol fuel to create a powerful explosion; the shockwave and consumption of oxygen is the mechanism of lethality

TOW-2B: A US tube-launched, optically tracked, wire-guided anti-tank missile, often referred to as a TOW

Troop: Military organization the size of a company, comprised of tanks and cavalry scouts for economy of force missions to protect larger units from enemy reconnaissance efforts

Tunguska: Russian-tracked vehicle mounted SAM and auto-cannon system; NATO calls it SA-19 Grison

UAS: Unmanned aerial system; a drone

UH-60 Black Hawk: A US troop carrier helicopter, crew of four and can carry either twelve passengers or four stretchers

WARNO: Warning Order; initial order to get troops moving and planning before the detailed operations order is ready

WIA: Wounded in Action

XO (executive officer): The military organization's second in command; focuses on logistics

About the Author

Galen D. Peterson is a West Pointer who went on to lead a tank platoon in combat in Iraq and later commanded a tank company. The M1A2 Abrams tank became his warrior's chariot and leading soldiers his passion. He was involved in some of the heaviest fighting of the war in Sadr City in 2008. In 2009, Galen was invited back to West Point as a guest lecturer to General Frank's Battle Command and Officership class. Suffering from the effects of a brain injury sustained in Iraq, he was medically retired.

Galen finds inner peace by spending time with his family, fishing, camping, biking, and model railroading. Not ready to give up on serving, Galen started a new career as a police officer in Colorado, serving in patrol, traffic, and SWAT. During his career, Galen received the Valor Award, Colorado State Patrol's highest award. After a total of twenty years in uniform, Galen settled down and now works for a municipal water department.

Combat Memoir

Strike Hard and Expect No Mercy

Global Response Force Series

REDCON ONE

Lightning Six

Task Force Thunderbolt

Printed in Dunstable, United Kingdom

79519431R00180